Realities

of

~

A Novel

Umm Zakiyyah

Realities of Submission
A Novel
By Umm Zakiyyah

ISBN 10:   0-9707667-4-2
ISBN 13:   978-0970766748

Library of Congress Control Number:
2008934411

Order information available online at
www.muslimfiction.com

Verses from Qur'an taken from Saheeh International,
Darussalam, and Yusuf Ali translations.

Published by Al-Walaa Publications
Suitland, Maryland USA
Printed in the USA

Acknowledgements

As always, all praise and thanks belong to Allah, my Creator, Who has entrusted me the gift of the pen so that I may use it in His cause. It is Him, *Ar-Rahmaan*, I must thank for my parents, Muhammad and Fareedah, who taught me as a child that Islam is the greatest gift, the greatest treasure a person could be endowed with in this life—and the Hereafter. The profundity of their lessons alone is a book in itself.

I too am indebted to my husband for his unwavering support and confidence in my writing, seeing in it a greater cause than I saw in it myself. I thank him for being my strength, confidant, and guide with every stroke of my pen. I too must thank our daughter for her patience and understanding as I dedicated many hours to composing this script.

I also thank those who took time from their busy schedules to peruse the manuscript and offer sincere advice. Thank you Rihana and Fatiha, who read and critiqued my words as I wrote them. I thank Debra Nasser and Amber Raszipovits whose suggestions and encouragement were much needed when I was indecisive. Thank you Dalida, Yasmin, Hudaifah, and Naeem for your comments and edits. I am especially grateful to Tarik Preston, graduate of the University of Medina and translator of the books *People of the Sunnah, Be Kind With One Another* and *The Signposts of the Propagated Sunnah,* whose feedback and insight were invaluable.

And I send my warmest thanks and heartfelt appreciation to all those who have remembered me in their *du'aa*—their private supplications to the One who holds with Him all good. I know, in the end, it is you to whom I am most deeply indebted.

~

Dedication

*For the stranger, whose life in this world is
that of a prisoner awaiting release.
May Paradise be your final abode.*

~

"The best of my nation is my generation
then those who follow them
and then those who follow them."
—Prophet Muhammad, peace be upon him (Bukhari)

~

Prologue

I have to admit, part of me is afraid to write this, to be so honest, to lay myself, my life and, ultimately, my faith so bare. My instinct is to hold on, to keep it to myself and protect it in the tattered cardboard boxes in which its ink-stroked testimonies had found refuge for so long, where I had found refuge from myself. In the basement of my home, in the dark, vacant basement of my heart. Yet, after countless tears and prayers, I've decided to come forward and hold onto the one thing I managed to hold onto throughout the sojourn—my faith. For part of my fear was due to those whose eyes would meticulously comb my every word and seek the fault lines, seek the hidden reason behind my struggles, a reason which, to them, was never hidden at all. For there are those who want to believe, in fact *must* believe, that this is an exposé of my religion more than myself. And for that, I would be heralded as their poster child for emancipation of the Muslim woman, of in fact Islam itself—even as I am, allegedly, unaware of my bondage.

But then I was, fortunately, reminded of the words of the Creator, the Most Wise, when He said, *"(They say) 'What does Allah mean by this parable?' By it He causes some to stray, and some He leads to the right path. But He causes not to stray, except those who forsake the Path."*

So for those who are destined to misguidance due to their contention upon forsaking the Path, there is nothing I can say or do to lead them aright. For the kindest word and the most definitive proof of Truth will lead them astray, because it is the path they have chosen for themselves. And, truly, there is nothing I can do for them, even if it is my ardent desire to clarify the veracity of my faith.

And for those who are destined to guidance due to their opening their minds and hearts to the Truth, there is nothing I can say or do to cause them to stray. For their destination is etched in something more lasting than stone. And my only prayer is that my name is there, too.

~

PART I

~

One

He doesn't know this, nor would it inspire in his heart any affinity for my decision, but it is my father who laid the foundation for my acceptance of Islam. He is the one who taught me about God and the angels and the Day of Judgment. He told me, us, about the universal message and spirituality of Christ. And it was he, during his weekly sermons at his church and daily guidance in his home, who insisted that we were Christians in the purest sense of the word, and that it was only this pure, unadulterated understanding of Jesus' message through which a person found salvation. It was a dishonoring, a disrespect, he said, to relegate God's religion to sects, to denominations, as if a person had a right to choose his method of submission, his extent of surrendering to God.

This made my childhood church, and upbringing, unique. It bore no Baptist, Episcopalian, or Methodist affiliation, nor did it bear the empty Protestant label. We were Christian, and in that term alone lay the essence of our belief, our existence. My father's church, like our religion, was not even Unitarian or non-denominational, nothing a person could fit easily into an ideological box or label. Christian. That was the only affiliation my father and his congregation ever used to differentiate themselves from the rest of the world, and from sectarian Christians.

It might be said, and certainly it has been, that my father's Christianity was his own, of his own making. Our church followed not only the injunctions of the Bible, but the injunctions of my father. It wasn't until years later, after I had already converted to Islam and married, that I came to realize that the rules with which I was brought up, the rules of our church, were not my father's inventions at all. They were, rather, a result of my father's sincere eclectic selection of true righteousness, much of which was borrowed from a host of world religions that he had, most probably, come across during his obtaining his master's and subsequent doctorate of theology and religious sciences at Harvard University.

Among the rules that I and my sisters, and later my younger brothers, followed, or at least were instructed to follow, was that of not listening to worldly music, of dressing modestly by never wearing tight or revealing clothes, and the women's covering their hair with a hat or loosely draped scarf at church. We were not allowed to date until we turned eighteen, and even then the date had to be chaperoned by my mother, father, or one of the trusted elders of the church. Needless to say, our social life was almost non-existent, and as could be expected, not all of us viewed this stringent lifestyle with fondness. Now, when I think back to those days, I realize that most of the congregation were married and over the age of forty. Which probably accounts for my and my siblings' restlessness to meet other youth, and my oldest sister's fate as a successful model who accepted a sectarian version of worshipping Christ after she secretly eloped, choosing to spend the rest of her life with a Christian professional athlete who truly felt Jesus died for his sins, thus relieving him of any responsibility for his.

It wasn't the religious parallels between my strict upbringing and the Islamic lifestyle that accounted for my childhood lessons laying the bricks in my path toward Islam. If anything, these parallels would have turned me away, for I longed for reprieve from an upbringing in which I felt I could, rightfully, do nothing. It was the purity of faith, the singleness of truth, the embracing of God's religion in the purest sense that opened my eyes, and heart, to Islam. Only then was I willing to submit, to fully embrace the lifestyle that I would have in youth viewed restrictive and suffocating. My only mistake, in retrospect, was in not taking it one step at a time, and not taking a breath between steps to examine, truly determine, whether or not the principles I was embracing, whether the choices I was making, or being encouraged or directed to make, were really a requirement of the God of my new faith.

When I look back on my life, I can find nothing to indicate that I was to stray from my parents' faith, from my Christian past. I had, for all intents and purposes, a normal childhood and youth. If anything, my life suggested that I would tread in my parents' footsteps.

My greatest joy in childhood was visiting or, more often, accepting a visit from my cousin, my neighbor, and my neighbor's good friend. Ironically, they were all boys. I had no female friends aside from the marginal friendships I'd formed at school; no girls my age were members of my father's church, not counting the ones who came once or twice a month at the behests, or pleas, of their devoted parents. My sisters had already decided, before I was yet twelve, that I was out of their league, or rather beneath theirs, mostly due to my "insistence" on siding with my parents, particularly my father. I, in sincere ignorance of their turmoil and concern, didn't understand that there were any battles to be fought, let alone sides to take, in the disagreements we had with my father and mother, or, more specifically, my father's church.

"You need to wake up," Courtney would say with a roll of her eyes.

In my mind's eye I see her then as I see her today, which is odd because we are both older now, and my image of her through a child's eyes is much fonder than the one I am burdened with today. Although, I cannot say I was ever enamored by her completely. Yet these two opposing images have somehow converged, allowing me to envision her in a kinder, gentler and in perhaps a more forgiving eye, than my current sentiments compel me.

As I hear her oft-repeated command to wake up echoing in my head, I see her deep brown skin, her dark luminescent eyes, outlined in full eyelashes and crowned with thick eyebrows that fade into each other rather than bear being completely separated. Her hair is straight, almost to a fault, because she spent hours with the cast iron hot comb wrestling its massive thickness until the tight, obstinate curls submitted to a plainness that allowed her hair to brush the collar of her shirt and resemble the photos of the Dark and Lovely models on the hair relaxer boxes.

"Wakefulness, my dear sister," I would respond with exaggerated boredom in her limited, erred vocabulary, "is the opposite of a lack of consciousness that the human body experiences in a state of slumber, often termed *sleep*. And unless this is a dream that only feels like reality, I don't think there's any need for me to wake up."

Because I was more into reading than watching television or listening to her forbidden music cassettes that she kept stashed in a jagged groove she cut into her mattress, I could get away with taking her words literally and feigning incomprehension. She really imagined I understood no subtleties of language, no inappropriate innuendoes that she and my oldest sister exchanged, nor any reality outside my father's church and my stacks of "theoretical, book knowledge."

"Renee," Patricia would snap, abruptly turning her attention to me from the mirror in which she was carefully applying mascara, "shut up."

I have often found it odd that Patricia would become the model. As a child, I never thought her beautiful, or attractive even. There were moments that I actually felt sorry for her, for her blandness. She looked too commonplace, too ordinary to earn any admiration in my heart for her physical attributes. Of course, I wasn't yet a devoted student of the world, the instructor who would soon enough teach me that my eyes had lied—that Patricia's pale skin was not sickly, that her tall, lankly shapelessness was not at all unpalatable or a cause for sympathy. That, in fact, it was my and Courtney's "disproportionate" body measurements and rich brown skin that should be pitied, although neither of us were unhealthy or overweight.

Occasionally, when I'm in the shopping market and pass a magazine bearing Patricia's image or catch a glimpse of her on a friend's television, I study the person I once thought of as my sister and am enveloped by sadness at what I see. My eyes and mind are now trained to at least comprehend, if not accept, that Patricia's light skin and long hair are, to many, tokens of beauty on Americans of African descent. But it is not what my eye beholds that inspires a sense of melancholy—I have long since developed an appreciation, if not pride, for beauty that is not limited or defined by the corporeal attributes of human flesh. It is what my heart beholds is beyond the deep brown of her eyes, beyond the skimpy fashions clinging to her anorexic torso and hips, that troubles me to near despondence. I am then overwhelmed in my own regret, and waning hope.

I know, perhaps too well, that her professed dedication to sectarian spirituality is a hypnotism she subjected herself to, to avoid the agonizing reality she would face if she were to truly submit to the guidance of her savior. I so ardently wish that I could tell her that the agony is brief, a stinging felt at only the moment of realization, lasting only as long as the heart procrastinates in facing its ultimate fate, and is lifted almost completely after formal submission.

Patricia knows, and actually had in one unguarded moment told me as such, that my path is the true path, the right path, the only one offering true salvation. And I know, although she has never told me directly, that it is my poor example in youth, and perhaps adulthood, that prevents her from proclaiming my truth—the truth—as *the* Truth.

I suppose I was too standoffish and self-absorbed, even before Islam graced my life, to afford me the gift of attracting others to what I would choose at any point in my life. Yet, it is my sincere prayer that she, as well as my parents, brothers, and Courtney, be guided in spite of me.

But I still search the annals of my past for what I could have done differently, and should do differently still.

In retrospect, I can see how they could have termed me standoffish and arrogant. But I was only defending myself. I was the youngest girl, only thirteen at the time of most of our exchanges, and I was tired of being treated like an afterthought in their familial connection to me. My brothers were still in diapers, at least one of them was, while the other was being potty trained. So they were of little benefit in my quest for acceptance or respect in the house.

Little did my sisters know, I didn't like my parents' rules any more than they, but I didn't have the heart to betray my father or mother, at least not in anything conspicuous. If I were to be completely honest, there was a part of me that feared the God that Dad had told us about, warned us about and preached about on Sunday mornings and Wednesday evenings, and I was terrified that if I did rebel, the divine vengeance of the All-Seeing would be unleashed when I least expected. So I resigned myself to the rebellion of mind and heart and, occasionally, the tongue whenever my neighbor or my cousin visited. I didn't yet trust my neighbor's good friend. Although I considered Reginald my best friend, and thus by extension that should mean I trusted his friends too, I could not bring myself to open up around William. It wasn't until college that I could safely admit my prejudice, that it was because he was White.

Our diversions were innocent enough, and we found refuge from my sisters' glares, sighs, and mutterings of how shameful it was that I was a "tomboy" by simply remaining out of their presence, or ignoring them altogether if their presence could not be avoided. The backyard, the front porch, or the smooth grains of the sidewalk or the black pavement of the street if my parents weren't looking, these were my places of escape that I found with my friends.

We did nothing special. We couldn't. That much they all, thankfully, understood. I didn't have to tell them. They knew. I was a member of "The Church." And that's exactly what it was called. The Church.

This simplicity in terminology was most likely due to my father's distaste for distinction in what should otherwise be implied in our pure Christian affiliation. Why *Baptist* church? Why *Episcopalian*? Why *Methodist*? Or worse, why *Christian* church or *Church of Christ*? Redundant, my father would say of the latter two. There was no church, no true house of worship, if it wasn't Christian.

It was a silent agreement among us, a kindness born of empathy, that they, my friends, would never mention The Church if I didn't bring it up first. To be truthful, they felt sorry for me, and I felt sorry for me. But I couldn't admit it at the time. I was making the best of it, not the worst. I refused to moan and groan, mope and complain, or to be shamelessly contumacious like my sisters. For that, I sensed that my friends respected me, that they were amazed and impressed that I could be so brave, so righteous while the rest of the world enjoyed the spontaneous joys of youth. But I didn't feel brave or righteous. I felt deprived, punished even, that I was born into such a bizarre family as to have a father inspired to further define the Christian-ness of my already loose, modest clothes that lacked even the suggestion of ostentation or style. It wasn't until years later that I looked back with intense gratefulness that God had spared me the impetuous nature of my peers, and the restless, worldly manner of my sisters.

One day William broke the agreement. He was staring at me with one eye squinted and the other only slightly open, making his slightly open eye appear more transparent than blue, as he often did when the sun was bright and the sky cloudless and he could see me more clearly than he did on other days, or at least better than the days spent inside the house. I suppose my jeans that I was keeping tight around my waist with a yellow-head safety pin borrowed from Michael's cloth diapers had inspired the forbidden inquiry. And I'm sure my oversized faded blue T-shirt didn't help in tempering his curiosity. I'd found the clothes in the church donation box, and they were for boys, I already knew, but I also knew the ones made for my female, thirteen-year-old past-puberty body would not meet my father's or mother's approval. Everyone else, at least the girls at my school, was sporting mismatched socks and revealing pants and shirts color coordinated to match their footwear. My baggy jeans were my truce. At least people were still wearing blue jeans. Certainly they would never go out of style, even if my personal selection would never be in.

"Why do you dress like that?"

I felt my face grow hot and was suddenly conscious of the awkward bulge that the gathered jean material held together by the pin was causing at my abdomen beneath the flimsy cotton of my shirt. I crossed my arms loosely in front of me and let my arms slide down, hopefully inconspicuously, to hide the bulge as I sat cross-legged on the front lawn. William was still staring at me while lying on his side, his head propped up by his elbow on the grass and fist on his cheek.

I opened my mouth to speak, but Darnell came to my rescue.

"Because she wants to. Everyone doesn't like your style, Billy Bob."

It wasn't true. I didn't want to dress like this, but my tacit acceptance of my cousin's response was less humiliating than the truth. I even giggled. He called Reggie's friend Billy Bob only when William said something Darnell felt stupid, funny, or inappropriate. I sensed Darnell enjoyed humiliating William, most likely for the same reason I couldn't bring myself to open up around him.

"Beats what most of the girls are wearing these days," Reggie said.

I smiled at him. I knew he too was lying, but I appreciated his coming to my defense even if Michelle, his girlfriend, dressed in the same fitting jeans and mismatched socks that every other girl was wearing those days.

William sat up, this time squinting both of his eyes in the sun. "I didn't say anything was wrong with it. I just wanted to know why she dressed like that."

In all fairness, William had a right to his curiosity. He was the only one who went to the same school as I. He was in two of my classes, so he saw the peculiarity of my taste in fashion more often than my best friend or my cousin. William and I both were students at MSGT—the Magnet School for Gifted and Talented—a high school almost thirty minutes from our homes in the middle class neighborhood in which he, Reginald, and I lived. Even at school, among the "freaks" and "nerds" in one of Indianapolis's most prestigious programs, I stood out in not being able to fit in even amongst them. Even the gifted and talented were up-to-date on what was in and what was not, and I couldn't measure up.

William was accepted amongst them as if it were second nature, and for the most part we kept our distance from each other except for an almost imperceptible smile of obligatory acknowledgement he or I would offer if we were passing in the halls when he was not among friends, other members of the tennis or baseball team. The racial segregation didn't help any. It was not a mandated segregation but a voluntary one, and no one questioned the logistics or ethics of it because it was only outside the classroom, that is if one dismissed the racial cliques in the seating selections themselves. My crowd, that is if I had found clothes and mannerisms to afford me one at all, would have been members of the basketball, track, or football (or flag football in the case of female students) teams. It was a silent agreement, much like that of my friends' not mentioning The Church, that the Whites would occupy particular sports teams, and the Blacks others.

The only racially integrated activities were honors programs, basketball or football games, and graduations. Even our proms were separate. But this was, technically, circumstantial. There were two proms every year: the junior prom and the senior prom, and they were sponsored by two separate school clubs. The junior prom was sponsored by the Bible Club, mostly Black, and the senior prom was sponsored by the Chess Club, mostly White. But when it came down to it, the Blacks—juniors and seniors— went to the junior prom, and the Whites—juniors and seniors—went to the senior prom. At the time, I never questioned the how's or why's of this practice.

Naturally, the Blacks had stricter rules than the Whites: Whites could come to our games, but we knew we were not welcomed at theirs. The other races sort of became one or the other based on the racial makeup of their social circles. If you were Korean and friends with Blacks, you held an honorary Black status. If you were Korean and friends with Whites, your status was likewise White.

I fit into neither, my small group of marginal friends was only three: Raksha, an international exchange junior who happened to be the only Indian I knew at the school and the first Hindu I'd met in real life; Carolyn, a petite biracial freshman with two painfully apparent and unpopular traits: a stutter and severe acne; Martha, a White sophomore whose only transgressions I could discern were bifocal glasses and more freckles than pale skin. William and I both were sophomores too, like Martha, but because of my clothes, my affiliation with The Church (which I later concluded no one knew most likely), and my natural hair that my parents forbade me from perming, I enjoyed no perks, no seniority, in my position of being, if nothing else, not a freshman.

If I had gone to a normal school, like Reggie's or Darnell's, I would most likely still not have enjoyed any privileges. I would be two years younger than most of my classmates, and I wouldn't be able to talk about my hair roots growing in, proof that it was time for me to get my hair permed yet again. Besides, I didn't see any benefit of going to a normal school because neither my cousin nor best friend would be there. They were both in middle school although Reggie, an eighth grader, was one year my senior in age while Darnell, a seventh grader, was thirteen like me. William, ironically, was the elder of our group. He was fifteen. But he didn't rub it in. I think he was so exhausted from distinguishing himself as part of the in-crowd at school that he was relieved to be himself when he was around us.

"Why do *you* dress like *that?*"

Exhausted from Darnell's insistence on taking offense, William sighed and tugged at the blades of grass in my lawn before saying hesitantly the most unexpected comment. "Congratulations on winning the algebra competition."

It took a second for me to realize he was talking to me. My love for math and all things academic was something else we never talked about, but it was not due to their empathy or feeling sorry for me but because neither Reggie nor Darnell knew this side of me.

My face grew warm.

"Thanks." My voice was barely above a whisper, and I sensed my best friend and my cousin staring at me, seeing me with new eyes. Although I wished one of them would say *something*, they didn't come to my rescue this time, I imagine, because they were just as taken aback by the comment as I was. But I was taken off guard because of who congratulated me, and they were taken off guard because of what he had congratulated me about. We all knew what school I went to, so it went without saying that my accomplishment was not insignificant.

That day in the front yard changed the current of my and Reginald's friendship. He visited more, stared at me more, and asked me more about my school and the things I did there. He even seemed to like William more, as if his friend's comment not only earned me admiration but William too.

One day, most likely because we were becoming better friends, I asked him outright why he was friends with a White boy. If I had known better, I would have waited until Darnell's father had finished visiting my mother before I asked. But it was too late, and Darnell, as usual, took this opportunity to insult William, and a second after I had asked, I regretted my inquiry.

"Because his father is a drunk and Reggie is Billy Bob's personal lord and savior."

I winced. I didn't like the way Darnell's comment not only disparaged William's honor but Jesus' too.

"Man, shut up." I could tell by the look in Reggie's eyes that he was not joking. Something Darnell had said had really gotten under his skin. He picked up a stone that had somehow found its way onto the steps of my family's back porch where we sat, and he threw it into the grass of the expansive backyard. I sensed he really wanted to throw it at my cousin. "I wish you would go home or get a life."

"I don't know what you all upset about. It's the truth. I think it's better that Ray knows the truth about her boyfriend before she—"

It happened so fast that I remembered only being knocked in the head by Reggie's knee and seeing Darnell's half smirk as his head scraped the wood of the banister and he braced himself for the fall onto the stone-lined garden next to where he had been sitting. When I realized what was happening, I shielded myself from their altercation and absentmindedly massaged the side of my head where Reggie had inadvertently hit me.

Darnell laughed, but I sensed the shock and nervousness in even that sound. "Damn, man. You really love that loser, don't you? Are you gay or something?"

"Go to hell."

"Maybe I will."

"Good riddance."

"See you there. And if we're lucky, Billy Bob will be there too. I don't think Hell is segregated."

Spent from Darnell's malicious determination, Reggie sat back on the step next to me, at that moment noticing his error. He seemed to forget about Darnell. His eyes widened slightly. "Did I hurt you?"

I shook my head and pretended not to feel the pain pulsating in my left temple, threatening to become a migraine. "No, I'm okay."

"Darnell!" It was Uncle Marvin's voice echoing through the screened door behind us. Inside I relaxed. I felt bad for wishing my cousin gone, but his presence reminded me that it was my fault that William's family life had been disparaged.

A few minutes after Darnell had gone home, my mother appeared in the doorway, her long, thin, locks that hung from her head silhouetted in the light from the kitchen. "Renee, it's time to come inside. It's dark out."

I knew what she really meant was that it was time for Reginald to go home. My heart sank. I was just beginning to enjoy our time together without my irritating cousin, which, of course, was most likely why my mother felt it was time to come in.

Reggie took the hint and gave me a reluctant wave before approaching with a slow run the fence that joined our yards and adeptly hopped over it in one movement as he held onto the top of the wire. I imagined Michelle was proud of him, seeing him run across their school's football field during practice for the real games in which he enjoyed his status as running back and his nickname "Missile." I wished I was able to perm my hair and wear stylish clothes. Then he wouldn't be too ashamed to invite me to games, even as I knew I wouldn't be able to go, at least not if my father or mother didn't have a previous engagement.

Two

In all honesty, it is Darnell to whom I'm indebted for my interest in Islam. It was he who introduced me to the term while I was still preoccupied in my world of The Church and the Sunday school classes I taught to the children of members, the only children still young enough to appreciate my words and admire me for them, and naïve enough to be oblivious to the unpopularity of my father's church and my weekly youth classes. My oldest student was ten years old.

I was fifteen and a senior in high school, the same school William and I had attended years before, and it was still winter break, two days after Christmas. It was too cold to go outside, at least to me it was. Reggie had stopped by earlier to ask if I wanted to join him and his friends in a snowball fight. I, who I suppose was always a bit pragmatic, decided that it was not judicious to join them. I figured, though not aloud, that it would take, at most, fifteen minutes before my fingers and toes would feel as if they weren't mine and my boots would be filled with snow, making the matter worse. Then I'd have to trudge home alone in the cold because Reggie would be just getting started, and he and his friends would most likely be unable to resist the one smack of a good, packed snowball across my face as I walked away in cowardice of, of all things, the weather.

I was in a bad mood anyway. For Christmas my aunt, who was a successful beautician, had taken Courtney and Patricia to her home and given them perms. They were college students, Courtney a freshman at Howard University and Patricia a junior at Ball State, but they were still haunted by my parents' rules, and despite their rebellious nature, they hadn't dared to stray so far as to show up in the house with a permanent although they kept their hair meticulously straight from a hot comb at all times. This, the forbidding of permed hair, was really more a rule of my mother than my father. I knew that much because none of the women in The Church's congregation followed it, and I'd never heard my father speak of it outside the home. Generally, if my father had a rule, it was a rule of The Church.

My mother was livid and my father nonchalant, which made my mother suspect that this was really his idea and not his sister's. But I couldn't care less about my mother's anger. I was nursing my own. Why had Aunt Juanita singled *them* out? They didn't deserve it. What had they done to earn such a priceless gift? If anything, their heads should be shaved for their relentless disobedience and disrespect of my parents.

"They're in college now," my father said, shooing his wife away as he tried to direct his attention back to the Bible he was reading to prepare for the after-Christmas sermon.

"But they are still our children. *My* children."

"They aren't *yours*. And they're not children."

"We talked about this, and you agreed that—"

"I didn't agree, Wilma, I *acquiesced*." He had looked up from his Bible to say that, and I grew disgusted and started for my room. But the sound of the doorbell stopped me. I headed to the front door instead.

"If that's Juanita," my mother shouted, "tell her we're not home."

It wasn't Juanita. It was my mother's brother Marvin, his wife Marcella, and their son Darnell. In keeping with the Christmas spirit, I smiled. But I didn't feel like being friendly.

"Thank God it's not *your* family," my mother said as she went to greet the guests.

Uncle Marvin laughed as he unbuttoned his coat. "What are you two arguing about this time?"

"Your brother-in-law has decided that God didn't know what He was doing when He gave our daughters beautiful, African hair."

My uncle's eyebrows rose. Disapproval was on his face although he wore a smile of cordiality. "You're kidding, right?"

Instinctively, I looked at my aunt's hair, and to my relief, at least for the sake of her comfort amid my mother's comment although I wasn't particularly in love with my African hair, I noticed the small braids pulled back into a bun, realizing at that moment that I'd never seen her with straight hair.

After removing his coat, Darnell pulled me by the elbow and led me to the kitchen. I sensed he had something urgent to tell me and I started to ask him when I noticed the bowtie on his neck. It was small and colorful and sat purposefully situated at the white collar of his button-up dress shirt. Thinking it was a joke of his, I started to laugh.

He ignored me. His face grew serious. "You're not going to do it, are you?"

I furrowed my brows and stopped laughing to regard him curiously. "What?"

"She's joking, right?"

I shook my head. "What are you talking about?"

"Your mother. She said your father is allowing you and your sisters to straighten your hair."

I grew defensive. "And what if he is?" What I meant to say was, *What's it to you?*

"Don't do it."

I decided against telling him that the decision had already been made for me. "Why shouldn't I? If my sisters can have a perm, why can't I?"

I felt myself growing upset as I thought of spending all my years in braids and a huge "Afro puff" at the back of my head when my mother was unable to braid my hair in time for school. I was tired of being laughed at, called Nappy Head, and listening to the taunting of the Black girls who would whisper, chant-like in my ear, "You need to get your hair done." If I were honest, *I* didn't mind my hair. In fact, there were moments that I loved it. But I did mind it creating an even greater barrier between me and normalcy at school.

"Because you're a goddess, Renee."

I grinned, enjoying his sense of humor in his attempt to flatter me.

"I'm serious."

It took me a moment to see it. But he really wasn't joking. Now I stared at him. Then I realized I must have heard him incorrectly.

"You're a goddess. A beautiful, Black African queen. Your hair is your honor, your crown. Don't put the White man's poison in it."

This time I withheld laughter. I had always thought Darnell a bit off, but this was over the top. Maybe he was the one addicted to intoxicants and not William's father. "Poison?"

"Yes, poison, Ray."

He sighed, deciding to take a rational approach. "Think about it. When did Black people start straightening their hair?"

I didn't have an answer.

"After slavery. After they were slaves of the White man. He didn't just chain our bodies, he chained our minds."

Stunned that Darnell was actually taking his words seriously, I stared at him, seeing him for the first time. He had the beginnings of a mustache and beard and the brown of his face glowed the color of cashews, and I noticed in his dark eyes a profundity—a profoundness of knowledge and worldly awareness—that I hadn't before. It was as if he'd matured overnight, even as the insanity of his words betrayed what I was sensing.

"—in your father's church for example."

At his reference to The Church, I felt my heart quicken and my defensiveness grew thick and tight in my chest. "What about my father's church?"

"Have you ever noticed, Ray? Look on the wall, in front of the church. What is there? What do you see?"

I could hardly think to answer his question because I was so offended that he had asked it. "What do you mean, what's there?"

"Think, Ray." It was as if I were the one losing my mind, not him, and for a moment I felt as if I were. His eyes were so concerned, so intense that I wondered if I had in fact done something wholly inappropriate to warrant such heartfelt directives to use my mental faculties.

"Think about *what?*"

"Your church." At the last word, he lowered his voice, as if suddenly aware that my parents were in the living room, within earshot, as if it were a bad word and we were exchanging a secret at their expense.

"There's nothing to think about." I intentionally raised my voice to let him know where my loyalties lay. If I wouldn't side against The Church for my own blood sisters' pleasure, I most certainly wasn't doing if for a thoughtless, cruel person like Darnell. In retrospect, I know I had judged him harshly, holding him accountable for the sins of that day on the back porch and sullying with it his image in the present. But I didn't know that I was being unjust, nor would I have cared, because I hated him for upsetting Reggie and insulting William. And now he had the nerve to attack my father, the lifeblood of my family and religious affiliation.

"There's a lot to think about, Ray. Too much to go over now."

As if I'd asked him to teach me. I could have spit on him right then.

"But it will behoove you to take one look at what's on your church wall to see what I mean. Then maybe you won't hate the beautiful, African skin and hair God has given you. Then maybe you'll wake up."

His last words reminded me of Courtney's and my offense was fierce. "Who the hell do you think you are?"

"No," he said so calmly, with so much concern that I too calmed, even if just to marvel at his audacity in remaining level-headed when I was unable to. "You are the one who needs to think about who you are. I already know who I am."

I laughed. Most likely because I didn't know what else to do to repair my injured pride. "And just who are you?"

"A Muslim."

I started to say something but stopped mid-sentence because he had used a word I did not know, and this startled me. The word sounded vaguely familiar as if I'd seen it in a book or heard it during a history lesson. The only images it conjured up were that of my former friend Raksha, but she had been Hindu.

"A what?" I was more curious than upset, momentarily forgetting our argument and what had angered me.

"Muslim." He said it calmly, more reserved this time, as if he was spent from all the arguing and realized just then he was making my affliction worse instead of better. There was a long pause as he tried to gather his thoughts, as if there was a confession he was about to make.

"Have you heard of the Honorable Elijah Muhammad?"

"No," I said, still a bit bemused.

"The Nation of Islam?"

I shook my head, but I couldn't take my eyes off of him. Why was there a sense of sorrow in his eyes? What had I done to deserve so much pity?

He sighed and started to leave the kitchen. "Wait here."

He returned a minute later with a book. *The Autobiography of Malcolm X.* He handed it to me. "You heard of Malcolm X?"

I laughed. Who hadn't? It had become the recent craze of Black youth to sport the "X" on their caps, and I had heard many Black students in hushed whispers talking about how "powerful" the movie had been. I had never seen it. I knew not to ask to see something like that. From the little I gathered from my schoolmates, it was a movie that The Church wouldn't permit, and thus one I wouldn't waste my time wanting to see. But at that moment, my interest was peaked.

I held the book in my hand and stared at it. I felt a connection to the serious-looking, intelligent man on the front cover. But I doubted I would read it. My father wouldn't approve.

"Read this, and do what I said."

I met his gaze, suddenly reminded why he had offended me a moment before. But for some reason I couldn't muster the same outrage at his implicit attack on The Church. And for the life of me, I couldn't figure out why he wanted me to stare, in judgment, at the walls of my father's church.

"And what have you gained in your Afro-centricity?" My father's voice was so distinct in its upset that his words cut through the pseudo-privacy my cousin and I had successfully forged only minutes before.

"A true understanding of God." It was my uncle's voice. *O Lord.* They were all arguing now.

"Put it away," Darnell whispered, as if sensing our family's current distraction would be my only opportunity to keep the book away from my father's attention.

Because I didn't want to hear the argument—it tore me apart to hear my family bickering—I left and did as Darnell said although I couldn't have, at that moment, cared less whether or not my father saw the book and reluctantly approved or told me to burn it.

In the quiet of my room, I locked the door. Darnell never ventured upstairs to my room, but I didn't want to take the chance of someone destroying my quiet. Why, I don't know, but I sat on my bed, my back supported by a pillow and began reading the autobiography. My reading was most likely to mollify the aching I felt in my chest as the voices from downstairs rose and stole their way into my room, burning my eyes and threatening to shatter my weakly fortified existence.

During the after-Christmas service, with thoughts of the racial suffering of Malcolm Little and his family floating in my mind, I stared at the wall above my father's head and saw what Darnell had told me to look for—a three-dimensional likeness of Jesus' crucifixion. Blood spilled from his hands on either side and his head dangled to his right in apparent pain, even as his eyes were peaceful, as if surrendering to this fate. It was the helplessness of my savior that I noticed before registering what Darnell wanted me to see. And I felt the perversity of it. How could he be my savior if he couldn't save himself?

I pushed the thought from my mind and concentrated on my hands. I couldn't look at my sisters on either side of me because the sight of their shiny, straight hair still inspired resentment. But I couldn't help noticing the likeness of their hair to that of Jesus' image on the wall.

White man's poison, Darnell had called the hair chemicals I envied.

White man. A White man. That's what Darnell wanted me to notice. Our savior was a White man.

That afternoon, I asked Reggie what he thought of Malcolm X and all this White man is the son of God business.

He sat in our dining room across from me and shrugged. "He has a point."

"Darnell?" I was shocked that Reggie had anything good to say about him after what he had said about William's father.

"Not just Darnell, all of 'em."

"All of who?"

"The Muslims."

"You know about them?"

"Of course." He paused and regarded me. "You don't?"

My pride was hurt, but I decided that satisfying my curiosity was more important than being the smart one this time. "No, I never heard of them before Darnell said he was one."

"Well, Darnell's a Black Muslim."

"As opposed to what?"

"A Muslim."

"What's the difference?"

"Black Muslims are members of the Nation of Islam, who believe Black people are gods and White people are devils. Regular Muslims are mostly Indians and Arabs who believe women shouldn't show their faces in public."

"What?" They both sounded like lunatics to me.

Reggie laughed and shrugged, as if saying, *You asked*.

"And exactly what makes you think they have a point?"

"I'm not talking about the Indians and Arabs. I'm talking about the Nation of Islam."

"You think William's family is full of devils?"

Reggie burst out laughing then settled for smiling at me. "Of course not. I just said they have a point. I didn't say they were right."

"How could you even say they have a point?"

"I'm not talking about the god and devil bit. I'm talking about Jesus being a White man. Why think of God's son like that?"

I didn't know what to say, suddenly reminded of my own doubts earlier that day.

"Who cares?" Reggie said finally, sparing me the agony of a further crisis of faith. "Who cares what color Jesus is?"

Reluctantly, I smiled. "Yeah, that's true."

But, somehow, although momentarily relieved, I hadn't convinced myself. I was thinking about the autobiography I was reading.

It was New Year's Eve, and following my father's sermon that evening, my parents had accepted an invitation to dinner. I was home with Patricia and Courtney, who were in our parents' room watching a movie that I suspected wouldn't be approved by The Church, and my younger brothers were asleep. Having already taken it upon myself to remove the dust jacket of the book and replace it with one of Mildred D. Taylor's, I was relaxing in the living room when the doorbell rang. Setting the book aside, I answered it and found William standing on the front porch holding a bag.

He smiled.

I stared at him. Most of the MSGT students were at a New Year's party, and I knew its most valued attendees were William's friends. Even Reggie had gone to a party of his own, and although he invited me to join him, I already knew my father wouldn't approve, and that even if he would, I couldn't put myself or Reggie through the humiliation of my being a tag-along with him and Shauna, his current girlfriend.

"Can I come in?"

I hesitated because I really didn't want to be disturbed, or more likely because I wasn't used to entertaining William if he wasn't with Reggie. But I felt it would be rude to say no. So I stepped aside and let him in.

"I won't stay long," he said, as if sensing my discomfort. He shrugged off his coat, carefully setting the bag on the foyer floor then picking it back up after hanging his coat. He walked over to the couch, sat down, and peered into the bag before pulling out a neatly wrapped gift. He faltered, glancing at my open book next to him, most likely because he was nervous to present the gift. But he did a double-take and read the words more closely, and my heart hammered in my chest, suddenly recalling the offensive passage I was reading.

His face colored slightly and he smiled, as if approving, but I knew he didn't. He couldn't approve of his race being talked about in such demeaning terms.

"*The Autobiography of Malcolm X*," he said, allaying my fears.

I couldn't get my question out from the shock I felt right then. But my eyes must have been indication enough.

"I'm reading it for history class."

"At MSGT?"

"Yes."

"They assign that there?"

He shook his head. "I'm doing a research paper."

"On Malcolm X?"

He nodded. "And Martin Luther King, Jr. I'm comparing them."

I didn't know what to say.

"Pretty good, isn't it?"

"You selected the topic or the teacher assigned it?" I was so intent on finding out more about the paper that it wasn't until after he had gone that I understood the weightiness of his last question concerning my reading.

"I selected it."

He held out the gift to me. "Merry Christmas."

I accepted the gift and studied it for sometime. "Thank you."

"No problem." He stood to go. For a moment he hesitated, then as if thinking better of it, decided to excuse himself.

"Tell your parents I said hello and merry Christmas," he said.

"And tell your parents the same."

He lifted his coat from the hook and shrugged it on, a smile on his face as he opened the door. "I hope you like it."

"I'm sure I will, William. Thank you." I paused. "I'm sorry I, uh, didn't have anything for you."

He waved his hand dismissively. "Don't worry about it." He laughed uncomfortably. "I'm sorry I'm giving it so late. It's just that we had to travel to Evansville and I—"

"It's okay. I understand."

There was a long pause. "Good night."

"Good night," I said as I closed the door.

Still recovering from surprise, inspired more by his research topic than his surprise visit, I sat down on the couch and stared at the box, too distracted by my shock to wonder, or care, what was inside, let alone ponder the reason for his giving it to me.

Mindlessly, I tugged at the bow and tore the shimmering red paper and opened the lid.

I blinked, staring at the gold necklace with a crucifix pendant. I pulled it from the box and noticed a single diamond in the middle of the cross. My eyes widened and I wondered how much he had to pay for something like this. Maybe the stone wasn't real, I considered, but I somehow sensed that I was wrong.

"Well, I guess you won't be needing my gift then," Reggie said late morning on New Year's Day. He had given me a pair of gloves with an "R" inscribed on each. I knew he couldn't afford William's gift, and I couldn't tell him the gloves meant more to me than the jewelry, even as the necklace sparkled on my neck and the gloves were stuffed away in a drawer in my room.

"Of course I'll need your gift. It's cold out there."

Reggie was silent from where he sat on the sofa a comfortable distance from me. His mustache was coming in against his deep brown skin and I found myself wishing I could dress like Shauna, or at least have my hair done like hers.

He was pensive, but at the time, I didn't know what was concerning him. "Your, uh, church..."

I held my breath, unable to understand my defensiveness at his breaking our unspoken rule. I forced myself to calm down. This was not Darnell, this was my best friend. If he was bringing up The Church, there must be a good reason.

"It doesn't allow you to date, huh?"

I dropped my gaze. "No. Not until you're eighteen."

He nodded. "So...you wouldn't go out with someone, I mean, not me, but someone like William if he asked?" His voice held a hint of hopefulness, as if he were asking me to make a promise.

At that, I looked at him, although he wouldn't meet my gaze, and laughed. "William?"

A reluctant smile tugged at one side of his mouth. He glanced at me momentarily then looked away. "Yeah, why not? It's obvious he likes you."

"*Likes* me?" I'd never heard those words used in reference to myself outside the punch lines of jokes at school.

"Don't tell me you can't see it." His gaze rested on the gold crucifix before he sighed of frustration. He started to say something but decided against it.

I fingered the necklace and shook my head. "He's *White.*"

Reggie looked at me as if disgusted. "So what?"

For a moment I thought I'd made the same mistake that Darnell had. I opened my mouth to clarify, but Reggie went on before I could.

"He's still a man."

I narrowed my eyes at the ridiculousness of my friend's claim. "Do you really think someone like William would give a second's thought about someone like me?"

He appeared even more disgusted. "What's that supposed to mean?"

I started to say something but realized he had a point. Why did I assume I was somehow inferior? "Well, for one," I began, unsure of what I would say until it came out, "I don't look like the Michelles or Shaunas of the world."

"They're not White."

True. And we were talking about William here. "That's beside the point."

"A second ago that seemed to *be* your point."

I was offended, but my pride prevented me from showing it. I decided to argue my point. "I don't know all the White girls' names at MSGT, but I see how they run after William and his friends. Cheerleaders, dance club, all of them."

"And?"

"And I have to walk around and make books and teachers my best friends. Christ, I can't even wear the clothes they wear or even style my hair how I want."

"And you think people like me or William care about stuff like that?"

I didn't know what to say. At his reference to himself, I was caught off-guard. But my insecurity reigned. He could not have meant what I thought, or hoped.

I shook my head. "I have no idea what goes on in your heads, but I know—"

"Then you don't *know* anything."

"I know what I'm not."

Reggie shook his head, apparently frustrated. But I didn't understand what was frustrating him. "You don't give yourself credit."

"For what? Being a nerd and an outcast?"

"See, that's what I mean. Maybe you should listen to Darnell a little more."

"For what? So I can lose my sanity and think I'm a god and William's a devil?"

"No, for Pete's sake, so you can see how—" He stopped himself. Aggravated, he stood and headed for the door, grabbing his coat so abruptly that the coat stand almost fell. He had to steady it with one hand while holding his coat in the other.

"Just don't do anything stupid," he said as he opened the door. "William's not the only one who knows a good thing when he sees it."

Before I could respond, the door slammed in my face. For a moment, I stood in the living room staring at the door as if it would give me the answers to the questions that flooded my mind right then. As my friend's words gradually took meaning, I felt hope. Not deflated hope. But pure, unadulterated desire that I was not misunderstanding.

After a moment's hesitation, I headed to the restroom and turned on the light. I stood before the mirror and squinted my eyes, closing then opening them, and finally rubbing them before I stared at my reflection, searching for what Reggie suspected William had seen.

I never thought much of my complexion, most likely because I didn't know where it fit into the color spectrum. My family never used the narrow terms that the Black students did at school. Light-skinned, dark-skinned, brown-skinned. I was only beginning to understand what they meant to my schoolmates, but they still meant little to me. What would my skin be considered?

In my ignorance, I didn't realize that these terms were not the only ones used when describing, or assessing, a person's beauty. My father talked of inner beauty. But, like most of what he said, I regarded it as just talk. The Church talk.

It didn't take long to rule out light-skinned. I thought of my sister Patricia and my biracial friend Carolyn whom I'd met when I was a sophomore. The term would be more fitting for them. Their skin was pale, Carolyn's almost yellow. My skin was certainly not in that color range.

I tried to see my skin as separate from myself. If I could compare it to anything, what would it resemble? I recalled thinking Darnell's color was of cashews. But did that make him light, brown, or dark? I rested my hand on the mirror and compared my hue to that of the wood framing the glass, a rich wood the color of Reggie's skin. Two different browns, and the wood was darker than mine. I then compared myself to Darnell and found that I was darker. As I stared, I concluded that my skin was the color of the chocolate milk enclosed in the cartons at school. That was the only thing I could come up with right then. And it didn't make me feel beautiful. Yet, still I prayed for a miracle, hoping that, regardless of what I was to the world, Reggie saw me as I couldn't see myself.

Three

Three things happened during my senior year in high school that would change the course of my life forever, as well as my outlook on it: While I was awaiting acceptance, or rejection, letters from the colleges I'd applied to, Darnell was registering himself for the military. William—and his good friend Reginald—asked me to the prom, an event I had long since divorced, in my mind, from having anything to do with me. I decided, or, rather, my parents decided for me, that I would go to Maryland for college, primarily because my sister Courtney would be a sophomore at Howard University and I would be near family.

What shocked me most about Darnell's registering for the military was the impossibility of it. He was only fifteen, and his newfound religious beliefs seemed, to me, at odds with such an apparently patriotic decision. Of course, I was biased. The Church forbade all forms of violence, reserving any infliction of bodily harm to cases of absolute necessity— that of self-defense when your life itself was threatened. One look at CNN, and I was convinced that, even if my father could use some adjustments in his taste of religious fashion, he was on point when it came to the world's need for peaceful resistance and each individual's responsibility to making it happen as opposed to just talking about it.

One afternoon in March during our schools' spring breaks, only weeks before either William or Reginald would shock me with their proposals to take me to the prom, I sat with my three friends in my living room playing Monopoly. It was raining outside, and my little brothers were wreaking havoc in the house. My father was out meeting with some "important people" about securing a spot on a local network, allowing him to have his Sunday sermons televised and broadcast in the metropolitan area. My mother was in her room nursing a headache and she'd asked me, and, by extension, my friends, to keep an eye on Michael, who was now two, and Elijah, who was approaching his fourth birthday.

I hated Monopoly. But it was the only game we had in the house. The Church hadn't yet lifted its ban on cards and video games, so we really had little options in amusing ourselves. My reason for loathing the game was that it did little to stoke my competitive spirit. I simply couldn't bring myself to be enthusiastic about it. I liked games that had a clear ending, and a clear winner, who I was determined should always be me, not games in which the only sign of their ending was a player's nodding off or another's finding interest in his fingernails.

Ten minutes into the game, I was more interested in the rain's pounding against the windows and in Michael's and Elijah's irritating playful shrieking, tireless running, and incessant fighting than the stacks of money before me and my competitors. In trying to avoid spoiling the mood of the men, who were getting more and more excited about the colorful cash stacked before them, I opted to release my unrest through talking.

"Where are you going for college?" I had to raise my voice above my brothers. They were getting noisier, and dangerously close to our game. Secretly, I hoped Michael would trip and fall onto the board.

I usually didn't talk directly to William. But he and I were the only ones graduating this year, and boredom emboldened me. Besides, I was still wearing the cross pendant he'd given me, and this made me feel more relaxed in his company.

It took a moment before he noticed me. It was his turn and he was hoping he wasn't going to be sent to jail—again. After taking a look at the card, he exhaled then glanced at me.

"Johns Hopkins. You?"

"University of Maryland."

"Baltimore?" His eyes lit up.

I shook my head. "College Park."

"Cool. That's not too far from Baltimore, I hear."

I nodded, not knowing what else I could say to keep the conversation going, and the game from continuing. "You going anywhere for the summer?"

"My parents were thinking about Evansville again."

"Who's there?"

"Aunts, cousins." He shrugged. "Nobody important."

"Sorry, White Boy," Darnell interjected, "but cousins are indeed important."

My cousin's voice startled me, both in its abruptness and its cruelty. Since joining the Nation of Islam, he had taken to replacing the usual "Billy Bob" with the derogatory "White Boy."

I rolled my eyes. At that point, I knew the Monopoly game was over, but this wasn't exactly my idea of its ending. I felt the tension build as Reggie stopped, mid-roll, and glared at Darnell. He started to speak, but this time I took the pleasure.

"Nobody's talking to you."

"And nobody's talking to you."

As if on cue, Michael came and ran carelessly across the board, sending our pieces askew. Elijah followed him, and our stacks of money scattered.

"Please tell me," I said in mock exhaustion, "that you plan to get a life sometime this year."

"Why are you all sensitive?" Darnell regarded me as if I'd insulted him. "Mrs. X-is-my-favorite-movie."

I glared at him and my cheeks grew hot. It was the ultimate betrayal. I hadn't even told Reggie I'd done the unthinkable: I'd watched the forbidden movie when my parents and aunt and uncle let me and Darnell go to the mall one Saturday while they went to a friend's house not too far from the shopping center. In my defense, I didn't know what movie we were going to see. Darnell said it was a surprise, and when we walked into the movie theater bearing Malcolm's infamous *X* title, I was too shocked, and too curious, to turn around and walk out.

It was as if time froze, and I wished I could disappear. In paranoia, or instinct, I glanced at Elijah, hoping—*praying*—that my little brother hadn't heard, or understood. His adult-like awareness was uncanny, and his mature speech was even more unsettling. In my mind, I could already hear him asking my mother or father, as if his inquiry's delay was solely for my personal public torment, *"Why does Cousin Darnell call Renee Mrs. X-is-my-favorite-movie?"*

To my dismay, Elijah was staring at us curiously and Michael, his shadow, stood next to him regarding me suspiciously. I couldn't look at William, and I certainly couldn't look at my best friend. So I did what my mind would register only later. I lifted the already tousled game board, turned it over, and kicked the money toward Darnell and stormed out the living room. I then ran upstairs to my room.

Once inside, I locked the door, and cried so pitifully that I couldn't keep my sobs from coming out as horrible whines and hiccups.

There was a knock at my door, but I couldn't—wouldn't—open it. I couldn't face Reggie right then, although he was the only person I imagined I would feel safe with at the moment.

The knocking became a pounding, an insistent pounding. But I was in my own world of selfish grief. At that moment, I'd lost all rationale, forgetting even that my little brothers were, technically, unsupervised downstairs. Minutes later, when I realized this, I felt an urgent obligation to go check on them, but still, I couldn't bring myself to move from my spot. To be honest, I was embarrassed that I'd made such a fool of myself. And in front of William, of all people. *Ugh!* I hated myself right then.

When the knocking ceased and I thought I couldn't hear anyone downstairs, I felt I'd better check on Michael and Elijah. I went to the bathroom in my room and washed my face, staring at my red, puffy eyes and tried to hide my sullied mood. I took a deep breath, left the bathroom, and passed through my room and opened the door before I could change my mind.

As I held the door open, I froze. Darnell stood with his arms folded and his head down, leaning against the wall next to my room. He looked up when the door opened.

When our gazes met, I saw in his eyes what I had never seen before. Desperation. For a moment, I stared at him, confused. Why should he feel desperate when I was the one whose life he'd just ruined?

"Denise, wait." He gently grabbed my arm as I tried to push past him when he stepped in front of my door.

I tried to shrug him off, slightly irritated by his calling me by the wrong name.

"Please, Renee."

It was the gentleness of his voice that softened me. But I couldn't show it.

"What?" I faced him, folding my arms across my chest defiantly, letting that motion free me of his grip.

"I..." He stammered, apparently taken aback that I'd given in, and so quickly. "I'm sorry."

My hurt and pride still stung in my chest, and my eyes burned in anger, but none of that prevented me from hearing the words I'd never heard come from him, and the sincerity in his tone.

"I'm sorry," he said again, softer this time, holding my gaze as if assessing my pain and reflecting it in his eyes.

Uncomfortable in not having reason to be upset or offended by him, I pushed past him and went downstairs, nursing my hurt feelings and fear that my sin would somehow be discovered by my father or mother.

When I reached the living room, I found that the Monopoly game had been cleared away and its box was on the dining room table, and that William had gone home. I heard the sounds of dishes clanking in the kitchen, ventured there, and found Reggie preparing a snack for my brothers. When he heard me, he met my gaze with a grin.

"You all right?"

I turned my lips in the beginning of a smile and shrugged, softened at the sight of him. "Yeah, I guess."

I heard the sound of footfalls on the steps. I quieted and cringed as I braced myself for Darnell's entry. A few seconds later, the front door opened and slammed close. I exhaled, unable to escape feeling relief at his exit. But Darnell's anger was potent. I could almost taste it. This disturbed me mostly because I knew whom he was most upset with—himself. This was not the Darnell I remembered.

Concealing my concern, I pretended to be offended. "What's his problem?"

Reggie placed a plastic bowl of dry cereal before Michael, who sat impatiently kicking in his high chair. He then placed a box of cookies before Elijah, whose eyes lit up. Michael, upon seeing his brother's meal, abruptly threw his cereal to the floor and screamed, "Cookies!"

I immediately grabbed the broom and began cleaning up the mess.

"Growing pains."

"What?" I paused sweeping and stared at Reggie with my brows furrowed. "Growing pains?"

"He just gave his future to Uncle Sam and doesn't know what to do with himself."

My eyebrows gathered in confusion, but before I could ask, Reggie explained.

"He's joining the army."

"The army?"

Reggie shrugged as he handed a cookie to Michael, who hummed in pleasure as he devoured it.

I was troubled and confused, and it took me a moment to realize the reason for the latter. "But he's only fifteen."

Reggie wore a hesitant, almost sad, expression on his face as he tried to smile but couldn't. He shook his head and apologized to me with his eyes. But I didn't understand what he was regretting. "He's eighteen."

Time seemed to stop. This couldn't be true. I tried to recall the first time my cousin and I met, when my mother's brother moved to Indianapolis when I was seven or eight years old. It was the same day I'd met Reginald. Yes, I was eight because I remember asking my mother if Darnell would be in my fifth grade class. My mother had grown quiet and said curtly that my cousin would be at a different school. I knew by her tone that I was to ask nothing further. But I didn't understand the relevance or justice in treating me as if I'd asked something inappropriate.

"What?" It came out as a whisper. I couldn't believe it. My cousin had lied to me. All these years.

"Why?" I asked, already feeling sorry for him, as if sensing there was more to this than I wanted to know.

Reggie paused, as if considering the ethics of sharing more. He raised his eyes to the ceiling then let out a deep breath. "He's...challenged in ways."

"What's that supposed to mean?" It was unjust getting angry with Reginald, but I couldn't help it. I felt as if everyone was keeping a secret and I was the only one left out.

When he didn't respond, I raised my voice. "What's that supposed to mean? Answer me, Reggie."

He shook his head, sighing, as if regretting what he'd already said. "Just forget it, okay?"

"I deserve an explanation."

"It's not my life to explain, Ray." I could see the hurt and frustration in his eyes. He was torn, between betraying my cousin and pleasing me. He started to give in, then thought better of it.

"Ask him, Ray." He wiped his hands on his pants and started out the kitchen. My heart fell as I realized he too was leaving. "Just consider his feelings before you satisfy your quest for information."

I followed him to the door. "Why are you leaving?" I sounded as if I were whining, and I hated myself for it. But I couldn't think about that right then.

"I have a lot on my mind."

Without glancing back at me, he left me with my guilt, confusion, and curiosity.

By the end of the week, after hours of sleepless torment, I decided that the only feelings I had a right to were my guilt and confusion. I realized in that moment as I lay in bed staring at the dark ceiling the night before school resumed, that Reggie had taught me a powerful spiritual lesson, the first I'd learned independent of The Church—that curiosity is sometimes a sin.

I respected Reginald in a way I couldn't fully express, even to myself. But I felt it and recognized years later that that night of the spiritual revelation was when I knew I wanted him as my husband, even if I had to wait a lifetime to fulfill that dream. My desire to marry my best friend was so visceral that it was painful. I imagined asking him, then my father if he could bend the rules and let me date before eighteen. Then I imagined cutting to the chase, saying to them both that I didn't want to be Michelle or Shauna. I wanted to be Mrs. Matthews. Nothing more, nothing less.

I cried when I realized I could never realize this dream. I was being foolish. My parents would never let me near a man before eighteen, especially for marriage. My mother was a success-driven, PhD-holding woman, and she wasn't about to let her intelligent, promising daughter throw her life away for some boy who was barely halfway through high school.

I cried more when I realized that it wasn't my mother or her dreams that I was up against, but Reggie's heart. He wouldn't be stupid enough to throw his life away and live like a high school drop-out to marry someone like me.

One night, in mid-April I sat watching my little brothers play in the living room, wondering what on earth someone like William had been thinking when he stopped by the night before to ask me to the prom, the senior prom. As I was regretting my response, which was more akin to speechless shock, I received a call from Reggie, which was weird because he rarely used the telephone to speak to me. But from the sound of his voice, it sounded serious. As his words slowly took meaning, I was speechless.

"But what about Shauna?" I hoped the pounding in my chest wouldn't make my voice falter.

"What about her?"

I didn't know what to say.

"She's a sophomore, like me."

My flattery and nervousness clouded my thinking, and I was unable to comprehend his meaning. But later I understood. Neither of them could go to their prom this year if it wasn't with someone in a senior grade, and they certainly could not attend with each other.

"She knows we're good friends."

The casualness of his voice made my heart sink. I was hoping for too much. Hurt, I told him about William.

"William?" The way he said William's name reminded me of Darnell. I flinched.

"Yeah, why not?"

"You can't be serious."

"I could go to both proms," I said, coming up with the idea right then. "You can come to our junior prom, and I could go with William to his senior one."

He was silent until I grew uncomfortable.

"You would really do that?"

"Why not? I'd get a kick out of the look on all the White girls' faces when we walk in." I wasn't serious, but I enjoyed seeing if I could hurt Reggie like he had me, by dating Michelle and Shauna, and saying we were "good friends." Secretly, I wanted to know if I had reason to hope for a future together.

"Fine." He breathed the word, giving in. "Suit yourself."

My heart raced. I immediately regretted my behavior. The sound of the dial tone in my ear was like a flat line. It took a few seconds, but I felt as if someone had punched me in the stomach. I saw, in that moment, as my clinched fist gripped the receiver, that I was the one who had inflicted the pain.

I didn't go to the prom that year. I never responded to William, and he never asked me again. I'd hurt Reggie's pride as I stoked my own. Too caught up in my own hurt, and if I'm honest—arrogance, I gave up the closest thing to a date my father would allow. It was the only boy-girl event my father or The Church permitted before the age of eighteen, and I missed out. But, more significantly, I gave up the last opportunity I would have to fulfill the only dream I had allowed myself to imagine could be reality.

Four

My first year of college was, for the most part, uneventful. I lived alone in a dorm room despite my assignment to a roommate that I saw, at most, once a week. I had been nervous and excited when my parents unloaded my belongings into the room and left, leaving me to fend for myself when I met my roommate late that night during the middle of August of 1993 in College Park, Maryland. My only solace when they left had been that I wouldn't be sleeping alone in the room—I had never lived alone before and wasn't looking forward to it. That first night, as trepidation gripped me, I realized that I had never even gone to as much as a sleepover at a friend's house during all my young adult years in Indianapolis. It wasn't The Church or my parents' strictness at fault for that, I knew, but myself, for having forged no meaningful friendships with females. Still, at sixteen years old, I had no female friend I could call to share my excitement and anxiety about living alone for the first time in my life.

I thought vaguely of Carolyn and wished I'd at least been sensible enough to exchange contact information with her. But because we had merely tolerated each other and had forged an alliance due to our shared unpopularity, I suspect we both silently agreed we didn't want to be permanent reminders to one another of who we had been, or, rather, who we had *not* been in high school. In all honesty, I think we were embarrassed by our friendship, and we thought it better that we part without pretending that we wanted each other as memories in a past we hoped college would allow us to deny and ultimately forget.

Yet, as I sat alone on the hard, bare bed feeling suffocated by the smallness of the room and the intensity of my apprehension, I longed for Carolyn's laughter, smile, or even sympathy. A flicker of pain was ignited in my chest as my mind, of its own accord, wandered to the raw truth of my suffering—that it was Reggie's laughter, smile, and sympathy that I wanted. But I extinguished the flame before its heat could cause me further discomfort and forced myself to focus on Carolyn's stutter and imperfect complexion, and I cried.

My sulking was disrupted by the sound of a key turning in the door, and I quickly wiped my face and saw a tall, shapely woman whose smooth, dark brown skin reminded me immediately of Reggie. Her hair was short, styled in attractive natural twists that pointed upward, and I instantly felt at ease. She smiled and extended her hand as she approached me.

"I'm Anita." Her accent was British, and for some reason I couldn't keep from chuckling. I'd never heard a Black person speak like English royalty.

I pretended my laughter was due to my joy in meeting her. "Renee."

"Where are you from?"

"Indiana. You?"

"London."

I was amazed. I liked her already. "You traveled far."

She shook her head. "My family moved to the states a few years ago. Right now, they live in New York."

"Oh." I stared at her. I couldn't get over the accent.

We talked for another hour before she decided she'd better remove her luggage from the lobby.

That was the longest conversation we had for the entire year. Apparently, she had a male friend who was more appealing than the dorm room and me, so I prided myself in only two benefits of making her acquaintance: I had ample time to myself, and she referred me to an Ethiopian friend of hers who styled natural hair for a nominal fee.

My first trip home was during Thanksgiving break. Courtney and I booked a flight together, and I surprised myself by genuinely enjoying her company and conversation. It was as if she and I were getting acquainted for the first time. I was actually saddened at the end of our return flight when we returned to our respective campuses. But we'd exchanged numbers, something we hadn't done before although we could have easily obtained the information from our parents.

I had wanted to see Reggie, but I didn't. My mother told me in passing—I'd hoped my melancholy wasn't that apparent—that he had traveled to visit relatives for the vacation.

William stopped by, but I couldn't have cared less. I could see him anytime I wanted since we were less than an hour apart from each other in Maryland. But both he and I were too busy with our studies to travel that distance, or to make it a priority. It was clear that we'd both moved on, and I had found myself wishing that I could see, at least, Darnell. But he was in the army now, in only-God-knows-what country and I couldn't bring myself to ask the specifics. I still hadn't gotten over that he was three years older than he'd let on, and that he had a life wholly unrelated to me. Still, I couldn't deny that I missed him, and I wished I'd thought to suggest keeping in touch through writing letters. But it was too late for that. Or at least I told myself it was too late.

In retrospect, I think my and Reggie's dying friendship cast a shadow on all my other relationships, and I couldn't muster the energy, or desire, to repair them. Life lost its luster, and I found love in the same mundane pursuit that characterized my childhood—academics.

During Christmas vacation, my second trip home, I saw Reggie. But my hopes were deflated as our time together took on the same note it always had: my listening to him talk blissfully about his most recent girlfriend. This time her name was Natalie. I feigned interest. We exchanged numbers, or rather I gave him mine, as he still lived at home, and we went our separate ways as if nothing had changed, or happened, in the year before I left to college.

I would be lying if I said I didn't beat myself up over not accepting his taking me to the prom. But right then, I was being an optimist, and I couldn't admit to myself that I cared. So I shrugged off my feelings and immersed myself into doing what I did best: relishing in the artificial glory of honors, awards, and professors' admiration and approval.

One night shortly before mid-terms were scheduled for second semester, Courtney called my room and when I answered, she said simply, "Pack tonight. We have to go home this weekend."

I felt my head pound and I tried to remain calm. Inside I tried to quell the panicked fear and dread that was causing my chest to hurt. "What happened?"

"It's Patricia."

I nearly fainted and had to readjust the phone to my ear. I asked Courtney to repeat what she had said.

"Her roommate called our parents. She's been gone a whole week. No one knows where she is."

I packed in a frenzy, fearing the worst. From what I gathered, she was last seen with her "boyfriend," a professional basketball player, and never heard from again. No note, no calls. Nothing. I imagined her body in some wooded area and her picture on a news flash. This couldn't be good news. I shivered as the word *boyfriend* echoed in my head. It wasn't a word we used in our home, at least not relating to any of us. *O Christ, this was definitely bad.*

I arrived home to find my mother in a daze and my father pacing restlessly. He and my mother were driving to Muncie first thing in the morning, a Wednesday. They were waiting for me and Courtney to arrive so we could keep an eye on Michael and Elijah, and, presumably, so our presence could inspire in our parents solace that at least we were still alive, well, and a healthy extension of the family.

The weekend dragged on, and the house felt lifeless, desolate even, although Michael and Elijah didn't change the rhythm of their activities. Their screaming, fighting, and rough play was mere background noise as Courtney and I couldn't find words to communicate our fear and premature grief.

Our parents returned Monday afternoon, a day shy of having been gone an entire week. Spent, after mumbling a stingy hello, they went directly to their room without a word of news. They remained there until late that night, when they woke me and Courtney and told us to come to the living room.

The boys asleep, the house was eerily quiet as we took our seats on the carpeted floor, reserving the couch for our parents. I envisioned what my father would divulge before he spoke: Her body was found strangled, violated, and abandoned, and her professional athlete boyfriend was at large.

Instead, my father said this: "We found your sister." He ran a hand over his face, and both my sister and I blinked back tears as we studied the sadness in our father's eyes. "She was pregnant." The use of the past tense sent me into immediate sobs, and I couldn't withhold or cease crying. But, thankfully, my father raised his voice above my dramatic display. "But she's Mrs. Something-or-the-other now, married to that sorry NBA friend of hers."

I was so overwhelmed by what I imagined had happened that it took me a full minute to register the truth. Overcome with relief, I cried more. I wasn't able to get a hold of myself until minutes later. When I did, my relief slowly gave way to shock, dismay, and, finally, anger.

My parents were already retreating to their room when Courtney stood, shaking her head, glassy-eyed, apparently nursing the same emotions as I.

"How could she do this to us?" I spat out, feeling the tears well in my eyes again.

She turned to me so quickly that I knew it was empathy or agreement she was offering when her hand gripped my shoulder and she turned me to face her, her fingers digging painfully into my skin. "What?"

The sound of her voice threw me off, and I lifted my gaze to see her eyes glistening in disbelief, apparently at what I'd said.

"How could she do this to us?" My repetition of the words was less heart-felt, and more uncertain, as if the question mark was in seeking Courtney's approval instead of agreement.

"No," she said in the same tone I'd used in my initial inquiry. "You mean, how could *they* do this to us?"

I stared at my sister, as if seeing her for the first time, and I felt that I didn't recognize her although nothing had changed of her copper brown skin and the attractive thickness of her eyebrows fading into one. "What?" My voice echoed the emotion I'd heard in her initial inquiry.

"You heard me the first time." She gripped both my shoulders and shook me, her eyes narrowing into slits.

"Listen to me," she said in a whisper that I understood was to keep my parents from overhearing and to temper the growing disgust she felt for me right then. "It's time for you to wake up and see the world for what it is."

Stunned, I listened.

"Patricia is twenty years old. She has a right to do whatever the hell she wants with her life, and it ain't a thing you, I, or our parents can do about it. If you have half the guts or sense as she does, then you'll do the same when you get the chance."

I opened my mouth to speak.

"Shut up, girl, and listen to me." Her grip didn't loosen, and I realized that in her own perverted way, Courtney was showing love and concern. Her voice was still a whisper, but I processed every word as if she were screaming in my face.

"If it wasn't for the stupid ideas Dad has about our life and The Church," she said, and I felt the warmness of her breath and the cruelty of her words, "she wouldn't have to hide anything at all. She could've told you, me, and the man and woman down the hall what she wanted to do with her life." She released my grip once she had secured my attention.

She sighed, shaking her head. "I feel sorry for her. And you. And me. For being born into this retarded family and Dad's fanaticism that he imagines is somehow paving our way to Heaven's golden gates." She contorted her face. "Who lives like this?" She motioned her hand to the house. "No music, no movies, no real clothes."

She rolled her eyes to the ceiling. "I swear to God, if I had someone love me like James loves Patricia." She paused, and it didn't escape me that Courtney was the only one in the household who knew the boy's name. "I'd leave this God-forsaken family and religion if I could."

I couldn't believe my ears. Certainly, she wasn't saying what I thought she was.

"I don't know if there's a God," she mused. "But if there is, it sure as hell ain't the God of *this* house."

I felt my hands tremble in realization of the magnitude of her sin. She was questioning the existence of her Creator. I was suddenly terrified of my older sister, and my repulsion for her sentiments was palpable in my throat. I feared I would vomit. But I stood stark still, unsure what other demons she had lurking within her.

Perhaps, she had known, had known the entire time, and was merely playing the role of a good daughter to appease our parents. As the theory materialized in my mind, it grew in plausibility until it was a certainty to me.

Even if she didn't disagree with our sister's actions, was it really humanly possible to react so viciously in support of her when only moments before we didn't even know if Patricia was alive? It would be only natural to first show relief, gratefulness, *something* to suggest a mental reality shift. But Courtney showed no shock, no relief, and no emotion upon hearing the news. As my mind retraced the events of the past week, I reinterpreted her quiet as, yes, nervousness, fear, and anxiety, but not for the same reasons I had felt these emotions. She was hoping Patricia could pull it off with the least amount of damage control.

I studied Courtney's eyes and saw nothing in their darkness except coldness and guilt, a testimony of being an accomplice in crime. I lowered my gaze, crawling inside myself and realizing that I was the only daughter left in the family. I was too upset to cry, too unsettled to grieve, and too aware of my predicament to be so foolish as to open my heart to someone I could not trust. So I did what I learned from my older sisters. I lied.

"Yes," I said as if subdued, "you're right." I nodded, feigning humility. "You're right. I'm sorry. Thank you."

A moment later, her glare softened and she half-heartedly threw an arm over my shoulder and walked me to my room. "It's all right. At least we know she's okay."

My peaked awareness allowed me to detect the obligatory tone of her last sentiment, as if expressed as an afterthought upon realizing, finally, that it was what she should have said initially, instead of the other way around.

Five

The year 1994 marked my second year in college, and while I was mulling over my choices in majors, I resigned myself to my heart's fate. I would forever be Reginald's "good friend," the one who listens to his talk of the women he loves and wants to marry, not a woman in either of those categories. We spent the summer together, much like old times, but knowledge of Natalie was always there, and he wasn't shy to talk enthusiastically about her beauty, talents, and promise.

Already, at the onset of the school year, she was the favored vote for Homecoming Queen, and the football season had barely begun. It was somewhat of a relief to return to school in the fall. Perhaps, part of my decreased apprehension was that I knew who my roommate would be. Anita's friend, my personal natural-hair stylist, and I turned out to be good friends. Her American name was Felicia, and although I hated the concept of foreigners changing their names or accepting Western nicknames to free Americans of the discomfort of a tongue twister, one look at her given name and I accepted my friend's selection of the name Felicia as one of God's small mercies. I never called her anything else. But my good memory rendered me able to recognize her birth name on postal mail and differentiate it from wrong addressees, even if their names were just as eccentric. Ironically, unlike Anita, Felicia had no distinct accent although I could detect a faint trace of her native language when she spoke.

Our only, and eventually most significant, point of diversion in shared interests was my increasing spirituality and love for Christ. Somehow the night my parents returned home with news of Patricia's whereabouts, my life changed and my faith increased. It was as if God sent Courtney as a personal sign to me that laxity in devotion to Him was a cancerous disease of the heart, and my nonchalance of that year would eventually lead me down my sister's destructive path.

I took heed and attended church services more regularly and joined an on-campus Bible study group that had a list of group members who volunteered to evangelize to the student body on a rotating monthly schedule. My group's week was mid-November, and already, only weeks after school commenced, we were meeting twice a week to discuss our strategies in calling people to accept Jesus in their lives. I wanted our group to be the best, utilizing both creativity and assertiveness as opposed to the half-hearted flyers tacked to campus message boards—passivity in inviting people to God.

38

I was planning my suggestions to present at the meeting one early October evening when I received yet another call from Courtney. There was in her voice the same urgency as she had had when phoning about Patricia the year before.

Too exhausted from her theatrics, I rolled my eyes and let my exaggerated exhale tell her that I wasn't game this time. "What now?"

She caught the hint. "In case you have time to be bothered," she said, and I could almost taste her cruelty, "your cousin Darnell is dead."

The dial tone was an ominous confirmation of what she had said. I gripped the receiver so desperately that my hand hurt. I felt my stomach churn and I grew lightheaded. Dropping the phone suddenly, I clutched my stomach and doubled over, feeling the heaving before I realized what was happening. The last thing I remember was vomiting and feeling sick all over again at the sight of it.

I woke in the nurse's office at school and was told that I had fainted. It took a moment to realize the reason for my fainting in the first place. At the reminder, I felt myself grow weak again but I mentally fought the urge until I felt strength and determination return to my body.

My family. *O God, my family!* I had to get home as soon as I could.

Not bothering to collaborate with my sister, I booked my own flight home and hoped, even in the wake of this personal tragedy, that we wouldn't cross paths at the airport.

We didn't. She was already home when I arrived.

The house held a distant, melancholy atmosphere, and I soon found my place in the slow motion of the days leading up to the funeral. I settled into my room and spent most of my time staring out the window, pondering the aloof manner of nature in continuing the mundane normalcy of dry, colored leaves of autumn as if nothing, absolutely nothing that upset the entire meaning of life, had occurred at all.

Two or three days after I arrived, I began to feel dizzy and lightheaded and my vision blurred. I woke, feeling a knotting pain in my head and a pulsing ache behind one of my eyes. Dull black spots appeared wherever I looked, but it took too much energy to keep narrowing my eyes to make out what I should be seeing, so I shut my eyes and wondered if I had the strength to make it to the window.

I thought little of my condition until I heard a lowered voice near my door, whispering in an apparent effort to keep me from hearing.

"Has she come out at all? Not even to *eat?*"

The last word inspired my opening my eyes. The voice sounded familiar. It was the voice of a woman, a mother.

The knotting in my head tightened until a throbbing pain pulsated in my temples. I was expending too much energy in trying to remember my last meal, and it hurt too much to attempt to discern whose voice I was hearing. I gave up.

The door opened.

The sound aggravated the pain, and the throbbing intensified. Slowly, I closed my lids, unable to turn my head in the direction of whoever had just entered. I hoped they wouldn't talk to me. I feared the slightest sound would make my head explode.

A warm hand settled on my forehead, and a familiar scent of perfume entered my nostrils, relaxing me, despite the pounding in my head. The kind gesture reminded me of Darnell, and I felt my stomach churn again. I gritted my teeth behind my closed lips and willed myself not to get sick. I didn't have the energy to sit up.

"Ray, honey," the voice whispered in a tone so soothing that the knot loosened and the pain subsided just slightly. "Have you eaten?"

The requirement of using my mental faculties made the knot tighten again. I turned my head slightly to one side but couldn't muster the energy to turn it all the way to the other to complete my response.

Soft lips brushed my forehead after she lifted her hand from it. "It's okay, honey. You don't have to talk. We'll bring you something."

Slowly, I fluttered my eyes open, but my vision was blurred and spotted, so I couldn't see her clearly. I felt the weight of her body ease off the bed, and immediately my head pounded more forcefully. I didn't want her to leave.

"It's okay honey," she said again. She gently loosened my tightened grip on her hand. "I'll just bring you a plate."

She stood upright and brushed the back of her hand on my cheek before starting for the door. I saw her blurred figure retreating and felt a lingering sense of sadness at seeing her go. She quietly slipped out without closing the door completely, as if sensing that that small bit of noise would be too much for me to bear. I felt tears well in my eyes.

Reggie.

I needed her to come back. The woman was Delores—Reginald's mother, and I wanted her by my side so I could hold her hand in mine.

As if God himself had told her what I needed most, Delores Matthews became my best friend that sober week in October, a month I would forever think of as one of the saddest. She held my hand, stroked my back, and held me without ever needing to ask what I wanted or needed at a given moment.

Years later I learned that the funeral preparation had been delayed, and that most of it was due to my family's disagreement over whether or not the casket should be open.   Neither Uncle Marvin nor Aunt Marcella was in a position to make the decision themselves.   Marcella was comatose for all intents and purposes and had to be drugged in order to sit calmly at the funeral.   My mother's brother, although holding the appearance of normalcy, was unable to decide.   In recognition of his limited abilities, he officially turned over the authority to my parents.

I knew none of this at the time.   I was engrossed in my own world of grief.   On the day of the funeral, I sat next to Delores in a limousine reserved for family and realized, too, only years later that she was the only non-family member in the limo that day.   And I understood that she had been there only for me.

Likewise, at the funeral, Delores sat next to me, in the section reserved for family, and held my left hand the entire time, alternating between squeezing it gently and massaging it with her own.   We sat in the front pew, only feet from the open glass-covered casket, and I felt sick, unable to understand how anyone could consider this unobstructed view as honoring the family.   At best, it was disturbing and, at worst, torturous.

I sat with my right hand lying limp in my lap as Delores coddled the other, and I was unable to lift my eyes from the dark cloth of my dress.   I willed myself not to gaze at the decorated, polished wood that enclosed the body of my cousin.   If I felt my head lifting instinctively, mostly at the accentuated words of the preacher of Marvin and Marcella's church, I forced my eyes to wander, to study the strangeness of a house of worship so familiar, yet so drastically different from The Church.

The church was smaller than my father's, and it bore none of the images with which I was familiar.   The only likeness of Christ was a painting hanging on the right wall. When my eyes grazed it the first time, I couldn't keep from staring at it, wondering if it was my blurred vision returning to me or if I were in fact seeing Jesus with brown, not white, skin.   As I studied the curly coarseness of this Jesus' dark hair that was strangely similar to mine, I concluded that it was not my vision.   Their Savior was a Black man.   The realization stunned and disturbed me.

Suddenly everything made sense.   The insistence on natural hair.   Their Afro-centricity.   Darnell's sudden interest in the Nation of Islam.   Even my mother herself took on a new persona.   Her natural hair.   Her own form of African pride.   Her forbidding me and my sisters permed hair.   Had this been her form of Christianity before she married my father?

The preacher's mention of Darnell prompted my turning my attention back to the tragic event that required our presence today. Sighing silently, I returned my gaze to my black dress.

I heard but couldn't bring myself to actually listen as the preacher droned on about my cousin being in a better place. Darnell was now in the company of angels. He was in eternal rest. His soul was roaming free in Heaven.

What if he isn't?

The question stunned me. I hadn't asked it of my own accord, but I couldn't deny that it had sat dormant at the back of my mind since I learned of Darnell's sudden death. Yet, at that moment, I found myself examining the query, as if outside my mind, and found that it had wedged a place for itself there, and I was unable, or perhaps unwilling, to remove it.

What if he isn't in a better place? What if he isn't in the company of angels? What if he doesn't even deserve Heaven?

The preacher described Darnell as intelligent, brave, determined, and admirable—adjectives eulogists reserved for occasions like these. I wondered if he really meant it. If he really believed what he was saying. I could think of a thousand words to describe my cousin right then, but there was only one that sat burning at the back of my mind and throat, inspiring the familiar knotting of a migraine.

Stupid.

My eyes welled as I realized just how much I hated Darnell right then. How utterly stupid, how outrageously idiotic of him to have joined the army, of all things. And for what? He hadn't even been in the service two full years and already he was proven dispensable. And what did we get in return for all his hopes and dreams of world travel, of pursuing a higher education? Meaningless trinkets. A red, white, and blue cloth and a cheap pendant to decorate our walls. And he'd see none of it.

If he was so damned brave, I wanted to scream to all who concocted wars for people like Darnell to die in, *then send your son, send your daughter to sacrifice their lives for what you believe so ardently in.*

Sniffles rippled throughout the church, and my anger was incensed. The mourners sat in obligatory grief, fighting tears and nodding pensively as the preacher's eulogy grew more poignant. But I hated all of the tissue-carrying, eye-dabbing grievers. There was no choice for them, for any of us. We *had* to mourn. It was grief born of obligation, not sentiment. It was only Marvin, Marcella, and my family who had a right to cry, to wail. We were the only ones who even knew Darnell well enough to have felt love, gratefulness, or irritation in his presence.

The melodious sound of the all-Black choir inspired my looking forward. Their words tormented me in their soulful gloom and beauty. The tears spilled from my eyes and I dropped my head as the soloist's sonorous gospel reverberated throughout the church, echoed by the powerful choir. I wanted them to keep singing, and I wanted them to stop.

But mostly, I wanted Darnell back so I could tell him how upset I was with him for leaving.

I hadn't seen Reginald the entire time except in passing until the night before I was scheduled to return to school. As usual, I was in my room staring at the ceiling and waiting for the throbbing in my head to cease. But it was my mother, not Reginald himself, who asked if I wanted to take a walk with him. I turned my head from where it lay on my pillow and met my mother's gaze. I saw softness in the dark eyes she and Darnell's father shared, and sadness overwhelmed me. I knew she was only trying to make me feel better.

I shook my head. I didn't feel like getting out of bed, let alone pulling clothes from my closet or packed luggage to wear during the stroll. "I'm fine."

She smiled gently and patted my hand. "I think you should go. Please."

Her last word prompted me to meet her gaze. I couldn't read her expression, but I understood that it was important to her that I took the walk.

Outside, Reggie and I walked in silence down the sidewalk for several minutes. The night was uncomfortably chilly, but the bitter cold of Indianapolis winter was still at least a month away.

"I didn't want to tell you," he said as if exhaling the words, breaking the silence. He lifted his gaze to the sky and tugged at the lapels of his thick coat and secured three buttons before pushing his bare hands into the pockets.

My gloved hands were already snug in the pockets of my coat, but I shivered as the wind blew in my face, lifting with it some dry leaves that scratched the sidewalk before rising and falling into the street. My curiosity heightened, I glanced at him and furrowed my brows. He wouldn't look at me.

"But I think—" He drew in a deep breath and exhaled, and I saw the soft cloud of breath even in the darkness. "Especially now, it's only fair that you know."

Unsure if I had the fortitude for more tragic news, I looked away, bracing myself for what I already knew I wouldn't view as justice, despite his or my mother's feelings on the matter. I didn't care anymore about knowing things, about, in fact, knowing at all. In its own way ignorance was a blessing. I was already wishing someone had told me that Darnell was in some far away country and would never return, instead of the raw ugliness of the truth.

"I'm sure you already know about his sister, but I don't know if you—"

"His sister?" I halted my slow steps to face him.

Reggie stared at me, eyes narrowed, blinking. Then his face contorted. "Nobody told you about her?"

"About who?"

"Darnell's sister."

"Darnell has a sister?"

Reggie's lids closed slowly as he shook his head and rolled his eyes toward the sky, apparently perturbed, as if this talk was to bear more than he could himself. He pursed his lips then cursed.

"Didn't your parents tell you *anything*?"

It was a rhetorical question, but even if it weren't, I would be unable to answer it. I had no idea what he was talking about. His frustration eventually dissipated and he told me more than I wanted to know. Not wanting to believe it, I cut the conversation short and ran to the house to confront my mother. Reluctantly, she confirmed what Reginald had told me and then went on to share a story of her own. Her primary reason, she said, for not telling me earlier was my father, and of course Reginald himself.

Here's what I learned that night: Darnell and Denise were twins, born while my aunt and uncle were part of the Nation of Islam, an organization that, as it turns out, had sparked my mother's interest briefly, though not my father's. Denise had some rare congenital disease that neither Reggie nor my mother knew much about. She died at the age of eight, two years after Marcella underwent a hysterectomy. Denise's death sent Darnell into a deep depression that resulted in his normally competitive academics turning to failures and an eventual expulsion from school for his behavior. His mother attempted to home-school him, but she re-entered him into the school system at age ten. However, he was placed in the "Special Education" stream, mostly because of his falling behind.

Unsatisfied with Darnell's progress, Marcella identified the primary problem: They needed a change. They couldn't expect Darnell, or themselves, to truly move on if they continued living in the same home and city where he and Denise grew up. The only problem was, *Now what?* Marcella suggested that Marvin phone his sister who lived in Indiana to see about moving there. But Marvin was keeping only cordial contact with her because her husband, my father, disassociated from the family years ago after Marvin chose to remain in the Nation of Islam instead of joining a proper church. My father's reason was simple. He didn't want his family "corrupted" by their religion. Although my uncle and his wife had long since left the Nation, the families remained at odds mostly due to what my mother called my father's stubbornness. Nevertheless, she welcomed the idea of having her brother close by. She felt that there was only so much my father could resist if they were neighbors.

Reginald's parents, having tired of Queens themselves for reasons unrelated to Darnell's family, job searched until they both landed jobs in Indianapolis. Due to "White Flight," the phenomenon wherein White people moved out of neighborhoods when Black families moved in, several houses were for sale in the neighborhood where my family lived. The original plan was for my aunt and uncle to live in the house the Matthews had found. However, Marvin and Marcella, who were not as educated or qualified as their friends, were not so lucky in securing jobs, so Carl and Delores Matthews bought the home themselves and agreed for the couple and their son to live with them until they could find work and purchase the home from them or buy themselves one of the available ones in the neighborhood.

Marvin eventually found work in a post office, but his salary couldn't cover the mortgage on a house, especially one in our neighborhood, so he and his wife moved with their son to a small apartment and took advantage of whatever government benefits they could to make a comfortable life for their now only child.

The change in Darnell was miraculous, and they attributed it to one thing: Me.

I reminded him of his sister. This was simply because Denise and I looked alike. I favored his sister most likely because I favored my mother and Denise her father. It was merely a matter of genetics. Nevertheless, upon meeting me, it was as if he had sister all over again, and he grew attached. Which explained why, when we first met, he had said he was my age—eight, the same age his twin sister had been when she died. It also explained why his family visited several times a week although the twenty-minute drive in my aunt and uncle's struggling car was inconvenient, not to mention their hectic job schedules.

The news both flattered and destroyed me. I wished I had known. That someone had told me. Perhaps, then, things would have turned out differently. But, my mother said this, as if it were supposed to make me feel better: It would have broken Darnell's heart for me to know, because then I might decide I didn't want to be his sister, and it would be as if he'd lost Denise all over again.

Six

I returned to school almost two weeks after I'd left for the funeral, and I was numb. While I was gone, I'd missed most of my mid-terms, and although I was given an extension for them all, it was difficult to study or remain attentive in classes. I was still coming to terms with all that had happened, and all that I had learned. My anger, naturally, was subsiding, but its slow retreat was giving way to a weighty melancholy laced in regret. The latter emotion I attributed mostly to the conversations I'd had with Reginald and my mother the night before my return.

I didn't know what to do with myself. I went to and from my classes and dorm room as if in a daze, and I kept playing and replaying in my mind the moments I spent with Darnell. In none of them could I recall appreciating or even liking him a great deal. Besides the day of the ruined Monopoly game, neither could I recall any of my aloofness in his presence perturbing him in the least. And that hurt most.

I resumed attending church and Bible study, but I couldn't bring myself to fully participate as I had before the funeral. Whenever the minister or Bible study members discussed the need for Jesus as a person's salvation, I thought of Darnell. I couldn't comprehend his receiving eternal damnation. Yet, I couldn't comprehend his receipt of eternal bliss either. He didn't seem to deserve either.

I fought these thoughts because I was doing what I had no right to, seeking to understand ultimate Judgment. I knew it was a task I could not succeed in, but that didn't prevent the incessant doubts and questions regarding Darnell's fate. They just wouldn't go away. I felt as if there were a missing piece in my own faith, as if I were somehow not whole.

One night I lay awake analyzing my unrest, determined to understand my self torment. I started by asking myself what I truly believed.

Do you believe Jesus is the son of God?
Yes.
Do you believe that it is through accepting his personal sacrifice on the cross that a person's goes to Heaven?
Yes.
Do you believe that Jesus is your Savior?
Yes.
Do you believe that Jesus is God?
No.

The last response didn't shock or disturb me because it was what I'd always believed, what I'd always been taught. It was one of the teachings of The Church. Of course, I never shared this with my Bible study members for the same reason I had kept to myself at school. They would never understand. It was sufficient for me to relax on the points of agreement instead of harp on those of disagreement. They believed in the divinity of all parts of the Trinity, and I simply believed in the Trinity as the Father—the Divine, the Son—Jesus, and the Holy Ghost—the divinely guided Spirit. All separate, but one in the sense of a unity of purpose in guiding people on earth. In my mind, I pictured a triangle, the Father at the top vertex and the Son and Spirit on opposite vertexes beneath Him.

It was this last thought that gave way to my understanding my unrest.

If they believed that a person had to accept Jesus as God to go to Heaven, and I believed you only had to accept him as the son of God and that it was in fact a form of idolatry to worship the cross or Jesus, then that would mean I believed that they were going to Hell, and that they believed I was going to Hell. And it was clear what we both believed about Darnell.

My cousin was merely a distraction, collateral damage in my search for faith, for truth.

I was disturbed because I was walking a thin line myself. Who was right? They or I?

Right then, I felt sick. Because, no matter who was right and who was wrong, one thing was for certain. I was a hypocrite. I was hiding in the ranks of sectarian Christians because it was the closest thing to belonging I'd had since high school—where I'd never, in fact, belonged at all.

I knew at that moment, whatever it was that I believed, I couldn't hide anymore, even if I would ultimately stand alone. I was determined to "wake up" and analyze my father's church with new eyes and compare it to all the "sects" of Christianity that I could read about in the library and talk to others about on campus. I absolutely had to know who was right. It felt awfully lonely holding on to The Church when the rest of the world held on to their own. At least for them, there were many branches of their sectarian beliefs. For me, there was only one. My father's. Could I rationally accept that my father's congregation would be the only ones to enter Heaven?

But perhaps, there were other congregations like The Church, those who believed in the purity of Jesus' message and in not corrupting it with their own.

It took me less than a week to conclude that my father's teachings were most closely related to those of Jehovah's Witnesses. All the other branches of the Protestant church, at least the ones I had read about, held fast to the belief that Jesus himself was God incarnate and that God himself was three-in-one. This latter belief was something I just could not bring myself to embrace, and it gave me solace to realize that it wasn't only the members of The Church who believed that Jesus was a separate persona from the Creator.

It was a late Wednesday afternoon in November and I was walking across campus to get something to eat when I saw my fellow Bible study members, my personal evangelical group, holding flyers and stopping to talk to students about Christ. I walked faster, not wanting to run into them for fear I would be asked to join their activities, especially since I had been the brainchild of the forum to be held next week. It was entitled, "So You *Think* You Know Jesus?" I was still debating whether or not I would go. I had already told Natasha, one of the members I'd grown close to, that they should find someone else to take my place since I was still nursing my grief over my cousin. She said that it was no problem, that she understood, and that she would just see me there.

Before reaching my destination, I was distracted by what sounded like a rally on the stone steps of the students' outside auditorium that resembled the Olympic theatres of old, except the school's was much smaller. Someone stood at a podium before the crowd on the steps, and near where I was passing, I noticed a table, set up much like the tables that I had begged my Bible study group not to do this year. Moving gently in the wind was a large paper banner taped to the table. In large letters, the sign read, "Ask About Islam" and in smaller letters, "Islamic Awareness Week November 1994."

I stopped, immediately reminded of Darnell, and approached the table instinctively. I had no intention of asking anything. I simply felt the need to be near my cousin, and the word *Islam* attracted my attention. I was only vaguely aware of someone sitting at the table as I sifted through the pamphlets and books neatly arranged on the cloth.

"You looking for anything in particular?"

I looked up and found a young man whose complexion and mannerism reminded me of my cousin. But then again, so much was reminding me of him these days that everyday I would think I saw Darnell himself, until my better senses kicked in. I studied the man carefully before concluding that he shared only my cousin's skin tone. He had a thin beard, my cousin did not. He wore glasses—Malcolm X-type, my cousin wore none. The collar of his shirt bore no bow tie, my cousin's sometimes did.

Suddenly conscious of my staring, I returned my gaze to the table and shook my head. "No, not really."

"You're a student here?"

I nodded. "You?"

"No."

I creased my forehead and looked at him, but this time he didn't meet my gaze. "Then why are you here?"

"For Islamic Awareness Week. I'm volunteering with the MSA."

"With the what?"

"MSA. Muslim Student Association."

Oh. I'd never heard of this Muslim denomination and imagined it to be somewhat like The Church, or a branch of Darnell's Nation of Islam. "Where are they based?"

He lifted his eyes briefly and registered confusion. "The students, you mean?"

"The association."

"Oh. Right here. They're Maryland students."

It had taken me sometime to get used to "Maryland" meaning the University of Maryland instead of the state of Maryland, depending on whom you were talking to. He must live in the area, I concluded and wondered if his branch of the organization was nearby. Perhaps this MSA had a house of worship not too far from campus.

There was an awkward pause.

"Are these free?" I asked, spotting a few pamphlets and books that I wanted to read.

"Yes, all of them." His voice was overly enthusiastic, but I understood it was his desire to be polite. "Take as many as you want."

"I will. Thank you." I took five pamphlets and three books, deciding that if they were truly free, the organization wouldn't mind if I took more than I had originally intended.

"You interested in Islam?"

The question was so bizarre that it took me a moment to register that it was directed at me. I contorted my face and shook my head. "No, never." I realized too late that I was being rude.

The weeks following the funeral required me not only to adjust to the knowledge of Darnell's absence, but to adjust to the sudden changes in myself. I was more tense and reactionary, as opposed to my previous quiet reserve and contemplation before speaking, if I spoke at all. The changes were most likely due to stress, but moments like these reminded me that I was better off with my bed covers pulled over my head.

To my relief, the volunteer laughed. "Okay, no problem. I hope the information is helpful anyway."

I wanted to apologize, but I could think of no way of saying how sorry I was without making a fool of myself. I didn't know this guy from Joe, so I owed him nothing. But, then again, I wasn't raised to talk to people like that. I sounded like Courtney, or Patricia, and I hated it. I tried to think of something to say to keep from leaving with his having a bad impression of me.

"Thanks." I turned then returned my attention to the table, as if I were intending to leave then decided against it as I recalled something.

"Excuse me," I said in the kindest tone I could muster, unsure what I would say.

He looked up momentarily then returned his gaze to the table as he nodded, letting me know he was listening.

"Is there a temple or something nearby I could go to to learn more?"

He smiled, and I sensed he was tempted to joke about my apparent disgust with the religion moments before. "Yes, there is a *masjid* close by."

"When is it open?"

He paused. "Uh, I'm not sure. But if you want, I can give you their number or I could take yours and have someone contact you."

"That sounds good."

A grin lingered on his face. "Which one? Taking their number or giving yours?"

I laughed self-consciously. "Both."

"O-kay," he said as he searched under papers and pamphlets until he found a small brochure and handed it to me. Then he slid a clipboard with a list of names and numbers of other students who wanted more information. "Just write your information there, and someone will call you *inshaAllaah.*"

I didn't understand his last words, but I nodded and lifted the pen attached to the board by a string and wrote the required information and slid it back to him.

"Renee," he read aloud and grinned. "That's my sister's name."

My heart pounded as the comment evoked memories of Darnell and what I'd learned of Denise. I tried to appear disinterested and nodded coolly. "You're twins?"

His broadening grin and chuckle made me see the silliness of the inquiry. "No. She's older."

"Is she part of the organization too?"

"No, she lives in Cleveland. She graduated from college a few years ago."

"I meant the Muslim organization."

He gathered his eyebrows and relaxed them seconds later. "Oh. No, she's not Muslim. She's still Christian, like the rest of my family."

My interest was peaked, but I didn't want to show it. "What sect are they?"

"You mean, denomination?"

"Yes, I'm sorry."

"Jehovah's Witnesses."

Oh. I didn't know what to say.

"Are you Christian?"

I shrugged. "Yes, I guess you can call it that."

He laughed. "You sound like me before I converted."

"No," I said, offended. "I meant I'm not part of any sect or denomination."

He nodded. "Non-denominational."

I shook my head. "No, just Christian."

He creased his forehead. "What do you believe?"

"About what?"

"Everything. Jesus. God. Heaven. Hell."

"Oh. That Jesus is the son of God." I didn't want to say more for fear of offending him.

"You believe in the Trinity?"

"No."

"Why not?"

"Because I don't believe a man can be God."

He appeared distracted. I lifted my gaze and saw two women approaching the table, at least I assumed they both were women. I could see the face of only one of them. I was immediately reminded of what Reggie had said about the Indian and Arab Muslims. That must be them. I decided that it was time for me to go.

"Thank you," I said as kindly as I could, abruptly turning and leaving, satisfied that I would not be thought of as rude.

Less than a week later I received a call from a Muslim named Sumayyah—I had to write down her name in order to remember it—inviting me to an open house at a local *masjid* (as I soon learned they called their church). After letting her know I appreciated the invitation, I told her I had no transportation and had no idea how to get around on the bus. She then offered to pick me up herself, and I didn't know what to say. I was uncomfortable accepting a ride from a stranger. I'd never done that before, but I couldn't tell her that, so I told her I'd think about it and get back to her. I took down her number and threw it in the trash the next morning.

Three days later, I was sitting against the headboard of my bed with my back supported by a pillow and reading from my advanced calculus book when the phone rang. I answered on the third ring.

"Hello?"

"May I speak to Renee?"

Not recognizing the voice, I paused then spoke cautiously. "This is she."

"Oh, hi Renee, this is Sumayyah."

I shut my eyes and rolled them before putting on my polite voice. "Oh, Sumayyah. I'm sorry I didn't call back. I was—"

"It's okay. I was just calling to see if you were still interested in coming to the open house tomorrow."

Tomorrow? Oh, that's right. She did mention that it was this Saturday. "Uh, I don't..." I didn't know what to say. Could I tell her the truth? That I really didn't feel like being bothered, that I wasn't at all interested in her organization, that I was only being polite to the volunteer?

"I know it's awkward to just pick up and go to a strange place with a stranger." She laughed.

I couldn't keep from smiling in embarrassment. "Yes, it is."

"That's why I figured I should call and tell you more about myself."

Instinctively, I glanced at the clock. It was almost seven o'clock, and I wanted to go out to eat with Felicia later that night. "Uh, I appreciate it, but I'm kind of busy right now."

"I'm sorry. When is a better time to call?"

She wasn't giving in that easily. I started to grow agitated. "I don't know. It's just that tonight's really busy and..." I sighed. Why should I have to explain myself to her?

"I'll tell you what," she said, as if reading my mind. "I'm going to be on campus tomorrow morning *inshaAllaah*. Do you mind if I stop by to introduce myself? It's no problem if you can't make it to the open house, but I at least want you to put a face with a name."

I didn't know what to say. "O-kay. That would be nice."

"Great. I can come anytime between nine and eleven. When is best for you?"

"Uh, anytime."

After giving her the name of my dorm and the number to my room, I hung up, relieved that the conversation was over. For a moment, I considered making certain I was out of the room at those times, but I dismissed the thought. Besides, I didn't like the idea of waking up early on a Saturday morning to hang out for two hours for no particular reason. And what was I running from anyway? Meeting another human being? I really did need to get over losing Darnell so I could relax and live life like a normal person.

Sumayyah knocked on my door at a quarter to eleven, which was good because I had been awake for less than thirty minutes and had just come from the shower. I was wearing a sweatshirt and running pants, and my damp twists were pulled back behind my head. Felicia was still sleeping but had told me the night before not to worry about finding anywhere else to meet the visitor.

I opened the door to find a young woman about my height dressed in a headscarf and a large dress, displaying only her face and hands. She wore a jacket over her outfit. She reminded me of the veil-less woman I'd seen approaching the "Ask About Islam" table the week before.

"Hi," she greeted and stepped inside. "I'm sorry about interrupting you." She brought a hand to her mouth when she saw Felicia with the covers pulled over her.

I waved my hand dismissively. "It's okay. She knows you were coming."

I closed the door and gestured my hand toward my desk chair. "Have a seat."

She removed her jacket and sat down. She laughed then extended her hand good-naturedly before reintroducing herself. "I'm Sumayyah."

I smiled, accepting the handshake. "Renee."

"I won't take too much of your time. But I did want to introduce myself in person."

I nodded respectfully. "I appreciate it."

"Well," she said with a grin, "I guess I'll just cut to the chase."

I sat down on the edge of my bed, hoping she really wouldn't take too much of my time.

"I'm from Baltimore originally, but my family lives in Columbia now. I grew up Christian and accepted Islam when I was thirteen. Now I'm a junior here at Maryland."

The last bit of information interested me most. "You're a student here?"

She nodded. "Yes. But I commute."

She paused, then asked, "What are you studying?"

"I plan to study math."

"Really? I'm a math major too."

I relaxed, my curiosity heightened. "You're American originally?"

"Yes, I come from your typical Black Christian family."

I was too shy to ask her race, so I was glad that she had offered the information freely. I knew from her bronze skin that she wasn't White, but I might've guessed Latina.

"My cousin was Muslim." I'm not sure what made me say it, but Sumayyah was easy to talk to.

"Really?" Her smile broadened. "How did he hear about it?"

I lifted a shoulder in a shrug and smiled uncomfortably. "I'm not sure. But his parents were in the Nation of Islam, so most likely he heard about it from them."

Her smile faded slightly. "Was he a Muslim or a part of the Nation?"

I furrowed my brows. Her question confused me. "I'm sorry?"

"Was he part of the Nation of Islam?"

"Yes."

Her eyebrows rose. "Oh, I see."

"Aren't you?"

Her eyes widened slightly but her kind expression made me feel better. She shook her head, smiling as if my words were a private joke. "No, no. I'm Muslim, orthodox Muslim."

I creased my forehead. "But you're American."

Her confused expression prompted me to continue. "I thought only Indians and Arabs were orthodox Muslims."

Her expression relaxed somewhat and she shook her head. "No, anyone can be Muslim."

"But you don't cover your face."

"You don't have to."

"So..." I didn't know how to form my question because I didn't know what I wanted to say. All I knew was that I wanted answers. "What sect are you?"

She looked at me quizzically as one side of her mouth creased in the beginning of a smile. "Sect? You mean what kind of Muslim am I?"

"Yes."

"Just Muslim."

Oh. It's what I would've said about my Christianity.

"But people would consider me Sunni. But that's what Islam is, to follow the guidance of the Prophet, peace be upon him."

"The Prophet?"

"Prophet Muhammad."

The name sounded familiar, and I suddenly remembered Darnell's conversation with me about my beautiful, African hair and the Malcolm X movie and book, which I never got around to finishing. "Oh yeah, Elijah Muhammad. My cousin mentioned him."

She grinned. "No, not him. I mean Prophet Muhammad, who was born in Arabia over a thousand years ago. Elijah Muhammad was a Black American who died in the seventies."

I stared at her. What was she talking about? I felt so ignorant. My speechlessness reminded me of how I felt when I'd first heard Darnell say the word *Muslim*.

"So which one believes women are forbidden to show their faces in public?"

"Some orthodox Muslims believe that the Prophet commanded women to cover their faces in front of men who aren't family."

Okay, good. At least I wasn't completely off base. "But why?"

She glanced at her wristwatch and stood. "Look, I'm sorry, but I have to go home to get ready for the open house."

My heart fell. I was just getting started.

A second later, she was opening the door to leave, and I remembered regretfully that I was the one who had given her the impression that she should keep it short.

I stood too and held the door for her.

"Thanks for letting me stop by."

"No problem."

A broad grin spread on her face as she met my gaze. "Why don't you just come with me? You can ask all the questions you want there."

My spirits lifted. I smiled. "Sure."

"Can you get dressed in five minutes?"

"Yes."

"Then I'll just wait for you in the hall, *inshaAllaah*."

As the door closed, I realized that her last words were the same ones the volunteer had used at the table.

Seven

Growing up we didn't have money
Or much of those other things
That don't grow on trees.
We didn't have acceptance
By friends or classmates
Or any of those others so many want to please.
Yet Daddy said we were rich
And Mommy smiled,
Pleased.
And although I knew we were not,
I knew every word he said was true.
Because our richness wasn't printed on green paper.
Nor did it grow like green leaves.
We had a treasure no one could take away.
We had
Heart
Determination
Will.
And yet
There was
So much
We wanted
Still.

At school I walked the halls in fear
And sought comfort in red checks and alphabet letters
atop papers
Written at the stroke of a pen held in a teacher's hand.
And never really expected
Them
To understand.
I hurt so much in the halls
But I pushed on
Knowing that after the red checks and scribbled A
My name would be on the wall
I grew to expect it
My name
Posted
As if the wall belonged to
Me
Perhaps I wanted to prove to them that I was better
Because of Mommy and Daddy
Or perhaps
It was I who needed proof of purpose
Worth
Sagacity

I have been called a fighter
And thought myself perhaps
A martyr of sorts
But now I know that I am merely a fool
With so much skin and flesh in my reflection
That it covers my
Soul
And hides it
From me.

I can no longer carry the sword of strength
Because my arms have grown weary beneath its weight
And now I am only
Sore.
I now must remove the mask that I mistook for my face
But I must keep my adornment of armor
Just in case.
Yet my armor is but ink
That flows from the pen
And acts as a shield between me and
My self.
Somehow the words are better spoken
And protected
That way.
But my prayer is only that they will be a shield
For me
That Day.
For then
I cannot pretend to see only skin over flesh
When my reflection is before me
Mirrored in strokes of pen
Once held in Angels' hands
And I won't find my name on a wall
And Mommy and Daddy can't give me
Heart
Determination
Or will
Should I fall.
Yet then
And only
Then
Will I have
The chance
To truly
See
Me.

I returned to my dorm room late Saturday night shaken and moved. I was relieved that Felicia had already gone, although as I lay in bed, I vaguely remembered asking her if I could come along with her and Anita, even as I had no idea where they were going.

I glanced at the clock. It was three minutes after ten.

Where had the time gone?

I slowly shut my eyes, hoping to digest everything better that way.

I let the events of the afternoon, evening, and night wash over me. I hoped to analyze my reason for unrest as I had earlier concerning my faith.

It was the young man's poem, I concluded, that affected me most.

As I recalled his monologue, I felt a storm of emotions that I couldn't give name to. I could think only of the lyrics to a song I'd heard Courtney playing over and over when my parents weren't home.

I felt all flushed with fever, embarrassed by the crowd
I felt he found my letters, and read each one aloud
I prayed that he would finish, but he just kept right on
Strumming my pain with his fingers
Singing my life with his words
Killing me softly with his song

Years later, I learned that these were the words to the song "Killing Me Softly" that I heard Lauryn Hill singing in my sister's cassette player, though I have no idea who wrote these words originally. But, at that moment, it didn't matter. And I didn't care.

All I knew was that these were the only words that could give name to the emotions I had felt as the young man I'd met at the "Ask About Islam" table stood on a portable stage in the basement of a local *masjid*. I couldn't remember his name—they had said it when they introduced him.

Naturally, he had not been the only performer. But he was the only one I remembered so vividly.

There had been children singing about their God "Allah" and His prophet Muhammad. A White woman talked about how she accepted Islam after being a feminist. An Indian man talked about converting from Hinduism. A Black man, an ex-preacher, shared his journey to Islam. A group of young men, who apparently were renowned in the Muslim community, sang a song, but I couldn't remember what it was about.

A boy recited from the Muslim holy book—the Qur'an. Although they explained that it was like the Bible was to Christians, I'd never heard our book chanted so melodiously before. They had translated what he'd recited, but that night I remembered only this part: *"We believe in God and what has been revealed to us and what was revealed to Abraham, Ishmael, Isaac...and in what was given to Moses, Jesus, and the prophets from their Lord..."*

What surprised me was that their holy book mentioned the same prophets that were mentioned in the Bible. And Jesus was among them. Someone explained later that Muslims believed that Jesus was a prophet and that they held him in high esteem.

But I couldn't get over that they believed in him at all.

This was so unlike the Islam that Darnell and Reginald had told me about that I was confounded. I now knew that the Nation of Islam and orthodox Islam were two completely different belief systems that were, at best, antipodes of one another. And that Reggie had had, at most, a marginal understanding of orthodox Islam. But I was still coming to terms with what that meant for me, and how it related to The Church and my Bible study group.

At that point, I wasn't interested in Islam for myself so much as I was interested in it so that I could put the world's religions into proper perspective. I felt an urgency to know the truth—*the* Truth. And I had no doubt that I was on the right track after discovering the parallels between The Church and the Jehovah's Witnesses. But my discovery that Islam recognized the same prophets of Christianity, and that they actually revered Jesus as an important individual in their faith, forced me to put them in a category with sectarian Christians. Before, I had relegated them to the mental category I had for Hindus, Buddhists, and other pagans. Now, I couldn't even categorize them with Jews because apparently Muslims did accept the validity of Christ's existence and were not awaiting the arrival of the "true Messiah."

They believed in Jesus, so to me, Muslims were in fact Christians, even if they, or others, didn't see it that way. And if they were not, then I had to come up with a new definition for Christianity because my belief about Jesus was closer to the Jehovah's Witnesses' and Muslim point of view than that of mainstream Christians. To me, Jesus was not God. To Jehovah's Witnesses, Jesus was not God. To Muslims, Jesus was not God. To most sectarian Christians, Jesus was God.

To all of us, belief in his divine purpose was essential to faith.

So, if a Muslim isn't a Christian, what makes someone a Christian in the first place?

I decided to attend my Bible study group for answers. I decided that I would call Sumayyah later to ask questions because I needed to figure out how to ask what I really wanted—how to get in touch with the young man who had read the poem. I had a lot I wanted to ask him.

At the meeting Monday evening I started by asking them the definition of a Christian.

"Someone who believes in the Trinity," Natasha said.

"But what about Jehovah's Witnesses?" I said. "They don't believe in the divinity of Jesus."

"Then they're not truly Christian."

Another member interjected. "A Christian is someone who believes Jesus is the son of God. But that's not enough. You have to accept him as your Lord and Savior."

"But what if someone believes in Jesus as a prophet. What are they?"

"A non-believer."

"Based on what?"

"The Bible."

The Bible study leader quoted passages about Jesus being the Light and the Way, and accepting him as the Lord and Savior being essential to salvation.

"So are Jehovah's Witnesses non-believers too?"

"Yes," she said.

I grew quiet, already knowing my fate in their eyes. I said nothing for the rest of the meeting. But I wasn't satisfied. I needed to know more. And I knew that the Bible study group wouldn't be able to help me.

I decided that night that I would not return. There was no sense in a non-believer masquerading as one of the chosen.

It hurt like hell, I cannot lie, to realize how they would see me—if they ever learned who I really was—a "non-believer." I had grown to love them like close friends, if not a second family. But I knew I could never be a part of them no matter how much I wanted their acceptance. I knew from the depths of my soul that Jesus was not God and that to believe in anyone, or anything, as God other than God himself was blasphemy. I couldn't sell my soul for their approval.

I returned to my room alone and felt the depths of my loneliness. I thought of Darnell, of Reggie, of Natasha. And I cried.

O God, in the name of your son Jesus, help me!
Help me find myself. Guide me to Your Light, Your Way.
Guide me to You.
Amen.

For the next two weeks, I read as many library books as I did school texts, and I didn't sleep as much as I would have liked. I sat with religion professors, history majors, and any other "experts" I deemed unbiased. I read encyclopedias and religious history texts like they were novels. I even read the Bible more closely. But mostly I prayed.

I had no idea what I was looking for exactly, or at what point I would stop and be satisfied that I'd found it. I knew only that I hadn't found it yet. So I had to keep searching.

If anything, my increased reading and research only added to my confusion. But what stuck out to me most was this, that allegedly the concept of Jesus as part of the Trinity was a concept not taught by Jesus himself, but by Paul, a man who never saw or met Jesus. I also discovered that all religious historians I'd come across stated that the concept of Jesus being God's son was first introduced by Paul too. I learned that the Bible I had was not even a book until long after the era of Jesus, and that it was the result of arguing and voting, a culmination of a decision that many monotheistic Christians of that era opposed on grounds that it did not represent Jesus' message. I also learned that most of these monotheistic Christians believed Jesus to be a prophet, and claimed that this was what Jesus claimed for himself. Also, I read that the entire idea of God having a son was a concept more akin to paganism and mythology than the Gospel. I learned further that December 25th was not Jesus' birthday, but the birthday of a pagan god.

I was overwhelmed.

I knew that no book, no historian, no human being, in fact, was completely unbiased, and that I had every right to question what I was reading and learning. There was no guarantee that they were not writing these things for their own personal benefit, and that their words could very well be false.

But that also meant that the same logic applied to The Church and the Bible study group.

I prayed again, this time more ardently. I realized only later that I had abandoned referring to Jesus as God's son.

O God, help me! Guide me to Your Light. Guide me to Your Way. Guide me to the Truth.
Amen.

The arrival of final exams followed by Christmas vacation freed me from my worries for the time being. However, upon arriving home, the lights glowing and decorations shimmering from the Christmas tree standing in our living room was a sore reminder that even the tree itself was originally a pagan practice.

For the two weeks I was home, I had a difficult time with the previously naturally recited phrase "Merry Christmas," and I was even less enthusiastic about attending and listening to my father's holiday sermons. I wanted so badly to talk to someone in my family about my troubles, but I didn't know whom I could turn to. But, mostly, I didn't know what I would say if I found that person.

Courtney's and Patricia's presence was, oddly, a welcome distraction for me. I enjoyed getting to know my sisters all over again, and I relished in my new role as aunt to my adorable, chubby nephew Emanuel. I even surprised myself by liking my brother-in-law James, who was personable and had a wicked sense of humor. I could easily see how Patricia fell in love with him. Although my father couldn't show it as much as he wanted, I caught the smile in his eyes and the subdued grin on his face whenever James said something funny. My mother, on the other hand, was unabashed in her welcoming her son-in-law into the family and doted over her grandchild as if he were a gift from Heaven above.

A few days before I was to return to school, Courtney entered my room after knocking lightly on the door. I was sitting cross-legged on my bed reading one of the books about Christianity that I had borrowed from the school library. Instinctively, I laid it face up to conceal the cover as I looked up to greet her. It took a moment for me to notice the neatly wrapped package in her hands. I narrowed my eyes in confusion because on Christmas Day she had already given me a gift, a hardcover collection of some books, including one I hadn't heard of.

She sat on the edge of my bed and wore a hesitant smile as she extended the package to me. "Here's your real gift."

I raised my eyebrows and grinned. "What?"

"Open it."

The rustling of the cellophane filled the silence between us until I reached the box beneath and lifted the lid. It took a moment to register what I was seeing. I wasn't accustomed to seeing compact disc cases and I was even less accustomed to reading names like Aretha Franklin, Mariah Carey, and Whitney Houston, so I took a full two minutes sifting through and reading each before it finally occurred to me that I was holding The Church's forbidden music in my hands.

My eyes widened slightly and I have no idea what expression my face held when I met my sister's gaze.

"Merry Christmas, little sister. Welcome to the real world."

I would be lying if I said that Courtney's gift was offensive or even unpalatable. I was ecstatic. The gift awakened all kinds of dormant emotions and desires inside of me. I couldn't wait to return to school to indulge in the previously forbidden and explore a world outside The Church. What surprised me most was that when I did return to school and put the CDs into Felicia's stereo system, I didn't feel even a thread of guilt. I danced and sashayed around the room until my legs and arms hurt and tears spilled from my eyes. It was as if God had answered my prayers, and I understood in a new light the meaning of the oft-repeated words of Martin Luther King, Jr: *Free at last! Free at last! Thank God Almighty, I'm free at last!*

Eight

With the addition of music in my life, I had a renewed confidence in myself and discovered that I actually had rhythm. On Felicia's urging, I signed up for an elective on popular dance and although it would become my favorite class, it wasn't long before I realized that it was African dance that would always be my love. When Anita told me about an African dance course in Washington, D.C., I was determined to sign up and get there somehow. I quickly learned the public transit system and took a bus to the College Park metro station once a week to arrive at my class in D.C. every Saturday morning.

I laughed more, had a renewed interest in my physical health, and even began to dress differently. I didn't have much money at my disposal, but the money my father was earning from the increased church membership after landing a spot to broadcast his Sunday sermons on national television helped me to build a modest savings. I wasn't accustomed to shopping for clothes and found the prices, even at outlet malls like Potomac Mills, far beyond my budget, so my forced frugality inspired my being acquainted with the most popular thrift stores in the area.

I would have permed my hair if it hadn't been for my friendship with Anita and Felicia, whose sophistication and self pride demanded they sport the latest fashions and proudly bask in the eccentricity of their natural hair styles. If I wanted "straight, limp hair," as they called it, I could simply subject my hair to the hot comb. And, they said, when I tired of the singularity of a hairstyle that offered nothing in the way of originality or true beauty, I could let the cool water reach my roots and enjoy the endless possibilities my naturally tightly curled hair offered.

I loved them for inspiring in me an awareness of beauty not measured by television, magazines, or movies—or the mirror. They scoffed at the society's so-called "most beautiful women" and mocked the shapelessness, paleness, and aesthetic sterility of the latest models, singers, and movie stars.

"The only reason people like us won't ever be next to these so called beauties," Anita would say, "is because, then, there would *be* no competition."

We would laugh until our stomachs hurt. What amazed me was that I actually saw what she was saying. Years later, as a Muslim, I would see the world with those same eyes, marveling at how if every woman and man covered as they should and if society didn't bombard people with images they literally *told* you were beautiful, human nature would kick in, and everyone's taste in beauty would vary.

Beauty would never be narrowly viewed or defined because there would simply be nothing with which to view or define it except your own heart, mind, and eyes—in that order.

With Anita's and Felicia's help, I selected clothes that struck a balance between my desire to be more stylish and my reluctance to divorce myself completely from how I was raised. In their words, my new wardrobe was "tastefully sophisticated." I wore loose-fitting pants and slightly fitting shirts, the kind of clothes that would never turn men's heads next to the more risqué styles worn at parties and clubs, but the kind that would confirm both my attractive physique and personal modesty. Occasionally, I wore wrap-around skirts and a short shirt that met the skirt at my waist, which strayed somewhat from my personal modesty.

For the first time in my life I felt both confident and beautiful. I was particularly proud that there was no man who had inspired this transition, and that I had freed myself from the shackles of a fickle society too caught up in others' definition of *pretty* and *ugly* and *good* and *bad* that people rarely took a moment to define those terms, and thus their lives, for themselves.

I was walking back to the metro station in D.C. after my African dance class one Saturday morning when I spotted some street vendors selling various Afro-centric paraphernalia. It was late February and the snow had melted but the air was still a bit cold, though nothing like I'd experienced back home. The weather hadn't kept me from dressing in my newfound style though. I was wearing a fitting button-up sweater that stopped at my waist and a wrap-around skirt that hid my knit pants I'd worn for class but accented what the pants had during class. I was conscious of how my low-heel black leather boots complimented the outfit, and I wasn't yet ready to get on the train and return to campus. I wanted to be noticed, so I lingered in front of the vendors, who were mostly African-American men, and pretended to be interested in buying something.

A shirt caught my eye and I immediately picked it up. "Some have brains. Some have beauty. Fortunately, I have both."

I grinned from ear-to-ear. This shirt definitely had my name written all over it. After finding out how much it cost, I handed the vendor a twenty-dollar bill and folded the T-shirt before putting it into my black shoulder bag I used for my dance class towel and clothes.

I heard the catcalling a moment after I decided that I had tired of being outside. I had never heard the derogatory whistling and sexual innuendoes directed at me before, so I actually turned and looked at the homeless man, who was obviously intoxicated. At the sight of him, my stomach churned and I quickly turned and walked faster, feeling my loneliness and vulnerability at that moment. He kept at it and complimented the curves Anita and Felicia had so meticulously directed me to accent "modestly" and he expressed desires so specific in their inappropriateness that my legs weakened. I found myself wishing I could hide in my usual clothes and be in my parents' home and church right then.

The man followed me to the train station, and unfortunately it was still too early in the afternoon for the station to be comfortably crowded. I wished someone, anyone, would tell him to mind his business, to leave me alone. But everyone walked on as if his harassment were as normal as the day itself. Even when he actually put his hands on me and I recoiled with a shriek, the most I received from passers-by was a double take or a frown. Not even the station security guard I spotted nearby raised an eyebrow although an expression of disapproval was clear on his face before he was distracted by something else.

My heart was drumming in my chest, and I was afraid to reach into my purse to retrieve the money I'd stashed there for the nominal train fare. I couldn't just jump over the rotating entrance bars although I so ardently wanted to in order to escape this sociopath, so I kept walking and pretended to look for someone as I found myself pacing back and forth in front of the payment area.

He continued his innuendoes and again he grew so close that I could smell his foul stench. My eyes burned in fear and frustration and I found myself guided by his surreptitious urging around a small corner that a great many people were not likely to venture. At this point, he moved to embrace me, and my survival instincts kicked in. My hands flew and I felt my purse and bag drop to the crease at my elbow, obstructing my abilities to defend myself fully. Unperturbed, he continued tugging at my sweater and touching me, as if I were his long lost girlfriend.

I finally found my voice enough to scream for help. His face changed and his actions halted, and he stared at me as if seeing me for the first time. I hollered again, and he frowned at me as though I'd misled and disappointed him. Cursing me, he turned and left me alone, mumbling something to himself and shaking his head in dismay as he walked away.

Spent, I fell to my knees and took concentrated breaths to steady myself. A moment later, the security guard rounded the corner, and the sight of him infuriated me. He asked if I was all right, and I told him to go to Hell.

Ignoring my rudeness, he helped me to my feet and asked again if I was all right. I yanked my arm free of him and felt the hotness in my cheeks and the familiar throbbing in my head. My eyes welled as I stumbled slightly then walked toward the payment area, where I retrieved my money and paid for my ride home. But I fought the tears, determined to get home without breaking down.

On the train ride home, I counted the seconds until the train arrived at College Park station. On the bus, I relaxed somewhat and felt myself shaking at the realization that I was almost home. The bus pulled in front of the stop nearest my dormitory, and I couldn't keep myself from walking at an unnaturally fast pace to my room.

Once inside, I found the room empty and I immediately broke down, not bothering to reach my bed before I collapsed. My crying was so terrible that my stomach heaved more than once and I lay on the floor relieved to be home. But more than anything I was horribly shaken and felt the depths of darkness that I'd fallen into in my search for spiritual freedom and self worth.

And I'd found neither.

I didn't attend my African dance classes after that. But I continued to exercise my freedom of choice in fashion although I didn't have enough courage to venture beyond University of Maryland grounds to share it with the world. I cannot lie, I was very tempted to crawl back into my shell of being a daughter of The Church and hide in my father's idea of modesty and appropriate dress. But I rebelled against this inclination. In my head, I heard my feminist psychology professors cautioning us to never blame the victim, to never blame the woman, to never blame *yourself*. But there was another voice in my head telling me that I was, somehow, at fault.

I knew that I wasn't culpable for the crime that the man could have easily seen to completion that day. But, intuitively, I also knew that divorcing myself from culpability entirely would do nothing to protect myself in the future.

Years later when, as a Muslim, I read in the Qur'an the verse commanding believing women to wear the *jilbaab*—the large, loose outer garment worn over a woman's normal clothes, I pondered the Creator's reason for this command: *"That is more suitable, that they will be known (as believers) and not abused."* As much as the feminist remnants in me wanted to argue that men did not discriminate between the covered and the uncovered, I knew my experience before and after wearing Islamic garb was testimony against this philosophy. Naturally, Islam recognized that there were those men who would verbally and physically harass women regardless of how they dressed, but it also recognized that women were respected most when they covered as pious women had for generations.

At the time of the train station incident, the words of my feminist professors were ones with which I agreed in theory but ones I found difficulty living in testimony to because of my experience. Yes, women *should* be respected regardless of how they dress, of where they work, or what they deem appropriate behavior. But *would* they?

In my head, I heard my father saying that there were only two types of respect in this world—the kind that is given from the goodness of a person's heart, and the kind that is earned by the virtuousness of a person's actions. "And the wise person puts himself in the second category before he expects others to put themselves in the first," he would say.

As much as I hated to admit it, my father was right.

You can ask the world to respect you for who you are on the inside, Renee, or you can show on the outside what's inside, so that they have no choice.

Despite having been terribly shaken following the incident in the metro station, the feeling slowly subsided until I was completely comfortable in my "tasteful sophistication" though I still didn't dare renew my trips to D.C. Honestly, I liked the way I looked when I dressed in slightly fitting clothes. Because there were so many other women around me dressing provocatively, tastelessly so, it was easy to feel modest, dignified even, in my new style.

In my dorm room, I would gaze at myself in the mirror, amazed that Renee Morris was actually attractive. I loved myself and couldn't get enough of seeing my reflection both in the room and out while passing glass windows and display cases. I knew I'd never pass the world's litmus test for beauty or be accepted amongst the stereotypical "norm"—I could barely find clothes that properly fit my Black figure—but I fell in love with myself nonetheless, even if one trip to the clothes store sent the clear message that my dimensions were not even worth considering in calculating numerical body sizes.

Nevertheless, after tiresome searching and trying on clothes whenever I had several hours to dedicate to shopping, I'd eventually find something that fit. However, there were occasions that I fit shopping into my schedule, even when it wasn't convenient.

Late March following Spring Break was one of those occasions, when Sumayyah called to invite me to a Muslim event in Baltimore. I immediately thought of the volunteer at the "Ask About Islam" table whom I'd subsequently seen deliver the poetic monologue. In the midst of my fashion and music fascination, I'd had nearly forgotten about Sumayyah, and him. But the sound of her voice and name brought back everything, and it was as if I were hearing the poem all over again. I felt the familiar desire to know more, but it was the young man I wanted to talk to and I had no idea if I'd ever get the opportunity. However, I did casually ask Sumayyah if she thought he and other performers from the open house would be there, and she said yes. She was sure that he would be presenting although she was unsure about the others. I couldn't care less about the others, but I did express a sense of disappointment at the news in order to veil my true desires.

Although I was still far from enjoying the luxury of having money at my disposal, I decided that the thrift store would not do this time. I was going to treat myself to real shopping. I already knew the selections at Beltway Plaza and Laurel Mall were too limited to waste my time going there. Besides, public transportation would take me to only the former, and it would be the latter I'd choose if I was left with only those two choices. And if I were to secure a ride with a kind friend, I would ask for what I really wanted, a trip to Potomac Mills, a thirty-minute drive that ended in Virginia.

Anita was the only friend I knew with a car, but I wasn't used to asking to go anywhere since I was usually invited whenever I rode with her. Of course, there were many other acquaintances with vehicles, but my relationship with them was more cordial than friendly.

When Sumayyah called again a few days before the Saturday event to confirm that I was going, I knew my dilemma was solved. She'd be happy to take me shopping. I was shy to ask, but once I did, my thoughts proved correct. She said that Thursday was best because she usually spent most of her Friday afternoons and evenings at the *masjid*. That worked perfectly for me, because I'd already asked Felicia to braid my hair Friday afternoon and my style would take a full eight hours to complete.

During the Thursday drive, Sumayyah told me the story of how she accepted Islam. The story was interesting, at least to pass time during the ride, but my knowledge of Islam was still rudimentary, so I couldn't fully comprehend the significance of her journey. But I was intrigued that at the age of eleven she was already doubting Christianity. I was impressed that a person so young had the ability to discern contradictions and decide that she didn't believe Jesus was God. My interest was sparked when she said that, in ways, it was easier for her to conclude that Jesus wasn't God's son than it was to conclude that Jesus wasn't God.

When I asked her why, she said, "People and animals have children, not the Creator."

Her answer was simple enough. I could see where she was coming from. But I didn't think of God's fatherhood in the human or animalistic sense. I told her that.

She shrugged, and I respected her for not arguing with me. She just continued to explain her feelings. "For me, I just couldn't agree with using the word *son* to explain the miracle of Jesus' birth. To me, even before I knew the Islamic explanation, it was as simple as God creating Jesus without a man's parentage. It's what He did with Adam. So why insist there had to be a father at all? It was like denying the miracle itself."

I pondered that. I never thought to compare Jesus' birth to Adam's.

At the mall, the conversation shifted to my clothes and occasionally my background. She found The Church's teachings intriguing and more than once expressed how blessed I was to have been raised like that. I couldn't understand that position and told her that I would've preferred a normal church and family.

She laughed and told me that if I knew what went on in most "normal" families, I wouldn't feel so inclined toward them. For some reason, her words made me think of what Darnell had said about William's father. I wondered if there was any truth to it. But I quickly dismissed the thought, immediately reminded of the lesson Reggie had taught me— that curiosity is sometimes a sin.

After I found the outfit I wanted, we sat down in the food court and ate warm pretzels and soft-serve ice cream. I discovered that Sumayyah used to be Simone and she had chosen the name Sumayyah because it was relatively close to her given name. I also learned that she never changed her name legally and didn't plan to. When I asked her why, she explained that it would hurt her parents too much and she wasn't willing to do that, especially since her name held no bad meaning and Islam didn't require her to change her name if that wasn't the case.

I sensed she was close to her parents and asked why she lived at home instead of on campus.

"I'm the only Muslim in my family," she said, "and I want my parents to eventually convert."

I didn't completely understand the explanation but I nodded as her explanation took vague meaning.

"I was a difficult child," she said, stirring her ice cream reflectively. "I want them to see that being Muslim means they mean more to me, not less, even if I can't embrace the religion they raised me to believe in." She sighed.

"I want to move out. It's hard praying and fasting and reading Qur'an while my family's watching crazy movies, blasting music, and drinking alcohol when guests come."

Her family sounded like how I'd imagined William's must be. The mention of movies, music, and alcohol always evoked an image of dysfunction in my mind, although years later I would learn those three things were part of the "normal" American household. It was simply a matter of moderation in most Americans' view. As long as they didn't waste their entire day in front of the movie or television screen, as long as they weren't alcoholics, then these activities could actually be "healthy" forms of relaxation.

"They don't mind you being Muslim?"

She gathered her eyebrows as a grin lingered on her face. "They think it's the worst thing that could've happened to them."

"Why?"

She lifted a shoulder in a shrug and toyed with the melting ice cream without meeting my gaze. "Honestly, I really don't know. I ask myself that everyday."

Friday after classes, my hair was to be braided into a style similar to what others would call micro-braids except for two things—the amount and thickness of my hair rendered the addition of false hair excessive, and I didn't have the patience to have my braids thinner than the already long session would allow for completion. Felicia blew dry my hair for maximum length then began the eight-hour session. As usual, I had a book ready, a few actually, and I began reading.

"I was awake that day that student stopped by the room," she said.

I was so engrossed in my reading that it took me a moment to register that she was talking to me, and about Sumayyah. "Oh, really? I thought you were asleep."

"Whatever you do, Renee," she said as if she didn't hear me, "don't convert to her religion."

I creased my forehead, but I couldn't turn to look at her without disrupting the hairstyle. I had no plans to convert to Islam, but her tone offended me. I immediately thought of what Sumayyah had said about her family thinking her conversion was the worst thing in the world.

"Why does it matter?" I asked.

There was a long pause. "Just don't. You'll regret it."

I didn't know what to say to that so I resumed reading, and we didn't discuss it any further. Felicia and I never discussed religion, and I had no idea what religion people from her country practiced. Before that moment I had no idea religion meant anything to her at all. I wanted to know what she knew about Islam and Muslims, but I decided against asking. The last time someone who wasn't Muslim explained Islam to me I was left thinking it was a religion of Indians and Arabs who thought women had to be stuffed under the floorboards of a house if the front door accidentally flew open while they were near it.

I was slowly learning the wisdom of my mother saying to me the night I learned of Darnell's sister and of her brief interest in the Nation of Islam, "If you want to understand someone's life and choices, ask them. Otherwise, you don't really want to understand."

Nine

Late Saturday morning I stepped out the passenger side door of Sumayyah's car feeling an air of confidence that permeated every part of me. Part of my confidence, I knew, was due to the outfit I had chosen so carefully. Heeding the advice of Sumayyah, I chose something that covered my body modestly; however, I could not completely abandon the sophistication with which Anita and Felicia had indoctrinated me. My jean skirt was fitting around the hips but was loose at my ankles. My feet bore the string ties of my white open-toe sandals that revealed meticulously applied maroon nail polish that matched my fingernails. My long sleeve white shirt too clung slightly to my form, but it was the low neck that I loved most. The gold crucifix William had given me glistened from the thin gold necklace against my brown skin, and I felt an air of both African and Christian pride as I took in the crowd.

The sight of so many cloth-covered heads made me conscious of my thin braids that fell to my shoulders and lifted gently with the breeze, inspiring in me a renewed self-assurance that I would indeed stand out in the crowd. It didn't occur to me, at least not then, that I should feel uncomfortable, or even ashamed, dressed like I was amid so many Muslims. It was most likely the festive, as opposed to religious, atmosphere that dulled my sensitivities where they would have normally been heightened. There was a moon bounce, pony rides, cotton candy, and tables of vendors. Music was coming from a portable platform where a group of young men performed songs and raps. In a way, I felt right at home.

Sumayyah handed me a program and I learned that at two thirty that afternoon, there would be a lecture entitled "Jesus, the Bridge and Divider of Monotheistic Religions Today." The topic interested me more than I let on, and I only vaguely noted that, following the lecture, there would be a panel of new Muslims sharing their journey to Islam. I knew I wanted to hear the talk, but I also knew I'd have to make up some excuse to leave before the panel. I had heard enough in College Park, and I was beginning to get a bit irritated that Muslims felt the need to make a public announcement every time someone left his childhood religion and accepted Islam.

Sumayyah introduced me to so many people that later I couldn't recall any of their names except a young woman named Shazia because she reminded me so much of my Hindu friend from high school. The only thing I recalled about the rest of them was that they had grown up Christian but converted to Islam. It did not escape me that each of them emphasized this point quite eloquently, as if the information would somehow inspire me to do the same. To be honest, I was offended and told them, frankly, I was happy as a Christian and was just here to enjoy the occasion. I decided against mentioning the "Ask About Islam" volunteer who had really inspired my desire to attend today's event. I hoped we wouldn't miss his performance.

As it turned out, I had no cause to worry, as Sumayyah primly seated herself, and me, in the front row opposite the portable stage fifteen minutes before he was scheduled to perform. I had already tired of perusing the items on the vendors' tables, and my stomach was full from barbeque chicken sandwiches and hot dogs that tasted better than any I remembered eating at home. I had even stood in line with children half my size to get cotton candy and tried my hand at the kiddy carnival games. So I was relieved when she tugged at my arm and guided me to the seats. I was becoming exhausted in the heat, surprised that it was already this warm in mid-March.

"Yusuf is up next," Sumayyah said to me in a whisper as we sat down before the platform of children performing what appeared to be martial arts.

"Who?"

"Yusuf."

"Who's that?"

"The brother who did the monologue at the open house."

Oh. My heart beat quickened, and I was surprised by how nervous I'd become all of a sudden. I found myself growing irritated at the childish flips, kicks, and tumbles the children performed at the calls of a man standing with his arms crossed authoritatively at the side of the stage.

When the time for Yusuf's performance grew near, I was taken aback by how packed the seats became all of a sudden. I was impressed. Apparently, he was well known in the area. I was grateful to Sumayyah for reserving our seats early on.

Yusuf was introduced as a renowned poet who had been featured in Essence and Ebony magazines, had won numerous oral and written poetry competitions, and even had a modest professional acting resume. Currently, he owned and operated Ihsan Productions, a Muslim performing arts company that donated most of its proceeds to Nourishing the Heart and Mind—NHM—a non-profit organization, which he had co-founded, specializing in giving minority youth the leadership, educational, and creative expression skills they needed to excel in society.

I was speechless by the time Yusuf finally stepped onto the stage. I barely noticed the three men seated at the rear of the platform, the one in the middle holding a small drum. But after Yusuf reached the microphone, their voices resonated in a harmonizing tenor above the gentle beating on the drum, reminding me of native music from South Africa. Yusuf wore a long white thobe that lifted and clung to him slightly with the wind, revealing his athletic form beneath the thin fabric. Yusuf's voice blended in with the men's even as it overpowered theirs, and it took me a second to realize he was singing.

"Amazing grace, how sweet the sound that saved a wretch like me." He paused, the background harmonizing continuing.

"Amazing." This time he spoke instead of sang, and the word came out as thunderous.

"Amazing," he said again, this time more subdued but the word still carrying the weight of his previous utterance.

"Amazing." It was a reflective whisper now, and his eyes narrowed in deep thought. "I once *was* lost. I once *was* blind." He drew in a deep breath and exhaled. "But now, *now*, I'm free."

Amazing that this grace that I sang about in church
wasn't found until I was free.
Amazing that its sweet sound that I sang for you wasn't
so sweet coming from me.
Amazing that when I was singing about not being blind,
I was wondering what it was like to see.
Amazing how sweet grace really is once its sweetness
graced me.

As I listened to his poem, which was part-song, part-monologue, I was entranced and moved at once. I could feel the pain of finding in adulthood the amazing grace of childhood only to feel the censure of the family who had taught him of grace. I was immediately reminded of what Sumayyah had said about her family and wondered if his family too viewed his conversion to Islam as the worst thing he could have possibly done.

After the performance, I wanted to approach Yusuf to ask questions, but before I could mention my intentions, Sumayyah said that it was time to pray and led me into the building on whose lot the festivities were being held. The coolness of the air conditioned indoors soothed me and I wondered why Sumayyah hadn't taken us inside earlier.

After using the bathroom, I emerged from the stall to check my appearance in the mirror while Sumayyah wet her hands, face, and arms in preparation for prayer like a few other women were doing at other sinks. When she removed her head covering to smooth down her hair and readjust the cloth, I did a double-take, having not seen her hair before. I was surprised to find her head full of small twists pulled back by a ponytail holder. I don't know what I expected her hair to look like, nor was I aware that I had expected anything at all, but I could not deny my intrigue as I realized how she looked fully African-American without the cloth on her head. She could have easily been a classmate of mine at school. Suddenly, I saw her as Simone and could relate to the heartbreak her parents must be enduring in the knowledge of her abandoning the church.

The sound of her voice interrupted my thoughts, and I found myself staring at her as she wrapped the cloth neatly around her head, transforming into Sumayyah.

"You can sit on the seats in the hall until we finish."

I nodded, wondering if there were any Simones-turned-Sumayyah at the school I had graduated from. The possibility lingered in my mind and remained as an intriguing possibility though I couldn't imagine how any of the personalities behind the confident, shy, and goofy faces in my high school yearbook could actually hide something as profound as converting to Islam.

I seated myself in the hall as directed and watched nonchalantly as scores of men and women passed me in preparation to pray. I had seen some of the Muslim prayer while I was at the open house and had wondered at the quiet contentment of so many different ages and races standing in solidarity next to each other with one arm folded over the other.

When a familiar face passed, I didn't realize I had spoken Yusuf's name aloud until he turned and searched the faces behind him for who had called him until his gaze met mine.

I smiled, feeling my heart pound as I realized he was looking at me.

"Hi," I said as if we'd known each other forever. "It's nice seeing you again."

I was only vaguely aware of others staring curiously at us, looking from Yusuf to me and from me to Yusuf, before entering the prayer area. One woman actually wrinkled her nose at us and said something I didn't understand at the time. Later I learned it was the Arabic expression *astaghfirullaah*, invoking God's forgiveness. However, I was too excited about my opportunity to talk to Yusuf to register that my greeting had broken any rule or offended anyone.

I do recall Yusuf quickly lowering his gaze and creasing his forehead in confusion. It was then that I realized that he didn't remember me.

"You too," he said hurriedly and disappeared into the prayer room.

I felt stupid and only then did I become aware of people's looks of disapproval that they were doing a poor job of hiding. It was the first moment I was self-conscious of my appearance. However, my discomfort was short-lived. A few minutes later, I spotted at least six other women uncovered, some with less shame than I. I exhaled in relief and dismissed the earlier looks as nothing, although I had a harder time downplaying Yusuf's eager exit after my greeting him. My face grew warm as I finally admitted the sentiment his face had displayed—embarrassment. I didn't understand why he had any reason to be ashamed, of all things. Had I said something wrong? Sacrilegious? Perhaps it was my greeting of *hi* instead of the Arabic greeting they exchanged that caused his shame in responding to me.

After prayer I had a difficult time finding Sumayyah. When I finally found her, I saw her talking to someone near the top of the steps that led outside. The crowd hid from me the person opposite her, and as I approached her, I kept losing sight of her behind the droves of people. But I knew where I had seen her, so I approached the stairs.

"Sumayyah," I called out when I saw her less than ten feet in front of me. She turned and tried to locate the voice when I waved. As she recognized me, she waved me over to her.

"This is Renee, who I was telling you about," she said as I reached her.

I turned and found myself staring into the face of Yusuf, whose eyebrows rose slightly in recognition, though I sensed he still didn't recall me from the "Ask About Islam" table. He immediately dropped his gaze and nodded politely.

"Nice to meet you."

I laughed uncomfortably. "We already met."

"Really?" He glanced up briefly and held the polite expression of one trying to place a face but unable to despite his greatest efforts.

"You probably don't remember. But I met you at Maryland when you were at a table during Islamic Awareness Week."

His expression softened somewhat as he nodded, remembering being at the table, but not in meeting me. I felt slighted and insignificant but hid my feelings with a broad smile.

"Congratulations," I said. "You're a really good poet."

"Thanks."

There was an awkward silence.

"Is it..." I didn't know how to finish my question. "Is it, uh, based on your conversion to Islam?"

"The poem?"

"Yes."

"Yes, this one is."

I nodded, unsure what I felt safe saying with Sumayyah standing right there. I wanted to know if we could keep in touch, if he didn't mind my calling him sometimes, but my senses told me that wasn't exactly proper etiquette for the moment. So I resigned myself to nodding, feeling stupid at not being able to think of anything else to say.

Sumayyah saved me from having to speak when she said we'd better get going. I wasn't quite ready to leave, but I could find no rational reason to protest, so I fell in stride next to her as she descended the steps. We still had thirty minutes until the lecture, she said as we approached the door, and she wanted to look at some clothes.

At two thirty, I sat in a chair in the third row opposite the podium in what looked like the building's cafeteria turned auditorium. To the right of the podium was an empty table with three vacant seats that I assumed were to be occupied by the panel of Muslims telling of their journey to Islam. However, my peaked interest was due to the topic of the lecture.

Delivering the lecture was, to my surprise, an African-American woman who had spent nearly twenty years as a Christian preacher before accepting Islam. I had been a bit taken aback by the former preacher who spoke at the open house, but for some reason, this woman's story really interested me. I was slightly disappointed when her story was abandoned to introduce the topic of the view of Jesus according to the three "Abrahamic faiths." I didn't think of Jesus as being a central point of belief for Jews, Christians, and Muslims, but the woman's talk made me see that he was. For Jews, it was their rejection of him as a Messiah that divided them from the Christians historically. For Christians, he was central to their belief system, but in time had become God himself although he never claimed divinity himself. According to the ex-preacher, it was only Muslims who believed in him as he believed in himself. Muslims accepted him as the Messiah prophet born of the Virgin Mary, but rejected the newly introduced concept of his divinity and God's fatherhood of him. What appealed to me was the historical proof she gave for her arguments, though some of them I recognized as similar to ones mentioned at the open house.

I was still reflecting on some of her points when a man stood before the microphone and introduced the panel. We were told that we were able to ask questions of the former preacher and the panelists once the converts had shared their stories. I was torn between remaining in the room and capitalizing on the opportunity to ask questions, and leaving to avoid sitting longer than I wanted.

The first panelist, a woman of Korean descent, approached the podium, but I had difficulty concentrating on her words because I couldn't decide whether or not I wanted to hear her story. As if mentally counting down until the end, my eyes grazed the panelists, and I saw that, naturally, there were only two speakers after her. I noticed that the last two were men, one White, the other African-

American, and I felt as if I were at the open house all over again.

When the woman finished, which was sooner than I had anticipated, the White man approached the podium. If I hadn't known this was a session on people accepting Islam, I would have assumed he was Arab although his skin was white and his eyes blue. He wore a small white skullcap, a long white robe like the one Yusuf had worn, and the beginnings of a beard shadowed his cheeks. I didn't understand the significance of the robe, which seemed Biblical to me, but I couldn't keep from feeling a sense of admiration and respect for the men who wore it. It made them appear righteous and dignified.

Since there was only one more speaker after the White man, I decided that it wouldn't be too torturous to sit through the rest of the panelists. I reluctantly relaxed and listened to the man tell of his journey to Islam, but it was his mention of Yusuf, the poet, being instrumental in his accepting Islam that made me pay closer attention. Yusuf had done an oral poetry performance on the man's college campus, after which the man had approached Yusuf due to the intriguing racial and religious turmoil expressed in the poem. They kept in touch, and slowly the man took baby steps to accepting that it wasn't only Yusuf's poetry that had captivated him, but Yusuf's spirituality.

The mention of Johns Hopkins being where the performance took place made me think of William, but only vaguely. It was then that the man's blue eyes held a distant familiarity, and the intonations of his voice, though foreign in their content and use of Muslim jargon, inspired a connection that was so intense that my breath caught. I sat forward and studied the contours of his face that were barely visible beneath the beard and suddenly his nose, his smile, even the gentle creases around his eyes made my heart quicken at the possibility.

When he mentioned growing up in Indianapolis and his reading of *The Autobiography of Malcolm X* as a project for class, I nearly stood up and screamed from the shock I felt at the realization. There was still a thread of doubt in my mind because he hadn't said his name, at least I didn't recall his saying it, and the Arab appearance made it difficult to confirm my suspicions.

I thought of Darnell and how I had so often felt I'd seen him, was so convinced that he was alive and well, only to walk up to a complete stranger and gawk at them for several seconds before Darnell's features faded to give way to the unfamiliar features of the stranger's face. Was it possible I was hallucinating about William too? If I was, it made no sense. No tragedy was connected to him, so there was no reason for me to mentally create him through the presence of another person. If anyone, it would be Reggie I'd see in my mind's eye, or was there some unknown connection I felt between William and myself that inspired the mirage?

I dropped my gaze and leaned back in my chair, realizing that my grief over Darnell's death was distorting my reality severely. I wondered if I was feeling nostalgic for home even. How often was it that I longed for connection to something familiar?

"Are you okay?"

I turned to the sound of the whisper and saw Sumayyah's concerned expression as her hand rested on my arm and she leaned close to me to keep others from overhearing.

Embarrassed that my internal turmoil was apparent, I sat up and turned my attention back to the speaker, who was now concluding. He left the podium, and my eyes followed him. But I was unwilling to trust my mind. It had failed me too many times. It was possible that he hadn't even said *Indianapolis* but *Minneapolis* for all I knew. And how popular had the reading of Malcolm X's autobiography become, for Black and White alike?

When the last speaker finished and the floor was opened for questions, I felt my heart throbbing in my chest. I had forgotten about the questions I had for the ex-preacher. I now had only one, and it was to the White man. *Are you William Garret, Reggie Matthews's good friend from Indianapolis?*

But I couldn't bring myself to take the risk. I sat through the question-and-answer session fighting the urge to raise my hand and convincing myself I could at least ask Sumayyah to ask for me. The host asked if there were anymore questions, and I felt defeated. When his hand pointed to me, I felt my face grow hot as I realized I had my hand half-heartedly raised as if I were unsure I wanted to participate.

Sumayyah nudged me playfully, apparently noticing my nervousness, and on shaky legs I stood. I had no idea what I would say, although I had no doubt what I wanted to know.

"My name is Renee Morris," I said, hearing the shakiness in my voice. I held on to the back of the seat in front of me to steady myself. The person in it was turned around facing me, so her back was not against its frame. "I'm from Indianapolis and I'm Christian, but I'm really interested in learning more about Islam." I tried to keep from looking at the White man, but it was difficult. I was hoping for some sense of connection, but from the corner of my eye, I saw none. He sat listening politely for my point as if my introduction did not faze him in the least. I decided against addressing him. "And my question is for the preacher." I fixed my gaze on her. "I heard what you said about Muslims following what Jesus taught, but how can you be sure of that? Every sect of Christianity claims the same."

I sat down, perhaps too quickly, and realized that my question sounded more like a challenge than an inquiry. But I also realized that what I had said was what I was feeling in my heart right then.

She approached the podium. "Thank you, Renee," she said. "I'm glad you asked. This is a very important question."

I stole a glance at the White man, but he was listening intently to the ex-preacher. My heart fell as I realized my mind, and eyes, had betrayed me, again. I returned my attentions to the woman, feeling a sense of obligation to at least feign interest in her answer since I was the one who had asked the question.

"Like I mentioned in my presentation, there is a lot of historical evidence to support the theory, if you will, of Jesus not claiming divinity or any blood relationship to the Creator. As I said, neither concept is traced to Jesus himself, but to other figures and councils in history." The sides of her mouth creased in the beginnings of a smile.

"But to respond to your question specifically: How can I be sure that the Muslim belief about Jesus is correct?" She rested her hand on her chest in emphasis of reference to herself. "I think what you really mean is, What evidence can I bring to make *you* or anyone else who is not Muslim convinced that the Muslim belief is correct, given that all religions claim ultimate truth?" She paused and lifted her eyebrows as she gestured a hand toward me. "Would you say that's a fair rephrasing of your question?"

I felt the eyes of the audience on me, and I willed myself not to look at them. I nodded my head, keeping my gaze locked with hers. "Yes." The confidence and challenge in my voice surprised me, but I remained calm as I folded one arm over my chest and rested the other's elbow on it with my chin resting on a loose fist, awaiting her response.

"It's not for any human to convince you of anything." She wore a smile of self-conviction, but her tone and expression suggested that she respected my conviction although it was different from hers. "In the Qur'an, God tells us to *invite*.

"As for the evidence of the truth of Islam," she said before pausing momentarily. "After studying from authentic sources, hearing Muslims share their journeys to the religion, and sincerely praying to God to guide you to His Truth," she said, her last words making my heart skip a beat as I recalled my prayers to God, "the answer to your question is simply this: Consult your heart. It is there you will find your answer." She paused. "If your intentions and prayers are sincere."

There was a roar of applause as she took her seat after whispering a thank you and a prayer that God be with me in my search. For some reason, I felt my eyes burn, as the urge to cry overtook me. But I didn't understand the feeling and fought it as I continued to smile and brought my hands together to join in the applause of the audience.

The crowd filed out the room to return to the outside festivities, which were drawing to a close in an hour, and I remained in my seat trying to get a hold of my emotions. I was relieved when Sumayyah stood and left without bothering me about joining her. It wasn't until several minutes later that I noticed her near the table with a small group of audience members talking to the ex-preacher and panelists, who were all standing now and gathering their notes as they carried on conversations with the questioners who remained in the room.

"Renee?"

I looked up and saw Sumayyah next to me with her hand resting gently on my shoulder. She wore a smile and she pointed behind her, where she stood in the narrow aisle of chairs.

The ex-preacher reached around her and extended a hand in greeting. Taken aback, I sat up and reached for her hand, standing with the motion.

They stepped out of the aisle, and I followed behind them until we were a small huddle next to the chairs.

"I just wanted to formally introduce myself," the woman said. "I know Sumayyah from working on projects with her and Yusuf. And she tells me that you are her guest."

I smiled. "Yes, I am."

"Welcome. I'm glad you could come."

I studied the walnut brown of her round face and the mole on her cheek and the dark green cloth on her head, trying to place her in a church before a congregation. I couldn't. It was too surreal.

"I'm Hadiyah, by the way." She chuckled. "Formerly Dr. Reverend Pauline Gregory."

I laughed, unable to escape the humor and unlikelihood of such an introduction. "I'm glad to meet you."

"My Muslim name means one who guides to righteousness, now that I can rightfully make that claim."

She paused as she opened her purse and withdrew a card. She handed it to me. "Feel free to call me any time, day or night. I don't mind late night calls. Whenever you want to talk, I'm here."

I didn't understand why I would want to talk to her, and so urgently, but I remained cordial. "Thank you. I appreciate it."

"I look forward to talking to you. You're free to stop over, even for dinner."

I continued to smile. "Thank you."

Hadiyah turned and shook Sumayyah's hand, exchanged the Arabic greeting, and excused herself. My eyes followed her retreat, unable to comprehend what could have convinced a studied reverend to change religions. I thought of my father and became even more perplexed by Hadiyah's journey.

"Sumayyah." It was the sound of a male's voice, and I turned instinctively although it was not my name being called.

Sumayyah turned and greeted Yusuf, saying, "Hey, what's up?"

"I have someone who wants to talk to you. Both of you," he added.

Her eyebrows rose and she grinned at me teasingly. I didn't understand her expression, but it was contagious, so I grinned back, suppressing a giggle.

My grin faded as the White man stepped forward.

"I believe you know each other," Yusuf said.

I could feel my heart in my throat. "William?" My eyes grew large and I was overcome with joy for some reason. I couldn't contain the happiness I felt for him right then, though it wasn't until later that I reflected on the reasons for that feeling. I could feel the tears stinging my eyes and I wanted to hug him in congratulations, but I withheld. Instead, a broad smile formed on my face as he nodded.

"Yep, it's me."

I laughed. "Wow. I don't know what to say."

His gaze was lowered, as if he were shy to talk to me. But he did a double take as the crucifix glistened and caught his attention.

Immediately, I was embarrassed. I had forgotten I had it on.

"You still have that?"

Instinctively, my hand went to my neck and I toyed with the pendant self-consciously. I shrugged. "Yeah, what can I say?" I laughed. "I like it a lot."

"I have to get you a star and crescent now."

A smile lingered on my face, but I didn't understand the joke that evoked their collective laughter. "A what?"

He waved his hand. "Never mind."

He changed the subject. "You still at UMD?"

I nodded. "Yes. And you're still at Johns Hopkins, I hear."

He creased his forehead. "Who did you hear that from?"

I laughed. "You. You mentioned it in your speech."

He laughed too.

"Are you really interested in Islam?" he asked a few seconds later, lifting his head to look me in the eye briefly, his eyes narrowed like he used to do in childhood.

I shook my head before I realized what I was saying. "Not really. At least not for myself."

He grew quiet and nodded.

"She's interested," Sumayyah said with a laugh that suggested we were good friends sharing a private joke. "She just hasn't admitted it yet."

I grinned and stared at her playfully. "Says who?"

"Says nobody. I just said you haven't admitted it yet."

They laughed and I nodded, chuckling, unsure what to say.

Someone called Yusuf's name, and he glanced back before excusing himself. Apparently feeling out of place, William excused himself too, and I was left feeling excited, curious, and fearful at once. But I understood only the first two feelings because their cause was easy to pinpoint: William. It was my fear that I didn't understand for another few weeks.

Because he was a friend of William's, I felt more comfortable mentioning Yusuf's name and asking about him whenever Sumayyah called or stopped by the room. When I finally felt comfortable with Sumayyah as a friend and mentioned my personal interest in Yusuf, she stared at me as if seeing me for the first time. It took a moment for her to recuperate, but when she did, her words were controlled but the message was heartbreaking in more ways than I could comprehend at the time.

In all words, she told me that Yusuf was interested in only Muslim women, and even amongst them, he considered only those who covered in Islamic garb, "*hijaab*." There had been many women, and still were, who were interested in him, but he refused to deviate from his conviction: His future wife would be one who wore *hijaab*. It was the one heartfelt advice his mentor had repeated over and over after Yusuf accepted Islam: "Never marry a woman who doesn't cover, no matter how beautiful she is to you."

I didn't understand why Sumayyah was sharing all of this with me, and I was offended that she felt I wanted to marry him. That was the furthest thing from my mind. I only wanted to talk to him on the phone and get to know him better. But I couldn't escape the stinging pain I felt in my heart upon realizing I didn't even stand a chance at attracting his attentions.

What Sumayyah didn't say right then, and what I would learn soon after the conversation, was that she and Yusuf were engaged to be married. After I was Muslim, she apologized for being so brusque with me that day. She said that my words of interest in Yusuf had cut her more deeply than she had let on. She then shared with me the cause for her emotional response. My words had evoked a pain that was felt by many Muslim women.

At the time of the initial conversation I wasn't Muslim, so I wouldn't have understood her sentiments, even if she had explained them to me. But as a Muslim, they resonated with me on some level although I must admit that, at the time of her apology, I viewed the mentor's advice as overly simplistic and superficial. As she spoke, I thought, *But there are many women who don't cover who are better Muslims than those who do.*

Today, my faith and knowledge have matured such that I can appreciate the advice of Yusuf's mentor, especially as I see in my own life the divine wisdom in Allah's commandment for women to wear *hijaab*.

In retrospect, I know I would not have viewed the mentor's advice as overly simplistic if he had said the same about a woman who drinks alcohol or is lax in her prayer. Even today I cannot completely explain this contradiction in my logic. But I think, at the time, my spiritual foundation was too weak to understand that Islamic wisdom is one. Upon hearing Allah's commands, the believer simply says, "I hear and I obey." Surely, anyone who is willing to openly say, "I hear your command, O Allah, and I disobey!" is not someone a mentor should encourage a Muslim to marry— regardless of the open sin he or she is committing.

I know now, too, that if I am guilty of open sin and point at others and say I am better, this is a clear indication that my understanding of faith in God is distorted—I'm measuring my piety by what others are doing and not by what my Lord asks me to do.

Sumayyah didn't mention any of this during her apology, but in retrospect I can see that it was implied by what she shared. For Sumayyah, it was merely irksome that Muslim men would date non-Muslims, teach them about Islam, and then marry them, or even marry non-Muslims themselves, effectively ignoring available Muslim women. It was also bothersome to her that Muslim men would marry non-practicing Muslim women in hopes of guiding them to religiosity, all of this in direct contrast to the prophetic advice to marry for the religion.

It was this sensitivity that my inquiry had sparked in Sumayyah, my words incensing a response from her that would normally have been more guarded and kind. However, at the time, I didn't understand any of that. But there was one thing that did not escape me as I slowly registered Yusuf's desire to marry someone so unlike me—

the irony of the different responses that my dress had evoked at the metro station and before a Muslim man. Clearly, this was a sign from God to take heed of my father's lessons that I had begun to ignore.

When you put yourself out there as bait, you'll only catch what likes what you're offering.

Ten

It took a full three weeks for me to come to terms with the fear that had become more suffocating by the day. It numbed me into inactivity. I wasn't inspired to go out with Felicia or Anita, and I withdrew from nearly everyone. I went to class, to the cafeteria, and back to my room, where I remained studying until I grew drowsy and fell asleep. I didn't even bother to dress in my "sophisticated" clothes and found myself caring only about wearing something clean and presentable. As I tried to escape the trepidation that was tightening in my chest, I was sleepless at night and anxious throughout the day. I had no desire to talk to even Sumayyah, but I still felt a lingering pull to speak to Yusuf. I hadn't yet learned of Sumayyah's engagement to him, so I didn't understand that this was impossible, at least if Sumayyah was to be our liaison.

It wasn't until a phone call two weeks before final exams were scheduled to begin that I realized both the cause for my fear, and the fact that I had abandoned even my regular prayers to God to guide me to His Light and Truth.

It was late one Friday night in early April when the phone rang. I was still awake, and its shrilling sound inspired an awareness that I was sitting in bed staring ahead pensively and hugging my knees that were drawn to my chest. A music CD that Courtney had given me was playing in the background, and I didn't want to get up. The phone was usually for Felicia even on my good days, so I wasn't in the mood to answer. But I did.

"Is this Renee?"

The voice sounded familiar, but I couldn't place it. I responded cautiously. "Yes."

"This is William."

At the sound of his name, I felt my senses return and my spirits lift. I stepped out of bed, the phone cord stretching behind me as I turned off the music.

"What's up?"

There was a long pause on the other end of the phone. "I'm sorry to call you so late. Your mother gave me the number."

That was shocking, but I didn't say anything to that.

"I just wanted to talk to you about something."

"Okay."

I recalled his asking me to the prom, but that seemed like ages ago. I wondered what it could be this time.

I heard him draw in a deep breath. "I don't know how to tell you this."

I couldn't contain the flattery welling inside of me, and the corners of my lips turned up in anticipation. I remembered how difficult it was for him to give me the necklace. I sensed it was something related to his attraction to me. I waited.

"You need to become Muslim."

His words registered seconds later, and they fell upon me until my heart dropped. My smile faded, and I felt my face burn with offense and shame. The burning sensation I'd felt upon hearing Hadiyah's response returned to me.

"*What?*" The word was a challenge, as if his statement had been a disgusting insult that I dared him to repeat.

"I'm sorry Renee," he said, sighing the words, "but I feel partly responsible."

"Responsible for what?"

"I gave you that necklace. You can't wear it anymore. It's wrong."

My heart beat pounded in fury as I realized this was not the conversation I'd expected. "If you don't want me to wear your stupid necklace, I won't."

"It's not that. It's that you shouldn't wear any necklace like that."

I tried to control my breaths as his insults grew visceral. "Who the hell do you think you are? My *father?*"

"Renee, listen to me."

His raised voice stunned me to silence although my lips had already parted in protest. I'd never heard so much frustration in his voice before.

"All I'm suggesting is that you do what you know in your heart is right. Don't you *want* to be guided to the truth?"

His question made me acutely aware of my prayers for guidance that I'd abandoned.

"What's that supposed to mean?"

"I'm just saying this because I care about you." He drew in a deep breath and exhaled as if this was taking more out of him than he could bear. "You need Islam, Renee. There's nothing else out there."

"I've heard enough." I slammed the receiver down with so much force that the phone nearly fell from the desk. I had to steady it and return it to its place.

Shaken, I stood in the quiet of the room, indignant. The heat of anger still warmed my face and body, but it was evaporating against my will, giving way to the tepidity of shame and frailty. My eyes welled and I let my weight fall onto the bed until I was sitting on its edge.

I resisted the urge to cry until my mind cleared. I couldn't understand why William's words had disturbed me, and so intensely. I lifted my head and my eyes caught the small stack of Islamic books and pamphlets I'd taken from the "Ask About Islam" table. For a moment, my gaze rested there, taken aback by their intrusion. It took me a moment to accept that I had placed the books there myself, at no one's urging but my own. But I hadn't read anything from them.

Instinctively, I stood and pulled the stack from the desk in irritation, feeling the anger well in my chest all over again. I walked to the trash can and dropped them all inside, the warm satisfaction of revenge soothing me at the thudding sound of their falling against its bottom. A tinge of guilt pinched my heart but I quickly dismissed it. In a show of contention for my decision, I lifted the plastic bag from the small bin and brought together the sides into a knot. I walked over to the door, opened it, and marched down to the end of the hall, where I tossed it into the large plastic garbage bin that would be emptied into the dumpster outside.

I returned to my room, and in a show of defiance, I resumed listening to the singer Aretha Franklin, humming along with her words, "Don't play that song for me..." as I sashayed in rhythm to my bed. I even pulled from my desk a text that I primly opened and skimmed as I continued singing and bobbing my head.

The song ended and in the brief silence before the start of the next song, I was struck by the sore emptiness that I felt. Sadness enveloped me until my throat closed.

What are you doing with your life?

The question hung in the air until my despondency was complete. When the next song began, I couldn't muster the energy to move my head to the music. I tried, but instead my head fell as if in exhaustion, or perhaps submission, at my pathetic state. What *was* I doing with my life, with myself?

I had no answer.

Don't you want to be guided to the truth?

I felt my teeth clench in recollection of the audacity of William's inquiry.

You need Islam, Renee. There's nothing else out there.

This time, the words were not coming from William, but from a dead weight that had lain dormant in me for years and was only now stirring to life. My right hand lifted and rested over the left side of my chest, an instinctive gesture to calm the growing discomfort there.

But I also knew it was an indication of where my last thoughts had emerged.

People prefer ambiguity to clarity and searching to submission. It was a realization so distinct that it paralyzed me momentarily as I sat in the cafeteria Saturday afternoon eating my lunch. Students gossiped, laughed, and snuggled with girlfriends and boyfriends, as if there was nothing to life but this. Their carefree manner upset me, and I couldn't help envying them for their ostensible denial of spiritual unrest. Were they pretending, or were they really oblivious to having a purpose in life, to having a Creator, to one day meeting Him to account for their sins? Perhaps, religion itself was a joke to them, or merely a prerogative with no actual implications beyond the constraints of one's mind.

I couldn't accept the possibility that a person actually believed in no accountability other than that which she carved for herself. It was almost painful to conceptualize this mindset as a person's concocted reality.

If only it were true.

I wished for an easier life, any life except the one before me. I didn't want to be Muslim. The very thought unnerved me. Imagining all the restrictions was more tormenting than any horrific memory I carried of The Church. I'd heard that the men married as many wives as they wanted, and I couldn't bear the thought of voluntarily relegating myself to someone's harem.

There was the tiniest flutter of a memory, that of a philosophy class I'd taken, and one I'd enjoyed thoroughly. It was empowering, rejuvenating to sit and ask questions for the sake of asking, reflect for the sake of reflecting, and never needing, or wanting, any definitive answer. The process. That's what distinguished philosophy from religion, or even beliefs themselves. Philosophy was an unfettering of religious and personal imprisonment, allowing the mind to wander at its own will and direction. It could rest at any place it pleased, or it might not rest at all. Because, in the end, philosophy was the search itself. By its nature, there was no end, no finish line, no arriving.

I recalled a feeling of exhilaration in the class, in not having to come to any conclusion, to not having to view my life through anyone's narrow lens, not The Church's, not my father's, and not even my own. In a word, I was *free*.

The fear that was afflicting me lately was in giving that up. My glorified rebellion against my upbringing was drawing to a close, and my search had actually led me where I had wanted, or at least where I had professed I wanted.

Had I really wanted to find the truth, or was my praying merely a selfish confirmation of a righteousness I had convinced myself of in childhood, but one that did not exist in truth? Had I merely wanted distinction from my sisters and classmates in that which intoxicated me with an air of superiority rather than endure the truth of my deepest desire—distinction in their world of which I could never be part?

The possibility terrified me. I knew this was my moment of truth. I'd asked God for guidance, and although I was still lost on all that Islam entailed, there was in my chest a deep, penetrating sensation that I had stumbled upon that Truth.

There was a thread of doubt as to whether or not this was what I had been searching for, but there was a lingering sense that told me, quite distinctly, that this was the end of the journey.

I felt betrayed. But this was a feeling I didn't understand. Or perhaps it was merely one that I was afraid to understand. For if I felt betrayed, there could be only one who betrayed me—the One who had brought me to this place of adjournment in the first place.

If only I could have continued in merely searching, in enjoying the insobriety of the ambiguous.

This was not the answer I craved. But I had already searched frantically for another option, another interpretation of God's answer, even as I was unaware of these actions of the heart.

Consult your heart, Hadiyah had said, and I hated her right then.

It is there you will find your answer—if your intentions and prayers are sincere.

Hadiyah's home was set in a lush cul-de-sac of Potomac, Maryland. The driveway curved around the side of the expansive brick house and disappeared somewhere behind. Hadiyah had told me that she would send her daughter Nicole to pick me up because Nicole was already out running errands near the campus.

During the drive, Nicole was cordial, but it was clear that she preferred the radio to conversation and staring ahead to acknowledging my presence. I sensed something about my presence was unsettling to her, but, naturally, I didn't inquire as to what it was.

Nicole's impeccable appearance did not escape me, and I couldn't help noticing how she was strikingly different from how I recalled her mother. Neatly cropped permed hair framed the walnut complexion she shared with Hadiyah. Small gold hoop earrings adorned her ears, and she wore a snug, low-neck white T-shirt and fitting jeans that accented her figure attractively. I wondered if she considered herself a Muslim, but again, it was not a question I felt I had right or place to voice.

I trailed behind Nicole to the front door, which apparently already unlocked because upon reaching it, she merely turned the handle and went inside.

"You can sit in there." She motioned a hand to the room to my left, but she did not wait to see me inside. She disappeared somewhere around a corner, and I walked into the room, admiring its beauty as I crossed the threshold.

The living room was mostly a soft peach color, its couch, loveseat, and curtains exuding an aura of coziness. For a moment I stood, studying the dark wood framed painting that extended almost the width of the couch. Soft peach strokes were delicately interspersed on the natural landscape, creating the illusion of blossoms all over, even where they could not logically be. On the waterfall, the rocks, and even on the glistening lake surrounded by lush greenery.

"Renee, it's good to see you again."

I turned at the sound of my name and found a woman entering the room with her hand extended toward me. It took a moment for me to realize I was looking at Hadiyah. The woman's hair bore the thinnest locks I had ever seen, and the most beautiful. Gray strands shimmered like silver threads in each. The small hair plaits curled and twisted, creating a fullness in her hair that fell to her neck. She wore an emerald green dress that reminded me of the wide-cut African styles I'd seen sold by vendors, but the fabric was so soft that it moved like silk as she approached.

I accepted her hand, suddenly conscious of my own braids whose grooming was much overdue. I'd brushed them and pulled them back by an elastic band and had realized how from a distance one would never know I had braids at all. Even my outfit was drab. I wore only a faded white University of Maryland T-shirt and baggy dark blue jeans.

"Please sit down," she said, gesturing to the couch.

I obeyed as she took a seat on a chair at an angle to me. She held an expectant smile, as if waiting for me to say something. My heart thumped in my chest, realizing I was the one who requested this visit. I had foolishly assumed she would do all the talking. But what could she say? She had, at best, only a vague idea what had prompted the visit in the first place. I would have to fill in the blanks.

"How are you?" she asked, relieving me of having to explain myself, at least for the moment.

One side of my mouth creased in an effort to be cordial, and I shrugged. "Okay I guess."

"You like school?"

I started to laugh but it came out as a humph. "Yes." I hoped my response made up for my expression.

"How are your studies going?"

I parted my lips to speak, but the sound of someone entering disrupted my thoughts. I lifted my gaze to find Nicole bringing a tray of juices and cookies. I remained silent, my lips parted, until Nicole left.

"Good."

"Where are you from?"

The shift in conversation took me off guard, but I replied as if it were natural. Our talk ran smoothly for several minutes as I told her of The Church, my family and my upbringing. When she asked about my first introduction to Islam, I thought briefly of Darnell but couldn't bring myself to mention him, so I mentioned talking to Yusuf at the "Ask About Islam" table. Without understanding the connection to Islam, I went on to share how impressed I was with Yusuf's poetry and monologues.

"Yes," she said, nodding, "Sumayyah has definitely found herself one talented young man."

The reference to Sumayyah confused me. I started to ask Hadiyah what she meant by that, but I stopped myself, unwilling to reveal that I cared as much as I did. Or perhaps a part of me already understood, but reluctantly. I didn't know what to say to satisfy my curiosity, or disappointment, so I said nothing at all, unsure where to redirect the conversation.

"So, what brings you here today?"

The inquiry was so abrupt, so unexpected that I was offended momentarily. I didn't want to talk about that yet.

I felt a laugh of discomfort escape my throat. "I don't know."

Hadiyah drew in a deep breath, and her eyes grew distant, resting briefly on the painting above me. She exhaled slowly as she shook her head. "Changing religions is a very difficult process. It involves more than you can prepare for." She pursed her lips before continuing. "I had the same feeling myself. I built my whole life around the church. My whole family, in fact."

I studied the way her eyes narrowed in deep thought, and I sensed she was recalling something painful.

"I can't give you any illusions about what this step will mean for you, Renee." The sound of my name made me realize her reflections were not completely separate from me, and the suffocating fear returned to me. "But I can tell you, in fact, I *must* tell you, that the step is necessary if you are to move forward spiritually."

"I don't want to change religions." My voice sounded awkward to my ears in this sudden outburst as I gave words to the plea that had burned at the back of my throat.

She nodded almost imperceptibly but still did not look at me, as if her mind was still elsewhere. "I know. No one does."

"I just want to find a way to be a better Christian."

The sides of her mouth turned up slightly. "Then you've come to the right place."

I suddenly remembered that Muslims viewed themselves as following the purest form of Christianity. "But it doesn't feel like the right place. I don't feel like a Muslim."

"Islam doesn't feel like the right place for you?" She met my gaze, wisdom emanating from her eyes as they met mine.

"No, it doesn't."

"What about it feels wrong?"

I bit my lower lip. "I don't know. I grew up with so many rules. I don't want to go back to that."

There was a slight pause. "What is it that you imagine Islam to be?"

I didn't know how to answer that. I thought of men marrying multiple women, but I couldn't find the right words to express that. "I don't know."

So much had changed since that day Darnell first uttered the word *Muslim* in my kitchen. I hadn't learned much more about Islam since then, but I had heard much more.

She reached toward the tray, lifted a glass of juice and handed it to me. I accepted it. She picked up a glass for herself and brought it to her lips to sip before setting it down again. Nervously, I sipped from my glass and was momentarily distracted by its pleasant taste. I imagined it must be natural or freshly squeezed.

"Do you believe that there is only one God?" She startled me with her directness.

I took another sip, delaying my response. I lowered the glass, holding it inches from my mouth, its coolness soothing my palm. "Yes."

"Do you believe that He is the Creator, and that He is not manifested in any part of His creation, even in spirit?"

I leaned forward to set down my glass, gathering confidence in that motion, her questions reminding me of church. "Yes."

"Do you believe that Jesus Christ is God?"

"No."

"Do you believe that Jesus Christ is His son?"

At that, I felt a throbbing at my temples as my head began to ache. It was a question I hadn't dared ask myself, let alone answer. But I was acutely aware that I had not referred to Jesus as such for at least a month. The aching in my head pulsated until I rubbed my eyes, which began to burn.

Consult your heart, Renee. It is there you will find your answer.

At that moment, I thought of what Sumayyah had said, of her abandoning the belief in God's fatherhood before the belief in His manifestation inside Jesus in flesh. *"People and animals have children, not the Creator."* But I didn't think of Jesus in that sense.

Then why was it so important to stick to the terminology of "son" if it wasn't fatherhood in which I believed? What did I mean when I said Jesus was God's son? If it wasn't a parent-child relationship, what was it? And if it was a parent-child relationship, then what was it that distinguished Jesus from Adam? Or from, in fact, any of the humans on earth? Weren't we all a result of His divine decree?

And why was it so hard to believe in him as a remarkable prophet? All prophets performed miracles by God's will. Why not look at Jesus' in the same light?

I became aware of Hadiyah's waiting and grew flustered. I didn't want to answer the question, but I found myself heeding the advice from her speech, to consult my heart.

I drew in a deep breath and exhaled.

"No," I said, my voice cracking, "I don't." The words made my heart beat quicken, but the throbbing in my head subsided, replaced by welling in my eyes. I felt relieved. Yet there was a weightier burden I'd accepted by removing that one. I couldn't bear to think of that.

Hadiyah, may God bless her, moved on to the next question before I could break down.

"Do you believe in the Day of Judgment?"

"Yes."

"In our entry into Paradise or Hell?"

"Yes."

"Do you believe in all of God's prophets, including Adam, Moses, Abraham, and Jesus?"

I drew in a deep breath, mentally preparing myself for the result of my heart consultation. I had already admitted that I no longer believed he was God's son. Could I say he was a prophet, a man inspired and taught by God, but a man nonetheless?

"Yes."

"And do you believe that Prophet Muhammad is God's Messenger, the last of all prophets and messengers?"

That question I wasn't prepared for. I met her gaze with my forehead creased. I shook my head. "I don't know."

She started to speak, but I continued.

"I don't know anything about him." I heard myself explaining, as if apologizing. "I heard that he married a lot of women, and I..." I shook my head. "How could a prophet do that?"

Hadiyah's eyes reflected the same kindness I saw there moments before. "Many prophets married more than one woman."

"But Jesus didn't."

"Jesus never married at all."

"Then doesn't that set him apart from them?" I had a distant sense of moving backward, of defending what I no longer believed. Perhaps it was my disbelief itself that gave me comfort in my argument.

"Yes," she said simply. "Each prophet has traits to set him apart from another." She paused.

"But Jesus will marry," she added.

My eyebrows rose.

"When he returns."

"Muslims believe he'll return?"

"Yes."

There was an awkward pause, and my thoughts drifted.

"I don't want to live in a harem." I contorted my face with the confession. "Do Muslim women have to do that?"

Her eyebrows rose. "A harem?"

"Polygamy."

She was silent momentarily, as if choosing her response carefully, or whether she should respond at all. "No," she said finally, "they do not."

I relaxed somewhat.

"Renee," she said, her voice sounding as if she had given a lot of thought to what she was about to say, "you need to read and study more if Prophet Muhammad, peace be upon him, is still unknown to you. God sent him as the last prophet and messenger, and each generation is held accountable for following their messenger." She sighed. "Our generation's prophet, like every generation now until the Day of Judgment, is Prophet Muhammad."

She shook her head. "But I must tell you, it is not necessary to know everything before you convert."

The last word took me aback, and I grew uncomfortable. Is that what I was doing? Preparing to convert?

"And honestly, I can't tell if you're holding back because you are really unsure whether or not Prophet Muhammad, peace be upon him, is a true prophet, or if it's out of the natural fear we all have of the unknown, even as we know it's what we need."

She pursed her lips before continuing. "This is something only you can determine. But remember, your time is measured on this earth, and there is no guarantee that when you leave here today, you'll wake to see another."

I felt myself growing defensive.

"And before you leave," she said before I could say anything to counter her, "I want you to think on this: Life is life. No matter what path you choose, you'll still have to endure all that it entails."

My eyebrows gathered, but I listened, searching for her meaning.

"And I also want you to answer this one question." She waited until I met her gaze. "And for this one, you can only consult your heart." She paused. "What is it that you want?"

Saturday evening I returned to my dorm, and before I made my way down the hall, I paused at the large dull grey garbage bin with black plastic spilling from its mouth. I knew it was the most disgusting thing to do, sanitarily speaking. But I also knew, rationally, it wouldn't be as bad as having waited another twenty-four hours for pungent glass bottles and God-knows-what to cover it up. Or worse, for God to remove the second chance from my life.

Willing myself not to look down the hall for the possible approach of another student or visitor who would judge me harshly, I calmly lifted the grey top and quickly surveyed the contents until I spotted the small white plastic bag. It was peering from beneath orange peels, torn paper, and pencil shavings. A black sticky substance sprinkled the top of it, but I reached in with my left hand and withdrew it from the bin, lifting it artfully, wrinkling my nose as it presented itself. I shook the bag free from crud as best I could and replaced the top before hurrying down the hall holding it away from me.

Instead of heading straight to my room, I went to the hall bathroom, tore the white plastic, withdrew the books, and tossed the soiled bag into the trashcan. I set the books on a sink, turned on the tap and lathered my hands with soap before holding them under the water.

In my room, I put the books back on my desk, but in another place, as if they would be more protected from my volatile emotions there. I then grabbed another outfit, tucked it under my arm, and made my way to the shower after throwing my towel over my shoulder. I wanted to start fresh, in body and mind, while I read.

PART II

~

Eleven

The lesson was the last of those taken that year and would represent the divider between those who would pass and those who would fail. We were terrified, all of us, because there was no choice, not for any of us enrolled in the program.

It wasn't the finality of the class that terrified us so completely, but the administering of the final exam that day. If we passed the exam, we passed not only the class in question, but the entire program itself, regardless of our exam marks in other classes. If we failed the exam, we failed not only the class in question, but the entire program itself, regardless of our other exam marks. But our passing the exam would mean other exemplary marks would raise our status in the program, although our failing would render our other marks, even if all exemplary, useless.

So it is understandable that I stood immobile outside the door, humbled and faltering before the wood, the divider between me and my fate. For this final exam, there was no procrastinating, no make-ups, no absentees, no excuses. There was no written excuse the teacher would accept, no claims of family illnesses or deaths, no tardy students given extra time.

There was only the exam.

I still faltered at the door though I now held the handle, trembling, knowing, and submitting to the reality of the final class, and exam. I was only vaguely aware of others surrounding me, they too hesitating for the same reason as I.

Somehow we all entered at once and took our seats without a word. I sat in the far back, imagining, I suppose, that my distance would delay the inevitable. But I realized as the teacher stood and opened the box enclosing the test papers that my seating far from the teacher's desk only meant I would extend my suffering until my turn came to be handed the paper.

The teacher did not lift the box after opening it as we expected her to do. Instead she set its lid on the desk and turned her back to us. There was sudden noise at the front of the room, and we all lifted our gazes to find the white screen being rolled up, the teacher releasing its string after a slight tugging, until the chalkboard lay exposed.

It took a moment for me to register what I was seeing. As my mind slowly defined what my eyes beheld, there were gasps, whispers, and even laughter, a final confirmation that I was not imagining this at all. All of the answers to the test were before us, written neatly, purposefully, on the board.

There were wisecracks, of course, asking the teacher if this was for real, or merely a trick. She did not smile or even

*meet our gazes as she quietly lifted the open box on her desk
and said, "This is no trick. The answers are all here." A
moment later, she was laying the papers before us, one by
one, each of us relieved that we would pass, excel even.*

*Yet, seconds later, I was stricken with fear, then
confusion, as I watched expressions on the faces of my
classmates upon receiving their papers. Someone said aloud,
"What's this supposed to mean?" Others compared their
papers to neighbors, mocking or complaining, based on what
they saw.*

"You expect me to write on this?"

*The question was coming from the girl next to me, and for
a moment I thought she was talking to me. But when I
turned, I saw she was glaring at the teacher, holding up a
limp, dirt stained paper that was crinkled, the obvious result
of having been balled up then flattened out.*

*"You have thirty minutes," the teacher said calmly,
glancing up at the large clock on the wall. "As you know, no
extra time will be given."*

*I barely paid attention to my own paper lying before me, I
was so distracted by the upset girl, and others. I stretched
my neck to see the various papers of my classmates. Some
had money, real money, pinned to the corners, backs, and
margins. Others had assortments of candies glued to theirs.
Some had what looked like jewelry decorating theirs. Some
had mud smeared across the front.*

*The teacher's sudden announcement of our having only
fifteen minutes remaining distracted me from the commotion
in the class. By now, students were out of their seats
marveling, laughing at, or even bragging about their or others'
papers. The girl next to me was now out of her seat standing
before the teacher demanding she be given a new paper.*

*It was then that I looked down at mine. I turned it over,
narrowed my eyes, straining to see what was before me. But
I saw nothing, only a clean white test paper. Conscious of
the time, I shrugged, picked up my pen and began writing,
looking up at the board each time. It was difficult to
concentrate, even with all the answers before me, because
there was so much laughing, talking, and complaining around
me. In my peripheral vision, I saw those with the money on
their papers, pulling at the staples and adhesive in efforts to
remove it and keep it for themselves. I looked up at the
teacher, who now sat watching us, unperturbed, as she
glanced at her wristwatch occasionally then back at us.*

*"Two minutes," she said, and I felt as if the pounding in
my chest would make me burst from the fear I felt right then.
I wasn't yet finished, but frantically, I copied the board, my
hand aching in the effort.*

"Give me my paper back!" someone called to a student marveling at, or criticizing, his test, the student suddenly aware that the time was expiring quickly.

"This isn't fair," the girl next to me said, collapsing into her seat just then. "We need more time."

"Time!" the teacher called, standing suddenly as she began collecting the papers.

My heart beat faster as I frantically filled in the last of the test, unsure if I was even copying the answers correctly. I had wasted so much time that I didn't have time to review my responses. Before I knew it, and before I was prepared, the teacher stood before me, hand outstretched.

And even as I knew that if I failed, it was merely the result of what my own hands put forth, it was with painful reluctance that I turned in my exam.

People have often asked me to recount the moment that I recited the *shahaadah*, the testimony of faith marking my soul's initial purification, my official entry into the religion of Islam. And each time that I part my lips to find words for the indescribable, I am met with the welling of tears instead. There are moments that I can blink them back and deny that they were ever there. But still, I detect them in the slight breaking of my voice at the onset of speech, or in the deep sigh I take to recover from my faltering emotions, or in the extended pause and purposeful smile I offer to appear as if I am deciding the best way to explain.

In reality, there are no breaks in my memory, no hesitations or pauses in my mind, and no mental breaths taken in preparation. There is only the memory, tenaciously engraved, of that day—that night, even as my present countenance masks its vividness. No matter how much time passes, my mind still holds on to that which I can't hope to forget—although there were moments, much later, that I wished that I could.

As compelling as the memory is, I have never relived it, at least not in the complete sense, even in recollection. Although, on occasion the moment haunts me, or rejuvenates me, in a dream as a symbolic reminder of my journey, or of life itself. The only parallel the moment has ever held to the present in truth is the welling of moisture behind my lids. Yet even then, my soul's bridge to that night is foggy, if not broken, and I wonder if I would ever be granted opportunity to rest my soles upon its splintering wood and gather strength from the purity God graced me with back then.

During those unfortunate moments of recollection that I cannot contain myself and my tears spill forth—their spilling forth a silent testimony louder and more profound than words—I know, even so, my tears are not fully comprehended, or understood, even by those who share the story of a soul lost then found, of an amazing grace granted to one who was once blind.

My tears, initially, were inspired by the lingering euphoria, that immense, uncontainable spiritual joy I felt at realizing that I had taken the step, had actually surrendered to the nagging of the spirit that had called from a voice deeply embedded within, to simply let go and submit.

Yet there are moments that the tears are evoked by guilt, that dead weight that sits in the pit of my stomach and grows heavier with each moment that I neglect my soul, and religion. It is these tears that come from a hollow space within, and hurt more than the neglect itself, enveloping me with the desire to blot, irrevocably, the moment from my mind. It is also these tears that I wonder at and I ask why my eyes haven't become dry, why my heart isn't sealed, and why, even as I am neglectful, the soft spot for that moment has not left my heart.

And there are still other moments that the tears are evoked by my sudden realization that I am still holding on, even as my palms burn from the hot coals of the religion in my hand. Or perhaps it is trepidation that I feel, that haranguing fear that my recital will be recited back to me on the Last Day and that I would have met the solitude of my grave without it on my tongue.

But never has anyone understood my tears. This I know because I do not understand them myself. Yet, there remains, in its own quiet space of my mind, the memory of that night, that life-altering moment that inspires a host of emotions depending upon the occasion for which it is called up.

The feeling I had that night is one I can relate to nothing I've known before it and nothing comparable, even still, that I have come to know following it. I recall repeating after Hadiyah and the sense that something inside me, something dark and corroding, was dissipating with the utterance. When I finished, there was only one word to describe how I felt, in body and soul—*pure.*

I remember the moisture of tears still behind my lids as I settled under my covers in my dorm room, sleep lulling me. I knew then, after the recital, that I could rest peacefully.

I also recall, quite precisely, that my slumber was disrupted by the shrilling of the phone, an unwelcome reminder that my spiritual seclusion, and euphoria, was limited to the confines of my own heart. I didn't want to answer it because it was most likely for Felicia, but then again, I thought, it could be Hadiyah calling me back, giving me one last officiating into the religion.

The truth was neither.

"Hello?" I could hear the grogginess in my voice and was stunned that, despite my spiritual transformation that set me apart from my former self and life, I was still subject to the mundane realities of this world.

"Thank God," a male voice crackled through the receiver. "I thought I had the wrong number."

The voice was faintly familiar, but I couldn't place it.

"I'm sorry. Who would you like to speak to?"

"Renee?"

The sound of my name jolted me awake, and I sat up, recognizing the voice. His voice was awkward in its familiarity and sent my heart racing at the reminder of a world separate from, but somehow loosely connected to, the new me. I thought momentarily that he had somehow heard of my conversion, although this was a logical impossibility given that I hadn't even been Muslim for a full hour right then. But fear has a way of perverting perception, making a possibility more palpable than it could be in truth.

So I sat alert in the darkness of my room, hoping that even if Reggie knew, he wouldn't have told my parents, and he wouldn't judge me for it.

"Yes," I said hesitantly.

There was an awkward silence. Because I was too distracted by the knowledge of my conversion and fear of its exposure, it wouldn't be until months later that I realized that the uncomfortable silence was foreign to us and, thus, I should have been prepared for the weightiness of what he was about to divulge. I should have known it would change everything between us, and prove a greater test of faith than my initial fear of being discovered.

"I can't talk long," he said, apologizing in his tone. "But I talked to your father and he said I could call."

I didn't know what to say, as his calling had never been a problem before although he had never called my room. Suddenly, there was a distant fear that something was wrong. But this fear was quickly assuaged as he spoke his next words.

It took several seconds for me to register what he was saying. It had been so long since I had spoken to him, thought of him even, that I didn't know what to say to his confession. It was then that his talking to my father became clear, because it was Reggie's only way of legitimizing his desire to date me that summer. I would be home in three weeks, he knew, and he would be finished high school, and he wanted to celebrate, or commemorate, this achievement by having what he had desired most for years—me by his side.

The heart, I believe, is the strangest and most phenomenal piece of flesh in the body. It can retain so many emotions at once, each contradictory in nature but somehow finding place, undisturbed and not at odds with each other there.

At the moment of his revelation, there was flattery nestling within, and a distant recollection of my heart years before. Yet there was the firmness of the faith I embraced, creating light years of distance between me and him, and a sense of sorrow in my heart that I could not respond favorably to his request. And still there was a visceral affection for him that I could not hope to ignore, even as I felt a twinge of pain that my answer would be no.

What words could convey my inability to fulfill his desire, a shared desire, without hurting a soul, his or mine?

Because I could neither bring myself to tell the truth nor hurt him, I chose a comfortable place in between.

"It's too much for me to consider right now," I said. "I have to think about it."

Although my words to Reggie hung heavy in the darkness of the room after placing the receiver on its base, by morning they were but a distant whisper as my thoughts were stampeded by impending final exams, and the weightiness of what I'd done the night before, for my soul.

Today I'm amazed at how quickly I forgot Reggie after that. I marvel still at how the maturing of the spirit transforms even the most intense desires of the heart.

Two days later I was sleeping in the guest room of Hadiyah's home and being carted to and from my exams in her car, even as my mind was far from being concerned with menial academics. I don't recall studying much for my exams, spending perhaps an hour, two at most, each evening preceding the final to be written the following day, a preparation most likely hurried through as a formality so I could focus on what I really wanted to study—Islam.

Because knowledge has a way of settling and becoming part of you, as if part of the plasma in one's blood, I cannot separate who I am today with what I learned back then, nor can I pinpoint each piece of information and credit it to a particular lesson or time. But what I know for sure is that those last three weeks of school were the most unforgettable, even as minor details escape my mind.

My most vivid memory is of waking early when the stillness of night had not yet completed its retreat for morning, and feeling the spiritual camaraderie of praying at dawn. I stood next to Hadiyah, the cloth of my *khimaar* brushing her at the shoulder from where the fabric fell around my head. I remember standing, unmoving, and listening to her husband recite *Al-Faatihah*, the opening chapter of the Qur'an. I also remember the *Qudsi* hadith I learned of this pillar of prayer and have, since then, never tired of hearing of the poetic conversation my Lord has with a lone worshipper standing before Him.

Allah has said,
"I have divided the prayer between Myself
and My servant into two halves,
and My servant shall have what he asks for."
When the servant says, "All praise belongs to Allah,
the Lord of the worlds,"
Allah, Mighty and Sublime, says,
"My servant has praised Me."
And when he says, "The Most Gracious,
the Most Merciful,"
Allah, Mighty and Sublime, says,
"My servant has extolled Me."
And when he says, "Master of the Day of Judgment,"
Allah says, "My servant has glorified Me."
And when he says, "You alone do we worship and
from You alone do we seek help,"
He says, "This is between Me and My servant,
and My servant shall have what he asks for."

There are moments, too, that I rather not remember of those last weeks of my sophomore year in college, but in all honesty, those moments would become significant, and painful, only later. During those few weeks, the unfavorable moments were like small blotches on a perfect image, and felt only like one feels the prick of a thorn on a fresh rose. Hadiyah, may God bless her, in her wisdom kept me distracted from those whose words and actions could have sullied my pure experience, or those who, in fact, could have shattered irrevocably the little confidence I was gaining in embracing my religion wholeheartedly.

In retrospect, I remember Hadiyah teaching me only about Allah and the prayer, and leaving all other issues unless they were somehow inextricably related to these two. Naturally, three weeks isn't an enormous amount of time, and the daily interruption of final exams didn't do much to quell my anxiety of not knowing enough before returning home. So even after I had a firm grasp of prayer, at least in the ostensible sense, she gave me but one parting piece of advice.

"The religion is easy, Renee, and in sticking firmly to the Qur'an and Sunnah is where you'll find your strength, and peace. Do not let the unrest and unhappiness of others distract you from this simple truth."

There are moments that, on occasion, these words settle upon me, and I feel the familiar throbbing at my temples and moisture building in my eyes as I recall my ignorance, and ultimate arrogance, in forgetting this deceptively small, yet profound, piece of advice. Or perhaps, it is just that, for me, it would take years of living in stark opposition to it before I could grasp, finally, the enormity of its meaning in full.

In my defense, I did not intend to oppose this simple wisdom or abandon my good sense. But convictions, like knowledge, have a way of seeping, unnoticed, into a person without her registering how they got there in the first place, and without her knowing on what they were founded, or why she had ever allowed something so wholly disconnected from righteousness and sense to find its way there at all.

In the beginning, I think, I had but one flaw—zeal. But it was the innocent zeal that one might count years later as an ailment of youth and inexperience more than ignorance or ill intention itself. It was the kind one could laugh about, decades later, reclining in her rocking chair as the chair's gentle movements creak the floorboards beneath, and the friend who sits knitting next to her nods in shared recollection of this innocent flaw that plagues, without exception, all of the young.

Yet, if zeal is an affliction, it is equally, if not more so, an antidote. It is that necessary cure for the diseases of the mind and heart, that might, if left festering, prevent one from going forward with what she knows is right, that might prevent one from overlooking the ominous obstacles in her path, obstacles thwarting her spiritual journey—within and without.

I've heard that one has not lived until she regrets, and although in my teens I hadn't time, or mind, to ponder the adages that so often peppered the tongues and lives of elders, I can say now without hesitation or thought, I have lived.

My sins are not ones that would turn the head of one immersed in the dark, cavernous channels of this world, drinking from the transient sweetness that poisons the heart. They would not earn me a spot opposite a talk show host, and, perhaps, they would not inspire even the slightest flicker of interest from a publisher of memoirs. But for me, they are real, and unalterable, as with all things past—and future, if one includes fate.

So it is with this knowledge that I uncover my past and try to understand in the strokes of my pen what I couldn't in the reflection of mind and heart.

Twelve

I returned to Indianapolis during the summer of 1995 a new person in many senses of the word, but my zeal had not yet inspired the youthful confidence that grants one such self-assurance as to not care what others think. So my Islam remained a secret that year, or for those few months at least. And I cannot honestly say I kept true to my commitment to, at least, perform all of my prayers. In reality—and how often does reality disrupt the purest intentions of heart?—I prayed only when it was safe to, when my siblings or parents or friends were dutifully distracted by the intricate affairs of their own lives.

So no one suspected. There was no reason or occasion to. I offered no information, and no one happened upon it, as I was careful to conceal all evidence of my conversion. Despite my being an avid reader, which would make for a plausible cover if any, I didn't carry with me even innocuous pamphlets or books on Islam. So there was, that summer, no one who discovered my new faith.

But Reggie came close.

The uneasiness that settled over the house one Wednesday night in mid-July should have been my first hint that I would be tested as to where I stood. My father's church was packed more than usual, which I attributed to the rows of cameras along the rear and sides of the church. I had been so engrossed in my own religious study that I forgot that this was what my father had worked so hard for, a televised casting of his sermons. I was unmoved, uncomfortable even, by this remarkable achievement. I hated the looming cameras, the businesslike manner of those situated behind them, and so many people's sudden interest in The Church. It was as if only after some reputable network decided its teachings were worth their time could others make it worth theirs.

Perhaps, my discomfort, and even harsh judgment, was due more to my realization that my hypocrisy could possibly be made public, my face on national television—a conspicuous testimony to my weakness of faith—than any real belief that the cameras and crowd were all for show. No one knew of my new religion, save Hadiyah and possibly Sumayyah, who I was sure would not waste their Sunday mornings viewing such evangelical programs as these. Yet, it was not Hadiyah or Sumayyah I feared would see my hypocrisy broadcast so plainly, but myself.

I felt I should have made up some excuse to miss church, but I could think of no plausible reason, at least not any reason that could be used twice a week for more than two months. So I sat, uncomfortably, in the front pew, head draped with a sheer headscarf, ashamed that I didn't do even that much for what I believed truly in my heart. Reggie sat next to me, his arm brushing mine, more at ease in my second home than I was myself. This summer marked his first visit to The Church, or at least his first visit with me; I sensed that he had been in attendance earlier this year, if for no other reason than to be granted permission to court me.

My father spoke of Jesus being the only path to Heaven, a person's only savior in the confusing sinfulness inevitable in this world. He spoke of Jesus' sacrifice on the cross, this remarkable gift to humanity, a gift that only the most blind and misguided would refuse.

I thought too of Jesus as being the only path to Heaven, as were all prophets and messengers, whose lives and words instructed us in the only means of atonement for the sins we would inevitably commit in this world. I thought of people's own sacrifices they would be asked to make, and of God's mercy, the remarkable gift to humanity that only the most blind and misguided would refuse.

He spoke of God, the Heavenly Father, who sent His son to bring the lost back to the path, and I thought of God, the Creator and Sender of prophets and messengers, sent to guide the lost back to His path. He spoke of the necessity of obedience to God's laws instead of relying on Jesus' sacrifice alone, and I thought of the necessity of obedience to divine laws instead of relying on God's mercy alone. He spoke of true faith being reflected in one's words and actions, and I too thought the same.

My mind drifted, and shortly thereafter, my eyes. My gaze rested on the likeness of Jesus before me, the blood spilling from his hands, his head cocked in exhaustion to the side, his sallow white skin, long hair. I thought of Darnell, then Hadiyah, then, finally, myself. I wondered at the different paths people took in life, and why they were so varied when the truth was one.

Was it possible that my father and my aunt and uncle truly believed their religion to be that one truth? My father's savoir a White man, my aunt and uncle's a Black? What was so wrong about believing in one God, the Sender of prophets and messengers, who were the torchbearers of truth sharing no attributes or kinship to the Divine?

The coolness of Reggie's palm on the back of my hand stunned me, and I, by instinct, pulled away. I stole a look at him, but at that moment, he turned his attention back to my father, apparently too ashamed to meet my gaze. My discomfort was suffocating then, and my heart pounded in my desire to be released from incarceration in the church and pew—and from the budding flattery in my chest. I couldn't bear the anxiety of my growing ease next to my former best friend. I felt myself falling into a place I thought I had left, thought I would never want to return.

My face grew warm in my desire to leave and stay at once, my curiosity for the possibility of a friendship turned fond threatening to overtake my newly born Islamic sense.

The choir sang a sweet spiritual and I relaxed in the sound, wishing this could be the entire sermon itself. Next to me, Reggie hummed along imperceptibly and patted his hand against his thigh. Other members swayed their heads, waved their hands, and some were not shy to sing along. This surprised me, as we'd never done that before. I attributed it to the cameras and crowd, as I did much else.

Upon arriving home, I sensed something was wrong when my father tugged thoughtfully at his tie in the foyer, something he normally did when retreating down the hall to his room. He paused in the living room, my mother already standing still there, arms crossed, disappointment written in the creases above her brow. Even Michael and Elijah looked on expectantly and Courtney halted her ascent up the stairs, distracted by what was about to unfold. For a moment, I thought I had been discovered, and I held my breath.

"Did you talk to William?" my father said. I started to respond until I saw him looking pointedly at Reggie.

Reggie dropped his head slightly and nodded in regret. "Yes, I did."

"So you know?"

A sigh. "Yes."

My father shook his head, pulling the tie from his collar then unfastening the top button. "I invited his parents to church. I'm not sure if they came."

"They didn't."

I stood silent, watching this exchange between my neighbor and my father, as if they were long time friends, only partly sensing the undercurrent of their words, only partly registering my dread. My heartbeat was a soft rhythm then, as if it too was fearful of discovery.

My father's shoulders lifted slightly as he tilted his head in sad reservation. "I don't know what else to do."

"There's nothing you can do." My mother's voice was awkward in its effeminate tone. It didn't seem to belong in this conversation. Or perhaps it was my own feminine voice that did not belong in the exchange.

"He called here asking for Ray's phone number some time ago." My heart skipped a beat at my father's words as I recalled vaguely that William had indeed said he'd gotten my number from my parents. "I hope it wasn't with ill intentions."

My father was looking at me now.

I furrowed my brows and shook my head, my heart beat now threatening to betray me. "What did William do?" I was surprised by the sincerity of my voice, the marked concern even, as if I had no idea in the world what was going on.

"I don't want him near my family, especially not in any romantic fashion."

Inside I exhaled. So the "ill intentions" my father was thinking of were ones of natural male affection for the female, and not of evangelical tendencies to a lost soul.

"He says he's Muslim," my mother said, her nose flaring as she rolled her eyes. There was the slightest sense of déjà-vu, as I recalled the melancholy atmosphere in the house after discovering Patricia's betrayal more than a year before. Why William's religious choice was any of our business, let alone concern, was lost on me.

"Did he call you?" my father asked, a look of intense concern on his face.

I narrowed my eyes as if trying to recall, shook my head slightly as if having trouble remembering, then said finally the truth. "Once that I can remember."

"About what?"

I felt as if I were on trial. I didn't know what to say, fearful that the tables would turn quickly, and I would be the culprit instead of William. Then, mercifully, the answer they wanted came to me in the form of truth. I chose my words carefully before I spoke. "The necklace he gave me a couple of years ago. He was asking about me wearing it."

Instinctively, their eyes rested on my neck.

"Thank God you had sense enough to take it off," my mother said. I knew what she meant—that my wearing it would give William a false impression of my feelings for him.

I nodded. "I took that off a long time ago."

"Good," my father said. He sighed.

"Now you and Reggie go out and get some fresh air. Your mother and I want to rest."

I knew what was happening. They were encouraging Reggie's pursuit to ensure that I had no opportunity to develop a relationship with William. I still had another month before I turned eighteen, but apparently desperate predicaments granted exceptions where they would not otherwise be bestowed.

"I can't believe he would do something like that," Reggie said from where he sat next to me on the back porch of my home.

"It is surprising." It was a weak response, but I didn't know what was safe, or right, to say, especially since I was guilty of the same crime.

"I can understand Darnell, but William?" He shook his head.

His mention of Darnell surprised and disturbed me. I was offended, perhaps, because Darnell was dead and because William's religious choice was so completely different from my cousin's.

"Why is it so hard to understand?" I looked at Reggie, brows furrowed. "People can believe whatever they want."

"That's not my point." Under the porch light, I saw his gaze lift thoughtfully, as if it pained him to explain. "It's just sad."

"Why?"

"Of all the things to choose in life." He shook his head, as if that were an explanation in itself.

"When Darnell joined the Nation of Islam, you told me you could see where they're coming from."

He met my gaze in confusion. "No I didn't."

"Yes you did."

"When?"

"When I asked you what you thought of Darnell's new religion."

"I don't remember that."

"I do."

He shrugged. "Anyway, that's not what I think now."

"What do you think now?" My question came out more challenging than I intended.

Reggie studied me curiously. "That Jesus is the son of God, my savior."

"So you joined The Church." It was more a statement than an inquiry, and it sounded mechanical, as if I was mocking.

"Yes." I could hear the defensiveness in his voice.

I couldn't mask the sneer on my face, revealing that I was humored. "Since when?"

"Since I thought of how Darnell wasted his life and I didn't want to do the same."

His words stunned me, in both their raw emotion and their uncanny parallel to my own emotions reflecting the same sentiment.

I didn't know what to say.

"Don't you ever think about his soul, Ray?"

I let my gaze fall to the grass glistening under the pale glow of the moon and the trees aligning the fence rustling softly in the gentle wind. "Yes."

There was a thoughtful pause. "I just don't want to make the same mistake."

I nodded, understanding, forgetting momentarily that Reggie wouldn't comprehend this gesture of agreement. "I had the same feeling."

"I just can't understand how someone could throw their soul away."

"I don't think he threw his soul away."

"I do."

"Instead of assuming, you should ask. You'd be surprised at what you'd learn."

A moment later, I had the sudden sense of Reggie studying me, and I met his curious gaze. "I was talking about Darnell."

Oh. And I was talking about William.

"Ray, what's going on?"

I could think of no sensible response. "What do you mean?"

"Why would I be surprised by what I learn?"

I shrugged, searching for some defense. "I was just saying."

"You weren't just saying, Ray. You said that as if you asked him yourself."

"Goodness, Reggie, what difference does it make to you?"

"It's not just about me, Ray. Your father wouldn't like to know you and William have talked more than you said."

I felt my face growing hot in anger. "You're not my keeper, Reggie."

"But is your father?"

"Since when do you care about my father?"

"When did I stop?"

"You didn't care about him when you were out drinking the sins of this world with all the Michelles and Shaunas it had to offer."

There was silence as he continued to study me, and I grew furious at this.

"Are you speaking of him or you, Ray?"

As I registered his meaning, I became more offended, more humiliated. "Who said I give a care about what you do? I'm talking about my father's church."

"The church isn't your father's. It's God's."

"And so is my soul. So mind your business."

"I didn't say anything about your soul."

My heart pounded in realization of what I'd implied. My upset at Reggie faded in comparison to this slip of the tongue. I didn't know what to say to cover it up. The quiet made my torment worse, and I wished he'd say something, anything to relieve me of the obligation to speak.

"What's going on with you, Ray?"

It's not what I had in mind, but it gave me a moment to gather my thoughts. I drew in a breath to calm myself, for fear I would slip again. Honesty was less perilous than shame, of covering the truth, so I chose that familiar middle ground.

"Look, Reggie. I'm just not ready to judge the world by my father's religion. I don't know what's right or wrong. And while I think Darnell's choice was definitely not right, I can't say that I think William's is completely wrong."

"How is William's religion different from Darnell's?"

It was my turn to study Reggie. Was it possible that in the last couple of years he knew nothing more of Islam than he had explained to me, that of the Nation of Islam and Arabs and Indians whose religion was nothing more than the belief in the sin of exposing a woman's face? Did he really imagine that William was a member of the former? Did my parents?

I felt suddenly that I had left the confines of childhood and matured, only to return and find that all that was once familiar, exemplary even, was infantile, and regressing.

No wonder my parents were so concerned for William's parents, especially if there was any truth to his father's addiction to alcohol. Who wouldn't be concerned for a young man who returns home to announce to his family that they were all devils, himself included? I could only imagine what my parents thought William's father's reaction to this would be.

"You really don't know what a Muslim is?" The question was so compelling to me that I didn't have time to discern whether or not it was judicious to put into words, and before Reggie.

"I know what Darnell said it is and—"

"—the Islam of Arabs and Indians," I finished for him.

He held my gaze for a moment, as if searching for something there. "Yes."

"There's only one Islam, Reggie," I said, surprised by the sound of my voice as instructor instead of student. "The one that teaches that there is only one God, the Creator, and that Jesus, like Noah, Abraham, and Moses, was a prophet." I stopped short of mentioning the last prophet. I didn't want to overwhelm him, or myself.

"Jesus is a prophet," he repeated, more out of shock at my words than any agreement on his part.

"Yes, he's a prophet, Reggie. What else would he be?"

He contorted his face. "You believe that?"

I parted my lips to speak, but caught myself, realizing the imprudence of such a confession. "I know that this is what his followers believed."

Silence created a wall between us, and I found myself comfortable, confident even, in my speech and spiritual distance from my friend.

"How do you know that?"

"I read, Reggie." It sounded sarcastic, but I didn't mean it that way. "You should too."

Despite his expressed disappointment with his friend's decision, Reginald spent time with William that summer, behind the walls of his home and that of his friend's. Other than the absence of Darnell, it was like old times, because I too was with Reggie when he was with William. I suppose my conversation on the back porch sparked questions Reggie hadn't thought to ask before.

I remember quite distinctly one day, a Monday afternoon, when our parents, at least our fathers, were at work, and we were sitting in Reggie's living room playing cards.

"So you don't believe that Elijah Muhammad is the messenger of God?"

William laughed. "No, I don't."

"I believe that Prophet Muhammad, peace be upon him, is the messenger of God. He was born in Arabia centuries ago and was the last prophet God sent."

"Is he a prophet or a messenger?"

William raised his gaze from his cards momentarily, that same look of shock that I had felt the night I realized his and my parents' confusion about true Islam. "Both."

"What's the difference?"

"All messengers are prophets, but not all prophets are messengers."

"So what?"

It sounded condescending, but I, like William, knew it was Reggie's way of getting a further explanation. "Messengers bring a new law, like the Torah or Gospel, and prophets are sent confirming what the messengers already brought."

"So anybody can be a prophet."

"No, they can't."

William's firmness stunned me, and I sensed he was offended. "Prophets are taught by God through the angel Gabriel. Anybody can't be a prophet."

"So Jesus was just a prophet." Reggie snorted at this.

"He was a messenger too. He was the one with the Gospel."

Reggie seemed to ponder this. I could tell he didn't agree, but he didn't know what to say. I knew, or at least I assumed, he was like I had been in devotion to The Church, not well versed in the Bible despite my professed belief in everything it said.

"That's not what the Bible says."

William shrugged, laying a card face up on the carpet in front of us. "Maybe it's not. Or maybe it is. It makes no difference to me."

"You can't be serious."

Because he was looking at William's card and not his face, I thought for a moment Reggie was speaking of William's play in the game.

"You're just going to throw away God's Word like it's nothing."

"I don't believe the Bible is God's Word." William kept his eyes on the game. "Partly maybe, but not entirely. So it makes no difference to me what is or isn't in there."

I could tell Reggie was bothered, and I imagined that he wanted to push William as he had Darnell on my porch years ago. But he laid down his card, and I followed suit, collecting all the cards because I'd played a spade. I remained a quiet observer of the argument, neither Reggie nor William knowing fully whose side I was on, though I'm sure both imagined they had a good idea.

"Don't you care about your soul?"

William met his gaze then. "Don't you?"

"Of course."

"Then why wouldn't I care about mine?"

"Because you just accept any religion that comes to you and throw away the truth."

"What makes you so sure you have the truth?"

"What reason do I have to doubt it?"

"Have you even read anything besides the Bible? The history of it even?"

"Why should I?"

"It seems to me if you're willing to give your soul to what it says, you'd at least want to know how it got here in the first place."

I grew uncomfortable in the tension. "Hey, we're trying to play a game here."

"Forget the game."

It was Reggie. In my recollection of this moment, I don't remember if he said "forget" or something inflammatory instead. It was most likely the latter, because I recall stiffening in realization that his anger was real.

"I want to know what your story is." It was a challenge, and I worried that Reggie's taunt would inspire the altercation to become physical. "Don't tell me you're tired of the whole White man is God thing."

"I never believed that in the first place." William's voice was decidedly calm, but I detected that his composure was the result of tremendous effort and conjured patience.

I laid my cards down, face up, in realization that, like the Monopoly game after my brother's feet had ruined it years before, the game was over, and not at all like I would have wanted—with my win. I was disappointed, angered even, that they would choose such a moment to quarrel. My hand was promising, and I was on my way to being victor.

"What exactly did you believe?"

"Nothing."

"Nothing?" I couldn't tell if Reggie was more perturbed with this news or with learning William's new religion itself.

"Yes, nothing."

"What about your family? Didn't they have some religion?"

"Yes, they did."

Still, Reggie's voice was on edge, William's calm. I couldn't understand why Reggie was so upset.

"They were Christian," William said. "If that's what you want to call it."

"What's that supposed to mean?"

"It means they went to church, hung a cross on their wall and around their necks, but it did nothing for their souls." It was the first indication that William was more bothered than he let on. His words were even and controlled, so much so that I could tell that he was one step from being infuriated himself.

"And what the hell has it done for yours?" It was William's question, his taunt this time.

"Nothing," Reggie said sarcastically, "nothing if you count this world. Your soul is saved in the next."

Reggie had a point. This even I couldn't deny. There was no way you could look at a person and see evidence of salvation. Only God could do that.

I looked at William, wondering what he would say to that.

He shrugged. "Then be happy and wait till your soul goes to Heaven, if that's where you think worshipping Jesus will take you. And leave me and my family alone."

"Worshipping Jesus?" The explosion of the inquiry was so sudden that my shoulders jerked, startled. "Who said anything about worshipping Jesus? We worship God."

"And so do we."

"You don't worship God." Reggie's face contorted. "You worship some man named Allah."

William grew silent, and I looked at Reggie, shocked again by his ignorance. Did he really believe that the Arabic word for the Creator was in reference to some man? I couldn't believe it. I was so stunned that I started to speak up myself. But William spoke instead, this time with a calmness devoid of effort, as if Reggie's comment took the last bit of impatience, and edge, from him.

"Allah," William said, "is not the name of some man. Arab Christians call God Allah. It's just Arabic for God."

Reggie just stared, upset still, but he listened nonetheless. Because William reminded me of Hadiyah right then, I too listened, taken aback by how much he knew.

"We say Allah because the English word *God* can be plural or refer to idols or people. The Arabic word can't be plural or used for anything but the Creator. A different word is used for other things people worship."

Reggie decided to leave Islam to William. "Still, we don't worship Jesus."

"Yes you do."

"How are you going to say what we worship? You shouldn't assume all Christians think Jesus is God. The Church doesn't."

His reference to my father's church took me aback momentarily. I had never before heard it defended, at least not by anyone other than myself.

But Reggie was right. We didn't worship Jesus, that was the divider between our church and Christian sects.

"If you believe Jesus is your savior, then you worship him."

Even I was lost on William's point.

I couldn't keep quiet any longer. "William," I said, conscious of the awkwardness of my voice, much like my mother's had been some nights ago, "The Church believes in worshipping only God."

"Do you pray in Jesus' name?"

I paused at that, mostly because of his use of the present tense and because the question was directed at me. I had wondered if he had any idea that I converted, now I knew he didn't. "Yes," I said, remembering that all our prayers had included *"in the name of Your son Jesus."*

"Then that's worshipping him." I started to say something, but William's point distracted me into silence.

It wasn't until some time later that I understood his point, that worship was not merely to whom or what you directed your prayers, but it included any intermediaries resorted to in the process, and also anything given divine attributes—like a physical kinship to God.

"Can we talk about something else?" I said, tiring of all the bickering.

"I'm not the one insisting on an argument," William said.

"I'm not arguing," Reggie said. "I just want to know why you don't care about leaving the church."

"I never was a part of the church."

Oh boy, I thought. *Here we go again.*

"Your family was."

"That's the difference between me and them. I never believed any of that crap."

I winced, embarrassed by William's bad choice of words. "What?"

"Reggie," I said, foreseeing a catastrophe in the sound of his voice, "I think what he means is that he never believed what you believed, so he didn't really choose Islam over Christianity. He just chose Islam."

"I did choose Islam over Christianity."

"But you just said you were never Christian," I said.

"That doesn't mean I didn't consider it."

"Whatever." I turned back to Reggie.

"You just believe different things."

"Who made you the peacemaker?"

I was growing irritated with Reggie's edginess. He wasn't usually like this.

Later, I would learn his fury was born of jealousy more than religious conviction. He feared that William's religion was more attractive to me than his, which included all sorts of obvious implications that he didn't want to face right then. But that afternoon, I hadn't the slightest clue why religion was so important to him.

"I'm just saying it's not worth arguing about," I said.

Reggie glared at me. "Not even for your soul?"

Okay, he had a point. "But you don't have to get angry."

"I'm not angry. I'm upset."

"But it's not worth it."

"I think it is."

Irritated, I stood and went for the door. "Then argue by yourselves. I want some peace."

"Don't you care about your religion?"

At the foyer, I turned to Reggie, who still sat on the floor. "I care about the truth." With that I opened the front door and let it slam behind me, hoping that I could contain myself for another four weeks, when I would return to school.

We didn't discuss The Church or religion after that. Or at least, Reggie and I didn't, and it was never again discussed in my presence when we were all together. But there were moments that we sat watching William excuse himself, even in Reggie's home, and go to the bathroom to prepare for prayer. It was at such moments that I felt unbearable shame, and urgency to do the same. We watched as he returned, face and arms moist, at times dripping wet. He quietly and dutifully performed prayer, unperturbed by our stares, Reggie's of curiosity (though I detected a sense of admiration), and mine of shame.

We never spoke during William's praying, and I would study how his forehead touched the carpet softly, his relaxing there for an extended time. The most intriguing moment was when we saw him pray at night and we heard his melodious recitation, a sound barely above a whisper, but moving nonetheless. There were moments I excused myself, giving in, saying I'd be right back, rushing home to lock myself in my room to pray myself, though I could never muster the calmness and intrigue of William's. I wasn't yet familiar with all the Arabic, or English even, of what I was supposed to say. Because I didn't want to be caught practicing Islam, I'd left all evidence of my religion along with my belongings in the storage room I was sharing with

Felicia, so I wasn't even able to improve my prayer by reading along with books or cue cards.

I spent most of my free time with Reggie, but William, interestingly, never acknowledged my presence beyond a simple hello or hey, and spoke nothing further unless I was with Reggie. It was as if I'd never seen him speak of his conversion, as if we'd never spoken after that. I was saddened somewhat, as if my hope was deflated somehow. But I could only understand this as my desire to learn more about Islam, and my thinking perhaps he could be the means for me to do just that.

The night before I returned to school, Reggie invited me on a walk, which wasn't unusual because we'd walked dozens of times before then. But during this one he asked, outright, if we could be officially a couple. He had been accepted at the University of DC, as well as other schools, but had chosen it because it enabled him to be closer to me, and also because they offered him a full scholarship whereas the others hadn't.

I was flattered, I can't deny, but I wasn't tormented any less. I don't know why I didn't just tell him outright my reason for hesitation. It would've made things much easier and less strained between us.

"I can't." I couldn't look at him. It would hurt too much.

"Why not?"

I shook my head. "It's too much to go into right now."

"That's the same thing you said on the phone."

"It is?" I looked at him then, trying to remember.

"Or something like that."

It pained me to see the hurt in his eyes. I looked away. "Well, it's true. I've got a lot on my mind."

There was a pause, the silence of the night falling around us as we heard the stirrings of others' homes. Soft music, a dog barking, distant laughter.

"Is there someone else?"

I creased my forehead and glanced at him. "No."

"Not even William?"

My heart fell, and I ached for him. I wished I could just come out and say what I wanted. But I couldn't risk my family finding out. "William?"

"Yes, William." He kicked at something on the ground, his hands pushed into his pockets.

"No. I don't talk to him like that."

"You act like you do."

"I do?"

"The way you're all quiet when he's around, and how you defend whatever he says."

That was the closest he came to mentioning religion. "Reggie," I sighed, shaking my head, "I do not. I'm just not the same Renee I was when I left. The world is a lot bigger than I imagined. You'll see what I'm saying when you leave too."

He exhaled abruptly, as if in contempt. "I'm not a baby, Renee. I know the world isn't as small as it seems."

I realized then that I'd insulted him. "That's not what I mean, Reggie. I'm just saying, you'll meet a lot of people, some of them far different from what you're used to. At first it may seem like they're the ones who have it all wrong, and then you'll think that maybe it's you who has to rethink things."

"Do I need to rethink what I said?"

"Said about what?"

"You and me?"

I grew silent at the reminder. "Maybe."

"Maybe or yes?"

"Maybe."

"And there's no one else?"

"I'm seventeen, remember?"

One side of his mouth creased in the hint of a grin. "Yeah, but you don't seem to care so much about that anymore."

"No, that's something I'm pretty much set on. No dating."

"Even in a month?"

"Even in a month."

Of course, I didn't say it was because of Islam. It was better, for the moment, to let him assume the best, at least what would appear like "the best" to him.

Thirteen

I remember the fall of 1995, the first term of my junior year in college, as the time I really embraced Islam. It was then that I recall my first flicker of zeal. It was also the year I turned eighteen, and when I felt as if I'd finally matured into an adult, a person with her own mind, soul, and heart. For the first time in my life, I didn't care about my position in the eyes of others, only my position before Allah, the Creator Himself.

My most evident show of spiritual maturity was my donning an African style wrap, worn like a turban or with a cloth bun at the nape of my neck. I chose clothes that fell loosely around me, even more modest than the ones I'd worn as a member of The Church. I preferred long shirts to waist length ones, wide legged pants to jeans, and skirts to pants themselves. I loved my new look and thought it more sophisticated than the style Felicia and Anita had introduced me to.

Because we had requested it, Felicia, Anita, and I were all roommates in a building that offered homely suites rather than the cramped dorm room of the previous years. In retrospect, this probably wasn't the best idea, given my newfound spirituality. It would have been, perhaps, easier to live with a complete stranger than to face the questions and opposition from friends. But I hadn't yet learned that one's desire for spiritual sanctity inspired a fire of rage in others' hearts, a rage that rendered silent or even respectful understanding an impossibility.

My friends' initial attacks were subtle, if not harmless. As late as October, during mid-terms, I hadn't yet told them of my conversion. However, the omission was not intentional. It simply did not occur to me that I should mention it. I was still Renee, and this was a personal decision I made for myself, and I never imagined that it would make any difference in the relationship I had with them.

I was wrong.

Their comments first took the form of jokes about my new dress. "Oh no, she's going straight African on us!" Anita would say. "Let's give her an African name," Felicia would respond. Or "What's wrong with your hair? You don't like the style I did for you?" "No, I think her hair is falling out." "Maybe she don't like her African hair after all."

I would laugh with them or shrug them off if I wasn't in the mood. Initially, I took it as the friendly humor that it appeared to be—until the day I excused myself to pray. That was the moment it hit me that they really didn't know. I had prayed many times in the suite before, but apparently, they had never been there or had been too distracted to pay attention to me.

"I have to pray," I said, standing abruptly one evening.

"You have to *what*?" It was Anita.

"Pray."

"Pray?"

"Yes. It's after sunset."

"And?"

"That's what I do at this time."

Felicia stiffened and grew silent, her eyes following my motions suspiciously. I could almost feel her disapproval burrowing into my chest.

That's when the realization suddenly came to me. *They don't know.*

Not much was said as I performed ablution, but I could hear their hushed whispers as I covered my hair and prayed a comfortable distance from them. It was almost impossible to concentrate, but I tried. It was the first time I was conscious of my every movement and how bizarre it must appear. My hands resting on my chest, my bowing until my torso was parallel to the floor, my head touching the ground.

I finished and found my space next to them, but the aura in the room had changed, as if I'd entered another reality entirely. They stared at me. I said nothing, forcing a smile but feeling a biting coldness that made me afraid to even move.

"What the hell was that?" Anita spoke as if I'd insulted her.

"What?"

She glared at me. "All that crap you were doing. Kissing the floor."

The comment stung. But I didn't show it. "It's prayer."

"I never saw anybody pray like that."

"Now you did." It was a weak attempt at humor, I admit, but I didn't know what to say. I was at a loss. It was similar to the feeling I had when my family was discussing William's conversion. I simply could not understand how my prayer had anything to do with them.

Despite her continued silence, one side of Felicia's lip turned up in a sneer. She snorted and rolled her eyes, turning from me.

"What church prays like that?" It was a rhetorical question, I knew, but there was a part of me that really believed Anita wanted to know.

"It's not a church prayer."

Anita's eyes studied me, her gaze taking in my every attribute, assessing each one—and finding fault.

"She's Muslim." Felicia's voice was matter of fact, and cold. She didn't look at me, refusing to.

"What the hell is that?" Anita wrinkled her nose.

"Just that," Felicia said.

"Just what?"

"Hell."

Felicia stood and picked up her keys. Anita, as if on cue, did too. They headed for the door. Opening it, Felicia turned and gave me one last look, contorting her face for so long that I thought she would remain there all night.

"I already warned you not to do it," she said, "so keep your miserable life to yourself. We're not interested."

The door slammed before I could register the cruelty of her words, and the meaning. Oddly, I felt sudden relief at my isolation, and I exhaled, having not realized I was holding my breath. My heart thumped, progressing in intensity with each second, until I felt the pounding in my throat and head. Because I hadn't yet come to recognize their contempt for what it was, I sat there, dumbfounded, wondering what I had done wrong.

Living in the suite became almost unbearable after that. I was cordial, they were cold. I would ask something, they would respond noncommittally, not even bothering to look me in the eye. I tried to strike up conversation, they would shrug and say they didn't know or would just shrug.

As much as I hated the cruelty of their words the day they saw me pray, I preferred speech, even if in disagreement, to this. The silence was overbearing. I felt shunned. But most excruciating was my inability to comprehend what I had done to offend them.

I imagined that Felicia, perhaps, had justification in feeling betrayed. She had advised me not to accept Sumayyah's religion, and I had. But the question that I couldn't answer was why it mattered to her at all.

Anita was an entirely different mystery. I could find no reason, no logic behind her treatment of me. A week before, she didn't even know what a Muslim was, so how was it possible to harbor so much animosity for a decision she knew nothing about?

Today, I cringe when I think back to my naiveté in seeking to reform the friendship I somehow felt responsible for ruining, even as I could find no plausible conclusion as to my particular crime. I compensated by apologizing through my actions. If I fixed dinner for myself, I made enough for three. If the phone rang in their absence, I took detailed messages and left a meticulously formed note for them on my best stationery. If the suite was untidy, I'd clean it before they had opportunity to. Even if I was doing laundry, I'd wash and dry their clothes with mine, even going as far as to fold theirs neatly and place it on their beds.

They never protested my actions or refused my food or services. But they never openly appreciated them either. They grew to expect it, and even occasionally requested I have their clothes or food ready at a certain time. I mistook their requests and acceptance of my kindness as signs that they had forgiven me and that we could again be friends. However, soon after, I learned that they were merely taking advantage of me. In their own perverted way, they saw servitude as my proper place before them. My religious choice had relegated me to a station beneath them.

Most humiliating is my memory of the day a few weeks after mid-terms, when I approached Felicia, having procrastinated as long as I could bear, and asked her what time was best for her to do my hair. My scalp was dry and itchy, despite daily oiling. My braids had once been secured tightly in small plaits against my head, exposing my scalp in rows. But the new growth was so much that I could see nothing but hair beneath the braids. It was as if I had a short Afro with frayed braids atop. I was often tempted to undo the plaits and wash my hair anew, but I resisted until I could secure a definite time shortly thereafter to have my hair freshly done. I knew the result of my tight curls drying to a frizz after a shower, especially if they were pulled by an elastic band at the back of my head.

Anita was out, and Felicia was studying at her desk, having just finished eating dinner, which I had made. I had done the laundry a day before, and she could have easily been wearing something I had dried and folded for her. I thought this was the most opportune time to ask, especially since, as we had eaten our meals within feet of each other, I had asked how everything was going for her, and she actually gave more than a terse remark and a shrug. She had joked about stealing past exams from the professor's file cabinet, and we had laughed.

The silence that followed made me acutely aware of every sound. Felicia's turning of a page in her text, the click of her pen as she prepared to write, my picking up the dishes and setting them aside, and my release of breath as I prepared to speak.

"I need my hair done." I heard nervousness in my voice, but I detected humor too. I was apparently on the verge of laughing at my pathetic state.

She didn't respond. I heard the rustling of a page turning. I went on.

"It's getting pretty bad. I might even have the beginnings of dreadlocks." The sound of my sudden laughter filled the room and made me more at ease, but a second later I was painfully aware of the awkwardness of my lone voice. Felicia had not even turned to acknowledge me.

"So," I said, "when do you have time?"

There was a long pause. She continued reading.

"Felicia?"

No response.

"Felicia?" I raised my voice.

She turned enough for me to meet her gaze. Her forehead was creased and her eyes narrowed in disapproval.

"When do you have time to do my hair?"

For a moment, we just looked at each other.

"I don't."

Now, I creased my forehead. "You don't do hair anymore?"

"I didn't say that."

My mouth opened to form a question, but I didn't know what to ask.

"I do hair," she said finally. "Just not yours."

The words were so unexpected that it took several seconds for me to register their cruelty. Because it was the only logical response to the ludicrous, I laughed. "You're kidding."

She just looked at me for a second more then turned back to her reading.

"Think what you want. I'm not doing your hair."

She continued reading as if her words had not created an impenetrable wall between us. I sat, unspeaking, too shell-shocked to know what to say in response, or if there was anything I should say at all.

"If you're ashamed of the styles I do, then I don't have time to do any."

"Ashamed?"

She said nothing, her face still turned away from me.

"You know this has nothing to do with your styles."

She slammed the book shut and turned to me, eyes fierce in agitation. "You want to be Muslim? Then live the Muslim life."

It wasn't until that moment that I felt something inside me rip open, exposing anger that I hadn't known was buried there. "*What?*"

To my ears, I sounded like Courtney, but it did not bother me in the least. I felt emboldened.

"Like I said, keep your misery to yourself."

"My misery?" I could have spit the words at her I was so livid.

"I grew up with that bull crap," she said, her words taking meaning even as I could not calm my rage. "I don't want it near me again."

I stared at her for several seconds, my emotions tempering momentarily as curiosity erupted. "You grew up Muslim?" My tone gave the impression that I was disgusted, but it was merely my inability to nurse two raging emotions at once—or perhaps, there was something that I found inherently repugnant in her words.

"I warned you," she said, ignoring my question. But I wasn't entirely sure she had registered it in the first place. "All fire and brimstone, and I don't want to hear any of it from you."

"Fire and brimstone?" I felt my defenses kicking in. "You mean *Hell?*"

"*Jahannam.*"

I was stunned by her use of the Arabic term, which was, even in her snide mockery of it, only vaguely familiar to me. For a moment I just stared at her, seeing in her eyes a pain I couldn't measure or define. I had no idea why my heart softened momentarily, but it did. I felt sorry for her. But even this I couldn't fully comprehend.

My knowledge of the religion was still somewhat rudimentary, but I couldn't understand how someone could abhor the same faith I had grown so fond of. There were several questions forming in my mind, but, of course, she wouldn't have answered them even if I could find words to give them voice.

"*Jahannam,*" I repeated in amazement, my voice barely above a whisper. I stared at her, feeling a brief connection—common ground. In a strange way, I felt more at ease, relaxing in the knowledge that my religion was not as foreign or bizarre as I had imagined.

I wanted to say something, anything to express this sudden realization. But Felicia rolled her eyes and turned from me as if my mere presence made it unbearable for her to remain in the room.

"I wish you would find somewhere else to live."

Her voice faltered, and I thought I detected a thwarted whimper. But I said nothing, turning my back as I stood, lifting the dishes and walking away.

Today, I wish I had had the fortitude to confront Felicia and draw the story out of her. But her history remained a mystery and I left well enough alone. I was too focused on my own spiritual growth to give energy or thought to another person's spiritual degeneration. To my knowledge, Felicia had no religion, but I suspected that Anita was Christian, at least in the way most Americans are members of the same faith—allegiance in only words, with no heart or actions following suit.

My suspicions would neither be confirmed nor denied. After the argument, they were never cordial to me again. Most days, they stayed out late at night, returning only to sleep and shower. Their words grew colder, their treatment crueler, and my faith grew stronger.

I often ponder the phenomenon of conviction in one's faith, how the greater the trial for a believer, the more fortified the faith, and not the other way around as one might expect.

I grew more reflective of my Creator and my purpose on earth, which I suppose was a natural response to their cruel abandonment of my friendship. I tried to understand them, empathize even, instead of submitting to the loathing that was growing in my heart.

It was difficult, I cannot lie, because there was no logical explanation for their treatment of me. I could have understood better if it had followed a heated argument in which I unwittingly insulted one or the both of them. But, as it stood, their attacks were preemptive, and I learned to always be on guard. I no longer felt safe or relaxed in the room, understanding for the first time the authenticity behind harassment claims, even as I didn't fear for my person or life.

I began to fear that no one would support my decision, or respect it even, and I wondered what that meant for me in both the short and long term, in school and in life. However, it never occurred to me to take back my *shahaadah.* My Islamic affiliation was not so much a choice as it was a submission to what God wanted from me, from all humans in fact, so the thought never entered my mind, at least not then.

It is these reflections that I carried with me as I made my way across campus one afternoon in late November, my hands nestled warmly in the pockets of my jacket, my book bag heavy with texts and notebooks at my back. My head was covered with a black cloth that was wound into a bun at the back of my head, and I wore black leather boots on my feet. My blue jeans were wide-legged, and my white sweater hung over them past my thighs. I was only vaguely conscious of my appearance, which I had grown to love, and as usual I was lost in thought.

Despite the cold, I was walking slowly. I was dreading returning to my room. Living there was becoming more unbearable by the day. My nights were mostly sleepless, my evenings tense, even when I was in the suite alone. The sound of voices or keys jingling in the hall made me stiffen, the noise portending Felicia's or Anita's entry at any moment. Most days, I studied in the library, but because I wasn't yet comfortable praying the daily prayers in public places, I'd eventually return to the suite, where I would resume studying after prayer.

Recently, I was having frequent headaches. Sometimes the mere sight of Felicia or Anita, even if from a distance, incited a painful throbbing in my head. I would go out of my way to avoid them, but it seemed they did the opposite for me.   But it's possible that this was not the case. Although the Maryland campus was by no means small, it was, after all, only a college campus, and the popular eateries and libraries were in definite locations, so our chances of passing each other wasn't low, especially since we lived in the same residence hall.

"Renee?"

My shoulders jerked slightly, and my heart pounded at the sound of my name. I was at that moment remembering Felicia's refusal to do my hair and my calling Hadiyah the next day and her giving me the number of someone who could.   I hadn't yet called the woman, having resigned myself to self hair care for the time being, but I was thinking how it was becoming too much for me and that I should give the woman a call.

I searched the eyes of the students around me, fearing that it was Felicia or Anita taunting me again. Instead, my eyes met those of a smiling student standing opposite me. She wore a UMD cap and sweatshirt that hung to the waist of her fitting jeans. In the dulling afternoon light, gold loop earrings sparkled on either side of her brown face, and permed hair was peaking out beneath her ears from where it had been tucked.

It was Natasha, my friend from the Bible study group. It took a moment for me to recognize her. In my new life, she belonged to an entirely different world, one that I had drifted from before I had even considered Islam.   I had forgotten about her and was amazed that she was still at the school although I saw no rational reason for her not to be.

"Oh, hi." I forced a smile, my heartbeat slowing to a normal pace.

"Girl, where have you been?   You just up and disappeared." She playfully slapped me on the arm, my hands still tucked in my jacket pockets.

"Just really busy."

"We have a potluck tonight at my place. Why don't you come?"

I shook my head, a hesitant smile on my face. "I can't."

"Why not?"

Her expression told me she had read more into my words than I intended.

For a second, she studied me, but I didn't know if my new dress would be suspect. A lot of African-American women covered their hair with a similar wrap, particularly when they were in between hair appointments.

I felt laughter escape my throat, surprised by how good it felt to laugh, and how strange it sounded coming from me. "Girl, you don't want me there."

"Why wouldn't I want you there? We miss you."

I grinned, unsure how to explain myself, and even less certain that I wanted to. But something inside me gave. I was tired of feeling alienated because of who I was.

"I don't believe in Jesus like you do, I never have actually." I was surprised by the honesty of my words. "I don't want to make anyone uncomfortable."

She was silent, but there was a smile still on her face, as if she was not bothered in the least by what I'd said. "Is that all?"

I creased my forehead. "What?"

"Is that all you're worried about?" She laughed, shaking her head, slapping me playfully again. "Girl, nobody cares. We're just there to eat."

I started to protest.

"I want you there." She squeezed my arm with a grin. "You look like you need a break anyway."

I grinned too, nodding. "Yeah, I do."

"It's at six."

She started to walk away. "Oh yeah," she said, and I met her gaze. "Do you mind coming to help me get ready?"

My eyebrows rose. "I don't know. I have—"

"I'm about to start now if you want to come along. That way you'll know where I'm staying."

Oh. I hadn't thought about her not being in the same room as the year before.

"You don't look like you're in the mood for studying anyway."

I considered it briefly, glancing toward my residence hall in the distance, realizing that I really wasn't ready to return there yet.

Before I could respond, Natasha looped her arm through mine and led me to where she lived.

As it turned out, Natasha had an apartment that year, and a car. When we arrived, the food was all ready, at least what she had prepared, so we were reheating and doing minor set-up until the guests arrived.

As we placed the dishes on the table and the food was being heated on the stove and in the oven, Natasha made a comment about how it was already after five o'clock. She frowned as she looked out the window into the growing darkness. "It looks like it's six already."

I too walked over to the window.

"Oh my God," I said, thinking aloud. "I need to pray."

It wasn't until Natasha stared at me in confusion that I realized what I'd said. "You need to pray?"

I hadn't planned on divulging my conversion. But it was too late. I dreaded another scene, so I decided that I didn't care what Natasha thought. I wasn't going to bow to others for the rest of my life.

"I'm Muslim."

The apartment grew silent and she stared at me, unable to keep from looking displeased. "Muslim?"

"Yes."

A second later, she shrugged. "Okay."

"Where's your bathroom?"

She pointed me to the hall. "The first door on the left."

I returned from ablution, and Natasha watched as I prayed. But she didn't stop setting up for the dinner.

My praying took longer than usual because I had to make up a prayer. I had forgotten about *Asr*, most likely because of the sudden change in plans.

When I finished, I rejoined Natasha in the dining room.

"Why do you pray like that?"

"It's how the Prophet prayed."

"The Prophet?"

"Prophet Muhammad."

She nodded, as if the name was familiar. "I heard of him."

"Not Elijah Muhammad."

She chuckled. "I know. That's the Nation of Islam. You're orthodox Muslim, right?"

I nodded, impressed by her knowledge.

"My uncle is Muslim."

"Really?"

She nodded. "I hear bits and pieces from my aunt."

"She's not Muslim too?"

"No. He converted a few years ago." Her eyes grew distant momentarily.

"It's causing a lot of problems in the family," she said.

I was unsure what to say, so I remained silent.

"They separated for a while, but now they're back together."

"They separated because he's Muslim?"

"Yeah. But my Mom's taking it really hard."

"Why?"

"She doesn't want them back together."

I couldn't conceal my shock. I chuckled at the ridiculousness of it. "What difference does it make?"

Natasha lifted a shoulder. "That's what my father says. But my mom's afraid for her sister." She paused. "And the children."

I thought of Sumayyah and what she had said about her family. I wondered if this family's sentiments were the same. I wanted to ask but didn't want to say too much.

"What is she afraid of?"

A grin formed on one side of Natasha's face, and she toyed with a fork amongst the silverware. "Him making them convert too."

I nodded, my gaze lifting toward the open curtains and seeing darkness there. I turned away, looking at her before I spoke. "Why does it matter? They're his children."

She was silent for some time. "To be honest, I'm afraid for them too."

She looked at me as if realizing that her comment may have hurt. "I'm sorry."

"It's okay. It's natural to feel like that. Before I studied, I would've felt the same."

She regarded me with her eyes narrowed in deep thought, a hurt expression on her face. "But why Islam, Renee? I know you said you never believed in Jesus, but—"

"I believe in Jesus."

"But you said you didn't."

"I never believed he was God, that's what I was saying."

"So you don't believe in the Trinity?"

"No. I was raised to believe in Jesus as God's son and God as God."

"What do you believe now?"

"The same, except I believe Jesus is a prophet, not the son of God."

Her face contorted slightly. "But how can you think he's just a prophet?"

I didn't know how to respond. Because I had read so much Islamic literature and had a new appreciation for prophets, I often forgot how insignificant they had been to me as a child. It was difficult hearing her say "just" as if being chosen as the student of God himself, as if being spoken to directly by the most respected angel in the heavens, and by the Creator himself, was not a venerated status, was not the highest position a human could attain on earth, as if it was not the nearest any creation would come to divine pleasure.

Her words reminded me of a Biblical image of one of the most revered prophets—that of drunkenness. Words could not convey how incorrect, and blasphemous, such portrayals were in light of my new knowledge. How far removed the prophets were from what humans had penned in the name of God. At that moment, I thought, too, of how loosely the word *prophet* was used. Buddha, Socrates, and Aristotle were referred to as prophets at times, and even the singer Bob Marley I'd heard referred to as such.

I wanted to share with Natasha what I'd recently read, a hadith, heartfelt words expressed by Prophet Muhammad on his deathbed. *Do not exaggerate your praise of me like the Christians praised the son of Mary.* I remember sitting on my bed, moved by his words. They made me think of the spiritual link between Jews, Christians, and Muslims, a bond broken only when someone deviated from the prophets' pure teachings, or rejected a prophet altogether.

It was a warning not to stray from the pure worship of God, to not fall into the errors of former peoples—and of people today.

But I doubted Natasha would understand.

"I don't think he's just a prophet," I said. "I believe that out of the thousands who were sent, he is among the best."

Natasha pursed her lips then sighed. "I don't understand how you can do it. I can't see myself throwing my religion away like that."

She paused. "Don't you fear for your soul?"

"Yes."

The response took her aback. "Then why do it?"

"Because I do fear for my soul. More than I ever did before. That's why I became Muslim."

I wondered how much she'd heard from her uncle about Islam.

"Well," she said with another sigh. "To each his own. I'm going to stick to what I know is true."

"But how do you know it's true?"

She looked as if I'd slapped her. "Because it's what God says."

"It's what people said God said. Jesus never claimed to be divine."

She started to respond, but the sound of the phone ringing interrupted her. She shook her head and made her way to the phone in the living room.

On the phone, she confirmed that she had plates and forks but asked the person to bring ice. She laughed at something and said, "Yeah right." A pause. "Not yet. But Renee's here." She wore a grin. "That's a long story. Later for that." "Okay." Another laugh. "Bye."

She returned to the table and said we'd better get the food set up. People were on their way.

We prepared the meal in silence, exchanging only polite words about classes and majors and what we planned to do after next year. Nonexistent was the cold atmosphere I lived in daily, although the atmosphere had undoubtedly changed. But I appreciated Natasha's affability, even in her disapproval of my choice. It was refreshing to remember I was human and actually had a right to choice in the first place.

Natasha and I remained acquainted, and she was amiable despite our differences. She stopped by my room periodically to say hello. Although it wasn't as often, she sometimes asked a question about Islam. She would talk freely about her aunt and uncle and her mother's fears. Her aunt, it seemed, was not only reconciling with her husband but being influenced by his beliefs. I didn't understand why Natasha felt comfortable sharing this information, especially with me. She knew I'd side with her uncle, but she spoke as if I would empathize with her.

I always gave another point of view and explained what Muslims believed on a matter, at least as I understood it at the time. Natasha seemed sincerely intrigued by what I shared. Occasionally, she reported to me that she was telling her mother what I'd told her.

Eventually, I told her of my stressful living situation, mostly because she witnessed my roommates' coldness on more than one occasion. She found it hard to believe that their cruelty was only because I'd become Muslim, and she pressed me for more details. I gave her as much I could recall, even sharing the conversation about my hair. She was a bit perplexed.

"I understand where they're coming from," she said one day, "but I don't agree with how they're showing it."

I was offended by her expression of understanding, but I didn't say anything.

"But you should really consider moving out," she said. "You look stressed every time you hear someone outside the door." She laughed. "If I didn't know you, I'd think you were abused by them or something."

I nodded, embarrassed that she noticed my discomfort and fear. "I don't have anywhere to go."

"Just go to the residence life office. They can help you. People switch roommates all the time."

Oh. I hadn't thought of that.

"If you go now, before break, they might have something for you by January." We were in mid-December, finishing our finals before Christmas vacation.

"It's best if you have someone willing to take you though." She paused.

"You don't know any Muslims on campus?"

I knew only Sumayyah, and she lived with her parents. I shook my head. "Not really."

"Check out MSA. They might know someone in the same situation."

I took Natasha's advice and decided to locate someone from the MSA before I approached the office. I wanted a definite placement before any official paperwork was put through. After a few phone calls, a Muslim student named Nasrin agreed to meet me after exams on the last day of finals. I had a flight to Indianapolis the next morning and was crunched for time. I had a hair appointment with the woman Hadiyah had referred to me, and the hairdresser had agreed to pick me up from Greenbelt metro station at eight for no extra cost. For obvious reasons, Nasrin and I agreed to meet in Nasrin's room instead of mine.

It was after four o'clock when I knocked at her door.

"Come in," I heard a voice call.

I turned the handle and peered in hesitantly before stepping inside.

"It's fine, you can come in."

The door closed behind me, and immediately I was pulled into an embrace. The show of affection took me off guard, and I mumbled a reply to the Arabic greeting she gave me as her cheek touched mine.

A half smile crept at one side of my mouth after Nasrin released me, still holding my right hand in hers. Her olive skin glowed bronze as she smiled broadly, shaking my hand to introduce herself even as I knew who she was.

"I'm Nasrin."

"I guess you know I'm Renee."

We laughed.

She motioned for me to sit down, and I took a desk chair while she prepared tea from a coffee maker and handed me a cup before sitting on the bed. Her jet black hair was pulled back into a thick braid, and I noticed that she was wearing a dark blue *shawar kameez* with gold trim at the neck and wrists.

"So what made you convert?"

I took a sip from the cup and set the tea aside, glancing at my watch, conscious that I didn't have a lot of time. I hadn't expected small talk. I started to change the subject to why I'd come, but one look at how her dark eyes glistened in anticipation made me change my mind.

I told her how I came to Islam, at least I summarized the story for her. Although I was impatient to get to the subject of moving to another room, I couldn't help feeling a bit relaxed as I spoke. It was the first time anyone had asked me my story, and it rejuvenated me to realize that it was an important story, and a good one. Living with Felicia and Anita had robbed me of feeling proud of my choice.

"Are you the only Muslim in your family?"

My eyes surveyed the walls of her room before they met hers. I started to speak but was surprised to see tears in her eyes, and a lingering smile on her face. I didn't know what to say. Until then, I didn't realize my story could be moving.

I told her that I was, and she wiped her eyes. "May Allah bless you."

The words settled over me in their kindness, and I felt a lump in my throat. I lifted my teacup again and sipped.

"I really admire you."

She was still smiling when our eyes met again. I set the teacup down and chuckled. "Well, there's not much to admire."

"No, I mean, how you accepted Islam. That's so beautiful."

I picked up my tea again, unaccustomed to compliments. But I couldn't help reflecting on what she was saying.

It was, indeed, beautiful.

"Sometimes I wish I could convert, just to see how it feels."

"You grew up Muslim?"

She nodded. "I'm from Pakistan. My whole family's Muslim."

"Everyone?"

"Yes."

"Even your aunts and uncles?"

"Yes."

My eyebrows rose in surprise. "You're the lucky one."

She shook her head. "But they don't all practice."

I creased my forehead. "What do you mean?"

"Some of them don't pray."

Her words confused me. "But I thought you said they're Muslim."

"They are."

"But..."

She waved her hand dismissively. "It doesn't make sense, I know."

I nodded though I could not comprehend what she was saying. Hadiyah had told me, and I had read, that prayer was a foundational aspect of Islam. I didn't understand how a person could be considered Muslim without this.

"But, *alhamdulillaah*," she said, "my family practices, and my parents' families too."

It took me a moment to realize she was now referring to sibling-parent relationships as opposed to extended family.

"Is your roommate Muslim?"

She furrowed her brows in disappointment, her gaze resting on something to her right before responding. "No." Her voice was quieter.

She sighed, and I wondered if my question was too personal. "She moved out a month ago."

Oh. "Why?"

Nasrin shook her head, a faint smile forming at her lips as she lifted her eyes to me. "I'm Muslim. She's not." She shrugged. "What can I say?"

I felt a smile tugging at my lips. "Yeah, I know what you mean."

"But she still lives here, at least on paper."

"I wish my roommates would move out."

She drew in a deep breath and exhaled. "I know you're looking to move out," she said as if apologizing. "But to be honest, I doubt Joni will agree to let you live here."

"But do you know anyone else looking for a roommate?" I didn't want to lose hope.

She shook her head. "Not on campus."

We were silent momentarily.

"But you're welcome to stay here," she said tentatively. "I don't think Joni will be back."

"Then why would it matter if I moved in officially?"

She shrugged. "That's just how she is. If she thinks it will be a favor to me, she won't do it." She sighed. "It's hard to explain."

I nodded in reflection. "I understand. That's how my roommates are." I laughed. "If I need something, they will do everything they can to make sure I don't get it. Otherwise," I sighed, "they don't have time for me."

"Yeah," she said with a shake of her head, "that sounds like Joni."

I paused as I considered her offer. "You don't think Joni will come back?"

She shook her head. "I doubt it. Unless she has no choice."

I studied the room. "But her things are here."

Nasrin shook her head. "She took it all out. I redid the room when she left." She turned and pointed to the other bed. "That's even my sheet and blanket."

I didn't know what to say.

"If you're sure it's not a problem..."

"Please come. I'd love to have some company once in awhile. Especially a Muslim."

The words were so heartwarming that I couldn't hide my pleasure. This would definitely be better than living with Felicia and Anita.

Fourteen

In December 1995, I returned home for break unashamed of my new faith. Knowing I was not alone endowed me with the strength to face my parents and family. At my hair appointment, I had met two other converts, Wadiah, the hairdresser, and Ghazwa, a customer I met only because she arrived while I was getting my hair done. Both were African Americans who came from Christian families who opposed their conversion to Islam. Wadiah, soft spoken and pleasant in nature, sighed in reflection whenever I asked a question about her and her family. "Allah is the best planner," she'd say. "I just pray Allah guides them." Ghazwa, on the other hand, was robust and unapologetic. "Forget them," she'd say, rolling her eyes. "I 'on't care what they think."

Wadiah was the elder, in her mid-forties, and had been Muslim for almost ten years. She was divorced from her first husband because he refused to accept Islam, and now she had been remarried for almost four years. Ghazwa was in her early twenties and had been married for almost two years and Muslim for one. She married her boyfriend after he accepted Islam and insisted they end their relationship or marry.

"You know you on the *haqq*," Ghazwa said in response to my concern about facing my family. "They ain't, so don't even worry about it."

It took me a moment to understand she meant that I was on the truth. I was still unfamiliar with most Arabic terminology.

"But it's hard," Wadiah's soft voice rose from behind my head, where she was braiding. She sighed. "I cried for three weeks when my mother said I wasn't her daughter anymore."

"Allah told Prophet Noah that his son wasn't his family." Ghazwa shrugged. "Good riddance."

Despite Ghazwa's no-nonsense encouragement and Wadiah's heartfelt empathy, my heart was pounding when I met my mother at my flight's gate upon arrival. I was wearing my black African head wrap and a heavy coat and gloves. She pulled me into an embrace, beaming.

"How was your trip?"

A bit surprised that she didn't notice my head cover, I answered coolly, my mind on my new dress. We talked casually on the way to baggage claim, and it wasn't until we had loaded my bags into the car that I realized why she didn't mention anything about my head cover. It was winter. Even she put her neck scarf over her head while we arranged the luggage.

It was just after sunset when we pulled out of the parking lot of the airport. The sky was dulling to a charcoal grey as I stared out the side window during the drive. My mother played Christmas music and sang along, oblivious to my far away thoughts. The songs aided in soothing my anxiety, as their cheerful and melodic tones reminded me that I was home and with family. But I couldn't escape feeling the painful distance between me and my mother. Part of me wanted to sing along too, if only to contribute to the merry atmosphere, but there was a stronger pull to stay quiet and gather my thoughts.

I decided that I would make no efforts to hide my Islam during this trip. I wouldn't go to church. I would say all my prayers. I would participate in no discussions that made me uncomfortable.

Holiday music was still wafting from the car speakers when we drove slowly down the streets of our neighborhood. My mother was now quiet, enjoying the mellow tunes without moving her lips. Colorful lights adorned the homes, and decorated trees could be seen through the open curtains of living rooms. Plastic snowmen and likenesses of Santa and his reindeer stood in the lawns patiently awaiting heavy snowfall for Christmas. One yard bore plastic models of a Muslim family.

I did a double take.

It took a few seconds for me to realize that this display was representing the birth of Jesus. I stared at these images intently, even turning my head as we passed. The woman covered in *hijaab*, the man in a *thobe*, his beard exuding a religiosity I associated with Muslims.

I had seen artificial likenesses like these dozens of times, but never before had I noticed how they were in stark contrast to how Christians portrayed themselves in life. Years later I would laugh at the irony of passing a yard with these images out front while the inhabitants of the home would glare at me and my husband for our appearance—which mirrored that of the people they venerated in their front lawn.

The sky was dark when we pulled into the driveway of our home, and I knew I'd have to pray *Maghrib* immediately. My mother and I dragged my luggage into the house, where we were met by Michael and Elijah. I stared at them, amazed by how much they had grown in such a short time. Michael was five now and Elijah was eight, but Elijah was almost as tall as me and Michael, although noticeably shorter than his brother, could have passed for eight himself.

Unabashed, Michael threw his arms around my waist, thrilled to see me.

"Merry Christmas," he sang out. His words complimented the cozy holiday atmosphere, made apparent by the decorated evergreen tree standing a few feet from us.

I burst into laughter, which relieved me from having to respond in kind. "Woe," I said as if I was losing my breath in his embrace. "I missed you too."

Elijah hung back after Michael finally let go, but I teased him. "Hey, you're ashamed to give me a hug?"

He grinned and walked over to hug me. "Merry Christmas."

I rubbed his head, aware that my silence was a bit awkward following his greeting.

"Hey, little sister."

I looked up to find Courtney leaning lazily against the entrance to the kitchen, her arms folded. She was wearing a fitting long sleeve white shirt with images of mistletoes all over, and a pair of form fitting jeans. Her permed hair was pulled away from her face to reveal a pair of mistletoe earrings to match her outfit, an outfit that could never pass The Church's litmus test for Christian modesty. I wasn't surprised that she would wear it, but I was surprised that she felt comfortable wearing it in our house.

"Hey," I said, smiling.

We met each other halfway in bestowing the obligatory hug.

My mother dragged one of my bags up the stairs to my room, and Courtney surprised me by taking the other.

"Come help us in the kitchen," my mother said after they returned. It was an offer to spend time together as a family, and I was happy that this was something I could participate in with a clear conscience. But I had to pray first.

"Okay," I said. "Just let me change."

I skipped the stairs two at a time, my nervousness shocking me. I had promised myself that I wouldn't lock the door while I prayed, but I was having second thoughts. After I performed ablution and changed, I covered my hair, deciding at the last minute not to lock the door.

I prayed *Maghrib*, but I had difficulty concentrating. I heard the door open during my last unit of prayer, and I froze. I was in the bowing position, so although the door was in front of me, I couldn't see who was there, at least not without lifting my head. Moving to the next position, I stood. It was then that I saw it was my brothers. But I didn't look them in the eye. My head was bowed humbly, and I mumbled the Arabic words to myself, hoping they couldn't hear.

I stood longer than I should have. I was stalling, hoping they'd lose interest and go downstairs to where my mother and sister were preparing dinner. But they didn't. My head began to pound, foreseeing what was about to occur.

Michael and Elijah were already staring at me curiously, but nothing could compare to the curiosity they'd feel once I moved to the next position—*sajdah.* I had to place my forehead on the ground.

Drawing in a deep breath and mentally telling myself that only God mattered, I prostrated, painfully aware of their staring. I sat too quickly then prostrated again, trying to get this over with, and hating myself for my weakness.

"What are you doing?" It was Michael's voice.

My head was still on the ground, but at the sound of his voice, I sat. My legs were folded under me, my forefinger of my right hand pointed as I whispered the last part of prayer.

A second later, I felt Michael standing directly in front of me.

"Renee?"

Although it was difficult, I ignored him, my face growing hot in embarrassment.

"Renee?"

He tilted his body sideways until his face was in front of mine.

"Are you okay?"

I could feel the warmth of his breath on my face, and I forgot what I had been saying. I started over, hating myself for being distracted.

He sat down in front of me and tapped my shoulder.

"Renee?" His voice sounded concerned now.

"Leave her alone," I heard Elijah say from the doorway.

"But something's wrong," Michael cried, turning slightly. "Maybe she's deaf."

"She's not deaf."

"Renee?"

For the closing part of prayer, I turned my head to the right then to the left, reciting the Arabic greetings of peace. Relieved to be finished, I exhaled, a smile playing at one side of my mouth as I met Michael's contorted face. He looked on the verge of tears. I reached out and rubbed his head, but he jerked slightly, as if unsure whether it was really me.

"Are you okay?" he whined.

"Yes, I'm fine." I laughed.

"What were you doing?" Elijah invited himself in, as if now knowing it was okay to enter. His arms were folded and he stood a comfortable distance from me.

"Praying."

He creased his forehead. "Praying?"

"Yes." I smiled widely now, pretending my praying was the most normal thing in the world.

"I never saw no prayer like that," Michael said.

"Shut up," Elijah said, turning to his brother abruptly before returning his attention to me.

"Is that a special Christmas prayer or something?" Elijah said once our gazes met.

I couldn't comprehend his expression. His forehead was still creased in curiosity, but his eyes looked hurt, as if I had betrayed him somehow. But I didn't understand what this meant.

"No. It's just prayer."

He studied me as if I were not being completely honest.

"Does Dad know you pray like that?"

Stunned, I didn't know what to say. I just looked at him.

"Michael! Elijah!"

It was our mother's voice. Apparently, she didn't know where they were.

They turned at the sound of their names and immediately started for the door. Michael ran out, disappearing into the hall, most likely anticipating dinner. But Elijah retreated out of obligation, giving me one last look before leaving, a look that told me he wasn't finished with me.

My father arrived late that night, after we all had eaten and my brothers were in bed. I had finished praying 'Ishaa minutes before and lay awake reflecting on my predicament. I had locked the door this time, having decided that it was better for my concentration. I was beginning to feel like a coward and wondered if I had the strength to be as open about my Islam as I had hoped.

There was a knock at my door followed by an attempt to open the door. But I hadn't yet unlocked it after praying. I swung my legs to the floor and hurried to the door.

I greeted my father with a hug and talked to him only briefly before he made his way to his room. He was exhausted, I could see it in his eyes, and I wondered if his growing church was beginning to take a toll on him.

A moment later I realized that in two days, it would be Sunday.

I groaned. Church. I didn't have too much of a choice in divulging my conversion.

I avoided church by saying I wasn't feeling well, but on Monday afternoon I was beginning to feel suffocated by my sin of omission. I was sitting on one of the twin beds in Courtney's room talking about school when she mentioned Patricia, who had graduated from Ball State a couple of years ago with a degree in interior design. It was known that my parents were disappointed with her major. Her love had always been political science, and before meeting James she had wanted to become a lawyer.

"I'm proud of her," Courtney said from where she sat cross-legged on the bed opposite me. Her hair was pulled away from her face by an elastic band, and she wore a white Christmas tree sweatshirt and jeans. Small gold earrings glistened at her ears, illuminating the brown of her face. Her eyebrows were still joined, and I faintly recalled her once saying she wouldn't separate them because she feared the hair would grow back thicker.

I too wore jeans and a sweatshirt, but my shirt was dull grey, bearing no tribute to the approaching holiday. In a week, Christmas would be here, and I felt no joy at the knowledge, only dread.

I nodded in response, not knowing what else to say. I always felt left out of their close relationship.

"She's modeling now."

"Modeling?" I wanted to make sure I'd heard Courtney correctly. "Modeling homes, you mean?"

Courtney rolled her eyes, a smirk on her face. "You would think that."

I was quiet momentarily.

"She's modeling. You know, like Naomi Campbell?" She studied my face for a few seconds as if making sure I'd heard of the model.

"I know."

"You don't sound happy."

I shook my head. "It's not that. I'm just..." I didn't know how to put my feelings into words. It wasn't that I disapproved, although I couldn't safely say I agreed with her choice; it just wasn't what I'd expected, especially given her newfound love for the church, even if it wasn't the one we grew up in. "...shocked."

"Why? 'Cause it's not what you'd do?"

It was a challenge, as if I were thirteen all over again. I chuckled to lighten the atmosphere. "Come on, Courtney, I'm a different person now."

Skeptical, she raised her eyebrows. "Really?"

I laughed loudly. "You're the one responsible for that."

"Me?"

"Yes. Giving me all those CDs."

"You listened to them?"

"I'm practically addicted." And I was. But this was before I read, much later, the hadith forbidding musical instruments.

She looked surprised. "I'm impressed."

"You're not the only one with a mind of your own."

She rolled her eyes playfully. "I already knew that. We were just waiting for you."

"To wake up?" I joked.

She creased her forehead, then relaxed it a second later as the memory came to her. She laughed. "Yeah, to wake up."

"Well," I grinned, "I definitely woke up."

"Good."

She didn't catch the hint in my words, but then again, I didn't really expect her to. She had no idea I was Muslim.

"I'm just glad Tricia is happy."

I nodded, thinking more of myself than my sister. "Me too."

An awkward silence followed. In the quiet, I realized it was probably a good time to confess to my actions.

"You ever think about religion?" I asked.

She gathered her eyebrows as she met my gaze. "Religion?"

"Yeah, you know, which one is true?"

She shrugged then answered honestly. "Sometimes. I know what Dad says, but then again, Tricia seems to have found the truth."

"But what about you?"

"Me?" She wrinkled her nose. "I don't like all this religion stuff."

"Really?" I don't know why I was surprised. A couple of years ago, she had openly speculated the existence of God.

"I think you should just do what makes you happy. Nobody can tell you what that is."

I considered her point briefly. "But you don't believe there's one religion that's the truth?"

She lifted a shoulder and shook her head. "To be honest, I don't know." She paused for a few seconds, her gaze distant for a moment. "And, honestly, I don't care. Not right now."

I leaned forward, intrigued, forgetting my troubles right then. "Why not?"

"You know," she said, looking at me in accusation. "You saw how we grew up. I don't think it's right to tell somebody how to live their life."

"Even your own children?"

"Especially your own children."

I was quiet as I took in her words. "But what do you teach them then?"

"That they have their own minds and can choose for themselves what to believe."

"What about their souls?"

"What about them?" She looked at me as if disgusted. "I'm not God."

"So you think all religions are true?"

She shook her head. "No, I think none of them are."

Taken aback, my eyes widened. "None of them?"

"You show me one that only believes in God and doesn't follow a whole bunch of manmade laws, then I'll eat my words."

"Islam."

Silence followed. I was surprised that I had said it. My heart raced and I reluctantly met my sister's gaze, but she just looked confused.

"What?"

"Islam."

"Islam?"

"Yes, you know, the religion."

"Like Darnell?"

I was offended by her mention of our cousin. She never seemed to like him. "No. His religion wasn't Islam. It was the Nation of Islam. There's a difference."

She stared at me, but I couldn't tell what she was thinking.

"There is?"

I briefly explained the difference, but she didn't seem satisfied.

"You're talking about that Middle Eastern religion?"

"It started in the Middle East, but it's not only for Arabs."

She shook her head. "That's worse than The Church."

Her comment stung, mostly because I knew how much she loathed our childhood church. It was the worst insult she could possibly give. I felt myself growing defensive. "Nothing's worse than The Church."

She looked at me with widened eyes. Even I couldn't believe what I'd said. I was trying to insult her, but it came out all wrong. I had insulted my father instead.

We said nothing for a few minutes, lost in our thoughts, and surprise.

"Well," she said after some time, as if trying to make me feel better, "like I said, people should be able to believe whatever they want."

I decided to leave it at that for the time being, unsure how the conversation would play out if I said more. Besides, it was time for *Asr*.

Monday evening, Reggie came over but I ignored him, leaving him to chat with my father. I said hello but nothing more, and returned to my room to read a book and pray. He came over almost everyday after that, and I grew irritated. My frustration was mostly because he came unannounced, and my brothers or sister let him in without telling me first. I had been covering my hair in front of males for months, and I hated feeling like I'd have to cover in my own home. But because I never knew when he was coming over, I never covered my hair. I merely excused myself after exchanging polite words when I ran into him. I made it clear that I had no desire for his company. Only when he called would he get a little more conversation out of me, but even that was strained.

The opportunity to chat with him wasn't even remotely appealing to me, and I found myself turned off by him more and more each day. He seemed so immature in his attempts to win me over, and I found myself wondering what I'd seen in him in the first place. He was still a dedicated member of my father's church, and even that seemed artificial to me. But then again, maybe he was really a believer.

I wasn't. So it didn't really matter.

On the morning of Christmas Eve, I avoided church again, but this time there was some arguing. I said I didn't want to go, and my parents insisted. Courtney stayed out of it, watching it all unfold with no apparent emotion either way.

"It's Christmas Eve," my mother said, as if it wasn't obvious.

"I know. And I'm not going."

"You are going," my father said, glaring at me.

"I'm not." For some reason, Courtney's presence encouraged me, and I was determined to get my way.

"Renee," my mother's voice rose in anger, "get dressed now."

"Mom, I said I'm not going."

"Now!"

My face grew hot, but I wasn't backing down. It was strangely refreshing to stand my ground for once. I shook my head.

A second later, my mother grabbed my arm and tried to lead me toward the steps to my room. I followed, unwilling to physically fight my mother. I stumbled up the stairs behind her, catching Elijah studying me from where he stood in the doorway to the kitchen. I held his gaze for a moment, my head turned awkwardly behind me. He held the same hurt expression from a week earlier, but now I detected understanding. I sensed he knew this act of rebellion was somehow related to my strange prayer. Michael stood next to him, dressed in an identical three-piece suit and tie, perplexed. He had no idea what was going on.

My mother nearly shoved me through the doorway to my room. A second later, my father stood behind her, shocking me. It was as if he merely appeared. I hadn't heard him behind us.

Crossing her arms, my mother repeated her command. "Get dressed."

I sat on the bed, feeling tears sting my eyes. "I'm not going."

"You are."

"I'm not."

She stormed into the room and stood towering over me as my father took her place in the doorway. "You'll put a dress on and get in the car."

"Why aren't you going?" My father's voice startled me in its abruptness.

I had to lean my head slightly to the right to see him. I blinked, trying to catch my breath. I didn't want to break down. "It's a pagan holiday."

For a minute, it felt as if all the air had been sucked from the room.

In the stillness, it took them several seconds to register what I'd said.

My mother stepped back, wounded. "What?"

My father's brows furrowed as he stepped inside the room. "Excuse me?"

For some reason his challenge emboldened me. I raised my voice. "It's a pagan holiday."

"What's a pagan holiday?" It was a dare. I had never opposed my father before, but I somehow felt a firm resolve to stick to my position.

"Christmas."

My mother was speechless.

"It's not Jesus' birthday. It's some sun god's. We shouldn't be celebrating it anyway. I thought we were following pure Christianity." My words were rushed, as if afraid I wouldn't get them out in time. I wanted my parents to feel the sting of every word.

Now, when I reflect on this moment, I cringe. I see my arrogance for what it was, and my gross lack of wisdom. It was the wrong thing to say, the wrong day, wrong in every possible way. It wasn't *da'wah* by any stretch of the imagination, and it certainly wasn't representative of the religion I'd embraced—a faith that considered dishonoring one's parents a grave sin. Perhaps I had read this somewhere, perhaps not. Either way, I was being hot headed, representative of nothing except my ignorant self. I could have called them ahead of time and told them of my religion, given them a heads-up, anything but this. But as it stands, I'll always remember this morning as the day I was afflicted with the infamous youthful zeal.

"Who do you think you are?" my father spat out.

"You taught us to follow pure Christianity, that's what I'm doing. Jesus never told us to decorate trees and celebrate paganism."

"And what makes you the scholar?"

"What makes you?"

My father smacked me so hard, and fast, that I didn't realize he could reach so far, and inflict so much pain. I fell to the side, holding my cheek in anger.

I could have left it at that. But now my pride was hurt, so I took the leap. I narrowed my eyes at him before I spoke.

"Is that what Jesus teaches?"

The silence that followed was biting, cold. I had won. I had to repress a snide grin.

They looked at me for a few more seconds, my mother's lip upturned, my father glaring, breathing heavily, trying to compose himself.

I had won.

When I heard the front door open and close a few minutes later, followed by the starting of the car, I laughed out loud. But was met with only the echoing of my own voice.

I had won.

But, strangely, I felt as if the walls were closing in on me. I felt the air shift, as if even it didn't want to be near me. It was then that I knew I was free to believe whatever I wanted. Just like Courtney had said.

Because I was no longer considered a part of the Morris family.

Christmas Eve came and went, and the excitement in the house grew as I heard Michael and Elijah scream in anticipation of opening their presents, oblivious to my crimes of the day before. I heard their restless feet pounding down the stairs after midnight and the whoops and hollers as they opened their presents. I was surprised to hear Courtney's motherly voice as she asked them questions and feigned surprise as they opened their presents. I didn't hear my parents at all, imagining them to be smiling off to the side, unable to offer more overt pleasure than that. I had taken that from them. I then understood what was happening. My sister was compensating for their inability to participate like they usually did.

I felt betrayed, enraged at Courtney for siding with them. She hadn't said a word to me since my refusal to attend church, and in my fury, I branded her a two-faced hypocrite. I was breathing fire as I sat alone in my room, still too zealous to realize I had dug my own grave. I blamed my sister, The Church, my father, my mother, and even Patricia. Anyone but myself.

Even now I recall how, although I was left to pray in peace, I was unable to relax as I stood before Allah. I had yet to learn this was because of my sins. It didn't occur to me then that I had displeased God in the least. I imagined that my actions had been for His sake.

This was soon to become a familiar theme in my zealous transgressions.

But, for the moment, I was drawing the battle lines, imagining that it was my new religion that they hated, not me. Yet, they hadn't even learned of my Islam.

Patricia and her husband arrived Christmas evening, apparently having wanted to be home for the morning. There was a lot of cheer in the house as James and his son filled the home with carefree laughter. I heard lots of *oohs* and *ahs*, which I later discovered were because Emanuel, who was now about fourteen months, was walking like a big boy, and talking like one too, at least in his own language.

Once again, I felt left out, and resentful.

I lay in my bed staring at the ceiling, too prideful to go downstairs and greet Patricia. I was tired, frustrated, and hungry. But I was paralyzed by loneliness and pride. So I suffered in silence.

I was surprised when I heard a knock at my door a couple of hours later. Not bothering to answer or get up, I raised my head and watched the brass handle turn and the door open.

Patricia peered in. Our eyes met immediately, and she smiled, stepping inside and closing the door behind her. Her skin was paler than I remembered, but then again, I was always taken aback by her white complexion. But she looked good, at least in the worldly sense, but I still couldn't picture her on a catwalk. She didn't seem to belong there, although her fitting black dress and long permed hair said that she did.

Her kind expression inspired me to sit up and smile weakly in return.

"Hey." She took a seat next to me and punched me playfully in the shoulder.

"Hey," I said.

"Why aren't you downstairs? For a second, I thought you were still in Maryland."

I tried to laugh, but I couldn't. "No, I'm here."

In the seconds that passed, we looked at each other. Her lips were closed tight in an expression of understanding, as if she felt sorrowful affection for me. She seemed older than I remembered, and more mature. Her eyes were tired but loving, and I felt something inside me go warm. I loved her. I hadn't really felt it so completely before.

I knew then that my parents had told her. I could have been angered by that, but, strangely, I was glad they did. Perhaps I was relieved that I hadn't been completely forgotten.

"What's going on with you?" Her expression changed to concern. She laid a hand on my thigh, a gesture to let me know she wanted to hear it from me and see my point of view.

I looked away from her momentarily, unsure how to respond. "Didn't they tell you?" I was being sarcastic, still too hurt to open up completely.

"They told me what you said, but that doesn't tell me anything."

I shrugged. "Well, what do you want to know?"

"What's going on."

"Nothing."

"Ray." Her voice was soft, as if she was leveling with me and saying, *Let's be real.*

I sighed, gathering my thoughts. But the words that came surprised me. They weren't the ones I'd planned in my mind. "I'm Muslim."

I wasn't looking at her at the moment, but her already still hand stiffened and slowly she moved it from my lap. After a few seconds, I met her gaze, unashamed by what I'd said. Her eyes were slightly widened, and I imagined that she had that expression frozen on her face.

She was speechless.

I was too.

Again, the seconds passed and we looked at each other. Then she blinked, the deliberate blinking that one does to ascertain they had heard correctly. Her gaze grew distant and concerned, and she bit her lower lip, shaking her head as if she couldn't process my words.

"Are you sure?"

It was the oddest question anyone has ever asked me after I shared my conversion. But I understood that she was simply trying to reconcile what was happening, what had happened. It simply made no sense.

She looked at me, brows furrowed. "Mom and Dad said you were some fundamentalist Christian now."

I furrowed my brows. "Fundamentalist?" I'd never heard the word used in real life. It was a term I associated with television, and it was never in the laudatory sense.

"Yes." She was still looking at me, demanding an explanation.

My expression softened as I realized the misunderstanding. "I said I was following pure Christianity."

She shook her head at a loss. "But you just said you're Muslim."

"I know. That's what a Muslim is."

"A fundamentalist Christian?"

"Patricia," I said, my voice on the verge of frustration, "I don't even know what a fundamentalist is."

"An extremist." Her voice rose in accusation and rebuke. "A person who takes things literally and life too seriously."

"You mean, like The Church?" Again, I was defending myself by insulting our childhood church. It wasn't right, but I was offended. I had no idea what she was getting at, but I knew it had nothing to do with what I truly believed.

"Ray," her voice was a plea now, "don't you know those people oppress and kill people in the name of their religion?"

My head pulled back in shock and disgust. "What people?"

"Muslims."

"What?" I almost jumped from where I was sitting I was so taken aback by her ludicrous statement. This was worse than Reggie saying women had to hide under the floorboards. "Where did you hear something like that?"

"Do you even watch the news, Ray?"

At that, I felt my chest grow hot in anger. "The *news*?"

"Yes."

"As in television?"

"Yes."

I contorted my face and made her taste my disappointment. "The same TV that did blackface comedy? The same TV that showed Blacks as animals? The same TV that still stereotypes us?"

"That's different."

"Why, Patricia, because it's you getting hurt? Did you even learn anything from what happened to us?"

"But look at what they do in their countries, Ray. That's not a stereotype."

"And look at what so-called Christians do in *this* country, what they've done for centuries." I wanted to yell, but I kept my voice as composed as I could manage. "It was the Bible they pointed to when they told us we weren't human. It was the Bible they used to justify oppressing us, Patricia, *killing* us, oppressing the whole world. Do you even study history? What about the Crusades? Or even what's happening today?"

Amazingly, she stayed calm, but I could tell I'd made her shift gears. "But Christ called to peace. Their religion calls to violence."

"Says who?"

She shook her head, clearly not up to arguing. "Look, Ray, all I'm saying is the only truth is through Jesus as your Lord and Savior."

"So now you think he's God?" I couldn't believe she'd actually regressed spiritually. "We never believed that, not even in The Church."

"But our church isn't a real church, Ray. It's heresy."

"Did you tell Dad that?"

She drew in a deep breath. "Dad and Mom know what I believe now. I just pray they accept the truth one day, for the sake of their souls."

For a moment, I was more infuriated with her than I was with my parents. At that point in my life, I couldn't fathom a person actually believing Jesus is God after being raised to worship God himself.

"So you believe in the Trinity now?"

She nodded. "Yes, I do. And I hope you'll find Christ too."

"But how can you believe that?"

"Because it's the truth, Ray. I can witness to that."

I stared at her, my eyes pleading. "But on the Day of Judgment, Patricia, can you witness to that then?"

I was hoping to spark something inside her, make her think about what she was saying, even fear standing before the Creator carrying the most grievous sin possible— associating partners with Him.

She smiled, rolling her eyes up to the ceiling in pleasant reflection. "God, Ray, if you knew all that Jesus has done for me, you'd know my answer to that." She sighed. "One day, hopefully, I can make you understand."

I was perplexed. I didn't know what to say.

Today, I'm more polished and can point out the inconsistencies in the belief that someone other than God answered one's prayers, even if a person calls on other than Him. As one convert reflected in a book I'd read, *"In His infinite Mercy, Allah answered my prayers when I called on other than Him, why shouldn't I answer His call to mercy that I can attain through worshipping only Him?"* But at the moment, I was too shell-shocked to even comprehend that she could believe that.

She patted my leg and our eyes met. In a truce, she grinned. "Let's go downstairs. Everyone's waiting. I miss you guys."

Dinner went more smoothly than I expected, although my parents' exaggerated laughter and intonations in James and Patricia's company made it clear that they hadn't forgotten, or forgiven, my impropriety. It was all they could do to deny my presence entirely. I was grateful.

Courtney wore a tight-lipped smile and kept looking at Emanuel, who was entertaining himself on the floor. I sensed that this too was an effort to avoid me. I sat directly across from her, but her eyes danced over me whenever she took a bite of food, preferring to turn at every sound of her nephew. Patricia sat next to me, her husband on her other side, and they made obvious efforts to include me, looking at me each time they shared a story or told a joke. There was something unsettling about this scene, particularly

Courtney's avoidance of my gaze, but I couldn't pinpoint what it was.

Whenever my and Elijah's eyes met, I made a weak attempt at looking pleasant. It was due more to unease than kindness. He couldn't stop staring at me from where he sat next to Courtney, Michael on his other side. Fortunately, my parents sat farthest from me, my father at the head and my mother at an awkward angle next to him, as if her chair placement had been an afterthought.

My Islam was not mentioned during the entire meal, and I couldn't help being impressed with Patricia for her silence. Or perhaps she had forgotten my confession, or simply viewed it as insignificant in light of what I had already been accused of.

I doubted it.

I waited for her to drop the news.

She didn't, at least not until we were relaxing in the living room after dinner. But I don't think she meant to betray me. It was the logical response to the flow of conversation at the moment.

"I see some unopened boxes under the tree," James had said, bending forward as he steered Emanuel from the gifts, his large hand on his son's back. My brother-in-law tilted his head as he read the name.

My heart sank as I realized what should have been obvious, logical even.

I was the only one who hadn't participated in this morning's activities. The boxes were mine.

I sat on a chair at the edge of the living room, facing my family. I didn't feel comfortable on the floor with Patricia and James, and certainly not on the couch with my parents, Courtney on the loveseat at an angle next to them. In any case, Michael was wedged between my mother and father, Elijah sitting lazily on the arm of the couch.

I didn't belong there. My presence was merely a necessary completion to the familial atmosphere.

At James's words, my mother stood immediately and walked over to the tree and scooped up the gifts in her arms, managing to carry all five somehow. My heart ached as I watched the boxes' shimmering paper—gold, red, and green—against her arms as she carried them to the foyer closet. I wasn't hurting because I wanted the presents, but because I knew how much effort must have gone into selecting them. I felt horrible. She deposited the gifts in the closet before returning to her place on the couch.

She grinned. But her gaze was on Emanuel. "There," she said. "Out of the way."

He laughed and ran to the tree again, this time tugging on the branches. Again, James stood, reaching to pick his son up before Emanuel pulled down the tree.

"Why are those the only ones left?" James was grinning, so I knew he meant no harm. He was preparing another joke. I cringed when he looked at me. "You have a special time you open yours that nobody knows about?"

The room grew quiet and I felt all eyes on me. My face grew hot and I tugged at the hem of my long-sleeve T-shirt. "Not really." I wished my parents had told James about my "Christian fundamentalism" when they had told Patricia. It would have saved me the headache.

I knew my parents wanted to steer the conversation in another direction. I could sense it. But no one knew what to say, so in a way, Patricia saved us.

"She's Muslim." Her words were soft, matter-of-fact, and non-judgmental. I remember that. But, still, it was a moment of revelation for everyone else. I think she was as confused by their reaction as they had been by her words, but I'm sure it was only a matter of seconds before it occurred to her that she was the only one who had known.

I twisted the hem of my shirt and glanced up, heart racing. I looked at my brother-in-law first. But he was looking at his wife. A half grin was still on his face and he was leaning sideways, tugging at the hand of his son, who was insisting on toppling the tree. His expression said, *No kidding?* but he said only, "What?"

"Muslims don't celebrate Christmas." Her voice remained kind, diplomatic even, as if her words explained it all.

My eyes darted in my parents' direction, and I found them glaring at me in disbelief, their firm set jaws demanding an explanation or a denial. I dropped my gaze then lifted it, willing myself to meet their stare. But I couldn't take it.

Inadvertently, my and Courtney's eyes met, and for a second I held her gaze, stunned by the seething anger I saw there. Her nose flared before she rolled her eyes, turning from me. But, like everyone else, she said nothing.

"Is that true?" my mother demanded, her eyes narrowing.

"Yes." I was surprised by how calm I felt, even as my hands were trembling slightly.

My father shook his head at me. Then he and my mother, as if on cue, looked at each other. I didn't know what they were thinking, but I sensed they felt that their fears had been confirmed.

"So you *were* talking to William?"

The mention of someone else took me off guard, and at first I didn't know whom my father was talking about.

"William?" I said his name as if I'd never heard of him.

"The time for games is over, Renee."

"I'm not playing."

"You know very well what I'm talking about."

I shook my head, my forehead creased as I struggled to understand my father's meaning. Seconds later, it occurred to me that I did know William. "You mean Reggie's friend?"

"Who else?"

"What about him?" I was genuinely confused.

"You told us you two haven't been talking."

It was then that I recalled our last conversation about religion. They had hoped William wasn't trying to convert me. "We haven't."

"Never?"

"I don't talk to him."

"That's not what I asked."

"But, Dad, this has nothing to do with him."

"Oh? So I suppose it's just a coincidence that you joined his religion?"

I felt myself growing agitated, but I tried to remain calm. "It's not his religion. It's Islam."

"I know what it is."

Defeated, I stared at him, growing more furious by the second. He couldn't be serious. Amid my raging emotions, I was offended. I had a mind of my own. I could think for myself. Why would I do something because of William? He meant nothing to me. We weren't even friends.

"I told you to stay away from him."

"I did."

"Don't lie to me." His voice rose in anger, daring me.

"I'm not lying."

"Daddy, what's a Muslim?" The innocence in Michael's voice softened the tension somewhat, derailing my father, at least for the moment.

My father's eyes glanced down at his son and softened slightly. "A heathen," he said, looking at me again. "That's what it is."

"It's a person who only prays to God and believes God doesn't have children," I said, my eyes on my little brother. "And who believes in all of God's prophets, including Jesus."

"What's wrong with that?" Michael asked innocently.

"Shut up."

For a second, I thought my father was talking to Michael, but when I looked at him, I saw that his eyes were on me. But Michael's eyes widened as he looked at our father in fear, realizing he had said something wrong.

"Don't corrupt my children."

"Corrupt?" I almost laughed, but I didn't. "But you don't even know anything about Islam, so how can you—"

"You don't know what I know. Don't forget, I know more about religion than you ever will."

Oh yeah. Harvard University. "Then why aren't you Muslim?"

If my father hadn't been rubbing Michael's back at that moment, I think he would have slapped me again. But this time, I wasn't trying to be caustic. I really wanted to know. I couldn't fathom a person studying the religion and not accepting it.

"Because it's a load of crap."

I started to say something, but I bit my lip. I didn't want a repeat of the day before.

"It's okay," James said, clearly unable to relax in a conversation devoid of laughter. A grin still lingered on his face, but he was sitting now, as was Emanuel, who appeared as engrossed in the exchange as everyone else.

"No," my father said, "it is not."

"But James and I believe differently than you," Patricia said, trying to patch up the wound she had unwittingly inflicted.

"Patricia," my mother cut in, her patience running thin, "don't make excuses for your sister. She has no right bringing a pagan religion into our home."

Out of respect, Patricia dropped her gaze, her fingers tugging at the carpet. I could tell she wanted to say more, but she wasn't willing to argue with her mother.

"It's not a pagan religion," I said.

My mother's finger pointed at me. "You, close your mouth. I don't want to hear another word from you."

I frowned. "But that's not fair."

"What did I say?"

I grunted, but I remained quiet. I didn't want to make things worse than they already were.

"Isn't Christmas supposed to me merry?" It was Elijah's question. His arms were folded, and he was pouting.

"Talk to your sister about that," my mother said. She gave me a sideways glance, placing all the blame on me in that gesture. "That's what happens when people leave the church. They ruin God's blessings for everyone."

How convenient, I thought. Blame the Muslim. I would get used to it over the years, but it wouldn't get easier. I would always feel it was a copout, a cruel one at that. I wasn't the first to get angry that Christmas evening, but somehow everyone's anger was my fault.

My fondest memories of my holiday vacation that year are two: Patricia's efforts to lighten the atmosphere that Christmas evening, and Elijah's undying curiosity about my new faith, even as he and Michael were forbidden to talk to me, something I discovered by accident.

A couple of days before New Year's Day, my mother went shopping, leaving Michael and Elijah in Courtney's care at home. My father was gone, as usual, working at the church. Patricia and James had gone the day before, so

Courtney had lost her companion, and the family had lost its mediator. Since Michael and Elijah were older now, they didn't need constant vigilance, only an adult presence in the home. So after my mother left, Courtney retired to our parents' bedroom to watch a movie, and I retired to mine to be alone. Since my secret was out, and since I wasn't the first choice of company in the home, I kept my room door unlocked, even when I prayed.

I had just finished praying *Dhuhr* when I sensed someone else's presence. I looked up to find Elijah in the doorway. This surprised me, mostly because I hadn't heard the door open.

When our eyes met, I started to greet him, but he spoke first.

"I'm not allowed to talk to you."

His words shocked me, not only because they were news to me, but because his very presence was in obvious contradiction to them.

I stared at him, his words hurting more than I let on. It cut deeply to know my parents would actually make such a rule, and behind my back. The hypocrisy upset me. When Patricia had done the unthinkable—got a boyfriend, eloped, *and* left the family's church—no such injunction was passed down. But I had done only the latter. Where was the justice in that?

Despite my hurt feelings, and pride, I couldn't help grinning at how more mature Elijah looked. The look on his face was grave, and if I didn't know any better, I'd think he was at least thirteen. His arms were crossed defiantly, and his face was twisted in a pout. His eyes were glassy as he glared at me, as if blaming me for the injustice of our parents' rule.

"Then why are you talking to me?"

I was only teasing him, but he seemed to grow more agitated. He pursed his lips and looked up momentarily, his arms still crossed in defiance.

"Can I come in?"

"Sure." I gestured my hand toward my bed although I still sat on the floor, where I had finished praying.

He stepped inside, closed the door behind him, and locked it. His movements were so deliberate in their seriousness that I brought a hand to my mouth to keep from laughing.

He let out a heavy sigh when he sat down on my bed, facing me.

I stared at him. He stared at me.

"Do you want to know why I'm talking to you even though I can't?" He was glaring at me, having resumed his pout, frowning with his arms crossed over his chest.

"Yes, please."

"I'm talking to you because I want to know why I can't talk to you."

"Ah," I said, unable to keep the humor out of my tone, "yes, of course." I paused.

"And you're sure the rule doesn't apply to the question at hand?"

He huffed and seemed to think seriously about it. "I don't know. But I want to know anyway."

"Okay..." I feigned concern. "But only if you're sure it's okay."

"It's fine, just hurry up. I don't want Michael to wake up."

"Oh yes, he might tell."

He narrowed his eyes. "Of course he'll tell."

"Okay, then, let me speak quickly." I drew in a deep breath and let it out, feeling my grin widen. "I don't know."

"What?" Clearly, this wasn't the answer he wanted.

"I don't know."

"What do you mean you don't know?"

"I don't know, Elijah. This is the first time I heard of the rule."

"That don't mean you don't know."

I furrowed my brows. "Why do you say that?"

"You know it's because you're that new religion now." It was an accusation, as if I were trying to withhold something from him.

"Oh, you mean, Muslim."

"Yeah, Muslim." He stumbled over the last word, trying to analyze its pronunciation for himself, but eventually it came out right.

"Then if you know the reason, why are you asking?"

"Renee," he said, frustrated, "I need to know what it means."

"Why?"

"Because I might get in trouble too."

I was silent for some time. "In trouble?"

"Yes, like you."

"Why would you get in trouble?"

"Because I think I might be one."

I studied him for a minute, unsure what he was saying. "You might be what?"

"A Muslim."

At that, I grew quiet, the reason for his distress becoming clear to me then. But so much of his unease was still a mystery. I had no idea if he knew what he was saying. After all, he was a child, only eight years old. It was possible that he was simply confused. Adults' arguing often had that effect on children.

"But why would you think that, Elijah?"

"Because of what you said."

I shook my head, squinting my eyes as I tried to grasp his meaning. I couldn't. "What did I say?"

"You remember. On Christmas."

"That I'm Muslim?"

"No." He groaned, growing impatient with me. "You said Muslims believe in God."

My eyebrows rose as the memory came back. I nodded. "Yes, I did."

"And you said they believe God doesn't have children."

I nodded again. "You're right. I remember saying that."

"So what am I supposed to do?"

"About what?"

"I think I'm Muslim, Renee." It came out as a whine.

I gathered my eyebrows. "But I'm the one who's Muslim, Elijah, not you. You can't get in trouble for that."

"But I believe that too."

I paused, staring at him as if seeing him for the first time. "You believe what?" I spoke slowly, wanting to make sure he understood my question clearly.

"That God doesn't have children."

I creased my forehead, concerned. "You don't believe Jesus is the son of God?"

He wrinkled his nose. "I never believed that."

"Even in church?"

"Church is stupid."

I blinked, his words stinging. Despite my newfound belief, it just didn't seem right for him to talk like that. "Don't say that, Elijah. It's not stupid, even if you don't agree with all of it."

"But it is stupid."

"Don't say stupid, Elijah." I spoke as gently as I could. "Just say what bothers you."

"When the ladies dance around like that."

Oh. He was referring to the Holy Ghost. That used to terrify me as a child too.

"And that statue with blood on it. I don't like it."

I nodded, unable to say anything to that. I didn't like it either. "But that doesn't mean you're Muslim."

He groaned, his eyes going to the window for some time. "Then what am I?"

At that moment, I remembered reading that each child is born upon the *fitrah*, the inborn nature to worship God alone and submit to Him. In essence, we were all born Muslims. It was our families who made us otherwise.

I got to my feet and walked over to the bed, sitting next to him. I put my arm around him. He relaxed somewhat.

"Look," I said, unsure what to say. I knew I'd be held accountable on the Day of Judgment if I didn't tell him the truth. "You want to hear a story?"

At first, he didn't respond. Then he shifted his shoulders in a shrug. "Okay."

When I didn't speak right away, he looked at me. Feeling his gaze on me, I pulled him closer and smiled.

"Before God put Adam's children on the earth, He did something very important." I looked at him then, and he blinked, waiting. "You know what it was?"

He shook his head.

"He asked all of us if we would testify that He alone is our Lord."

"How many children did Adam have?"

I shook my head, still smiling. "I don't know. But every person is from Adam, so we were all there when this happened, even me and you, and Mom and Dad. You heard of Adam and Eve, right?"

"Yes."

"They're everyone's parents. Even yours and mine. But this was way before Mom and Dad were born."

"I know. I read about that."

"Adam and Eve, you mean?"

"Yes."

"Well, good, because that makes the story easier to tell." I took a deep breath before continuing, surprised by the slight pounding in my chest.

"So," I said, "everybody said, 'Yes, we testify that You are our Lord.' And then God told them why He asked them to do this." I paused. "You know why He made them testify?"

"No, why?"

"He told everyone to do this so they'll have no excuse on the Day of Judgment if they blame their parents for worshipping something other than Him."

"But I don't remember that."

"I know. I don't either."

He looked confused.

"Nobody remembers, Elijah. Not in our minds. But in our hearts," I reached over and touched his chest, "that's where you hold the memory."

"How?"

"Well, in everyone's heart is the truth. God created us like that. This is so that we don't have to guess which religion is right. We know when we learn about it."

His eyes were intent as he studied me, listening.

"So, I'm going to tell you something very important." I met his gaze, an intent expression on my face. "But it's something you can't talk about until you're big enough to go to college. Can you wait that long?"

He shrugged. "Okay."

I paused, gathering my words. "You were right, Elijah."

"About what?"

"Being Muslim. You are Muslim."

He grinned hesitantly. "I am?"

"Yes, you are. Because you still believe in God like you're supposed to."

"I don't want to get in trouble though."

"Don't worry about that. Just pray to God to help you learn more about being Muslim, and don't say anything to anyone until you're bigger, and God will take care of you."

"Can you teach me about being Muslim?"

I hesitated, but nodded seconds later. "Yes, but only if no one knows."

"I want to learn how to pray that special prayer you do."

"Okay, but you remember what I said?"

"I won't say anything."

"Except to God."

He nodded, grinning widely now. "Except to God."

Before I returned to Maryland, I gave Elijah a small book on Islam and told him to keep it in a safe place. It was a pretty basic book, about the oneness of God, the five pillars, and the importance of prayer. I had no idea if I was digging my grave in the family or merely being an instrument of guidance to my brother who was Muslim at heart. Either way, my heart was at ease. I did the right thing, that I was sure about.

Fifteen

Standing at an oceanfront at sunrise can be a powerfully moving experience, as one is left in awe at the magnificent beauty of the sun stretching out over the horizon and announcing its presence to the world. The gentle ripples of the ocean glow and twinkle, moistened stars moving calmly upon the water.

At such a moment, one may marvel at what great power sustains a creation as magnificent as the sun. One may ponder what great force sets it in motion each day, a force causing it to rise and set on an infallible course, never falling short of its schedule.

A spiritual person credits this phenomenon to a Creator, feeling at that moment a closeness that reminds her that she is not alone in this world. Others may credit Mother Nature or science. Regardless of one's explanation, no eyes can behold such splendor and truthfully believe it all occurred by chance, that there is no power setting it in motion and sustaining it each day.

For a Muslim, the majestic exhibition at sunrise evokes more than speculation as to the power behind its brilliance. The display is, undoubtedly, a sign from the Creator, a reminder of Allah's eternal presence—and the reminder that she has a duty to Him.

She, at that moment, will know with certainty that life is not without purpose, and that her time is measured on the earth. Regret or sadness may well within because she recalls Allah's countless mercies and blessings, and that she ever falls short in showing gratefulness to Him.

She may even feel fear, as the sight may have triggered thoughts of life beyond. Life in the grave, standing before Allah on the Day of Judgment, and one's ultimate abode in Paradise...or Hell.

If she was afflicted with depression—that immense weight of shouldering life's burdens—she may begin to feel a tinge of hope, or even joy. A smile may crease the sides of her mouth, because the magnificence reminds her that Allah is always near, as is His help. It is not unlikely that she will weep as the sun makes its way overhead. Her tears may be of joy or of sadness, or both.

The reason for such a poignant reaction to this simple solar movement rests in her knowledge of her Creator, of His attributes, of His sole right to worship, of His being far above having a son or daughter attributed to His Glory. The poignancy rests also in the camaraderie she feels in embracing the religion of Adam, Abraham, Jesus, and Muhammad, a faith untainted by falsehood or the finite constraints of the human mind.

The core of this knowledge of God, this firm belief, is formed by a unique concept that is the foundation of a religion whose concept of the Creator goes beyond the realms of mere emotion or spiritual experience.
It is one that is, above all, rooted in Truth.

The year 1996 will always hold a special place in my memory. It is, for me, the year of enlightenment. It is the year that the light of Islam illuminated my heart, broadened my mind, and guided me on a path that would remain my fortitude in life, even in times of difficulty. It is also the year that I first understood truly the meaning of my *shahaadah*. What I learned that year has become so much a part of me that the knowledge permeates my very being and directs my words and actions. Yet, it is life experience—my triumphs and errors, the suffering of bumps and bruises, and the simmering of my youthful zeal—that would transform my spiritual knowledge into the light of wisdom.

The year began routinely, with my returning to the University of Maryland in the middle of January to complete the second semester of my third year. I was a math major, but my love for algebra and trigonometry and statistics and calculus settled in a place at the far back of my mind as I moved on to embrace more completely my new faith.

I was still sore over what had happened on vacation, but it didn't abate my inspiration to delve deeply into the world of Islam. I was hungry for Muslim companionship and wanted badly to be in the company of Sumayyah and Hadiyah. It felt like years since I'd last seen them.

Because the term had just begun, I withheld calling Nasrin. Less than a week into the new term Felicia and Anita became cruelly unbearable again. But now I was less intimidated than I was irritated in their presence. Perhaps it was because I now had a choice to sleep elsewhere, or perhaps it was simply because I began to see them for what they were—heartless and immature. Till today, I cannot understand how a person's religious choice can spark so much animosity in the hearts of others. Or perhaps, the sight of someone openly choosing a different faith doesn't inspire animosity at all but instead incites a deep, painful reminder of one's own shortcomings. I imagine that, left alone, this insecurity can lead to a host of unpleasant eruptions in the heart.

This, I can relate to.

There was a time, after the youthful euphoria had tempered, that I became so spiritually discontented that I no longer recognized myself, let alone the turmoil of my heart.

But that wasn't so in 1996. That year, I hadn't yet learned the authenticity of internal struggle or its intricacy. I was on a high, and my inevitable dips in faith were diminutive. My spiritual lows amounted to, at worst, my lessening the amount of voluntary prayers I performed in a day. I didn't imagine it could, or would, get worse than that.

My year of enlightenment began with my experiencing Ramadan for the first time. The month of fasting began on the twenty-second of January—although I didn't discover this until the twenty-fifth.

I was in the suite furiously throwing my important belongings into a black garbage bag, mumbling under my breath with each motion. I was so aggravated that I didn't even think about the suitcase that I had tucked away in my closet. I had decided minutes earlier that I couldn't stand Felicia or Anita any longer. I didn't even call Nasrin. I was going to simply show up at her door. If I had tears in my eyes when I knocked, so be it. Maybe then she'd have sympathy on me and forgive the sudden intrusion.

The phone rang, the sound making my heart leap. My eyes immediately shot in the direction of the door—an irrational reaction, but that's how on edge I was at the moment. My roommates' treatment was becoming more and more condescending, and we hadn't even been back to school a good two weeks.

The phone rang again. This time I let out a sigh, my left hand over my heart as I rolled my eyes to the ceiling in relief that it wasn't my former friends returning.

On the third ring, I walked over and lifted the receiver from its cradle.

"Hello?" I could hear the edginess in my voice, expecting the call to be for Felicia or Anita.

"As-salaamu'alaikum."

I was so unaccustomed to hearing the Islamic greeting of peace, especially on the telephone, that it took me a moment to realize that I understood the foreign phrase.

I replied, my broken Arabic pathetic even to my novice ears.

"This is Nasrin. How was your vacation?"

Her voice was chipper, a sharp contrast to the atmosphere of my room right then. I was delighted to hear a familiar voice, especially a Muslim one. I often think back to how, at that moment, I felt an instant connection with Nasrin, despite having met her only once. Inside, the stress that was constricting my chest eased, and my heart opened. I forgot my troubles and felt a grin spread on my face.

I exhaled audibly and shook my head, still grinning. "Don't ask."

I heard her chuckle. "Okay, never mind."

"Thanks."

"No problem." There was a brief pause.

"How's everything?"

"Could be better," I said. "How are you and Joni getting along these days?"

At that, she laughed. "Oh, you know, inseparable. Like always."

"She's back for good?"

"Hmm. Don't think so. You know, absence makes the heart grow fonder."

"Yes, of course." I twisted the black plastic in my fist as nervousness overtook me. "You up to knowing the opposite of that?"

"Of what?"

"Absence."

When she didn't catch on, I said, "Right before you called, I was just thinking how you were growing too fond of me."

"Really?" Her high pitch told me she understood the joke. "Great. I was beginning to like you a lot. It was making me uncomfortable."

We laughed.

"So you really don't mind?" My voice was serious now, on the verge of a plea.

"Of course not. I already told you that. When will you come?"

I hesitated. "Now?"

She laughed again. "No problem. That works out better anyway."

"Better than what?"

"Me coming to you."

"You were thinking of coming *here*?"

"I meant to pick you up, not live." There was amusement in her voice.

"Oh." I didn't know what she meant by picking me up but I didn't want her to know that, sensing this was something I was supposed to already know.

An awkward silence followed.

"Don't you want to know why I was coming to pick you up?"

I coughed in embarrassment, but I was still smiling. "Oh yeah. Sure."

"There's an *iftaar* tomorrow night. I can't stay long though. But Sumayyah said it's no problem for her to take you home."

I creased my forehead and adjusted the phone at my ear. "There's a what tomorrow?"

"An *iftaar*, you know? That's what we call it when we break our fast."

"Your fast?"

For a few seconds Nasrin said nothing. When she spoke again, she sounded concerned. "You know Ramadan started Monday, right?"

For a moment I didn't understand the question. Then, vaguely, I recalled reading about Ramadan, the month of fasting. "Ramadan started on Monday?" It was Thursday.

"Nobody told you?"

I felt my head begin to ache. "No, I... This is the first time I heard about it."

"Are you serious?" Nasrin sounded upset, but it was clear that she wasn't blaming me. "I'm so sorry, Renee. *Astaghfirullaah.* I just assumed... I mean, we should've known..."

Feeling guilty that she was beating herself up about this, I said, "Don't worry. I should've called you when I first got back."

"No, it's my fault. I'm the one who should've called. But..." She drew in a deep breath. "Well... what's important is that you know now."

"Yes, true."

"When you get here, I'll make sure you have *suhoor* and *iftaar* everyday *inshaAllaah.* That way at least you don't have to go emergency shopping for your meals."

Minutes before sunset on Friday evening, Nasrin and I pulled in front of a large brick home. I was slightly self-conscious as the car slowed, aware of the *khimaar* that I wore in place of my favored African wrap. The fabric was soft against the sides of my face and beneath my chin, where it was pinned with a small silver brooch. Nasrin had helped me arrange the white fabric about my head so that the cloth fell over my shoulders and my neck was concealed. She had told me briefly about the *hijaab* and its conditions, and I felt embarrassed as I recalled reading about *hijaab* in a book. I don't know why it never occurred to me that my wrap was not consistent with the Islamic injunction to display, at most, "face and hands" in front of unrelated males. Later, when I read the Qur'anic verses on *hijaab*, I realized my mistake immediately. I hadn't used the head cover itself to cover my neck and chest.

I self-consciously ran a hand over the cloth on my head as my attention was drawn to the massive house, a feeling of awe overtaking me as I gazed at it through the passenger side window. A circular window glowed above the double doors of the home, displaying a massive chandelier sparkling and winking in illumination. Four white pillars stood proudly from the roof to the ground, guarding the expansive front porch.

Next to me, Nasrin was nonchalant as she slowly guided the car into a space along the dark winding driveway aligned with small heaps of snow. Three cars—a Lexus, BMW, and Mercedes—were already parked along the curved drive that was shaped like a *U*, facilitating passage to and from the home. We got out of the Camry and walked together up the cement path leading to the front door.

"The sister hosting the *iftaar* is Sister Desta," Nasrin told me, her breath white clouds that appeared gray next to the white *khimaar* she wore on her head. "But most people call her Umm Muhammad because her oldest son is Muhammad."

"She lives here?"

"Yes. Her son and daughter live here too with their families."

Nasrin pressed the doorbell with a gloved finger, setting off the sound of a tune playing behind the door. Pushing my hands deep into my pockets, I turned to admire the other homes, some of which still bore elaborate decorations for Christmas.

"She said her niece goes to Maryland."

"Really?" My voice was of feigned interest. The cold was beginning to cut through my coat and I wanted to go inside.

"But I'm not sure if she's practicing."

"They converted?"

"No, their family's Muslim, like mine. They're from—"

The door opened. "*As-salaamu'alaikum.*" A woman with a broad smile greeted us, stepping aside as we entered, the warmth of the house drifting toward us in that motion. I relaxed, relieved to be out of the cold.

The woman wore a large gray *khimaar* that hung to her knees, revealing only the cinnamon brown of her face. I'd never seen a garment like it. It appeared as though she was wearing two gray skirts, one on her head and the other at her waist. It was beautiful.

The soft fabric gathered at the wrist of her henna-dyed hands, revealing gold bangles as she extended her palm to greet me and Nasrin before pulling each of us into a hug. She smelled faintly of food, the same rich aroma that filled the foyer, tickling our nostrils and reminding us of how hungry we were.

She took our coats and gestured for us to put our shoes in the room to our right. We stepped inside the room, removing our shoes before placing them on a small shelf reserved for that purpose.

"Renee, this is Fana, Sister Desta's daughter," Nasrin said when we returned to the foyer, gesturing toward the sister who greeted us. "And Fana, this is Renee. She took her *shahaadah* a few months ago." Nasrin broke into a grin, her face glowing with pride as she turned to me.

Fana's eyes widened and brightened, and she embraced me again. "*Mabrook!*"

"Actually," I said as she released me, "it's been like a year now."

"She goes to Maryland," Nasrin chimed.

"Really?" Fana was so excited that it was contagious. I couldn't keep from grinning. I was unaccustomed to people being intrigued by me. "My cousin goes there too."

I nodded, remembering Nasrin telling me that. "Yes, I know."

"You know her?" Her eyes sparkled in anticipation of having something in common.

"What's her name?"

"Abrinet." I'm not sure if this is the name Fana said. The pronunciation was so awkward to my ears that I can't be certain that I'm remembering it correctly, or putting the right vowels and consonants in order. This would remain a struggle for me for the next couple of years, my ears and mind adjusting to learning so many foreign names at once. After becoming Muslim, I was thrust into a world of true multiculturalism after living in Black and White all my life. It wasn't easy. Despite my good memory, recalling names and saying them properly were true challenges for me.

I shook my head, my eyes squinted, a smile still on my face. "I don't think so. Nasrin and Sumayyah are the only Muslims I know there."

Fana looked as if she were about to say something but withheld.

"She's here," Fana said, tugging my hand. "Let me introduce you."

She led me to an expansive living room, where she directed me and Nasrin to sit, the smell of exotic food burning my nostrils as my stomach growled. Fana disappeared down a hall, and Nasrin, who sat beside me, glanced at her watch.

"I think it's time," she whispered.

"I hope so."

A minute later, Fana emerged from the hall carrying a tray, behind her a young woman who wore a wide light blue traditional dress of some sort. The woman's hair was uncovered, synthetic braids spilling over a shoulder and behind her neck. Red lipstick glowed from her lips that bore a wide cordial smile, but the dark makeup around her eyes did not hide her displeasure with her cousin having dragged her out to greet us. Nevertheless, her hand was extended as she approached where Nasrin and I sat, Fana's cheerful voice explaining that Nasrin brought a new Muslim with her who went to Maryland. Nasrin and I stood to greet her, polite smiles on our faces.

Abrinet stood before us, and my eyes met hers, recognition coming to me slowly, mostly because the face was completely out of context. Abrinet's face fell, her hand dropping just as I extended mine. A scowl replaced her smile and her nose flared. Abruptly, she rolled her eyes, turned her back on us and walked out, angry footfalls heavy on the steps as she retreated.

Dumbfounded, I stood with my hand still extended, my smile fading as I realized what had just happened—and who she was. My face grew hot and I felt the beginning of a headache. The realization came to me in blurred pieces, fogging my perception. It took, perhaps, a full minute for it all to make sense to me.

I remember Fana's mouth falling open in shock and her eyes widening in disbelief. A second later, her eyes narrowed in anger, a tray of dates still in her hands.

"It's time," I remember Nasrin saying softly, reaching for two dates and handing one to me. Mechanically, I took the strange fruit, my eyes burning behind my lids, my mind elsewhere.

Fana set the tray on a table in front of us, saying quickly, "The sisters are eating downstairs" before she disappeared up the stairs.

The doorbell rang, and I saw Nasrin hasten to get it, aware that Fana would not be able to. The door opened and the sounds of cheerful greetings filled the house. My chest tightened as I recalled the painful encounter.

Felicia was the last person I expected to see there that night.

I didn't go downstairs to join the other sisters, not for another hour. I was too shaken. Instead, Fana returned minutes later apologizing profusely and guiding me out of the living room—out of view of other guests. Her hand was gently on my back as she ushered me into a room down the hall where she and her cousin had entered minutes before.

Nasrin had grown quiet and hung back, unsure what to do. She had no idea what was going on. She had never met my roommates, so it wasn't possible for her to make sense of anything.

In the room, I sat on a soft bed, the date still in my hand.

"Eat," Fana said, seating herself cross-legged on the floor in front of me. "You have to break your fast."

I brought the date to my mouth and took a small bite, the soft brown fruit delicious on my tongue. I had never tasted a date before, but I couldn't savor the moment. The thought of Felicia made my stomach churn.

"I'm sorry," Fana said again. "I had no idea you knew each other."

The sound of her voice brought me back and I forced a smile. "Me either."

Fana bit her lower lip and glanced around the room for a second. "Let me bring you a plate." She stood, and a second later, she was gone.

I exhaled, the reality of what had happened coming to me suddenly. I felt myself growing infuriated with Felicia, but I thought of Ramadan, knowing I'd have to temper my emotions for the time being.

Fana entered the room with a large plate. I was amazed that she could carry it. The sight of it reminded me that I hadn't eaten for the entire day. I had just completed my first day of Ramadan. This thought soothed me. I could hardly believe it. I don't know how I would've survived my first day without someone like Nasrin. She had kept me busy, reading from Qur'an then reading the English, then bringing up various Islamic topics, even going over my Arabic pronunciation of the prayer.

Steam rose from reddish soup that filled a large bowl, small chunks of meat or chicken thickening the soup. Beside the bowl was a stack of thin spongy bread folded at one side. Brown rice, at least it looked like rice to me, was on the other side of the bowl. Fana placed this on the floor of the room then disappeared again. She returned with a tray of salad and a white mat tucked under an arm.

She spread out the plastic-coated floral mat then placed the food on it. She closed the door and tugged at her *khimaar*, removing it from her head in one motion. A small gray triangular scarf was still on her head, revealing thick curly hair pulled back by an elastic band. She pushed up the sleeves of her fitting white shirt and waved me to the floor, a broad smile on her face.

"Eat. We'll pray in a few minutes, *inshaAllaah.*"

Because I didn't want to soil it, I too removed my head cover and pushed up the sleeves of my blouse before seating myself across from her on the floor.

Using the spongy bread instead of silverware, we ate until she asked me if I'd had enough, the tasty food still on my tongue. I nodded, not wanting to appear greedy although I wanted more. I didn't know that she was asking if I had had enough to satisfy me for prayer, so after she led me in *Maghrib*, I was pleasantly surprised when she sat back down and removed her *khimaar* in preparation to continue our meal. I followed suit.

"I'm sorry about Abrinet," she said after licking her fingers.

I shrugged, disappointed at the reminder. "It's okay. I just..."

"No, don't apologize. It's her. We don't know what to do with her."

I dropped my gaze to the plate and continued eating although my curiosity was peaked. "I didn't know her name was Abr..."

"Abrinet."

"She said her name was Felicia." But I recalled seeing the name on her mail.

Fana shrugged. "I'm not surprised. Ever since high school, she hasn't been the same." She sighed.

"She didn't want to wear *hijaab*. Her parents fought with her about it, but she still refused to wear it." She shook her head. "She has four sisters, and she's the only one who doesn't wear *hijaab*."

There was a long pause as we ate in silence.

"She told me she used to be Muslim."

"Used to be?" Fana's hand halted inches from her mouth, taken aback by what I'd said.

My forehead creased. "Oh, I thought that's what you were saying..."

"No. I never heard this before."

I began to doubt myself then, my brows gathering as I tried to remember her exact words. Perhaps I had heard her wrong. "Maybe I misunderstood..."

"What did she say to you?"

Eyes squinted, I shook my head, unable to recall. For some reason, even as my memory failed me, I felt guilty, as if I was betraying her through the mere effort of recollection. Part of me hoped I wouldn't be able to remember.

Keep your misery to yourself. I grew up with that bull crap. I don't want it near me ever again.

The words returned to me so suddenly that I stiffened at the painful reminder. Had she really referred to Islam as "misery" and "crap"? I didn't want to repeat it.

"What?" Fana's expression was tight with concern.

"Renee, tell me. It's for her own good that we know."

I was reluctant at first but eventually my mouth formed the words.

Fana's eyes narrowed in disbelief. *"What?"*

I didn't know what to say.

"Why would she say something like that? What happened?"

Hell. She also called Allah's religion hell. I shuddered as I recalled this being her answer to Anita's asking what a Muslim was.

I told this to Fana, strangely enjoying the power I had over Felicia at that moment.

Felicia's cousin shook her head in dismay, wounded. Her face contorted, unable to fully digest my words, and I thought I saw her eyes glisten in sadness.

"Are you sure?"

"Yes," I said. "But maybe she didn't mean it."

"She said *hell*, that being Muslim is *hell*?"

For some reason, I felt a sudden urge to come to my roommate's defense. I feared I had exaggerated her errors by sharing only two exchanges. Maybe I wasn't being fair.

"I think she was trying to be funny."

Her eyes glistened more, a hurt expression on her face. "But that's not something to joke about."

"I know. It's just that I think..." I didn't know what to say. I couldn't conjure a single positive image of Felicia, not in the spiritual sense anyway. My heart ached as I saw the pain in Fana's eyes.

"Her mother would die if she knew this."

"I'm sorry. I thought you knew."

"We knew she didn't like *hijaab*, but..." Her eyes grew distant and she drew in a deep breath and exhaled, trying to recover from the weight of my words.

"Maybe she never got over that boy," she said with a shake of her head. "He was—" She stopped, realizing she was sharing too much. "Never mind."

We finished eating in silence, my mind wandering to the boy Fana had alluded to.

When it was clear I couldn't eat anymore, Fana pulled the *khimaar* back over her head and lifted the large plate, setting the salad tray on top. She set it on the floor as she opened the door then carried it out of the room.

She returned and folded the mat to keep the fallen food from dropping to the floor.

"Let's go downstairs," she said with a smile, clearly wanting to make up for our somber discussion. "I don't want to keep you from mingling with everyone. I think they have all the drinks down there anyway."

I stood, preparing to follow her to the door. But she waited, looking at me.

"Put your *hijaab* on," she said. "We have to pass the brothers."

After I covered my hair, we made our way down the hall. She deposited the mat in the kitchen before turning to walk toward where Nasrin and I had been sitting earlier. As we approached the living room, the noise level rose so high that I was surprised that we hadn't heard the men talking and laughing while we were in the room.

The sound of people passing distracted some of them, but only momentarily. After they saw us, they turned their attention back to their friends and lowered their voices slightly to continue their banter. The room was packed with dozens of men, several on the couches along the wall, others on the floor, plates of food before them. I had never seen so many people in one room.

In front of me, Fana's head was down, and she was moving quickly. I quickened my steps too, but I slowed them when my eyes met those of a young man who was laughing with a brother whose back was to me. It was Yusuf.

Instinctively, I smiled in recognition and waved. It was my second mistake of this fashion, and I realized it only when his expression changed to embarrassed cordiality and he responded with the faintest motion of his hand. Fortunately, everyone else was too engrossed in their own conversations to notice my error. But the brother across from him turned to see what had distracted his friend.

I had started to move along, but I did a double take as my gaze met that of Yusuf's friend. I recognized the blue eyes and dark beard immediately.

William.

I quickly lowered my gaze, not wanting to embarrass him too, but in my peripheral vision, I saw that he was still turned, his eyes following me, a shocked expression on his face.

"This way," Fana whispered, gesturing me in the direction of a door around a small corner on the far side of the living room.

It wasn't until I was halfway down the carpeted steps that William's reaction made sense to me.

Until that moment, he had no idea that I had accepted Islam.

Despite my unfortunate run-in with Felicia, I managed to enjoy myself for the remainder of the evening. I met several sisters I hadn't met before, and I was even able to spend time with Sumayyah and Hadiyah. They both were there.

I was surprised that Nicole had come with Hadiyah, but I could tell she hadn't come voluntarily. She sat in a corner near her mother, but she interacted with no one.

Shortly before it was time to go, I decided to say hello, so I moved to the space next to her, although I was already in earshot from where I sat across from Hadiyah. But I sensed that Nicole wouldn't feel comfortable including too many people in a conversation, so I decided to go to her.

We exchanged small talk, and I noticed Hadiyah glancing in our direction often. But I could tell she was pleased I had taken the time to sit with her daughter.

"How was it for you when your family converted to Islam?" I asked.

"Okay, I guess."

"Was it hard for you?"

Nicole shrugged. "They can do what they want. It doesn't matter to me." It was clear from her tone that she wasn't being honest with herself.

"Nikki is not taking our lifestyle change too well," Hadiyah said, moving over and turning herself to us.

"Oh," I said, though this wasn't news at all. I had suspected as much. "Your whole family didn't convert?"

"Everyone except Nikki." Hadiyah reached out and pinched her daughter's cheek playfully. "She's always been the stubborn one."

Nicole brushed her mother's hand away, but a slight grin creased a corner of her mouth. "I'm not stubborn."

"You are. I've known you since the day you were born."

"Still, I'm not stubborn."

"See? You just proved my point." Hadiyah laughed at her own words, and her daughter fought the urge to respond in kind. A second later, Nicole's expression conveyed frustration.

"For twenty years, I did everything you said, and you call me stubborn? Even now, I'm still doing what you taught me. You're the one who changed."

"Yes, you're right." Hadiyah was still smiling as she spoke.

"Why didn't you convert?" It was my question.

Nikki shrugged. "Ask my mom. She loves to talk about it."

"No, I mean seriously," I said. "You don't believe Islam is true?"

"I don't know what I think about the religion."

"You believe in the Trinity?"

She rolled her eyes. "I've already been through this a zillion times with Mom and Dad."

"But I'm curious. A lot of Christians don't really believe in it. They just accept it on faith."

"Well, I don't accept things on faith. I follow clear evidence."

"So, you're no religion now?"

"I'm Christian."

My forehead creased in interest. "But the evidence says that a true Christian is Muslim."

She raised an eyebrow as she met my eyes with a sneer. "I don't think so."

"You ever heard of the Nicene Council?"

"Yes." Her voice was flat with boredom. "I know all about the meeting."

My eyes widened. "What about Paul and how—"

"He never met Jesus," she droned, rolling her eyes as she recited the information monotone, "and was the first to teach about the Trinity, blah blah blah."

I was stunned. "And you still believe the Bible is God's Word?"

"Yes."

I didn't know what to say.

"Like I said," Hadiyah interjected. She pursed her lips and looked at her daughter, defeated from years of exhausted efforts. "Stubborn."

Sixteen

Nasrin proved to be a tremendous blessing for me that Ramadan, and year. Selflessly she drove me from lecture to lecture, class to class, and even sacrificed sleep to answer my questions about Islam. Hadiyah too was a blessing, a phone call or car ride away. And I cannot forget Sumayyah, for whom I am most grateful to Allah for choosing to help guide me to Islam.

In those names alone lie so many blessings that I am at a loss when enumerating them, let alone in counting the blessings in the dozens of Muslims I met thereafter.

Amidst my enlightenment and spiritual high, my regrets of 1996 are only three. In not seeing then what I see now in the value of a university degree in this world, in not realizing the value of family in my life and Islam, and most painfully, not holding onto the simple lesson of life and faith so eloquently conveyed to me in Hadiyah's words a year before.

The religion is easy. In sticking firmly to the Qur'an and Sunnah is where you'll find your strength, and peace. Do not let the unrest and unhappiness of others distract you from this simple truth.

SubhaanAllaah. If only I knew the weighty value, and relevance, of those words before I tread a path in stark contrast to the immense Islamic faith and wisdom conveyed in them.

In retrospect, I do not know from whence my confusion was born. Before I cultivated a relationship with anyone who would be my rope to transgression, I knew already simple Islamic truths.

I knew that Allah alone is my Lord.

I knew that He is the only One I should call on in prayer.

I knew, already, that no creation, no imam, no sheikh, no pious person on this earth, or in the grave, can hear my supplications, let alone respond to them, and that, even if they could hear them, they would be as effective in answering my prayer as they had been in disrupting their appointment with the Angel of Death.

I knew, already, that He is above the Heavens on His Throne in a manner befitting His Majesty and Glory.

I knew that He, in His infinite knowledge, is closer to me than my jugular vein, even as He is above the seven heavens that He constructed as a canopy in the sky.

I knew, already, of His Qadr, His Divine Decree, recorded in the Preserved Tablet.

I knew too that Allah's first creation was the Pen. And that His first command was, *Write.* And that the Pen, in obedience to its Creator, wrote everything that was to happen until the Day of Judgment.

I knew, already, that His Qur'an, His Speech, is not created.

I knew, already, that the true Religion is one. And that Islam is the only path to Paradise.

I knew too that Allah's last revelation was two, both the Book—the Qur'an—and the Wisdom—the Sunnah.

I knew, already, that in the Qur'an and Sunnah lay the only path to true Islam and that those who lived and understood it best were Allah's Messenger and his companions, and the students of his companions, and the students of the students of his companions. And that, even as Prophet Jesus returned before the Day of Judgment and lived a life in testimony to the guidance of his brother Prophet Muhammad, the religion of Allah would remain unaltered and that the scholars of Islam, the inheritors of the Prophets, were only those whose knowledge moved them to live more firmly in testimony to this.

Fortunately, it would be months before I would be diverted away from even simpler truths than these, a diversion called to by those who came under the guise of calling me to the truths in which I already believed.

My year was fulfilling and blessed before that, by the mercy of Allah, and it is these earlier memories of that year that make 1996 the year of spiritual growth and guidance for me, and the year that would always hold a special place in my heart.

It too was the year that the idea of marriage was introduced to me, an idea that had not even crossed my mind. Today, I cannot decide whether or not this is a regret because I know now the tremendous blessings marriage can bring. Yet, I still do not see why it couldn't have waited another year, at least until I finished school. I am still trying to come to terms with the urgency with which my Muslim sisters exhorted me to marry, even as there was no candidate in my heart or mind. And I too am trying to come to terms with my naiveté in listening to those who made me believe that there was somehow a contradiction between my newfound faith and my desire for a university degree in math.

It is true that I was more enamored with Islam than school, but by no means would I have given up my matriculation had I known more about the value that degree would be for me in life, and in Islam.

In later years, when my desire to settle in a Muslim land took root in my heart, I shuddered to think what I would have done had I not had the sense and wherewithal to go back and complete my degree even as I was years late. I cannot count how many Muslims I know who had the same desire to live in a land of Islam, only to return back to the very land they left, all this to obtain the piece of paper that would grant them passage into the place they felt they belonged.

So while I am in doubt as to whether or not my marriage so soon is a cause for regret, I am in no doubt as to my regret that I allowed this tremendous blessing, along with the even greater blessing of my firm belief in Islam, to disrupt my obtaining my degree in 1997, when neither of these blessings was mutually exclusive to the degree in math that I had for so long desired to earn.

"Girl, you crazy, you better get married."

These words came from Ghazwa, the feisty sister I'd met at Wadiah's when I was getting my hair done the year before. It was now a Saturday in mid-March, less than a month after Ramadan had ended, and I was at a gathering Ghazwa had invited me to. I was sitting on the floor holding my paper plate of half-eaten fried chicken, potato salad, and collard greens, a plastic fork in my right hand. The two couches in the apartment living room were filled with sisters chatting and laughing amongst themselves.

I rolled my eyes and grinned, responding a second before I lifted a forkful of salad to my mouth. "Whatever."

"I ain't playing. I 'on't know what you waiting for."

"Maybe the right person?" Wadiah teased, nudging her friend.

Ghazwa sucked her teeth. "What she need the right person for if she ain't trying to get married?"

At that moment, Ghazwa reminded me of Patricia, but even today I don't understand why. Aside from their pale skin they had nothing in common, in personality or appearance. Patricia's complexion was unblemished, while Ghazwa's was disrupted by mild acne sprinkling her cheeks and forehead. Patricia's hair was black, while Ghazwa's held a tint of brown. Patricia's lips were thin and Ghazwa's attractively full, and Patricia was of average height, around five-six while Ghazwa towered near six feet.

Although Patricia definitely had her moments of being strong-minded and stubborn, even her worst moments couldn't compare to the boisterous vibe Ghazwa sent off when she as much as walked into the room. It was as if every word Ghazwa spoke was emphatic, and there was no middle ground. If I didn't know her, I'd think she was in a heated altercation with whomever she happened to be talking to.

I was never comfortable around Ghazwa, but I never told her this. Given that she made me a bit nervous at times, my discomfort only made sense. I didn't speak my mind around her. She didn't really give me chance to in any case. I was known as quiet at school, but the people who knew me well knew that I didn't fare too well with keeping my opinions to myself, let alone in exercising humility in sharing them. But I wasn't myself around Ghazwa.

Perhaps it was that we came from completely different worlds, I from a middleclass college degreed family while she was a daughter of "the hood" as she called it. But I know even this distinction is being overly simplistic, if not unjust, because in the months and years that followed I would meet others with the same background as Ghazwa and have no difficulty in relaxing completely around them and even sharing a love for academics and strong family background.

Oddly, despite my discomfort, I loved hearing Ghazwa talk, being near her in a gathering, and most importantly I loved being in her good graces. Her stories were intriguing and humorous, sending me into fits of laughter or pensive silence depending on what she had shared. More than anything, it gave me a sense of calm knowing she counted me as a friend, even if I could never open up to her enough to feel the same.

"You know what I heard?"

I lifted my gaze to see a sister smirking and leaning herself forward from where she sat on the opposite side of the room. She met Ghazwa's eyes and glanced at me as if she and I were sharing a private joke.

"What?" Ghazwa asked, raising her voice, inviting the rest of the room to stop mid-sentence to hear what the sister was about to say.

"There's this White boy she's talking to for marriage." The sister's smirk spread on her face as she met my eyes that were now widened in disbelief. "That's why she ain't saying nothing to you."

Like a scene from high school, the room was filled with taunting *ooh*s as if her comment was somehow "fighting words."

Ghazwa exploded in laughter. "Girl," she said to the one who had spoken. "You smoking something. Renee ain't talking to no White boy. Wadiah getting her hooked up with her cousin."

I was too confused to be mortified, so I looked at Wadiah, a question mark on my face. Wadiah shrugged and shook her head, as if saying, *Girl, don't ask me. You know better than to pay attention to anything Ghazwa says.*

"Where'd you get that from?" I said to the sister who spoke the rumor, aware that my voice was a cross between playing along and taking offense.

"Don't worry," she teased, looking at me over the glasses she was wearing. "I got my ways."

There was more laughter.

I didn't even know who she was.

"Don't pay no attention to Lisan," someone said in a tone that was obviously meant more as a friendly tease to the sister than any consolation to me. "She always talking about something she heard. That's how she got her name."

"Forget you, Arwa. Ain't nobody talking to you."

"Don't be trying to make yourself look good. We all know the truth."

"You know that's right," someone else said.

"Renee," Lisan said as if we were lifelong friends, "don't let these sisters get to you. The truth is they jealous 'cause they don't got no man."

There was another round of *ooh*s in the room. That was when I lost track of who was saying what. I resigned myself to finishing my food and counting down to when Wadiah, my ride, was leaving so I could leave too.

"Oh, no you didn't."

"I got a man!"

"He don't count."

Ooh.

"If she want to marry a White boy, what's it to you?"

"I ain't say nothing was wrong with it."

"Then why you acting like something wrong?"

"Who's acting like something's wrong except you?"

"I'm just happy she getting married."

"Girl, no you ain't."

"Who said she's getting married?"

"Wadiah's cousin is good for her, I think."

"How you know what's good for her? Worry about yourself!"

Ooh.

"I know you didn't just say that."

"Yes I did."

Laughter.

"You know what I think? What she need to do is..."

Needless to say, in the car later that night, I asked Wadiah if she had any extra-strength Tylenol in her purse.

She handed her handbag to me and told me I could find a small bottle in the right hand pocket. I found it and retrieved two pills, not bothering to worry about washing them down with water. Besides, there wasn't any in the car.

Wadiah drove in silence, occasional streetlights illuminating the walnut brown of her face in the dark. Her gaze was on the road beyond the windshield and mine on the night beyond my passenger side window. I listened to the soothing calm of the car's soft engine as we rode down the interstate leading to the exit for College Park, where we both lived. Tonight's conversation was bothering me, but only slightly, as my mind was on school and the fact that

William had indeed been calling me often. Once or twice he mentioned the future, but that's exactly how I thought of it—something too detached from the present to hold any real meaning in the now. As for me, I was just enjoying the conversations because it gave me the opportunity to relax and discuss Islam. It was relieving to have someone to relate to, especially someone from my hometown.

It would always remain a mystery to me how the sister Lisan heard anything of these conversations, let alone a rumor that we were planning to marry, something neither William nor I ever discussed. But this misunderstanding of our activities doesn't bother me as much as it astounds. Even today, I am amazed by the phenomenon of hearsay, and how humans so often place in it more value and faith than they do wisdom, experience, or truth.

Of all people in the world today, I think Muslims know this irony best—how their true beliefs or lifestyle is of no consequence next to that which is claimed of them through radio airways, newspaper print houses, and the infamous plug-in box that never has a dearth of talking heads to tell viewers what they should hold true in their minds and hearts.

But even the transgressions of those who rely on a colorful entertainment box more than they do their sense is not as phenomenal to me as the damaging powerful of hearsay amongst those who don't fall prey to talking heads and tantalizing headlines.

Had I not experienced for myself, had I not been poisoned myself, and had I not suffered myself, from a small but pernicious group of people who recited the same religious truths as those spoken from the lips of believers who actually held them to be true—in word and deed—instead of merely making the claim, I would have laughed in the face of anyone who claimed that such inanity existed at all amongst the best people on earth. Yet, I learned a painful lesson over the next few years—that the difference between a scholar and a worshipper is indeed vast, and that the difference between a label and its truism is even greater.

And that sometimes the most powerful aid you have in navigating darkness under the guise of light is that slight flutter within, that wavering in the heart, that acts as a pulsating warning to call you back to true righteousness. Back to Allah's Book and Wisdom.

I know now that it is this flutter that is sometimes the lone indicator in your heart that Allah wishes for you good.

PART III

~

Seventeen

Who is your Lord?
My Lord is Allah.
What is your religion?
My religion is Islam.
Who is your prophet?
My prophet is Muhammad ibn Abdullah
Sallallaahu'alayhi wasallam

You, O Allah, sent him with the Book,
The Light for mankind
You sent him with the Wisdom,
The Guide for mankind
And I, O Allah, have believed in him
Though I have not seen him
And I have believed in You
Though I have not seen You
And I have left my family, my home, and my former life
Coming to You with nothing
Except my faith in You alone,
And I have testified, my Lord!
That none has the right to be worshipped but You
And I have testified, my Lord!
That You have no son, no daughter,
no partner or intermediary
And I have believed in Your mercy
I have believed in Your generosity
I have believed in Jibreel, Mika'eel, and Israfeel
I have believed in Noah, in Abraham, in Moses,
Jesus and Muhammad
And I have believed in Your promise of forgiveness
For all those who bear witness to
Your sole right to worship
And those who die reciting this on their tongue

So, I ask You, O Allah,
Do not call me to account for my
shortcomings in praising You
For no amount of praise honors Your Glory in truth
And, I ask You, O Allah!
Do not call me to account for my
shortcomings in worshipping You
For no amount of worship is sufficient in
honoring Your Worth
And, O Allah, Hearer of Prayers,
Forgiver of all sins except shirk!
Do not call me to account for my
shortcomings in remembering You

For no amount of remembrance does
justice to You in truth,
For You are the All-Seeing, the All-Knowing, the Wise
Master of the Day of Judgment,
Preserver and Granter of wealth
And lives
You are the One who has sole power to decree
You set a matter in motion by simply saying, Be!
You send the angel of death to the young and the old
And you hold in Your power the affair
of every human soul
So, I ask You, O Allah!
For You are the only One with power to condemn or save
Write me down amongst those who answer with firmness
The questions in the Grave

One of the matters that kept me up many nights in my year of enlightenment was knowledge of life in the *Barzakh*—that barrier less penetrable than an iron curtain as wide as the heaven and earth. It is the *Barzakh*, the life in the grave, that separates the world of actions without knowledge from the world of knowledge without actions.

It is a dream I read about that so eloquently defined this separation of the two worlds. In the man's dream, he saw a relative who had recently died, so he asked her, "Tell me about your world." She said, "You have actions without knowledge, and we have knowledge without actions."

The profundity of this statement was so great that I was immobilized by my hope and fear. I thought of my predicament, knowing that I, like everyone possessing a soul would meet Munkar and Nakir, the two angels of the grave. They would ask me the three questions asked of every person who lived, from the time of Adam to the last of those to whom Prophet Muhammad was sent.

Those to whom Noah was sent must answer the third question, *My prophet is Noah.* And those to whom Moses was sent, *My prophet is Moses.* And those to whom Jesus was sent, *My prophet is Jesus.* And all of those who lived during and after Prophet Muhammad must answer, *My prophet is Muhammad.*

I reflected on this for hours, for days, and months, moved by how Allah sent His Messenger to inform us of the simplest of details—that of the angels sitting us up in the grave because we would be unable to move ourselves, and to inform of the greatest of matters—that of Allah, and that our sincerity of faith in Him alone and our righteous actions according to the Prophet's Sunnah are our only hope for salvation, and our only hope in responding to the questions—the three fundamentals of life itself.

I knew then with certainty, even as I had certainty of faith before, that Islam is the religion of truth and no other is a path to Allah's mercy. I was pained to think of anyone dying on a faith other than Islam. I was tormented in thinking of a person hearing the message of their prophet and rejecting him in favor of a religion of man. I cried imagining the mere possibility that anyone in my family would not be able to answer even one of the questions with firmness of heart.

My faith soared in the knowledge that a simple recitation on my tongue and complimentary actions of my limbs secured for me a place in Paradise if I died upon this. I imagined being under the Shade of Allah's Throne on the Day when there would be no shade but His. I imagined drinking from *Al-Hawd* when the sun is but a mile or two from the earth, and of never being thirsty again—even as the Day of Judgment stretched on for fifty thousand years. I imagined my deeds being weighed in the Scale, and my testimony of Allah's Oneness tipping it with the immensity of its weight. I imagined my book of deeds falling in my right hand and my pleasure overcoming me such that I couldn't contain myself. I would announce for every soul to look and see that the promise of my Lord is true. I thought too of those who denied this Day and would then say, *Woe, what book is this that leaves out nothing small or great, except that it has enumerated it here!* who when perceiving their imminent destruction would wish, more than anything, they could become the dust of the earth.

My thoughts inspired me to say, *SubhaanAllaahi wabihamdih* and *SubhaanAllahil-'Atheem* because these simple utterances of praise and glorification of the Creator are light on the tongue and heavy on the Scale.

These thoughts and hopes filled my days and nights and inspired me with the steadfastness to continue endless Islamic studies even as I came upon demanding mid-term and final exams. These worldly distractions I attended to only so I could move on to quench my thirst for knowledge of Islam—in preparation for the true Final Exam.

These are the days of which I carry not a single regret. Along with my *shahaadah* itself, by Allah's mercy, these would be my fortitude in holding onto what I knew to be true and would endow me with the determination to never let go.

Yet these are also the days that inspired me with such a high, such a desire to stay upon the Truth, such a determination to be in the mercy of Allah, that my fear of falling into falsehood clouded my more subtle sense in protecting myself from those whose call to Truth was more a word than a heartfelt reality that they committed themselves to living.

I was never a person of labels in lieu of the authentic purity of truth. My very upbringing forbade even Christian sectarianism in which Jesus' message was relegated to sects instead of what he actually called his followers to believe.

Yet, I was soon to learn that I was, more than anything, human, after all—and subject to error and utter stupidity like all other souls on the earth.

Eighteen

In my first testimony of humanness, I married William Garret in a small Indianapolis *masjid* on Thursday, August 15, 1996, just two weeks before either of us returned to school. Our only witnesses were a kindhearted imam William had met and two witnesses neither of us knew. Even as I share this, there are regrets that linger in my heart. The greatest of these is in not consulting my Lord before I took this step, and a distant second is in not consulting my family or friends. I am, after all, a woman, and what woman does not dream of her wedding day?

I was no different. I had imagined in childhood my elaborate dress, the floral arrangements on the tables and walls, the layered white cake, a romantic ornament atop, and of course next to me a man of my dreams with whom I was deeply in love and he with me. Naturally, he would have been on his knee when he asked to marry me, and when he slipped the diamond ring on my finger.

Although I know I would have adjusted the reality to more authentically reflect who I was at that time, I still wish I had not, at only a moment's consideration, given up that dream. I hadn't even dated a single man in my life, so for me, this moment was precious in a way I think only a pious person committed to chastity can understand.

Part of this arbitrary decision, I think in retrospect, was due to resentment and frustration on my part. That summer, although spiritually a high for me, was the most disheartening in terms of discord with my parents and Courtney.

My school year even ended a bit tense, as I had my first real argument with Nasrin, who felt my use of the phone to talk "privately" with William was crossing Islamic bounds. Had I known then the cultural undercurrent of this misunderstanding, I perhaps would have been more diplomatic in listening to her words. But because neither she nor I had yet understood the fundamental, and vast, difference between our realities and worlds, our friendship was tainted that day.

Till today, I don't think those who come from large Muslim families can comprehend the tremendous difficulty it would be for a convert to Islam to not use even the telephone to talk to a potential mate. In the absence of a male relative representing us, not to mention the dearth of Muslim family themselves, marriage becomes an unimaginably delicate and complicated pursuit that cannot be held to stringencies that are, in many cases, more ideal than they are religious mandates.

Yet, still, I cannot help but feel a tinge of jealousy for those with Muslim fathers, uncles, cousins, and siblings. How I wish I had the luxury of knowing someone who loved me would take care of finding a suitable mate on my behalf. As a teenager I would have scoffed at what I saw as an "arranged marriage," but today experience has taught me that it is most prudent to have someone who knows and cares for me sift through potential mates before bringing them before me. Then and only then should I select a lifelong mate. This method is so much more promising, not to mention successful long-term, in pursuing marriage than feeling your way in the dark—even with a well-intended imam by your side. Internet sites, I-heard-of-a-good-brother-my-friend-knows, green-card marriages, and sheer "luck" have truly taken their toll on those who have accepted Islam. The problems suffered by converts who have no Muslim relatives is so rampant that I now believe it is wisest, though not obligatory, to include trustworthy non-Muslim family in the process of marriage, seeking their advice and approval before embarking on such a tremendous life change.

"You know it's not right to talk on the phone like that," Nasrin said to me as I was smiling to myself after hanging up from talking to William. Her head was turned to me with her elbow propped on the desk and a fist at her cheek, her other hand holding a pen she had been using to write something in a notebook. As usual, her hair was pulled back in a thick braid and she was wearing a beige *shawar kameez.* Her eyes looked tired, but I couldn't tell if it was because of the exams or lack of sleep.

I creased my forehead, a faint smile still on my face. "What?"

"Talking to a brother like that." She shifted, removing her fist from her face and sitting up straighter as her eyes grew concerned. "It's not allowed."

For a moment, I just looked at her. I didn't know what to say. Part of me feared she was correct, that this was something else I needed to learn about Islam. But another part of me was skeptical, unwilling to take her on her word.

"I never heard that before."

"It's known."

"Where?"

"In the Sunnah. A man and a woman who aren't married can't be alone, even if they're just talking."

"I thought that was if they're in a room by themselves."

"It is," she said, turning herself in the chair so her body faced me instead of facing the desk. "But it's not only a room. It's any talking if others aren't there."

My eyebrows rose. Perhaps she was right.

A thought came to me suddenly, and I furrowed my brows. "So when you answer the phone and it's William, you're committing a sin?"

"But I'm not talking to him, Renee."

"What if I'm not here and you take a message?"

"That's different." Nasrin looked more exhausted all of a sudden. Clearly, she hadn't been expecting a challenge. Usually, she simply instructed and I listened and nodded in reflection.

"But you're still talking to him to take the message."

She sighed. "Renee, this isn't a joke. You don't want to be in trouble with Allah on the Day of Judgment."

"Joking?" I stared at her, my eyes squinted in confusion. "I'm not joking, Nasrin. I really don't see what you're saying."

"Yes you do. You're making fun of the rule."

"But Nasrin, if it's a rule, it wouldn't be allowed for you to answer the phone because a man could be on the other line."

"That's not true."

"Yes it is."

I decided to take a different approach. "Let's say I wanted to give a brother a message from his wife, can I go into a room, close the door, and explain it to him?"

She frowned. "Of course not."

"Because it's breaking a rule."

"I know."

"Then why are you treating the phone like it's the same?"

"It's not the same, but—"

"If it's not the same, then it's not wrong."

"It's about your intentions though."

"I can have good intentions alone in a room with a man."

Her jaw stiffened. "Look, Renee, if you want to talk to the brother on the phone, it's up to you. I just can't let you do it in here."

"What?" I couldn't believe what I was hearing.

"I don't want to support this. It's wrong." She turned back to her notebook and narrowed her eyes as she read something on the page, but her frustration was apparent. Her mind wasn't on what she was reading.

"I'll talk to him any time I want."

"Not in here." She didn't look at me.

I laughed. "Do you really think I'm going to stop talking to him just because you *feel* it's wrong?"

"I was hoping Allah would matter to you," she said, her gaze still fixed on the page.

At that, I was offended, remembering how Ghazwa and Wadiah had once discussed how Muslims from Islamic countries often confused their customs with Islam.

"Is this about Allah or your culture?"

She was silent for sometime, but I could see her eyes blinking in shock. Slowly she turned to me. "My culture? This has nothing to do with my country."

"Really?" I folded my arms over my chest. "Then give me the verse or hadith that forbids talking when I'm not alone with a man. Last thing I read, even the Companions talked to the wives of the Prophet with only a curtain separating them. That's a lot closer than a phone."

"But they weren't flirting and talking for fun."

I glared at her. "Flirting?"

"Yes, Renee. That's what you're doing. I see you laughing when you're on the phone."

"So?"

"That's wrong."

"To *laugh?*"

"With a man, yes."

"So now it's a sin to *laugh?* Oh my goodness, Nasrin. You've got to be kidding."

Defeated, she shrugged. "Do what you want, Renee. I'm just surprised you find some of your religion so unbelievable. I really thought you wanted to do what's right."

"Islam? You can't make up a rule in your mind, and when I don't follow it, you say I'm not doing what's right."

"Whatever you think. Just don't do it in here."

"When I moved here, this became *our* room. If that's still the case, I'll talk to whoever I want. But if you think I'm homeless and under your personal rules, I'll pack my things and go back to the suite."

"All I'm saying, Renee, is don't talk to him in here. I don't want to be in trouble on Judgment Day."

"If it's wrong, I'm the one who'll be in trouble, not you."

"But it's my phone."

"It's the school's line. I can bring my phone from the suite if you want."

She slammed her pen down. "Can you please leave me alone? I'm trying to study."

I threw my hands in the air. "You're the one who bothered me, but hey, as you like."

Nasrin's disappointment in me after the argument cut me deeply. I felt I had let her down. I sensed she had really admired me for my dedication to Islam and eagerness to learn. That day, I think she saw a fault in me that she couldn't reconcile with her initial impression. Although I still didn't agree with her perspective, I couldn't help feeling lousy for being unable to live up to her good expectations.

Today I can appreciate what Nasrin was trying to say, and even understand where she was coming from. I haven't yet embraced the opinion that talking on the phone is sinful, but I can see that the absence of a male guardian in such interactions can lead to a lot of problems—and sins. If I had grown up in a Muslim family like Nasrin's, I wouldn't need the phone. I could meet William in the living room of my house and talk to him until my heart's content, even laughing at something he said—while my father, brother, or uncle sat next to me. But I couldn't do that, and she probably would never understand that most of the other options available to me were far more nocuous than a phone call.

Despite my disagreeing with Nasrin, her disapproval made me more cautious in my conversations with William, and I stopped talking to him while she was around. A part of me was ashamed that I was doing something that could be considered inappropriate, even if there was no specific proof to support Nasrin's misgivings. I was also aware of that wavering in my heart whenever the conversation grew too personal, and I knew that it was closer to righteousness to shorten the talks if not strive to eliminate them altogether, unless it was necessary to discuss something, which was rare.

If I'm completely honest, I was talking for enjoyment anyway, not for marriage. William had begun to mention wanting to marry me, but I always laughed him off, saying I didn't want to. But, really, I wasn't joking.

William and I never saw each other in person after the *iftaar* at Sister Desta's home, at least not until the summer. I was invited to several gatherings by Sumayyah, and more than once he and I were at the same function, but we never actually saw each other. It was always a disappointment, but then again, what would we have done if we did see each other? Wave?

Oddly, it was actually Nasrin who led me to finally agree to marry William. I kept playing the argument we had had over and over in my head, and the more I thought about it, the more I realized that we should be talking for a purpose. This I didn't need religious proof for. This was common sense.

When I mentioned my thoughts to Hadiyah one day, she advised me to wait until I finished school. She even offered to help me plan a ceremony for the following summer if I decided to accept William's proposal. I could tell that she was afraid I would marry before I graduated, and I was offended. In my head, I heard Ghazwa talking about marriage: *"Forget school. Marriage is the Sunnah. That's half your deen. We don't need to be all caught up in this dunya."* In my naiveté, I imagined Hadiyah to be influenced by the world, and I dismissed even her suggestion to do the marriage contract now if I wanted but wait to live together and be "fully married" until I graduated.

When I talked to Sumayyah, she said the same thing Hadiyah had said, and again I was offended. I thought to myself, *Of course that's what Sumayyah will say because that's what she and Yusuf are doing.* How could I have forgotten? Sumayyah and Yusuf's wedding was that June because she would have graduated in May.

I called Wadiah too. She didn't want to commit to a position, but she said that it was better to get married than to keep talking on the phone. Apparently, Wadiah called Ghazwa, because Ghazwa called me less than an hour after I hung up from Wadiah, and as usual, there was no middle ground for her.

"Girl, you better get married. Is it that White boy?"

I hesitated. "I was thinking about it."

"Thinking about it? Girl, ain't nothing to think about. Just get married. You don't wanna do *haraam.*"

I was torn. I didn't know what to do. Today I still can't make sense of why I was so offended by Hadiyah's and Sumayyah's advice. Looking back, I think theirs was the most wise. With the writing of the contract, I could have both avoided *haraam* and finished school without the worry of possible pregnancy or even normal newly wed distractions, particularly for me and William, who were still getting to know each other.

I wouldn't remain indecisive for too long. I was about to return home for the summer.

Nineteen

The arguments started almost immediately, so it was a blessing that Courtney was home for only two weeks before leaving for an internship. She was an instigator. Unfortunately, Patricia could not be a mediator for any of us because she had her own life to deal with. She was home for four weeks with Emanuel, but it wasn't a typical visit. I overheard many of her conversations with my parents, and it was clear that she and James were having problems. At that time, I wasn't surprised, given her husband's career. I assumed it was part of the package when you married a celebrity, although James was known better for his bench warming than shooting baskets. Apparently, women didn't make the distinction and neither did he.

My heart went out to her, I cannot lie. But it was mostly because I felt sorry for her. I was saddened that she had imagined that it could be any other way. James was her first boyfriend, but who was she to him? She had been so naïve that it was tormenting to imagine her hurt. James was an active member of his church and was committed to Christ and so on. Here's the question that stuck in my mind: *If Jesus died for his sins, what motivation does he have to avoid them?*

But on this, I remained quiet. I was still trying to get over her leaving my father's church for sectarian Christianity. At least in The Church, Christianity was a way of life. There were rules. Jesus' sacrifice was real there, but only insomuch as your life itself reflected a commitment to sacrifice. Mere acknowledgement of accepting Jesus never cut it in my family.

Of course I never discussed my thoughts with Patricia and did not intend to. These were merely thoughts and I left them that way. She had enough to worry about.

And so did I.

"You're not in church, Renee," my mother said one day in late June after I returned from a walk around the neighborhood.

I groaned. "I know that, Mom."

I lifted my chin as I unfastened the pin on my *khimaar*. I then slipped it off my head and walked into the kitchen, where Courtney was sitting reading a book and eating some cookies.

"Then why are you covering your hair like an Arab?"

I was quiet. My mother already knew I was Muslim, so these were rhetorical questions. I didn't want a repeat of Christmas. I was already walking on thin ice.

Opening the refrigerator, I took out some juice and found a glass in a cabinet and poured some for myself.

"I'm talking to you."

"It makes you look like an old lady," Courtney said, wrinkling her nose as she glanced at me.

I rolled my eyes at her, but she had already turned her attentions back to the book.

"You certainly don't look like a Christian."

I closed the top of the juice and looked at Courtney. She wore a fitting tank top and tight jeans. "If Jesus were here right now," I said, "I think I'd be the only one he wouldn't be ashamed of."

I was referring to me and my sister, hoping to make my mother see the illogic of her perception, but my mother's expression told me she thought I was talking about her too.

"You need to watch your mouth, child."

I bit my lip, putting the juice back into the refrigerator.

"Why do you dress like that anyway?" Courtney asked. "It's so tacky."

"Why do you dress like that?" I grimaced as I regarded her. "It's so slutty."

"I don't like that language in my house."

I lifted my glass of juice from the counter and started to leave the kitchen. I really didn't want to argue with my mother. I had told Hadiyah about the incident on Christmas and she lectured me for over an hour on the rights of parents, especially the mother, and how I had to respect them no matter what. I was offended because I felt they had been wrong, but she said it didn't matter. Right or wrong, parents deserve respect.

"All I ask is that you don't wear that in our neighborhood," my mother said as I approached the steps. "I don't want you announcing your dissent with The Church. Your father has worked too hard to get where he is now for you to go making it more difficult. The least you can do is not wear that rag on your head."

"It's not a rag." My voice was as even as I could manage, but I didn't turn around. I kept going up the stairs.

"Renee." Her voice was soft.

I turned in the middle of the stairs. "Yes?"

"Please don't do this to us."

I gave a tight lipped smile and finished my ascension. I was beginning to get irritated. I couldn't believe my mother saw this as having anything to do with them.

Fortunately, no one bothered me after I closed the door to my room. I thought of Michael and Elijah, but my parents had put them in a sports day camp, so they wouldn't be home until later that evening. I didn't have the chance to talk to Elijah much because we were rarely home alone. I think my mother intentionally kept them out of the house and away from me. If she ran to the store, she took them with her. Naturally, I was hurt by this, but not too much. In my heart I knew that the conversation I had with Elijah at the beginning of the year had not been forgotten. I prayed for him everyday to be guided to Islam.

In my room, I set my juice on my dresser and pulled out a book about marriage in Islam. I then settled on my bed, juice in hand, and began reading. My mind drifted to my conversation with William earlier. We had discussed Patricia and James. It was a pretty heated discussion because I took offense to a comment he had made.

"That's a really hard life for a man," he had said from where he sat a comfortable distance from me on his back porch.

I was taken aback. "Hard life for a *man*? What about the woman? Seems to me James isn't having it hard at all."

"That's not what I meant."

"But that's what you said."

"I wasn't talking about James. I was thinking about men in general."

"But still. How is it hard for him? I can understand if he's Muslim and fearing Allah. But he's not doing any of that. How is it hard?"

"It's still hard, Renee. You think a man wants to commit a sin like that?"

My eyes widened. "Apparently. That's what he's doing."

"But people don't always do what they want. They're weak."

"If he's weak, then he's doing what he wants."

"It's not that simple."

"It is to me."

"But it isn't really."

"In this case it is. He could have resisted temptation and moved on. He's supposed to be Christian."

"But that doesn't mean anything. He's human."

"And so are Muslims."

He chuckled. "And you think if he was Muslim, he wouldn't have done the same thing?"

"Yes."

William shook his head, a half smile on his face. "You don't know anything about men, do you?"

"Well, according to you, James is a good teacher."

"I didn't say that."

"You didn't have to. You're saying even a Muslim would do that."

"I didn't mean it like that."

"Then what do you mean?"

"Look, it doesn't matter what religion you are, Renee. Men are men."

"So you're telling me that you're still dating like you were before?"

"No."

"So you changed?"

"Of course, but—"

"But nothing. You're Muslim, so you fear Allah."

"Okay," he conceded, "a Muslim definitely is going to do a better job than someone else, if he's really practicing. But I'm saying, inside we're all human. We can be weak at times."

"But, come on, William, he has a wife already. So there's no excuse."

He creased his forehead. "You think marriage means you stop being human?"

"Human? That's not being human. That's sick."

"It's not sick, Renee, it's sinful."

"The same thing."

He shrugged. "Anyway, you can't compare James to a Muslim man. If he were Muslim, he could just marry another wife."

I felt as if someone had punched me in the stomach. I glared at him, overcome with anger and shock. "What?"

"Why are you looking at me like that? It's true." He laughed as if it were a joke, and enjoying it.

"That's not funny."

"I'm laughing at you."

"It's still not funny." My face was hot with anger. "I hope you don't plan on doing something like that."

His smile faded. "Doing something like what?"

"Marrying another wife."

He was quiet for some time. "Of course not."

"Good." I folded my arms across my chest. "Anyway, I read that I can put a no-polygamy clause in my contract."

He nodded slowly. "I read that too."

"I hope you know I'm putting it in there."

"Really?"

"Yes."

We didn't speak for some time.

"What if I don't want to sign it?"

I shrugged. "It doesn't matter to me. I just won't marry you."

"You would turn down a good brother for something like that?"

"If he's a good brother, he wouldn't mind signing it."

"Now, that's not true."

I shrugged again. "Whatever. It's what I think."

"Some brothers I know think it's *haraam* to sign it."

"So?"

"So I'm not sure if it's okay."

"Honestly, William, I don't care what you think. All I know is that whoever I marry is going to sign that, *inshaAllaah*. Otherwise, we won't be getting married."

"And if no one signs it?"

"I just won't get married. It doesn't matter to me."

There was an awkward silence.

"You're really serious, huh?"

"Yes."

"Does it really mean that much to you?"

"Yes."

"But why?"

I looked at him. "Would you want your wife with someone else?"

"But that's different—"

"How is it different?"

"Polygamy is *halaal.*"

"I didn't say adultery. I said someone else. She could divorce you and marry your friend. That's *halaal.* But would you like it?"

His eyebrows rose as he thought about what I said. "No, I wouldn't."

"Then why are you surprised when I feel the same way?"

"But it's in the Qur'an. That means it's not the same for you. Obviously, women can handle it."

"Just because it's in the Qur'an doesn't mean everyone should do it."

"Then who should?"

"Honestly, William, I don't care. I just know it's not me."

"But how do you know?"

At that I grew impatient. "How do you know you can handle another woman?" Before he could answer, I went on. "You don't. So why do it? Or, better yet, why not just be patient and see how you can handle just one?"

He shrugged. "You have a point."

"I know I do. And you don't."

A grin formed on his face and he shook his head. "Okay, you win."

Because I didn't know what to say and was too upset to smile with him, though I did feel the urge to laugh at myself, I got up. "I should get home. I told my mother I'm going for a walk. I don't want her to think I'm kidnapped or something."

"Or to know the truth."

Unwilling to display amusement, I nodded. "*As-salaamu'alaikum.*" I didn't wait to hear his reply.

In my room, I reflected on what I'd said and wondered if it was the full truth. I certainly was not willing to live in polygamy, but I doubted I'd turn down the opportunity to marry someone I really wanted just because he didn't sign the no-polygamy contract. Still, I refused to get married without the clause in there.

Twenty

Love is not a word, and hate is not a word. Each is a definite reality, a truth firmly rooted in the heart. Each emotion possesses a warmth or rage that is cultivated there. Love and hate manifest themselves first in that undeniable stirring within, of affection or repulsion, at the reminder of or encounter with that which evokes them. One's love or hate is either suppressed, with great effort or patience, or let loose— by volition or weakness, and the testimony for each is in one's actions and interactions with the object of adoration or disgust.

Loving everyone is not possible, not sensible even. Everyone is not equal, everyone is not good. Everyone is not deserving of the same emotion of the heart. Even those who argue against this have as their contester the very piece of flesh they assign false love.

A week after my discussion with William, I had another argument with my parents. But this time, my mother sat silent, her arms crossed, clearly unnerved, and my father did all the talking. Apparently, this dispute was to convince me that Christianity was better than Islam. When I told him that they were the same religion, if we're going by the definition of Christianity he was teaching in The Church, he grew furious.

"How could you even think something like that? Just look at how you view God. All this hate and punishment and fear, fear, fear. Where is the love in your religion?"

As I thought of all the love and mercy in Islam, I didn't know where to begin. Should I mention that all a person's past sins are wiped away at the recitation of the *shahaadah*? Or should I mention that the mere utterance of a verse from the Qur'an meant ten blessings per letter? Or should I tell him how 113 verses in the Qur'an start with "In the name of God, the Most Gracious, Most Merciful"? I wanted him to show me just one in the Bible that started with something even close. Or, better yet, show me any Christian source replete with even half as many promises of mercy and forgiveness as easily found in thousands of *ahadith*—statements from the Prophet Muhammad, not to mention all the verses of love and forgiveness from God himself in the Qur'an.

Where this idea of a vengeful God of Islam and loving God of Christianity came from, I have no idea. Especially since there is, according to both religions, only One God.

I didn't waste my time arguing with my father, except to say, "That's not true" whenever he said something wholly untrue about Allah's religion, which was so often that I thought I sounded like a parrot.

I knew from my father's mannerisms, the way his eyes narrowed in rage and his voice rose thunderously and his hands gestured angrily, that he had no intention of knowing the answer to any of his questions or hearing specific proof against his false claims.

I wondered what sort of religious program Harvard had and thought I'd be doing them a favor by volunteering myself, right then, as a professor on Islam. But, to be fair, this probably wasn't the result of Harvard at all. They'd probably renege his degree if they heard the ludicrous claims he was making about Islam, and even Christianity. It was the first time I understood Patricia's embracing a sectarian belief in Christ. At least then she had a leg to stand on in terms of her beliefs. My father was pulling his out of thin air. If he wasn't so serious, and so insulting, I would have laughed. No wonder his Sunday broadcast was going so well. He was, more than anything, really entertaining.

When he ran out of breath—evidenced by his huffing and puffing as he paced the living room, having exhausted himself of spewing all the stereotypes and mendacity he held in his head, I was excused. Well, not excused so much as shooed off ("Get out of my sight!").

I had won, again. But, this time, my victory was in not saying a word. Apparently, it was more powerful for me to sit patiently unperturbed saying nothing more than a calm "That's not true" than to even dignify his tirade with a response. I think he was better able to hear the contradictions in his words that way. I learned a lot from this moment. When a person is talking more from their emotions than rationale, let them speak, and only look at them with raised eyebrows, feigning interest. They'll have a wavering in their heart, I believe, and know that they are, more than anything, as far from righteousness that a person could possibly be. That's because they would be, in the absence of dialogue, forced to listen to their heart as the sole response to their words.

Although I didn't show it, I was fuming when I made my way upstairs. As my father's arguments against Islam stampeded my mind, I was angry with myself for remaining quiet. I closed my door, locked it, and groaned so loud that I hoped they heard me downstairs. Now, it was my turn to pace and huff and puff. I then imagined the argument in my head as it should have been minutes before: his false claim, my smooth refutation; his angry outburst, my patient reply.

Why didn't I do that?

Because I couldn't contain myself any longer and maintain sanity at the same time, I took out my journal and wrote furiously, letting my smooth pen strokes temper the anger bubbling beneath the surface of every word.

My father claims that his is a God of love and mine is a God of vengeance. Yet he professes a belief in Paradise and Hell. He even claims to love everyone, even his enemies, and that Muslims preach hate. Love and hate are just words to him. They mean nothing. He thinks that just because he says he loves everyone that he actually does. Apparently he isn't looking in the mirror. Since I walked in the door, I haven't felt one ounce of love in this house. If this is how he loves his "enemies," I feel sorry for his friends, who surely must be deserving of even more love than I'm getting right now.

I wanted to ask, if your God is a God of only love, then why does He have a Hell Fire? Or maybe you think God created only Heaven, and that Hell has another creator? That's not too hard to believe. You're already claiming Prophet Jesus is His son. So why not just keep on going and strip God of one more of His Divine attributes and say there's another creator, a god just for Hell?

I'm not sure what "Hah-vahd" taught you, but in Islam God has at least ninety-nine names, but you choose to focus on only one—that of punishment. He is All-Knowing, All-Seeing, All-Wise. He is Most Gracious, Most Merciful, Most Compassionate. He is Most Generous, Most Kind, Possessor of Majesty and Bounty. He is All-Forgiving, Most Patient, Hearer of Prayers and the Bestower. Should I go on? Or maybe you have a list like this in the Bible?

But you're right about one thing, Dad. Muslims do fear God. A lot. That's exactly why I can't accept your invitation to disbelieve. I'm scared. Maybe your all-loving, touchy feely, I-love-everybody mantra makes you feel safe now. But on the Day of Judgment it won't. Because there's no feeling safe now and being safe then. There are only two groups of people, those who feel safe now and fear later, and those who fear now and feel safe later. I choose to be the latter.

And guess what? One more thing about love. God certainly is full of love. But He doesn't love everybody. He only loves the people committed to Him. ...Are you one of them?

In the weeks that followed, my parents' "Christian" unconditional love for everyone, including me the "heathen," got so intense that they stopped short of only throwing me through the wall to show just how much they couldn't contain the love for me that was swelling in their hearts. They talked so cruelly about Islam and Prophet Muhammad, peace be upon him, that I don't even care to repeat the indignities. Their words aggravated me, no doubt, but I was stricken with more fear than offense because I was really concerned for their souls. Even by Christian standards, they were crossing the line. Lying isn't okay in any religion.

Today I'm baffled when in religious disagreement so many people have no qualms about lying against Islam or cruelly insulting Allah's Messenger. My theory is that since each person carries within themselves the knowledge of Islam's veracity, the only way to attack it is to apply to it what it does not contain within itself—falsehood. I also think people are groping for some reason to reject Islam for themselves. I remember my feeling of anger when discovering that my search for truth brought me to Islam. I think they're going through something similar.

But I am at a loss to explain the rationale behind my parents' animosity. They hadn't even given me a chance to explain what Islam is in the first place. Since becoming Muslim, I've heard similar stories from converts about their families, some who've even been physically beaten, others put out of their homes. Each time, I think of my dad's religious claim of unconditional love and say to myself, *Where is the love?*

Of course there are those Christian, and non-Christian, families who have internalized the universal concept of tolerance and respect for others. But the only ones like this that I got to know personally were William's parents.

Whenever his mother was home, William and I would sit and talk to her for over an hour, and she showed genuine curiosity and respect for our beliefs. Because his father was often not home, I didn't have the opportunity to talk to him as much as I did to Audrey. But on the rare occasions Horace was home when I visited, he listened with his forehead creased in intense interest and his arms folded across his chest. He didn't talk much, but when he did speak, he'd say, "Well, there's something worth considering."

I came to understand this was one of the greatest compliments he could give. If he was bothered, he'd say nothing, making his feelings known by simply leaving the room.

From William I learned some intriguing things about Horace and Audrey. In high school, before he learned about Islam, William often heard his parents discuss possibly moving to Saudi Arabia. Their reasons were primarily two. One, there were great financial opportunities there for Americans. But, most importantly, Horace felt it was the best place for him to overcome his addiction to alcohol. According to William, this was a phenomenal step for his father. For years he was in denial of his problem, and only in the last five years did he join help groups and openly discuss options for moving beyond the disease.

I also learned a bit of family history, which softened my heart to marrying him. Horace's father was a White anti-racist from Mississippi, a place known for its anti-Black sentiments, during a time when civil rights were fought for by very few and was almost unheard of as a priority among Whites. Horace's father's fate was death, having been killed along with a group of Black men he had befriended. After the lynching, Horace's mother took him, his older brother, and his younger sister to Indiana, where she had family who took them in.

The move did little to soothe the grief in the house, as schoolmates were unrelenting in their cruelty, saying often, "I heard your father was a nigger lover," despite the man being in his grave and his children suffering the loss. As I listened, I was reminded of scenes from the book *To Kill a Mockingbird* and imagined Horace's father as a real-life Atticus.

Horace's drinking began when his older brother committed suicide. William was around four years old and remembered his uncle only vaguely but the funeral vividly. No one but Horace, his sister, and his mother understood what the man's friends could not. William's uncle had been a successful, wealthy corporate lawyer with a wife who was a stay-at-home mom and kids who played tee-ball and soccer. It was the American dream fulfilled. But it hadn't been enough to erase the grief of his past.

When I asked William why he never talked about his grandfather, who had been an American martyr of sorts, he said, "It's not something my people take pride in."

I knew what he meant and was saddened by the reminder.

"White people don't get a lot of recognition for civil rights," William said in another conversation, his eyes distant as he sat on his back porch. "But my father says that's how it should be. We had our moment of glory, let them have theirs."

Listening to William gave the term "White guilt" a whole new meaning. I simply didn't realize that a White person could hurt so much because of their history. I heard stories from my father about Blacks' being sprayed with water hoses, dogs tearing into their flesh, their being put in jail, and of course enduring the cruelty of a form of slavery that would have been unethical for even animals.

Once, when we were discussing race, I was telling William about the stereotype of Whites being intellectually superior.

"It's not a stereotype," he said. "It's what a lot of people really believe."

I didn't know what to say. Of course, I already knew this, but I didn't want to say that. I remember being angered by a teacher in high school who actually said intelligence was a matter of racial genetics. I was so offended that I could hardly sleep.

I remember waking the morning after, a sense of peace in my heart, and smiling at his perverted conclusion that I knew he wasn't alone in thinking. *It's their coping mechanism*, I said to myself, *so let them have it*. It's their way of avoiding seeing themselves for what they are, of avoiding responsibility, of avoiding the *self*. By believing others are, by birth, inferior, they can sleep at night, walk their dogs, and clock into work without ever giving a second's thought to the blood in the very bowels of their homes, pets, and jobs. It was their way of seeking solace. Through more corruption itself.

One day William showed me an article his grandfather had written in a small anti-racist publication he and some of his White friends had started. The article was in response to Whites who said that they were guilty of nothing in terms of Black people's predicament, so they felt no need to work to repair something they hadn't broken in the first place. The only part I remember is this:

"No, it is not your fault, not at all—as long as you think of yourself, and in fact live, as you, the individual, and nothing and no one else. But once you think of yourself, accept yourself, or even live as a beneficiary of the privileged majority, the white majority, then the blood is on your hands for anything and everything the whites have, and have not done. So until you can effectively subtract your whiteness from your existence, then you cannot, entirely, subtract the guilt and fault from yourself."

"Will you marry me?" William asked for the umpteenth time one day in late July. I had gotten into another argument with my parents earlier that day, but this time neither my mom nor I stayed quiet. It was a heated two-against-one, and Michael and Elijah were there to witness it. My father was enraged that I was shaming the family and my mother demanded I not pray in the house.

"No," I said to William, rolling my eyes to the sky in exhausted frustration as I thought of the disagreement with my family. I didn't know how I was going to survive another month in that house.

"Why not?"

I was too agitated to be prudent in my words, so I told him the truth. "I want my husband to be Black."

He was silent for some time. It took me several minutes to grow uncomfortable in the quiet. My mind was still on my parents. I didn't have the energy to think about William.

"Why does it matter?" he asked finally.

"Because it does."

"But you're Muslim now."

"That's all the more reason to have a Black husband."

He creased his forehead. "Why's that?"

"Because now I know what my people need to get out of the mental slavery they're in."

His jaw tightened, unsure what to say.

"You don't think the same about your people?"

"When I became Muslim," he said, hurt apparent in his voice, "my people became the believers."

"I feel the same."

"Then why would you refuse a brother just because of his race?"

"It's too complicated to explain, William. You'll never understand."

"Probably not. But try me."

I considered it for a moment then shook my head. "No, I can't make you understand."

"I think I understand already."

I braced myself for the "How can you be Black and prejudiced?" tirade, prepared to refute it. But it didn't come.

"I think that's how my grandparents saw it. White families need to be taught anti-racism, that's the only way to root out the disease. If they all marry other races, who will teach the next generation?"

I started to nod, but realized I could only understand to a point. I wasn't White.

"But, Renee, that's not how I think."

"How do you think?"

"I think it's ideal to marry your own race, but it's not for everyone."

"I agree with that."

"Then how do you know you're not an exception?"

I shrugged. "I guess I don't."

"Do you have a Black brother who proposed?"

I thought of the people Ghazwa and Wadiah said were interested in me. "Some."

"What did you say?" His voice sounded pained, as if he had feared there was indeed someone else.

"I didn't say anything. I barely know them."

"But you know me."

"Not really."

The sound of a dog barking filled the silence for a few seconds.

"You know we can't keep talking like this?"

I thought immediately of what Nasrin had said about the phone. "Yes, I know."

"It's either marriage or nothing, you know."

"Yes."

"So think about it, okay?"

I shrugged. "Okay."

I thought about it a lot, at least between my fights with my parents. Then one day I decided, *Why not?* We were both Muslim. Nothing else should really matter.

So I agreed.

The date was set so soon because it was becoming clear to both of us that our interactions were beyond "talking for necessity." We were enjoying ourselves a bit more than we should have. I wasn't sure I wanted to marry him, but I had no doubt I didn't want to give up the company.

Reggie was home for only a few weeks that summer, but it appeared that he had moved on, at least superficially, so I wasn't inconvenienced by dealing with his potential reaction to my refusing us as a couple. However, on several occasions he had tried to talk to me, but I brushed him off, irritated that he wouldn't leave me alone. But for some reason, he wasn't as annoying as he was before, his entire aura having changed to a humble maturity I detected whenever he spoke to me, or at least whenever he tried to speak to me. I wouldn't let him get beyond my name.

Once William and I decided to elope, I didn't want my parents to think I had vanished. I feared they would file a missing person's report if I didn't let them know our plans, so I told them on August 14th in the middle of a somewhat mellow argument. I said that I was going back early to Maryland and was marrying William the next day.

They nearly hit the roof. They were so irrational that they even asked me what happened to me and Reggie, as if the mere mention of my father's latest addition to The Church would change my mind about marrying William. It irked me that they actually hoped that I'd one day marry

Reginald. I knew they thought the relationship would guide me back to my father's church.

But I had all my things already packed and felt a surge of power and relief in knowing I didn't have to live like this anymore. I could have peace, and under my own roof.

But I had no idea just how hard it would be to have my own roof in the first place.

Twenty-one

William and I took a flight to Baltimore the next day and spent our time on the harbor and toured the city enjoying ourselves like two normal newly weds. Given our financial predicament during our first year, I have no idea where William got the money to cover the hotel we stayed in for those two weeks. But I had a good time. It was rejuvenating to actually be on my own, and with William of all people. We dined at Afghani and seafood restaurants, took walks by the water (more than once responding to the salaams offered by fellow Muslims), and laughed at how it had been growing up. But William never mentioned Reggie, so I didn't either. I sensed that mentioning my former best friend was too uncomfortable a subject for us right then. Mostly we spent our time getting to know each other and marveling at how weird it was to actually be a couple.

I even had my first lesson in understanding the saying, *You don't know someone until you live with them.* Well, had I not lived with William, I would have never believed there was a such thing as methyphobia or potophobia, the two names for his affliction—fear of alcohol.

The phobia was severe. I've never seen anything like it. If even an empty wine glass was on the table of a restaurant, his hands started shaking and he'd have the waiter remove it, saying he liked water or juice glasses better. If someone at a nearby table started drinking alcohol, he'd change seats until his back was to them. Once when we walked into a restaurant and the smell of alcohol was in the air, his face went pale and he did everything he could to hide his growing nausea.

Initially, he tried to be inconspicuous, but I knew something was up when I pointed to a bird flying in the sky, coincidentally above a Budweiser billboard advertisement, and he couldn't even focus on the bird because his eyes kept skipping to the sign, sending his hands shivering. If I didn't know him, I wouldn't even have recognized his hands shaking. It was almost imperceptible. But living with someone magnifies even the smallest details.

It suddenly made sense why he had always been around Reggie when we were growing up. A person with methyphobia can't possibly stay long in a house with an alcoholic. I knew too that Reggie must have known, not only of William's father's alcoholism, but of William's phobia too, which was why Reggie went out of his way to keep William around him and not at home. I also recalled the night—a New Year's Eve—when William gave me the necklace. I thought it odd he wasn't at the MSGT party where most of his friends were. Now I knew why. Alcohol would be there.

I began to admire Reggie for his kindness and my heart softened to him. I was no longer attracted to him, but I couldn't help liking him as a person for being selfless with William. Seeing how much William struggled around even the word *alcohol* made me understand Reggie's fury when Darnell called William's father a drunk. You can't reduce human beings to derogatory labels, especially people who mean something to you.

School began and I registered as a senior, having no idea that I would be there only until I finished my mid-terms. I lived on-campus with Nasrin, who was beginning her junior year as a pre-med biology major. In the brief time that I lived with her that term, I grew to appreciate her generosity more. I learned that the lectures she took me to the previous semester were against her parents' wishes, at least against her mother's. Her mother's brother had died in a car accident before Nasrin was born, and since then Nasrin's mother had anxiety whenever anyone she loved was on the road. Even though Nasrin lived in a suburb of Baltimore, less than thirty minutes away from campus, it was her mother's anxiety that made her parents decide to have Nasrin live on campus. Her mother couldn't stomach the idea of her daughter on the road every morning and afternoon. Although Nasrin had a car, she was allowed to use it only on campus and as transportation to and from home on the weekends.

"My father knows I cheat," Nasrin told me with a grin one day. "I always let him know what's going on. But we don't say anything to my mother."

"I'm sorry, Nasrin. I didn't know."

"Why are you sorry? I'm happy to get the blessings. It's important to learn about Islam."

I nodded. "I certainly learned a lot, thanks to you."

"*Alhamdulillaah*," she said in praise of Allah instead of herself. "I'm just glad I was able to help."

I thought of Hadiyah and Sumayyah and wondered what I'd have done without them too. "May Allah bless you," I said.

Before I decided to leave school, I went to a few more lectures with Nasrin and met three sisters who would become close to my heart for years to come: Arifah, a twenty-three-year-old who was born to parents who converted to Islam after being part of the Nation of Islam. Bashirah, an African-American woman in her late forties, and Jadwa, Bashirah's best friend and neighbor who was originally from Brazil but could pass for a biracial American.

Arifah and I bonded almost immediately because we had such similar upbringings that we found it hard to believe that we hadn't grown up in the same house. Even her husband Ibrahim, who also grew up Muslim, got along well with William. It was as if the relationship was meant to be. Arifah and Ibrahim had been married for almost two years when we met and they had a four-month-old son, Rashad. I myself was pregnant but didn't know it although I was feeling less energetic and wasn't my normal self.

When I visited Arifah one day in late September, she joked that I was acting like I was pregnant. The possibility hadn't even occurred to me until that moment. I was embarrassed by her teasing, having not yet learned that this was normal heckling amongst married sisters. At the moment, it felt too personal for someone to say. But because Arifah's character was so pleasant and her toffee brown skin ever aglow with a smile, I couldn't take offense. Her pleasant nature was contagious, so I grinned.

"I don't think so."

"You better take the test to make sure." She was still smiling when she said it, patiently changing Rashad's diaper on the floor of her living room.

I didn't take the test because I was too shy to go to the store to buy one. But after I was two weeks late for my cycle, I decided that Arifah's suspicions were probably correct.

Ghazwa invited me to a gathering in early October and as usual Wadiah offered to pick me up. I had already confirmed through a clinic that I was pregnant, and I didn't feel well. I dreaded the idea of riding in a car for any period of time. But because I didn't know how to say no to Ghazwa, I agreed to go. When I hung up, I realized I'd made a mistake. My heart wasn't in it. The mere thought of sitting in a gathering with Ghazwa and her friends made my stomach churn. I wasn't in the mood. There was also this sinking feeling that I would not enjoy myself and would dread waiting until Wadiah felt like leaving.

Years later I would think back to this feeling and wonder if this in itself was a sign from Allah. This is mere speculation, I know, but twenty-twenty hindsight does that to you. You look back and see signs and warnings that you couldn't at the time, and you wish you knew back then what you know now. For I was about to embark on one of the most life-altering experiences that would define my life for the next few years.

The night of the gathering, I compromised with myself. If I was going to go, at least I should bring a book in case I got bored or sick, or both. My love for books had never died and they proved a medicine for me throughout pregnancy because they distracted me from my discomfort. Because the thought itself of impending mid-terms made me ill, I decided against bringing a school book and instead chose one I wanted to read—a book about Allah. I had borrowed it from William who had gotten it from Yusuf shortly before becoming Muslim.

The gathering was at a townhouse about twenty minutes from the campus, but I was too nauseated to pay attention to the exact "city." In Maryland, the city names could easily change three times during a twenty-minute drive down a main road.

I remember smiling politely and greeting everyone and waiting for Ghazwa and Wadiah to sit down so I could find a place far from them to be spared obligatory conversation. I found a space on the side of a couch near a floor plant where no one could sit on either side of me. I settled there with my plate of food, which I really didn't have the appetite for. After I felt everyone was distracted by their own conversations, I began to read.

I was so engrossed in the book—I was reading about the three categories of *Tawheed* that scholars often used to explain the Oneness of Allah—that I didn't realize someone was talking to me.

"Renee, girl, don't act like you can't hear!"

It was Ghazwa, shouting from the other side of the room. I looked up, realizing that sitting here was probably a bad idea. Now, anything she said to me would be public—not that it wouldn't normally be since her voice was never low. Even her whispers were louder than most people's normal tones.

"What?"

"I said, don't be acting like no stranger over there. Don't you know it's rude to read when people trying to talk to you?"

I forced a smile but couldn't think of anything to say.

"What you reading anyway?"

Thinking nothing of it, I lifted the book and showed it to her. She squinted her eyes but couldn't make out the title or the author.

"What that say?"

I told her, a second later resuming my reading.

"Girl!"

My heart leaped at her tone. My eyes shot up in concern, thinking something terrible had happened.

"You can't read that!"

The room grew quiet, and all eyes were on me.

"Don't you know he off?"

I creased my forehead, feeling embarrassed and self-conscious but unsure what I had done. "What?"

"He off. You ain't allowed to take from him."

208

"Yeah, Renee," the sister I remembered as Lisan said. "You need to throw that book away."

Because I was already feeling unwell, it took me some time to register what they were saying.

"Throw the book away?"

"Yeah, girl. He ain't right."

"Who's not right?"

"That author."

My heart pounded in my chest. Fear engulfed me. "What did he do?"

"Girl, I 'on't know," Ghazwa said, as if merely knowing was a crime. "I 'on't read nothin' from him."

I stared at her, blinking in confusion. "Then how do you know he did anything wrong?"

"Fulan said he off, that's all I need to know." Of course, she didn't say "Fulan," which is an Arabic term for "so-and-so." She actually said a name, but now the name escapes me. But even if my memory did not betray me, I don't think I would repeat the brother's name because there's so much I know now that turns out to be untrue in this sort of hearsay.

"Who's that?"

"Girl, you don't know Fulan!"

Ooh, I could almost hear everyone crowing although they didn't say a word.

Everyone in the room, it seemed, bowed their head in pity for me.

"What other books you got at home?"

I gathered my eyebrows, more confused than I had been a moment before. "Books? I have lots of them."

"But who are the authors?"

"Maya Angelou, Mildred D. Taylor, Ja—"

"Girl, I ain't talking 'bout them. I'm talking 'bout Muslims."

I shook my head, unsure how this was relevant to anything. "I don't know."

"You better check!"

I felt myself growing irritated. I didn't understand what her point was. "Why should I check?"

"'Cause you don't wanna be reading nothing from people who off."

I nodded, exhausted suddenly. We were going in circles, and clearly, that's where Ghazwa was going to stay. No answers, no whys, no whats, just "Fulan said it, so it's the truth."

"Okay," I said because I was beginning to feel like the sisters' eyes were pins sticking me all over. "I appreciate you letting me know."

"No prob'm. You just stick with us and we'll make sure you on it, girl. Don't e'en worry 'bout it. Ain't no going wrong with us."

I felt the urge to laugh suddenly, not because her comment was funny, but because it was so ridiculous. For a second, I thought she was joking. In my mind, no one would say something like that with the confidence Ghazwa did and be serious. I had read enough about Islam to know that, although there were naturally Muslims, even if well-intentioned, who called people to something completely different from the Qur'an and Sunnah, no believer in her right mind would be confident that she was so free from error that she could be someone's guide and not ever go wrong. I thought of Ghazwa trying to keep me on the straight and narrow and smiled to myself.

But I soon learned there was not an ounce of doubt or humor in anything she had said.

On the ride home, Wadiah was quiet for the first few minutes then spoke as if she had been reflecting for some time.

"You know, Renee, Ghazwa's right."

"About what?"

"Listening to Fulan."

"Wadiah, I'm almost finished with this book and haven't seen anything wrong with it." At that moment, I was aware how comfortable I felt speaking my mind around Wadiah while I was almost tongue-tied around her feisty friend.

"But you wouldn't know if you saw anything wrong. You don't have knowledge like Sheikh Fulan."

"Wadiah, please tell me what's wrong with someone saying to worship Allah and stay away from *shirk*. That's all he's talking about. He even references everything with Qur'an and authentic hadith."

"But there could be something wrong that you don't pick up."

"If it's that hidden, then what am I trying to stay away from?"

She sighed. "I can't answer that, Renee, because I'm like you. I'm not knowledgeable like Fulan. He knows, so we listen."

"How do we know he knows? What if he's mistaken?"

She looked at me sideways, a shocked look on her face. "He's not mistaken, Renee. He studied Islam for years, and he knows Arabic and Qur'an."

"This author does too."

"But he went astray. Fulan didn't. Fulan stuck to the right path."

I sighed, shaking my head, feeling the nausea come on again. "But don't you think it only makes sense to know at least *something* this author did that's clearly wrong before you toss out all of his books?"

"I know what you're saying, Renee, but we don't have the knowledge to understand what he did wrong, so we just go to someone who knows."

I was quiet for a few seconds. "That just doesn't seem fair. I mean, why Fulan and no one else?"

"There are a lot of people like Fulan. Fulan has all the knowledgeable people in the world listed on his website."

I laughed. "What?"

She glanced at me, hurt. "This isn't a joke, Renee. Don't take your religion lightly."

I was reminded suddenly of my argument with Nasrin months before. "It's not my religion I'm laughing at, Wadiah."

"I don't see anything funny."

I stared at her, a half grin on my face. "You mean to tell me you believe that Fulan knows all the righteous imams in the world and listed them on his site?"

"Why not? If you're on the right path, you know who is and who isn't."

Because I could tell she was serious, I grew quiet, confounded. Did she really believe what she was saying? It scared me. How could she think some www dot whatever dot com had a complete listing of something that only Allah could know in full?

Days passed and I pushed the incident at the gathering to the back of my mind. My focus was now on approaching mid-terms. One day I was studying at my desk in the room when the phone rang. Nasrin was sitting on her bed, her back supported by a pillow. I was closest to my phone, so I answered.

It was Ghazwa. We exchanged the Islamic greeting and she, in keeping with her character, got straight to the point.

"Girl, I called the imam, and he called a brother who knows somebody who sits in the classes with Fulan, so you cool."

It took a full ten seconds for my mind to register her words and determine that they made absolutely no sense. I blinked, a bit irritated by the disruption. "What?"

"I asked about you, and he says you okay as long as you repent and throw away the book."

I pulled the receiver from my ear, stared at it, and grimaced before putting it back in place.

"Ghazwa," I said with as much patience as I could muster, realizing that I wasn't tongue-tied on the phone, "why wouldn't I be okay in the first place?"

"'Cause you off. But he said you're ignorant, so you're excused. But you gotta repent."

I drew in a deep breath and exhaled, my eyes grazing the math text I needed to get back to. "And exactly what would I be repenting for?"

"Being off the *haqq*, girl! Don't you know?"

No, I didn't.

"But when I asked about you being in school without your husband," she said, "he said it ain't right. You can't do that. Anyway, it's too much free mixing up in there, so you can't live there anymore. Plus, Renee, you gotta get your mind out the *dunya*."

I felt myself growing agitated. What was she worrying about my life for? And what made her think my mind was focused on this worldly life, and not my soul? I was offended. I felt violated by her talking about my life to someone else, and on *my* behalf. I started to respond, but something stopped me.

I didn't know Ghazwa. It suddenly occurred to me that she might not realize what she was saying. Maybe she was chemically imbalanced.

The thought scared me, but it seemed plausible. She certainly wasn't making any sense.

I tossed this idea around in my head until I realized that it was unlikely, but possible nonetheless. I couldn't imagine anyone in her right mind worrying about someone's private relationship with her husband or whether or not this person finished school, especially growing worried enough to make phone calls in hopes of solving their problems for them.

"Okay," I said, these new concerns for Ghazwa's mindset fresh in my mind. "Thank you."

"Girl, you know I love you! You my sister. I don't want you off the *haqq*."

"Thank you, Ghazwa. I appreciate your concern."

"No prob'm!"

"Okay, then. *As-salaamu'alaikum*."

"*Wa'alaiku mus-salaam!*"

After returning the receiver to its place, I exhaled, rubbing a hand over my face. The conversation played itself in my mind, and I chuckled, shaking my head. I thought of Ghazwa and a grin creased the sides of my mouth. A second later I was laughing to myself.

Apparently, my laughter was contagious because I heard Nasrin chuckling too.

"What?" An expectant grin was on her face as she looked at me.

"That sister..." I shook my head, unsure how to explain. I laughed again.

"What?"

I was finally able to formulate the words enough to summarize the conversation, including the background of it from the gathering. I was only slightly aware of Nasrin's fading smile and widening eyes, a look of trepidation overtaking her.

"Renee," she whispered with so much concern that I thought I'd accidentally hurt myself while talking.

Instinctively, my gaze scanned my body, and a hand went to my face to make sure it was intact. "What?"

"No, I mean, what you said."

Oh. "What about it?"

"Those people, they're for real."

I gathered my eyebrows, her fear contagious in the room. "What do you mean?"

"You need to be careful, Renee. It's not a joke to them."

"What's not a joke?"

"What they're saying."

I stared at her, unsure what to say.

"Just be careful."

"Nasrin," I said, leveling with her, "what are you talking about?"

"They're known for causing a lot of problems, Renee. You don't want to be around them."

"Who's *they*?"

"Those people."

"What people, Nasrin?" I was beginning to get irritated.

"People like that."

It was as if she were speaking in code and I needed to decipher it. "You know them?"

"I've met people like them. And it's not good."

"What happened?"

She drew in a breath and exhaled, shaking her head, clearly unable to explain all that was on her mind. "So much."

"Like what?"

"They'll say all the right things about Islam." Her eyes grew distant, and I saw pain there. My heart grew heavy with dread. "But that's pretty much it. It's like they memorized all the scholars' books on 'aqeedah and that's the whole religion for them."

"'*Aqeedah*?" The word sounded familiar, but I couldn't place it.

"Islamic creed. It's a person's belief about the religion."

I nodded, suddenly remembering attending lectures and reading books on the topic. It was what differentiated the people of the Sunnah from Muslims who believed in Islam differently from the Prophet and his Companions.

"But they'll backbite and slander people," Nasrin said sadly, "even scholars. And if you don't do it too, they'll backbite and slander you." She looked at me, her concerned eyes meeting mine. "They think if you don't join in, you're not following the Sunnah."

213

Stunned, I stared at her, my mouth agape in disbelief, unwilling to believe such an enormity. Finally, I shook my head, my face contorted. "I don't believe that."

"I'm telling you, Renee." Her voice was a plea. "I'm not lying. Be careful. A lot of people get confused about Islam from them."

At that moment, it was as if a cloud of darkness hovered in the room, and I had a gut feeling that Nasrin was right. Today, I think back on this feeling and wonder at how pervasive it was, another clear sign in hindsight. Feelings are not definitive indicators of right and wrong, I know, but in the course of life, they are but one of many signs God gives a person to steer her from sin.

Because I couldn't vouch for anything my roommate was saying and hadn't seen anything to verify it in the actions of Ghazwa and her friends, I nodded in response to Nasrin although I was confounded by it all. The gut feeling never left. Yet, still, I didn't know what to believe.

"No, Renee, don't." Arifah's eyes glistened as she pleaded with me from where she sat on the opposite side of the couch. Rashad was sleeping soundly on his blanket between us. Another soft cover covered him to keep him warm.

"It's just for a semester." I averted my gaze and played with the hem of the shirt I was wearing. "Until I feel better."

"But you don't know if you'll ever go back."

"I already talked to my professors. They're willing to hold my mid-term grades and give me an incomplete."

"But you'll be further along then. What if you can't finish the year after the baby's born?"

"I don't know. I'll figure something out."

Even William was telling me not to take off that semester. But I was vomiting every morning when I woke up and every night before I went to bed and feeling nauseated for every second of the day. My headaches were constant and severe, and I resisted taking medication, fearing for the baby's health. I was also lethargic. I barely had energy to get out of bed, let alone pay attention in class.

"But where will you go?"

"I'm not sure..." My gaze grew distant. William lived on campus in Baltimore—with a roommate, so staying with him was out of the question.

"I know a sister who I can ask," I said tentatively. I was thinking of Hadiyah, but I was doubtful. I knew she would disapprove of my taking off school, even if it was only until January, as was my plan. I figured by then I would be over "morning" sickness, at least this was my prayer. So much of what I was reading about what to expect during pregnancy was turning out to be untrue, so I wasn't counting on it.

The truth was that school was becoming less significant to me in the scheme of things. Although I knew William was still in school, I felt I should focus on my marriage and make Islam a priority in my life. Talking to Nasrin and Ghazwa and Wadiah made me realize there was so much more I needed to learn. My confusion was exhausting me, and I questioned my intentions in getting a degree. Marriage was half my religion, a math degree wasn't. So why was I putting myself through this?

"But what about your scholarship?"

I'd thought of that. "As long as I don't take off more than a year, I can keep it."

She frowned, shaking her head, her gaze falling on Rashad. "I don't know, Renee. I just know so many sisters who did the same thing and regretted it for the rest of their lives. My mother always told me not to do that."

"But why is school so important? What about Islam?"

Her eyes were squinted when she met my gaze. "But Renee, Islam is life. It's not separate from it."

"It is if I focus on the *dunya*."

"You can drop out of school and still focus on the *dunya*."

"But I want to take this time to study my religion. There's so much I don't know."

"And even if you're a scholar, Renee, there'll always be so much you don't know. Seeking knowledge is a lifelong pursuit. It never ends."

"That's why I should start now."

"But you already started. There are tons of classes you can go to on the weekend and still be in school."

"But I won't learn as much as I will if I'm not so distracted."

"But you're almost finished. Why would you stop now?"

"I'm not stopping. I'm taking a break."

"Just make *du'aa*, Renee. A lot. Make sure you're making the right decision."

I nodded, but I had no intention of praying on it. I had read that if something is religiously mandated or recommended, there is no need to pray *Istikhaarah*. Of course, now I know that the exception for performing the prayer of making a decision is specifically related to matters clearly outlined in the Qur'an and Sunnah, like prayer and fasting, but I didn't know that at the time.

Rashad stirred, and for a moment, we gazed at him as he resumed sleeping peacefully.

"What does your husband think?"

I sighed. "He thinks I should stay in school."

She shook her head. "And don't you think it's closer to Islam to take his advice?"

I shrugged. "Not if it compromises my Islam."

"Renee!" A grin was on her face, as if saying, *I know you can't be serious!*

"I'm serious. Why should he come between me and Allah?"

"He's not, *ukhtee.* He's just saying what he thinks is best for you."

"Maybe. But that doesn't mean he's right."

"I think he is."

I chuckled. "Yes, I know you do."

She smiled then sighed. "I just pray everything works out for you."

"I believe it will."

"*InshaAllaah.*"

I nodded. "Yes, *inshaAllaah.*"

Hadiyah agreed to let me stay with her although they were preparing the house for the market. They planned to renovate it and sell it by summer. She was reluctant to agree, not because she was unwilling to share her home, but because, as I expected, she disagreed with my taking off school. She expressed the same concerns as Arifah had, but I had already made up my mind. William wasn't excited about my decision, and he let me know it. But he made it clear it was up to me. I sensed my living with Hadiyah made him feel guilty for not having an apartment for us. I felt a tinge of guilt for making him feel bad but that wasn't my intention. I didn't fault him for that. I knew when I married him we had another year of school before we could enjoy the comforts of other married couples.

Although I was sick, I told Hadiyah I wanted to learn as much as I could about Islam. I shared with her my fear of not understanding Islam well enough to differentiate between truth and falsehood on matters that could cause someone to stray. But I didn't mention my experiences with Ghazwa and Wadiah because part of me feared she might react like Nasrin had and I didn't want to relive that sinking feeling that something was definitely askew.

Hadiyah was busy most days because she and her husband were starting a family business. During the day, her husband (who called himself Mumin but hadn't changed his name legally) taught chemistry at a university in D.C. and spent his evenings tying up loose ends for their business venture. Apparently, Hadiyah's acceptance of Islam took a huge toll on their financial situation, as their suburban home was made possible from profits from her church more than his job as a professor. Learning this made me admire her more, and increased my gratefulness to Allah for guiding me in youth. I couldn't imagine being faced with Hadiyah's decision—to accept Islam and give up everything she built her life around, or remain the preacher of her church and continue the comfortable life she had built. Of course, spiritually, the answer was simple, but practically, the reality was something different entirely.

Because of her hectic schedule, Hadiyah and I sat down for class only once each week, focusing on perfecting my prayer—from understanding its great importance to knowing effortlessly what to say in each position (Yes, I was still a bit rusty). But she told me about an Egyptian sister who lived in walking distance from the house who could teach me Arabic and Qur'an. Nicole walked with me the first day to show me the way, and it took us thirteen minutes to get there. When I walked alone for the next class, it took me only nine minutes, so it wasn't bad at all.

In Hadiyah's home, I lived in one of the guest rooms (there were three) near Nicole's room on the third floor, while Hadiyah and her husband slept on the opposite side of the house on the second level. The house was beautifully designed and spacious, and I found myself wishing that William and I had enough money to buy it from them. This was wishful thinking that bordered on a fairy tale, but it felt good imagining how it would be if we could.

There was a phone in my room, and I learned that it was separate from Hadiyah and her husband's line. This was exciting to learn, until I realized the second phone number was really for Nicole, who had gotten the line under the agreement that it would be the line for the entire third floor. Since Hadiyah left the church, guests were few and far between, except for faithful family members who visited at least once a year. I never saw any of them except Hadiyah's oldest son Javon who often visited with his wife and two children who were both under four. They lived in Fredrick, which was about forty minutes away, so the trip was not completely out of the way. But I soon learned his trips were due to his strong desire for his wife to accept Islam.

Yolanda was reluctant because she felt the religion was too restrictive, but she was a good listener and had a pleasant disposition. However, whenever Hadiyah and Mumin were both gone, Yolanda and Nicole were inseparable, spending hours outside by the pool or inside at the kitchen table, and on many occasions I overheard them talking about how they "could *never* live like that."

I lived in a seclusion of sorts for almost two months, having given Nicole's phone number to only William, Nasrin, and Arifah. My reluctance to call Ghazwa or Wadiah and give them the information or even let them know where I was staying would be yet another indicator in retrospect that Allah was telling me that my relationship with them would bring little good. When I called to give Nasrin the number to Hadiyah's, I told her not to give the phone number out. She had laughed and said she wouldn't have given it out anyway. May Allah bless her, that's just how she was, very considerate.

Naturally, William called most often, and almost every evening Nicole would come to my room and let me know he had called while she was on the phone. Fortunately, she was cordial and didn't seem bothered by this and had even let me know it wasn't a problem when I apologized to her for his calls. I sensed it was the least of her concerns. She had her moments of stubbornness, but it was only when religion was discussed.

Arifah called me at least three times a week, and I called her almost everyday, going on and on about how much I was learning from Hadiyah and how much I loved Sister Saliha, my teacher of Arabic and Qur'an. It was as if Allah had chosen to bless me and sent me all these people at once. At moments, Arifah and I would be in tears as I shared the moving lessons from Qur'an, hadith, and stories from believers of the past and present. Sister Saliha, may Allah preserve her, would not only teach me how to recite Qur'an but would give me the *tafseer* of the chapters and share any hadith about them. I was learning the small chapters at the end of the Qur'an, yet there was so much to learn. My lessons in Arabic were similar and were often based on a Qur'anic verse, hadith, or a statement from a righteous scholar from the past.

I was on a spiritual high and felt my faith soar in love, hope, and fear of my Creator. My love for my Muslim brothers and sisters grew, and I learned to overlook faults, pray for their forgiveness, and always wish them well, even when they were in error. I was overcome with an intense desire for my Christian family to be guided to Islam and spent my days and nights in prostration praying for them, Elijah being foremost in my mind and heart.

Periodically, Saliha or Hadiyah told me about major errors of belief to stay away from, always referencing their statements with clear proof so that I understood why the belief was wrong. So I learned the intricacies of *shirk*—that good luck charms and amulets, swearing by other than Allah, and calling on an intermediary in prayer were serious mistakes that contradicted *Tawheed*. I learned the importance of understanding and practicing Islam as the Prophet did and that his Companions were foremost in their understanding of Islam. I learned about life in the grave, signs of the Day of Judgment, and the events of the Last Day. I learned the basic principle of establishing proof on *halaal* and *haraam*—that all acts of worship are forbidden unless there is Qur'anic or Sunnah proof for them, and that all worldly matters are permissible unless there is Qur'anic or Sunnah proof against them.

And the list goes on.

So clearly, when I had gone shopping with Arifah in mid-December and ran into Ghazwa and Wadiah at the mall, I was not in need of religious direction. But I had no idea until a week later at the "dinner" they invited me to that that's exactly where they thought I was lacking.

I often think back to the moment I saw them and how my heart was a thunderstorm in my chest. Because we saw each other at the same time, I couldn't avoid them like I wanted (another twenty-twenty hindsight sign), so I had to "suck it up" and put on a fake show of pleasant surprise.

"Girl, where you been!" Hands on her hips, Ghazwa stared at me as if I'd wronged her. She looked so out of place in full *hijaab* talking like someone from a low budget rap video that I was momentarily embarrassed to be standing opposite her. I glanced around to make sure no one was staring at us. But of course they were.

I forced a smile and nodded my greeting to Wadiah who stood quietly beside her, a pleasant expression on her face. "Busy."

In the corner of my eye, I saw Arifah do a double take from where she was pushing the baby stroller near a clothes rack and walk cautiously toward us. She stopped a few feet behind me, close enough to make it clear that we were together but far enough not to be invited into the conversation. I remember Ghazwa looking Arifah up and down before frowning and turning her attention back to me.

"I been calling and you ain't never there."

"I'm not at school anymore." I spoke quietly because I noticed a store worker pretending to be occupied by something as she moved closer and closer to us.

"You dropped out?" She looked hopeful, as if on the verge of congratulating me.

I nodded slightly, hoping the store clerk didn't see my affirmative gesture. At that moment, I felt ashamed of myself.

"Good, now you on it." She paused as she thought of something.

"Did you repent?" she said.

I creased my forehead, growing more self-conscious of how we looked—and sounded. I thought of Arifah standing behind me and hearing every word. My face grew hot. I was too distracted by my mortification to register what Ghazwa was talking about.

"Repent?"

"Yeah, girl, about that book you had."

My stomach bubbled like lava beneath the earth's surface. I felt like I was going to throw up. I was nineteen years old, but at that moment I felt like a scolded toddler. "No..."

"What!"

"I, uh, forgot." I lowered my voice and glanced around nervously, noticing the clerk crossing her arms next to us. Clearly, we were not wanted here anymore. I started to inconspicuously point this out to Ghazwa, but, as usual, she was in her own world.

"You forgot! How you forget?" She turned to Wadiah.

"We gotta bring her over on Saturday."

Wadiah nodded. "I have somebody for a hair appointment at four but I can pick her up at six, *inshaAllaah.*"

"Wadiah gonna pick you up for dinner on Saturday. Where you at now?"

"I'm...not sure exactly where."

"Gimme the number and we'll call you." She turned to Wadiah again.

"You got a pen?"

Wadiah rummaged through her purse until she withdrew a pen and a torn piece of paper and handed them to her friend, who handed them to me.

"Write it on there and I'll call you *inshaAllaah.*"

Holding the pen, I hesitated, my mind stormed with all the reasons I shouldn't give out the number but unable to find the words, or guts, to tell her.

"Hurry up, girl, we got things to do!"

I quickly wrote the number and Ghazwa took the paper from me. I felt a sharp pain in my head as I realized what I had done.

"Don't e'en worry about it," Ghazwa said as she folded the paper and put it into her purse. "We'll hook you up."

She gave the Islamic greeting and looked Arifah up and down once more before frowning again and walking away.

Instinctively, I dropped my head and rubbed a hand over my face.

"Who was that?" Arifah whispered, concern in her voice as we made our way to another part of the store, away from the clerk.

"Ghazwa and Wadiah." Defeated, my voice was void of emotion.

"What's this about repenting over some book?"

I shook my head, as if saying, *Don't ask.* I sighed. "If I only knew."

There was a brief pause.

"Be careful though." Her gaze was now on Wadiah's and Ghazwa's fading images in the distance. Arifah sounded like she wanted to say more but withheld.

Inside I thought of Nasrin's warnings and said, *Yes, yes, I know. I already know.*

Twenty-two

"I have met many scholars, and the affair of one was different from that of the other, and their knowledge was of varying levels. And the one whom I benefited from his company the most was the one who used to apply what he knew, even though there were those more knowledgeable than he. I met a group...who memorized and knew a lot, however they would permit backbiting under the guise of jarh wa ta'deel; they would take monetary payment for narrating hadith, and they would be hasty in giving answers, even if they are wrong, lest their status diminishes."
—Ibn Jawzi

"Whoever does not guard his tongue does not understand his religion"
—Abu Haatim

On Saturday evening shortly after seven o'clock, I sat on the floor of Wadiah's living room surrounded by about seven sisters, if I don't count Ghazwa or Wadiah. But Wadiah wasn't in the living room at that time because she was preparing the meal in the kitchen. I could hear the clanking of pots and pans, and the aroma of food filled the house. Although I hadn't eaten, I lost my appetite upon walking in the door minutes before and seeing Ghazwa talking conspiratorially in hushed whispers with the other sisters. When they noticed my presence, they stopped immediately and Ghazwa gave me a thunderous greeting, and the other sisters forced smiles, that look of discomfort on their faces that people often have when they realize you overhead them gossiping about you.

I sat down, feeling like I was about to be hazed in initiation to a sorority I wanted no part of. The dark cloud that had hovered in the dorm room when Nasrin had warned me was now so thick in the room that even my memories of this evening are of a murky room full of people wishing me harm. I was once tormented by a nightmare of this moment, in which all the sisters smiled at me at once, revealing human flesh between their teeth, a minute later telling me to stay away from every single person I'd come to love and trust because of their devotion to Islam and me as their Muslim sister.

Ghazwa started the meeting with an opening supplication that, before then, I associated with the *khutbah* on Fridays, the lectures I'd attended with Nasrin and Sumayyah, and the start of Sister Saliha's class.

Ghazwa then said, "I heard you staying with that sister named Hadiyah?"

Cautiously, I nodded, taken aback by hearing Hadiyah's name mentioned. It sounded out of place here.

"Is she the one who live in that mansion and used to be a preacher?"

Again, I nodded cautiously, feeling that it was a horrible idea to have come. Hadiyah had already invited me somewhere, but I canceled because I was too ashamed to tell Ghazwa I already had plans when she abruptly scheduled this dinner.

"Well, she off."

My jaw tightened. But I didn't speak. Clearly, I was outnumbered.

"And anyway, it's *haraam* to live like that. All these poor Muslims and look at her! Acting like she some damn celebrity. I ain't get no *sadaqah* from her. Did you?"

The sisters chuckled and shook their heads. Someone said, "Uh uh, not me. I ain't get a dime."

I winced. This was cruelty in the worst form.

"Well, first thing, you gotta get out of there. You 'on't wanna be in sin too. Anyway, like I said, she off, so it ain't permissible for you to sit with her."

"What did she do?" My voice was pained. I knew she had done nothing, but I wanted to come to her defense somehow. I felt like a hypocrite listening to her name being maligned.

Ghazwa glared at me. "Didn't I just say she off? That's what she did."

"But what did she *do*?"

"Am I speaking Chinese? Or maybe you off too?"

It was a hit below the belt—*Keep talking and I'll put you "off the haqq" with her.* Of course, if this was really about being "on" or "off," then Ghazwa would have no power to put me there; I'd have to go myself. But, apparently, that's not how things worked in this sorority.

I shut my mouth.

Ghazwa rolled her eyes, as if saying, *I thought so.* Thus, I passed the first phase of hazing.

Phase two: Interrogation and Defamation of Character.

"Who you take from?"

Anger was already boiling in my chest from her insult moments before, but I managed to at least appear calm. But I felt myself clenching my teeth between questions. I narrowed my eyes, feigning confusion but I was really just infuriated. "What do you mean, who do I take from?"

"Like what speakers you listen to? What *masjid* you go to?"

Feeling like a complete idiot, I told her.

The room grew quiet and they all looked at each other, their eyes widening in fear: *Ooh, she really off!*

"You were seen with Sumayyah."

I narrowed my eyes again. "What?"

"We got witnesses. You know Sumayyah, married to that fool Yusuf?"

"I know a sister Sumayyah married to a brother Yusuf." It was a weak defense of their characters. But I couldn't forget that I needed a ride home after they were finished harassing me. So I had to maintain a middle ground.

"They off too. Stay away from them."

Phase three: More Interrogation and Defamation of Character.

"Did you throw away that book?"

"No."

"Throw it away and repent. I told you he off, didn't I?"

Silence. I imagined shoving her from her seat.

"Now, what other authors you got?"

Idiotically, I answered, mostly because I felt cornered. But I spoke through gritted teeth.

"They off too. They enemies of the Sunnah, all of 'em. Throw the books away."

Phase four: Initiation.

"Are you part of the saved sect?"

I creased my forehead. "The what?"

Again, the room grew quiet, and they all looked at each other, that fear in their eyes: *Ooh, she really, really off! Don't even know what it means!*

"You have to bear witness that you are part of the saved."

"I already took my *shahaadah*." I was being sarcastic, but her arrogance was so pungent that she thought I was confusing the two.

"The *shahaadah* is for becoming Muslim. This is for being saved."

In my mind I said, *Saying I'm saved doesn't mean I am.* But, clearly, this was not a group of people you could contend with, not if you wanted to go home in one piece. So I acquiesced.

I nodded.

"You have to say it."

"Say what?"

"I am saved."

If I wasn't so intimidated, I would have laughed. I felt like I was in church. If it was this easy, I could've remained Christian.

The sisters stared at me, blinking expectantly. Ghazwa looked like she was going to throw me across the room if I didn't say the words.

Meekly, I opened my mouth and whispered the words, feeling like a complete fool. In my heart, there was a heavy knowledge, a conspicuous voice saying: *Renee, are you out of your mind?* This was a thousand light-years beyond that mere wavering within. It was more like a jet plane flying a banner across the sky. This wasn't a *feeling.* I knew: *This is plain stupid. These people are mentally ill.*

Phase five: Let's eat!

As if robots on a timer, the sisters all smiled and cheered at my words, their grim faces having disappeared. Wadiah served the food, and they talked freely with me, asking me about my marriage, bursting into easy laughter as if I was a long lost friend. Oddly, I found myself laughing and talking too, intoxicated by the change in atmosphere as we ate.

I was in—or "on it" as Ghazwa would say. And I was relieved that they didn't think I was "off."

When I got home, I exhaled in relief that it was all over.

Little did I know, this was just the beginning.

What is odd in my recollection of the weeks that followed is that the feeling of uneasiness never left me while I was in the presence of Ghazwa and her friends. In retrospect, I see clearly that my faith was beginning to dip dangerously low. I had no desire to learn more about my religion. I actually began to dread it, fearing that I'd have to throw yet another book away or stay away from yet another sister who loved Allah and His Messenger.

I gradually showed less interest in Hadiyah's class and called more often to Saliha to say I was sick, all the while seething at the illogic of Ghazwa's arguments against scholars, authors, and sisters who committed no crime. I didn't throw away any books or stop talking to my friends, at least not yet, but I had already been contaminated by one of Satan's most powerful weapons: doubt.

Initially, I didn't even know that's what it was, and I didn't even pinpoint Ghazwa's crowd as the source. At the time, I remember feeling more and more lethargic, and I attributed it to pregnancy. But, physiologically, I was less nauseated and was vomiting only once each day, sometimes going a full two days without getting sick. But because I was expecting, Hadiyah and Saliha attributed my waning inspiration and deflated energy to pregnancy. And, for me, it was a convenient excuse. It gave me time to think.

It was during Ramadan at the beginning of January 1997 that I realized my affliction. Despite my clear disagreement with Ghazwa and her friends, I was beginning to wonder if there was something to what they were saying. Okay, it was clear that they were lacking in good character, to say the least, but did that mean they were wrong about my books and friends? Was I going astray without knowing it?

These would be the questions that would ultimately lead me astray. Until today, I have not one ounce of concrete proof that I had reason to question any of the books or people they said I should, hence the verse in the Qur'an saying that suspicion, in some cases, is a sin. I know now this was definitely one of those cases.

Ghazwa and her friends would constantly argue, "But it don't matter if they ain't say nothing wrong. They sit with heretics!" That's literally what they would say was their crime: they "sit with" so-and-so. This crime of "sitting" could range from literally sitting in a room with a "heretic" or actually, God forbid, quoting from one (Bear in mind that, for them, a "heretic" was defined by whoever they don't "see" at their *masjid* or a certain lecture or conference, so this was an extremely large group of people considering the amount of Muslims on earth).

One person who found his way on the "off" list committed the crime of saying in a lecture, "Do unto others as you'll have others do unto you." The crime in this? Well, here's a hint: You won't find this quote in the Qur'an, hadith, or on Fulan's www dot whatever dot com.

Another person's crime: When prompted, he wouldn't say the line: "I am saved." The crime in this? *If he ashamed of it, he must be off!*

For the most part, it didn't matter whether or not the person actually was exhibiting characteristics of a person who is "saved." If a person who made the declaration of being "saved" made a mistake (like saying it was permissible to backbite and slander from dawn to dusk), we were to excuse them because they're human, and after all, what human doesn't make mistakes? Or, better yet, we just say, *Let's backbite and slander, there's a new ruling that says we can!*

But if a person who didn't make the declaration was seen even buying a box of Wheaties, the brother who knows a brother who knows someone who has a friend who knows a brother who sits in the same class as Fulan receives an emergency call to clarify whether or not the cereal purchase could be indicative of a "mistake" in the religion.

My life after Ramadan is a time I don't like to recall, mainly because it involves so much of what I'm ashamed of now. Today, I'm amazed by how I decided to actually join Ghazwa's *"Girl, I know you off it!"* anti-sisterhood sorority. Despite having been blessed with Hadiyah, Arifah, Nasrin, and Sumayyah in my life, I actually joined this exclusive club under the rationale, "Well, I just want to be safe"—after I saw *clearly* that it was not even remotely related to true

Islam (if you subtract how fast they could recite from authentic books on *'aqeedah*).

My joining the sorority after seeing clear signs of misguidance was such an amazing phenomenon to me that when I returned to school, I actually double majored in math and psychology. In my mind, things just didn't add up.

There are many times that I reflect on my days of ignorance, the ones that came after my "enlightenment" and, naturally, before my wisdom. What I ponder most is my and my sorority sisters' remarkable abandonment of three basics of Islam: fearing Allah, focusing on your soul, and guarding the tongue.

I know there will be many who wonder at my use of terms of endearment in place of those specific labels that my sorority sisters prefer to use in reference to themselves. But I steer clear of this for the same reason I am no longer part of the club: I fear Allah. Referring to them as they refer to themselves would be committing the same crime I repented when the hazing wore off: using labels to simplify the complicated—and pervert reality.

In the sorority, a person was damned or saved by the mere application of a label (a right exercised by only the sorority or its mirror fraternity whose primary job was to seek the faults of others, especially if none were apparent, hence the necessity of interrogation phases at all "heart dissection" appointments for potential members). If the sorority sisters labeled a person "saved," they were saved. If they labeled a person "damned," they were damned. It was, really, that simple. Reality, the possibility of error, or even the fact that the role of saving and damning a person belonged only to Allah was never discussed.

The more I became a part of the damning and saving, I realized just how loose these terms were—both the terms used in labeling, and the terms followed as criteria in blessing or cursing a person. In addition to obvious religious infractions, a person could be damned as "off" for any of the following reasons: having "too much" money (Hadiyah), being "too popular" (Yusuf), being "too nice" (trust me, I'm not exaggerating. I was at a fault-seeking meeting when this was a person's only crime), being from a country deemed too "cultural" (Nasrin), wanting to get "too many *dunya* degrees" (Nasrin again, poor soul), not backbiting or slandering anyone pronounced as "off" by Fulan or by the sorority/fraternity (all Muslims not seen regularly at the *masjid* of "the saved" or at least carrying a valid excuse: "I was at the other *masjid* spying on others to see who was masquerading as "saved" so I can report them to you"— again, not an exaggeration; our sorority had bona fide spies who would even visit homes of Muslims for the sole purpose of scanning their shelves for "off" books so the person can be announced as "off" at the next event), winning an argument against a "saved" brother/sister (even if the argument wasn't related to Islam), giving salaams to a Muslim who's on the "off" list (you're excused if you didn't know they were "off," but you have to repent and promise to grimace at them from now on), going to any site besides Fulan's www dot whatever dot com (matrimony sites are excluded from this rule, especially the ones with "off" sisters' pictures all over them because brothers might want to guide them to the *haqq*).

I know it sounds like I'm being facetious, but I'm not. This is actually an abbreviated list of bona fide infractions. Some may find this list hilarious, but I don't. I know people still drowned in the confusion, so I don't have the luxury of a good laugh. As I wrote this list, I was actually trying to keep myself from crying. It hurts that much. Still.

But I don't fault anyone who laughs. It is ludicrous, I know. I wish I had the luxury of being so far removed from it as to find it comical. But it's too personal for me. I simply can't find humor in a direct reminder of my sins, especially as I know there are scores of people for whom I may be held on the bridge to Paradise until I can come up with proof for the tales I actually spread, and dozens of others I helped to be spread. Every e-mail I forwarded, every bulletin I posted, every flyer I distributed, and every word I spoke on the phone and amongst sisters will come back to haunt me on the Day when even the smallest weight of good—or evil—will be brought forth.

What tears me apart inside and evokes long periods of weeping over my sins is this: During the years I spent as a card-carrying member of the "hate for His sake" club, I learned less Islam, less Arabic, and less Qur'an than I did in the few months of enlightenment in 1996 alone. And in the sorority, my faith actually decreased, *plummeted* would be a more accurate term.

To be fair, there were many classes on Islam, and I attended almost all of them. But I don't recall learning a single matter about Islam that I hadn't already learned from the lectures I'd gone to with Nasrin and Sumayyah or from the classes I took with Hadiyah and Saliha. However, every single class in the sorority/fraternity, even if under the guise of "Qur'an," was peppered with tale-carrying, backbiting, and slander—the appetizer (or dessert) was always the "drum roll" announcement of the most recent addition to the "off" list (one's possible infractions I've already gone over).

Today, one of the most difficult sorority recruits to offer advice in hopes of keeping her from drowning in the "on/off" ocean of confusion is the one who, before meeting the likes of Ghazwa and sorors, never heard of their actually being a saved sect or their being genuine heresy amongst Muslims. The person often arrives to the *"Are you on it doggonit?"* meeting straight from the *masjid* (or street) after taking their *shahaadah.* During interrogation phases one through four (remember phase five is simply "let's eat!"), they're pumped with all the "off it" names and books and websites and people before they even know how to pray or pronounce a single letter of Qur'an. Some of them never learn these things properly or completely because, like the bow-tie wearing newspaper boys at stoplights, they're too busy passing out Fulan's latest bulletin of *"You off the haqq, ak!"* to realize they actually have a soul and the Angel of Death will not be as much as a fraction of a second late when what is written overtakes them.

Because there *is* such a thing as having correct belief, being a part of the "saved group," and staying away from misguidance, clarification on what is true Islam and cautioning new (and sometimes veteran) Muslims to stay away from the damnation club is excruciatingly difficult. There's no label you can really say that would make things clear, at least not without stripping the beautiful truth of that label from those who actually live it—rather than offer mere lip service to it while calling to something entirely foreign to Islam and good sense.

Here's one of my journal reflections on this whole label business, written after I had left, at least internally, the "saved by the label" group:

Renee, from now on just call yourself Muslim or believer, because these are the names that Allah and His Messenger taught. If you wish to add an adjective to these terms, feel free, but make sure you don't forget that the adjective is something you're striving for, not what you really are in truth.

Distinguish yourself in your faith and actions. A label means nothing without these two.

And know it's not the label that's the problem. In fact, the label is necessary if I'm thinking of correct belief and what I <u>hope</u> my actions attest to. The call to the label may actually be good, even necessary at times. But my hesitation is only one:

If I use a label, how do I define it to someone? For someone to find out what it means, they must go to those with the loudest voices, to the books and Internet sites that come up under my label's name, and to the communities who've affixed the label on themselves. And I'm apprehensive about what they'll find. Because I know very few of them would represent who I am, and far too many of them would call to what I hope to God I'll never again be.

Even as the label itself points to a purity of Islam.

But who would know that after a simple Internet search or a visit to the "fraternity house"? There is just too much to explain, and refute. And I don't have the energy anymore.

And am I really to believe that I'll be closer to Allah for focusing more on a word than on my soul? What if the label I choose contradicts who I really am? And what if the adjective I use for myself is defined, by others, in a way that contradicts Islam?

And, really, are Muslims that astray, are we that lost and clueless, that we can't see that Islam is only the Islam revealed to the Prophet by Allah? That the Prophet and his companions were and will always be the exemplars of this religion? If we are this far gone, then our words and actions alone testify against us in the religion we claim.

Do I really need a distinct label for others to see such an obvious fact?

If so… I accept the label. And I'll wear it with pride.

I'll only need to find the right one, where no one, and I mean no one except the ones truly exemplifying that righteous label will claim.

My only questions are: What is that label, and who of us are truly of these people?

I know, for sure, it's a compelling question whether I am.

Twenty-three

"...Be all of you as fellow brothers and servants of Allah.
A Muslim is the brother of a Muslim. He does not oppress him
or betray him, nor does he look down upon him.
Righteousness is here [and he pointed to his heart].
It is enough as a serious evil for a Muslim to
despise his Muslim brother. All of the Muslim's
property is sacred to the Muslim—his blood, his wealth,
and his honor."
—Prophet Muhammad, peace be upon him (Muslim)

Somehow amidst all the confusion in my life, I managed to achieve some sense of normalcy. After living with Hadiyah until June 1997 (a month after William graduated), I moved to live with William in the basement in-law suite of the home of Yusuf and Sumayyah, where we lived for two years. Then in August 1999, William and I moved into our own apartment. At that time Luqman, my firstborn, was two years old, and I was pregnant with my second child and was due in the second week of December.

Our move was not out of necessity or wisdom. Yusuf and Sumayyah had made it clear that we could stay there as long as we wanted. We were paying rent, so it wasn't charity, but the fee was nominal, almost half the price of any other one-bedroom apartment in Rockville or in any of the D.C. suburbs. We had our own entrance to the home by descending a cement staircase that led to a small walkway ending at the basement door. In the home, almost everything was separate, so we rarely crossed paths with Yusuf or Sumayyah except outside. We shared only the laundry room, which separated the suite from the stairway leading to the kitchen of their house, but in our rental paperwork, we agreed that only the women in the household could wash, dry, or retrieve any clothes.

The decision to move was a painful one financially because William, who had majored in economics as an undergrad, was working part-time in the evenings and going to school for his master's of business administration during the day. He had originally registered with plans to complete the MBA in one and half years, but the demands of wife and children forced him to lessen his load with new plans to complete the degree by 2003.

The primary reason for our move was simple: The damnation fraternity had met and decided it wasn't permissible for us to give "heretics" money for rent because they "might" use it for Yusuf's various projects and entrepreneurships that made him popular (an infraction) in the first place. It didn't matter that his programs were responsible for hundreds of youth becoming Muslim or that he was one of the few Muslim faces active in community service in disadvantaged areas.

To be fair in my recollection of this time, William had always been skeptical of the fraternity although he had, like me, decided that it was best to "be safe." However, he was much too busy to keep up with the latest books and people who were to be abandoned. Although he had been "warned," he refused to give up his friendship with Yusuf, but, wisely, he never told the fraternity. He would listen politely and say, "*Akhee,* I hear you." He'd then hang up the phone (or leave the fraternity house) and say to me that he was going to play basketball with Yusuf or help him at the youth center.

Things like this infuriated me, mostly because I had already made it clear to Sumayyah that my association with her would contaminate my "pure" status in Islam. I didn't say this outright, but I did have a private interrogation meeting with her to test her commitment to being saved. She didn't pass, so I told her my associations with her from hereon would be that of only salaams, but I told her that I was being nice because I really shouldn't even be giving her the Islamic greeting until she threw away her books, repented, and said "I am saved."

Sumayyah, in response, sighed and gazed at me with an expression that I later understood as pity, a sympathetic smile creasing the corners of her mouth, and said simply, "Renee, I love you for the sake of Allah. If you ever need anything, I'm here."

The Islamic response to this expression of love, aside from the natural human instinct to respond in kind, is: "May the One for whom you love me love you." But I just stared at her, too drunken in the sorority's hazing to use either Islamic or human sense, and said, "I already warned you, so now you know."

Years later, I called Sumayyah on the phone and cried my eyes out, begging her to forgive me for all I had done. She then chuckled as if nothing at all happened in all those years and said, "Renee, I already have." Then she invited me to her daughter's *'aqeeqah,* a gathering to eat the meat sacrificed after a baby is born.

My studies in psychology have given me a basic understanding of the mindset of the sorority and fraternity, as well as the mindset of reluctant recruits like myself. As with labels, nothing is as simple as a scientific explanation, but psychological studies do offer some plausible explanations that are quite compelling. According to my research, the anti-sister/brotherhood damnation club is striking in that it shares these characteristics with that of cults: members are often youth; members are cut off from friends and family and must give complete allegiance to a leader who often is believed to have direct communication with God; illogical fear is the primary intimidation to keep members away from "enemies"; defamation of all non-members is established to reduce the chances of a member straying; the leader secures his position by discrediting all other leaders who may challenge or refute his claims; mental and physical abuse are the primary means of maintaining group membership and control; there is a psychological connection—a "fraternity"—established after being abused and then embraced. (The last characteristics are why some apparently harmless college sororities and fraternities are also questionable ethically.)

My breaking free of the sorority was a gradual wearing down of the human spirit, a testimony to the veracity of the Prophet's words, *"...whoever overburdens himself in his religion will not be able to continue in that way."* The excruciating pain of carrying the load of the self was becoming too much for me to bear. I was sore and spent. I simply could not go on like that any longer.

When I had met with Sumayyah privately and given her an ultimatum, my heart wasn't even in it, which is why I didn't turn her over to the fault-seeking committee themselves. I had gone to the meetings less and less and was beginning to grow tired of their righteous façade and non-existent Sunnah (except for what they could recite from books). They had even begun in-fighting amongst themselves. Ghazwa accused fellow sorors of being "too soft" with non-members, and Wadiah accused Ghazwa and her likes of being "too harsh." When the imam at the fraternity house (they didn't have funds to afford an actual *masjid*) had announced that there was a new ruling by Fulan that members were to be "kind," there was a huge split in the club. Ghazwa and her friends announced that both the imam and Fulan were "off" and started a new fraternity house. Wadiah and her friends remained but inserted phrases like *SubhaanAllaah* and *Alhamdulillaah* when backbiting or slandering a non-member.

"*SubhaanAllah*," Wadiah said reflectively to me one day, her voice in its usual soft tone, "I know it must be hard for you living with Sumayyah while she's an enemy of the Sunnah." She sighed. "What do you think we can say to guide her to be of the saved?"

That was one of the last times I saw Wadiah in person. I was beginning to wonder what it was that Sumayyah had done in the first place. As I thought about it, I realized that Sumayyah was most likely sincere, so my heart softened, hence my decision to give her a chance by meeting her privately.

Now, I cry in my *sajdah* as I recall just how contaminated I had been when I spoke to my sister in Islam, a woman who had shown nothing except commitment to Allah's Book and His Messenger. For Sumayyah—like Arifah, Hadiyah, and Nasrin—Islam was a way of life, a belief that permeated their hearts and minds, a belief that guided them to kindness, forgiveness, making excuses for others, and displaying good character and sincerity as they lived in love, hope, and fear of Allah, their most ardent desire in life being to die in a state pleasing to their Lord.

Nevertheless, there are two incidents that would lead to my final abandonment of the sorority. It was then, following these events, that I realized, finally, what I had known intuitively all along—that the "saved sect" mentioned in the Sunnah is not a physical group of people living in one place, attending a particular *masjid*, and who all befriended and knew each other.

In truth, all those who are a part of this group are known only to Allah. A person truly of this group would never feel secure moving her tongue to admit or dismiss anyone from it, as a person herself will live either in testimony to the truth or in testimony against it. The characteristics of this righteous group are conveyed to us in the Qur'an and hadith. These righteous worshippers' most distinct traits are a correct belief in Allah, commitment to the Prophet's Sunnah, good character, a tongue stilled except for speaking good and reminding of Allah, speaking only with knowledge, a forgiving nature, love for Islam and the Muslims, and an ever present concern that he or she has fallen short of being saved—from punishment in the Hereafter.

The first incident was when William and I were in a financial crisis. When we moved, William had increased his hours at his job until he was full-time, thus giving us enough money to live from paycheck to paycheck in the new apartment. We had health insurance, but when we received our bill weeks after my daughter Rahma was born in the first week of December, we discovered that it did not cover the entire bill. We scraped up what monies we could and paid the remainder of the bill, but we found ourselves at the beginning of January unable to pay the rent in full.

It was the last ten days of Ramadan, so William and I prayed to Allah sincerely and were at ease that we would be taken care of, as this is the time of year when the Prophet's ever-present generosity had increased the most. We knew that there would be hundreds of Muslims rushing to follow his Sunnah in hope of earning Allah's mercy and forgiveness.

My instinct was to call Arifah or Sumayyah, but I cursed myself for not thinking to consult the saved members first. In my mind, my sorority represented true Islam, so I shouldn't go to heretics. When I called Wadiah (I was a member of the "be kind while you malign" group), she hesitated and said she'd have to ask the imam if it was permissible to collect the money (which amounted to less than three hundred dollars after William and I paid what we could).

I was stumped. Wasn't I a bona fide member? What did she need to ask about?

She called me periodically, giving me the updates. As it turns out, there were questions as to whether or not I would use the money for my rent or if I'd use it to support "deviants" like Arifah and Sumayyah, whom they believed I wasn't being strict enough with (kindly strict, of course).

The verdict came down on the twenty-seventh night: The imam had called a brother who called a brother who was friends with a "student" who sat in classes down the street from Fulan (no joke), and they said if my status as being saved was in question, then it wouldn't be permissible to give me the money. But if I was willing to come to the fraternity house (along with William) and do an open testimony and clarification of being saved, while bearing witness that I would never speak to Arifah and Sumayyah (or in William's case, Ibrahim and Yusuf) again until they repented and testified too, they would consider giving me some money from what they collected at Eid, but only after a meeting of the saved to determine whether or not my testimony was sincere.

I hung up the phone and cried my heart out. I was all chokes and hiccups, asthmatic breaths and whimpers. William was at work, so I had no one to complain to.

Spent, I raised my hands and prayed to Allah.

O Allah, Hearer of Prayers, Owner of all Provision, Most Generous, Most Kind! These are the last ten days of the month in which You sent down Your Qur'an. You made a promise of mercy to those who ask, forgiveness for those who ask, and exhorted us to beg of You because You are the One Who bestows and bestows without account. I ask You to have mercy on me and William, forgive me and William, and I beg you to shower Your generosity upon us. We came to You after worshipping other than You. We have believed in You after disbelieving in You. And we come to you, testifying to Your Oneness after being in the darkness of shirk. So, I ask You, Ar-Rahmaan, I beg You, Ar-Razzaaq, to relieve our burdens, for there is no one to relieve our burdens but You. Yaa Rabb! Respond to my prayer!

After my supplication, I continued crying on the couch in my apartment. Rahma was sleeping in her crib, but Luqman was running around entertaining himself by making "vrooming" noises with the car he was holding. But when he saw me, he approached the couch with a concerned look in his eyes.

"Ummi, what's wong?"

I forced a smile, but the tears continued to slip down my cheeks. I rubbed his head to assure him I was okay. He looked hesitant.

"Why you cwying?"

"Because I want something."

"I got some money. I can buy for you." He reached into his pocket and pulled out three pennies and a nickel and presented them to me.

I laughed, evoking more tears as I thought of how his eight cents could actually help us just a bit. "Thank you, Luqman." I accepted the coins and held them in my palm, still smiling at him. "I'll give it to Abi when he gets home *inshaAllaah.*"

"Allah said don't cwy."

"Really?" I was amused and moved at once.

"Yes. 'Cause He already give you what you want."

I nodded, immediately ashamed that I was being ungrateful in front of my son. "Yes, He did, Luqman. I don't need anything else."

He nodded emphatically. "That's wight, Ummi." He was distracted by his car suddenly and ran off resuming "vrooming" it around the room. "No more cwy baby!"

"Yes, Luqman." I shook my head, smiling. "No more cry baby."

I took a deep breath, my heart more at ease and leaned back on the couch, knowing without a doubt that Allah had heard my prayer and would respond to it.

The phone rang as I thought this. I walked over to it and picked it up. It was Arifah.

"I was just thinking about you," she said after we exchanged the Arabic greetings.

"Really?" My voice was exhausted despite trying to sound normal.

"Is it okay if I stop by?"

I hesitated, immediately fearing that one of the members might see. But then a feeling came over me. *Allah is my Judge.* "Sure, I'd love that."

Arifah and I still talked to each other during the years of my membership in the sorority though the relationship was naturally a bit strained. Oddly, I never felt the inclination to give her an interrogation meeting, even like the half-hearted one I'd given Sumayyah. It was as if each time our gazes met, she was saying, "*Ukhtee,* I know you're just going through something. Don't worry about it. I love you anyway."

She never gave up on me, even when I was nonchalant about our friendship and even neglectful at times. I rarely called her, and out of respect, she rarely called me, though her calls came more often than mine. I saw her at most once in a month, and I never went to anything she invited me to, and I never invited her to any sorority functions. She had visited me at the apartment one time in the months I had lived there, and that was because she had some household items and children's clothes she thought I could use. The visit had been short, and she didn't bother with too much small talk. She just wanted to see Luqman (Rahma wasn't yet born) and spent less than twenty minutes talking baby talk to him. I hadn't even called to tell her I had had the baby. So this offer for a visit was not a part of our usual routine. But I was pleased.

When Arifah arrived, she wore a broad grin and embraced me warmly. Her sons Rashad and Musa were with her. Rashad was around three years old, and Musa was about eight months. She had called me when Musa was born, but I hadn't gone to visit. As usual, I had been under the haze of the damnation association.

This evening, she acted as if nothing had changed between us. She talked about Rashad and Musa driving her nuts and how she couldn't wait until they grew up. I laughed and told her that Luqman was a handful himself.

Upon seeing Rashad, Luqman ran to him and they chased each other around the room, and I thought of how sisters in the sorority went as far as to forbid their children from playing with children of non-members and would even coach their pre-school aged children until they ran around saying, "I am safed" and "So-and-so is a hair-a-tic." I had never done that. It just seemed so vile. Those poor children didn't even know any of the ninety-nine names of their Lord, yet they could run around saying "Yusuf is a hair-a-tic!" I didn't understand the logic. What if Yusuf one day joined the "saved"? Allah had created minds of children such that teaching them something was like writing in stone, and I couldn't imagine cementing there anything other than basic religious knowledge and good human sense. That's what they would need in life, not a photographic memory of the "off" list. I feared for the children's mental states as adults.

With the increased noise, Rahma began to cry and I quickly excused myself to get her. I returned with my daughter, and Arifah squealed in excitement, laying Musa next to her on the couch before stretching out her arms to hold my daughter.

"Aw," Arifah said, gazing lovingly at Rahma. She held the back of Rahma's head while her other hand was at the baby's back to get a good look at Rahma on her lap. "*BarakAllaahufeehaa*," she said, invoking Allah's blessing. "She's beautiful. She looks just like you."

I laughed self-consciously. "No she doesn't."

"She does." Arifah glanced at Luqman running around the room. "Luqman has your husband's eyes, but Rahma definitely has yours."

I gazed at my son for a moment, unable to keep from grinning from how much I loved him. Caramel brown skin, black curly hair, and blue eyes. He was a sight to see. Rahma still had the pale skin tone of newborns, but rich brown stroked the soft of her ear, hinting at the color she would be graced with later in life. Her eyes were ebony, like mine and already she had thick eyelashes and a head full of hair.

"May Allah preserve them," I said.

"And mine too."

We were quiet as Arifah cooed at Rahma, and I gazed at the baby too, smiling all the while.

"Did you eat?" I asked. It was already after seven thirty that night, far past *iftaar*, but I wanted to be a good hostess.

She nodded. "I'm stuffed. I can't eat a single bite right now."

I stood anyway. "Then I'll just bring you something to drink."

I returned with water, juice, and a tray of snacks. We didn't have much to offer, but I was pleased that I could place the attractive array of crackers, cookies, and candy before her.

"*JazaakAllaahukhair*," she said, invoking Allah's reward for me as was customary in a Muslim's expressing thanks.

"*Wa iyyak*."

Rahma started to squirm and cry, and I took her from Arifah, placing her in position to nurse. Rahma immediately accepted the meal and grew content as I nestled her in the crook of my elbow as she ate.

"Renee," Arifah said, now holding Musa and nursing him next to me. Her voice was reflective, as if lost in thought.

"Mm, hm." I was gently petting Rahma's hair and gazing at her with a warm expression on my face.

"I wanted to apologize to you."

I creased my forehead and glanced at her before turning my attention back to my daughter. "For what?"

I heard her sigh next to me, and I looked at her. "For everything."

I shook my head. "What do you mean?"

"I feel bad for not being there for you when you became Muslim."

I laughed. "You didn't even know me at that time."

"No, I don't mean right after. I mean when we met."

"But still, you were there for me a lot."

She shook her head. "No I wasn't. I was caught up in my own life."

"I don't remember it like that."

"Well, I do. And I feel bad."

"Well, you shouldn't. I don't. You didn't do anything wrong."

"Yes I did."

I looked at her intensely, a slight grin on my face. "What are you talking about?"

Her eyes grew distant as she stared at her son, but it was clear her mind was somewhere else. "I never said anything when I saw Ghazwa and Wadiah at the mall."

I stared at her. "You know them?"

She shook her head. "Only Wadiah. She used to do my hair. I only saw Ghazwa in passing a couple of times. But I know about her."

I was quiet, sadness overtaking me. I know now this was the beginning of my regret, my heart nagging me to turn to Allah in repentance. I hadn't even had a flicker of temptation to correct Arifah and say she was wrong. Because, deep inside, I knew she had been the true Muslim all along.

"I should've said something," she said. "But it's really hard, you know, with all that's going on. I guess I felt like there was nothing I could do."

Her words touched me, and a lump developed in my throat. But even at that moment, I didn't know it was because the burden of misguidance was being lifted and her words were evoking an awareness of self. I didn't know I was getting a glimpse at my aching soul, the first flicker of light since the damnation sorority had blinded me from the enlightenment of my faith.

"I've seen so many sisters get involved in that and never come back."

I dropped my gaze to Rahma, swallowing to keep the lump from growing more. I concentrated my attention there to keep my eyes from burning behind my lids. I didn't want to hear any more but my words of protest were lost in my throat.

"I even know some who left Islam. I mean, I..."

Her voice cracked, and I willed myself not to look at her because I didn't want to see the tears welling in her eyes. I heard her take a deep breath before continuing.

"And I just didn't know what to say. I mean, I knew it was wrong. But when I tried to tell the sisters, they thought I meant it was wrong to be *saved*. They thought I was saying the group's *'aqeedah* was wrong." She breathed again.

"So they thought something was wrong with my beliefs."

She paused, and in the silence, I looked at her, our gazes locking—in that moment our hearts connecting as fellow sisters in Islam. My heart swelled with love for her at that moment, but I didn't say anything. We just looked at each other, her eyes brimmed with tears, mine on the verge.

I looked away, biting my lower lip as Rahma nursed.

"I just wanted to say I'm sorry. I should've told you before. I don't know what you think now, or what's happening with them. But I just felt compelled to apologize and ask your forgiveness." I heard her exhale. "Because I want Allah to forgive me."

I nodded, unable to speak for fear that I would break down. The irony of this moment has never escaped me. I should have been the one asking her forgiveness, not the other way around. I knew she was holding her breath, fearing that I wouldn't forgive her for the wrong she imagined she had done, and that fear, her raw sincere fear, pierced my heart as I realized that this is what it meant to fear Allah. It was the end of Ramadan and she wanted her sins forgiven and her supplications answered, and she feared that the wrong she had done to me was standing as a barrier between her and Allah's mercy.

Wronging another human being is a sin that Allah withholds forgiveness until the rights of the person are restored and the wronged forgives her oppressor. If the wronged isn't given their rights or they don't forgive the one who wronged them, Allah does not forgive that sin, and on the Day of Judgment the wronged takes from the oppressor's good deeds, and if he runs out of good deeds, the sins of the one he oppressed are piled on him. Seeking forgiveness from a person whom you wronged, while repenting to Allah, is one of the characteristics of those whom Allah has truly written down as saved.

The irony was astounding.

I had spent years giving my time and energy to wronging others, never once imagining I was earning sin, and was in fact drilled with the belief that we were actually getting blessings for each "off" person we slandered and maligned. Once we were actually told, "Come, let's backbite for the sake of Allah." Even when a person accused of being "off" defended themselves against the accusations levied against them, we were told that they were lying and couldn't be trusted...even when they were speaking of their own beliefs of the heart! So there was no opportunity to be exonerated by the damnation association unless they decided you had repented and testified to being saved enough and were now worthy of *their* forgiveness and admission into the club.

"I forgive you." I whispered the words as I had uttered *"I am saved"* a couple of years before. But this time my shame wasn't in knowing that I was not speaking from my heart, but in knowing that I was. Even as it was really I who needed to hear Arifah say those same words to me.

Before she left, she stood at the door, Musa in her arms and Rashad at her legs. She was asking if I needed anything, anything at all, and I shook my head, holding Rahma as she rested her head on my shoulder. "No, I don't need anything."

She nodded and parted her lips to speak but was interrupted by Luqman.

"But Ummi you were cwying!" He was pulling on my pant leg.

I stared at him, trying to register what he was saying and its relevance. "Sweetie," I said, embarrassed. "Auntie has to go."

"But you were cwying. You need money."

My eyes widened in embarrassment as I realized what he was saying and why. I glanced at Arifah, whose eyes were slightly widened too as she listened to his words, and understood that they were in response to her.

I forced a smile. "*JazaakAllaahukhair* for stopping by."

Her forehead creased in concern. "*Ukhtee*, if you need something let me know."

I shook my head. "No, I'm fine."

Luqman stomped his feet. "You were cwying! Allah answer your prayer."

"Renee, really it's not a pro—"

"Allah answer your prayer when you cwy!"

"Luq-*man!*" My voice rose tensely in my mortification. I wanted him to stop.

He cried louder. "Allah answer your prayer, Ummi. He send Auntie 'Rifah!"

My heart nearly leapt from my chest in realization of what he was saying. I stared at him as if seeing him for the first time. I think every parent has a moment where their very heart trembles at the phenomenal prodigy exhibited in the words or actions of their child. This was that moment for me.

His voice lowered when he saw he had our attention. "You cwy for money, Ummi," he whined, his eyes glistening with tears. He was sounding like himself again, but the maturity in his meaning was uncanny. "But Allah give and you say no."

My breath caught, and I didn't know what to say.

"I better go," Arifah said.

I nodded, greeting her as she ushered Rashad out the door with one hand while Musa leaned his head against her as she held him with her other.

Two days later, on the twenty-ninth night, I found an envelope stuck under my door. Inside was a card stuffed with five one-hundred dollar bills and a simple handwritten note:

"You cried to Allah, and He answered your prayer. So you can't say no."

I cried when I read it and then prayed to Allah to preserve Arifah and her family and give them *Janna-tul Fir-Daws*—the highest level of Paradise.

Twenty-four

*"There has come upon you the disease of
the nations before you: envy and hatred.
These are the shavers. I do not mean that they
shave hair, but they shave away religious commitment.
By the One in Whose Hand is my soul,
you will not enter Paradise until you believe,
and you will not believe until you love one another."*
—Prophet Muhammad, peace be upon him (Tirmidhi)

*"Those who disagree the least among themselves are the
people of the Sunnah and hadith, since they build their
actions upon that foundation. The further a group is from
hadith, the higher the level of disagreement among them.
For whoever leaves the truth finds himself in a state of
confusion, unsure what the truth is or where to find it."*
—Ibn Qayyim

I'll always remember the year 2000 as one of my most confusing and depressing years. For three years I had given my energy, time, and heart to the sorority, thinking I was being "safe" in the company of those who claimed to be saved. But I found myself with lower faith, increased distrust of Muslims, and unable to even rekindle my thirst in seeking knowledge because I didn't know which books were okay to read, which lecturers were okay to listen to, or even what *masjid* I could attend to learn Arabic or Qur'an. The fraternity house made constant efforts to secure classes in Arabic and Qur'an but the infighting among the members made consistency an impossibility in any class. Sometimes a teacher was dismissed after only one session because the imam realized that he was a recent addition to the "off" list, so he couldn't be allowed to teach anymore. Sometimes sisters gathered in the home of a "saved" Arab sister only to realize three sessions into the class that she wasn't committed to the sorority like she should, or that her teacher had been a scholar on the "off" list overseas.

Even the innocent mention of an inspirational book made me wince, because I knew the routine. We'd get motivated, start reading and benefiting from it, only to be told weeks later we had to throw the book away and buy nothing from the author again. My Islamic bookshelf bore only three books, the Qur'an, an abridged *Sahih Bukhari*, and a lone, thin publication on *'aqeedah* distributed by Fulan's website.

Meanwhile, Arifah, Sumayyah, and Nasrin were memorizing more and more Qur'an, learning more and more

Arabic, and attending lectures and conferences I'd never heard of. It was as if my life was passing me by as I wasted away sitting at a worn desk in an abandoned preschool while my former friends were getting ready to graduate from high school.

Periodically, I would buy an Islamic book, but the doubts and questions that gripped me, not from the content but from the illogical fear drilled into me by the sorority, prevented me from ever finishing or gaining anything from a book. Occasionally, I would actually come across genuine misguidance (like the worshipping of "saints" or making pilgrimage or religious rites around a grave or a call to abandon hadith), and I'd feel fear grip my chest. Where was the knowledge? Where could I learn my religion? Was the sorority *right*? Was there no one upon the truth except the likes of Ghazwa and Wadiah, who barely knew how to recite Qur'an well enough to pray, let alone teach a class, and had perfected nothing that could be passed on to others except the art of making people's lives difficult and miserable?

After some time, I just stopped buying books on Islam and when I felt the urge to read, I would read a novel or review my math texts (my love for formulas and derivatives never died), drawing a temporary high from engrossing myself in a fictional world or from solving math problems in books I held onto because I didn't want to lose my knack. I had also started tutoring middle and high school students in math at the local library, so this was also part of my incentive in perusing the texts.

My interaction with the world was limited because my heart was hardening from ignorance and unrest, and my sowing the seeds of discord as part of the sorority was coming back to haunt me. People stopped calling me for fear of the problems I would cause them, and even the sorority itself was growing in distrust of me because I hadn't been seen at any lectures or events in the past three months. I imagined they were about to have an official meeting about me, if they hadn't already, but I couldn't bring myself to care. It wasn't their companionship I was craving, it was that of normal people like Nasrin, Hadiyah, and Sumayyah. But they had stopped talking to me, because I couldn't open my mouth without sounding like a hypnotic robot as I recited the sorority mantra, exhorting them to say the magic phrase, in hopes they'd be "saved" so I could talk to them again.

I ached for some female company to distract me from my life, but I had only three companions in my life right then. And when I say companions I don't mean three close friends and a dozen associates, I mean these three were the sum total of all the people I could call if wanted to have a lavish dinner at my home or picnic at the local park. There was

Arifah, who gave her all in trying to revive my spiritual life but to no avail because I was becoming more and more despondent by the day. She would come to visit, and I'd just sit next to her, unable to muster the energy to even hold a decent conversation. My only moments of liveliness were when I was playing with Luqman or Rahma or when I was tutoring at the library—while Arifah or William watched the children.

My other two companions were the best friends who were each other's neighbor—Bashirah, the African-American, and Jadwa, the Brazilian who looked biracial. When I couldn't take staying in the apartment a moment longer, I'd put both Luqman and Rahma in the single-seat stroller and walk fifteen minutes to Bashirah's and Jadwa's townhouse community. Because Jadwa was often at Bashirah's house or would come over the minute she found out I was there, I always went to Bashirah's home and had never been inside Jadwa's. They were both a lot older than me, but I enjoyed their company like I did Arifah's, and sometimes even more so because I couldn't get away with sitting off alone and feeling sorry for myself. Their personalities simply didn't allow it. I also was getting closer to Bashirah's sixteen-year-old daughter Ihsan, who shared my love for math. That knowledge alone rejuvenated me whenever I visited. They also had no idea of my affiliation with the sorority, and I wanted to keep it that way.

It was early March when I got a surprise visit at my home—the first phase of the second incident that would prove my undoing in the sorority, but I, of course, didn't know it at the time. When I looked through the peephole and saw a sister in *hijaab* and glasses, I opened the door and was surprised to see Lisan standing opposite me. Not only was the sorority all but abandoning me now, but after the split, Lisan had joined the ranks of Ghazwa and labeled Fulan himself "off." So I was twice removed from the sister at my door, first by my status and second by hers.

Next to Lisan was a pale, freckled sister with a mass of red curly hair that was covered with a thin *khimaar* that kept slipping from her head. The sister was wearing jeans and a long-sleeve fitting shirt, something definitely not approved by the sorority. I assumed she was a new Muslim, and when Lisan introduced her as Annette who had taken her *shahaadah* two months ago, I wasn't surprised. When Annette spoke, it was clear she wasn't American, but I couldn't place her accent, which held a hint of her being "street smart." I was too distracted by the surprise visit itself to relax enough to ask her background.

Lisan explained that Annette had heard of me and was eager to meet me, especially since she heard I tutored in math. This took me aback because I had only recently started tutoring and was a bit uncomfortable with someone like Lisan knowing this information. I wanted to ask where she had heard this, but it would have been out of place. Lisan went on to explain that Annette wanted to get her GED and was having trouble in math but she didn't have any money to pay, and would I be willing to help her for the sake of Allah?

Of course, I agreed, because you can't exactly say no to a question posed like that. And I was too shy to point out to Lisan that she hadn't even asked if I would be able to tutor Annette at all. It was like having a flashback from Ghazwa and Wadiah in the mall, planning my Saturday for me without even taking a moment to consider that I had a life and that my schedule was possibly already full. I withheld my thoughts on this for Annette's sake, but I doubt that I would have had the guts to speak my mind to Lisan even if Annette wasn't there. The sorority had already shown me what they were capable of, and if I'm completely honest about this period of my life, the mere sight of one of them gave me an instant migraine because I was that scared of the misery they could evoke by their presence.

The entire visit confused me because not once did Lisan acknowledge the sorority or their split, or that she and Ghazwa had cited me by name as one of the people who were "suck ups" to non-members. I kept my mouth shut on this because, again, Annette was there (and, of course, there was my cowardice that would prevent me from sticking up for myself anyway).

They left almost as quickly as they had come, and I sat for a full five minutes, perplexed by the senselessness of it all. I knew Lisan lived in D.C. and would have had to take both a metro train and a bus to get to my apartment after which she would have to walk a distance inside the complex itself. Apparently, Annette lived close to Lisan, and they both had made the trek without even as much as a phone call to alert me. It was sheer luck for them that I had been home. I could easily have been at Arifah's or Bashirah's, or even tutoring in the library. This was unsettling, and I couldn't shake the feeling that something didn't add up about the whole ordeal.

Because I was trying to keep myself afloat mentally, I pushed the doubts out of my mind and focused on what I knew: Annette would come once a week to my house (I had no more timeslots when Arifah or William could watch the children while I went to the library). I was having a difficult time understanding how a person in such dire straits as Annette could afford to take the train and bus twice a day each week, all for sitting with me for two hours when there had to be dozens of people who could help her in D.C. Yes, private tutoring was expensive but there were many non-profit organizations and *masjid* programs that could easily secure her a tutor. But because it was a part of good Islam to think the best, I tried to keep from suspecting anything, and I put my energy into helping her pass the GED.

However, I'm human, and curiosity got the better of me, so I asked her how she became Muslim. She told me that she passed the *masjid* (a small row house) often and would see women covered, and she walked in one day. She said she met Lisan, Ghazwa, and some other sisters who taught her about Islam, so she took her *shahaadah*.

My heart softened toward her after hearing her story. Till today, I never tire of hearing how someone came to accept Islam. Each story is so intricate and beautiful as it traces the smallest details that Allah decreed to guide someone to Him.

"You know how to pray?" I asked her, wanting to help as much as I could.

"I'm learning," she said. "But it's hard. I'm really busy at work."

My eyebrows rose in surprise. "Oh, *mashaAllaah*, where do you work?"

"At a youth center. I'm a basketball coach."

"That's really nice."

"Well, the kids are twelve and thirteen, so it's not much. But they have competitions."

I nodded. "That's really nice."

"I told them I became Muslim."

"*MashaAllaah*, that's good!"

"Let's just hope they get the point."

We laughed then continued the session where we sat at the table in the dining area. After class, she played with Luqman for a few minutes and asked to hold Rahma before she left.

Things went on like this until one day I received a call from Wadiah.

"I just want to let you know that we got a ruling from the brother who knows the brother who sits with the brother who knows Fulan, and we can't speak to you anymore." Her voice was soft, in keeping with her commitment to being kind.

I rolled my eyes to the ceiling. I had expected this. But it still hurt. "Thanks for letting me know."

She was silent, as if taken aback by my unwillingness to argue. "It's not that easy," she said before hanging up.

Less than fifteen minutes later, Lisan called. There was no salaams, and I figured that was in keeping with her commitment to being cruel. "I hope you know it ain't permissible for a heretic to be married to one of the saved."

She hung up. Dial tone humming from the receiver, I stared at the phone as if it had fallen from the sky. I couldn't figure out the sense of her words because, last I knew, William was less enthusiastic about the fraternity than I had been.

It all made sense when I was about to go to bed. They were trying to get Annette acquainted with my family in hopes of introducing her to William, who they hoped would divorce me and marry her. It was the most ridiculous of theories, but the possible reality of its cruelty made me shudder. Would they stoop *that* low? I had no fear that William would pay them any mind, but it did hurt to think he had known their plan and had not shared it with me.

At that moment, I recalled with intense relief the no-polygamy clause we had put in our contract before marrying. Up until then, I had pretty much forgotten about it. But during this period it became crucial in my growing insecurity with my life. At least I didn't have to worry about that distraction. Annette had no idea what she was up against.

When William came home, I asked him about my theory as to their plan. He affirmed it, and I was taken aback, stung.

"Why didn't you say anything to me about it?"

He regarded me with his eyebrows gathered. "For what? I'm not going to divorce you just because they say I should. They're nuts."

Oh. Well... "Still, you should have told me."

He laughed and shook his head. "Renee, right now, I just want to eat and go to bed."

"Do you know she's coming here for tutoring?"

"You mentioned that before."

"I mean, did they tell you that too?"

"They said she was trying to get her GED."

"Why didn't you tell me?" I walked to the kitchen and began preparing his meal, glancing over my shoulder as I spoke. "I mean, that's pretty serious."

"You tutoring her in math? I didn't think it was a big deal."

I carried his plate to the table. "It is to me."

"Is it too much for you?"

I shook my head. "Not really. But with the children, it's a handful."

"I didn't know she brought her son."

I stared at him. "Her son?"

"She never mentioned him?"

"No."

He shrugged. "Well, she has a four-year-old."

"How do you know?"

Realizing my reason for the question, he smiled at me. "Relax, Renee, of course I would know that. If they're trying to get me to start over with her, don't you think I'd know all the stats?"

"Whatever." I was too upset to make sense of it.

When Annette came to the house for the next session, I stood in the doorway with my arms folded across my chest.

"Why are you here?"

She looked confused. "For tutoring."

"Is it a GED you want or a husband?"

Her jaw dropped. "Renee, it's not like you think. I didn't kn—"

I slammed the door in her face. I was shaking for a few seconds, overcome by what I'd done. This wasn't my personality at all.

A few hours later the phone rang. It was Annette.

"Renee, really, I didn't know what they were planning. I found out when—"

"Yeah, right, Annette. And I was born on Mars."

"I'm sorry that I—"

"If you were sorry, you would've never come to this house and pretended to be a student of mine." I was talking through gritted teeth.

"I really didn't mean to do any—"

"*As-salaamu 'alaikum.*"

I hung up on her.

The phone rang again and again but I didn't answer. Finally the ringing ceased.

It rang again an hour later, and I answered.

"I hope you know you wrong." It was Lisan's voice. Then she hung up.

I shivered as I heard the dial tone.

I told William about it later that night but he shrugged it off, saying it wasn't a big deal.

It was months before Annette's name was out of my house and the phone calls ceased. By then I was exasperated by all that had happened. I was officially fed up and told William I was finished with everything that had anything to do with that group.

"Don't say that, Ray. They're Muslim."

"And so are Yusuf and Sumayyah."

"No one said they're not."

"But to them they're heretics."

He laughed. "Listen to who's talking. Not too long ago, you told me that we had to move from their basement because of that very reason. Now, you're arguing with me saying they're not. I never said they were."

"I'm just tired of all the *fitnah.*"

"I am too, especially because of what it's done to you."

I looked at him with my forehead creased. "What?"

"You're not the same, Ray."

He moved to embrace me, but I pulled away, too hurt by his words.

"You never told me that before."

"I couldn't. You were too caught up."

I didn't know what to say. He moved to embrace me again, and this time I didn't resist. I relaxed in his arms, realizing that I had wasted my life.

"I want to go back to school," I said, my voice a moan.

I had no idea this is what I would say, and I was a bit startled by the honesty of my words.

"But we can't afford it right now." He sounded pained that he couldn't help me fulfill this small dream.

"I can wait," I said, my heart aching in realization that I had made him feel bad. He had been working so hard to keep us afloat, he didn't need my added stress. "It's more important for you to finish right now."

As I said this, I sensed he was feeling the same as I— that we both could have finished undergraduate school together. Regret tightened in my chest, but it was too painful to dwell on. I thought of how everyone had told me not to withdraw and I ignored them, preferring the advice of those with whom I felt "safe." What had I become? Even my own husband saw the harm my affiliation with the group had done to me, and he hadn't been able to reach me because I was too caught up in the haze.

I was overcome by sadness as I wondered how I had looked to him. I feared that my worth was shrinking in William's eyes. The possibility terrified me. I wondered if he wished he could have Renee Morris back—the academic full of promise, destined to do something remarkable with her life. What if in losing myself I lost my husband too? I felt my chest tighten at the thought, fear gripping me as I realized I had no control at all over his heart.

"I'm glad you married me." His voice was so sincere in its reflective tone that I felt tears well in my eyes at the words. "You're a really special person. Please don't leave me again."

His words inspired a whole new perspective on my insobriety in the club. I was so engrossed in seeking the faults of others and warning against them that I didn't see the crumbling of myself. Till today I have never brought myself to actually ask William what abnormalities he had seen in me for those few years. The pain is still that raw. I think everyone has an experience in life they cannot bring themselves to relive. When I returned to school and read stories of abused women, it terrified me that I could actually relate, though the concept of an abusive husband was beyond my comprehension or experience.

I was also incensed at the reminder of all the sorority had stripped from me and what they wanted to strip from me still. I began to see their behavior as vindictive and spiteful instead of representative of anything in which I could feel safe. When I recounted those believers the sorority was most intent on maligning, they were almost always Muslims who had something commendable going for them that many of the sorors didn't have themselves. *"Dunya"* degrees, popularity, prominence among Muslims, money, a nice home, a good husband, good character, self contentment, success in *da'wah*, success in teaching the Sunnah, a lucrative business, strong family background, and the list goes on. Why it never occurred to me before was beyond me. Even my first induction into the club was after I had, in their view, taken Ghazwa's advice to abandon my pursuit of a college degree. Upon joining, I found that other recruits were asked to do the same. If they already had a bachelor's, the sorority made certain the recruit didn't "waste" her time pursuing any other degree. If a recruit had a good husband, they labeled her "off" or busied themselves finding him a "saved" second wife if they didn't sabotage the marriage altogether.

Envy. That was the undercurrent of almost every ruling of someone being "off." Naturally, by sheer statistical probability, there were those they labeled as "off" who actually had some glaring error. But, oddly, those with the glaring errors were not defamed nearly as much as those without. It was like the inclusion of those with genuine crimes was to mask who they really wanted to despise. Most of our time had been spent attacking believers who, like Wadiah had said, only Fulan had knowledge to understand the intricacies of their crimes. Obviously, this left us stripped completely of our right to use our own good sense or even apply what we already knew of right and wrong.

Years later when I attended a class with Nasrin and Sumayyah, the teacher, in order to illustrate a common error in belief, had read a quote from someone with that error, but he didn't give the name. This both stunned and impressed me, and it was some time before I could fully appreciate his wisdom. We were laypeople and didn't have a firm foundation in Islamic sciences, so it wasn't personalities we needed to know but concepts. By equipping me with an understanding of the *concepts* of right and wrong, I could then detect soundness and error regardless of *who* it came from.

Only after a person reaches a certain level of knowledge can people's names be freely mentioned because only then will the student have a strong enough foundation to understand that very rarely can a person be placed in a definite category of correct or mistaken in the complete sense. There are just too many things to take into account, the most obvious of which is that everyone makes mistakes. It simply wouldn't be just to define people by their errors. Otherwise, who is left as trustworthy on the face of the earth?

So even if I could actually quote from someone's book or lecture to "prove" they were "off," I'm overlooking four very basic explanations that a scholar would consider by instinct: He made a mistake. He didn't mean it as we're understanding it. He may have changed his opinion since then. And most profound: *I could be the one who is wrong.*

There is also the disagreement amongst scholars on zillions of matters, but as I learned after leaving the sorority: The people of the Sunnah disagree in a manner that does not harm them in the least—because they are firmly grounded in those things that are not open to disagreement. And they know this is the foundation from which sisterhood and brotherhood is established in Islam.

It can be likened to the differences of opinions between husband and wife or among good friends. The people of the Sunnah are not in disagreement about where Allah is, but they will disagree about the details of Islamic garb. And even as they are in no doubt concerning that Allah is above the heavens, they will disagree about where to place the hands while praying to Him.

There are simply so many possibilities to take into consideration in explaining a person's error, the most obvious of which is...maybe he never learned that.

Here's another thing I learned after leaving the sorority: The people of the Sunnah do not unite based on personalities, and they do not abandon based on personalities. Their focus is one: to clarify the truth. When someone speaks the truth, they say, *This is the truth,* even if it comes from the mouth of a liar. When someone speaks falsehood, they say, *This is falsehood,* even if it comes from the mouth of the most trustworthy, sincere scholar on the face of the earth.

SubhaanAllaah. I reflect often on the meaning of Allah's words, "Nay! We hurl Truth against falsehood, and it destroys it, and behold, falsehood does depart!" For certainly, after learning the truth of Islam and the Sunnah, the falsehood that I'd been taught during those years departed and has since never returned.

O Allah! I ask You for knowledge that benefits, a heart that is humble, conviction upon truth, and a tongue that moves in constant remembrance of You!

Twenty-five

"Say, O My slaves who have wronged their souls!
Despair not of the mercy of Allah.
Verily, Allah forgives all sins.
Truly, He is Oft-Forgiving, Most Merciful."
—Qur'an, 39:53

If the year 2000 is my year of confusion, then 2001 is my year of despair. I remember listening to a woman who became Muslim tell the story of how she was forced to leave her homeland and family, even a two-year-old daughter, her firstborn, who had been the joy of her life, because her life and safety had been jeopardized so severely after accepting Islam that her only option was this or remain and die. When she returned years later to see her child, her daughter didn't even know who she was. Later, the woman was granted asylum in America, where she met a Muslim man to whom she had been married now for over thirty years. The couple had two tenacious teenager daughters with whom they were constantly arguing and a twenty-five-year-old son who was married but had left Islam.

When asked how she copes with these struggles, she said thoughtfully, "I think of it as a lesson to learn from. With young children, you carry them for nine long months, pamper them, and love them until it hurts, only to have them forget all about you if you can't continue like this. And with the older ones who you raised through all the ups and downs, they won't forget you. But, still, it's almost the same. Because they're sometimes so ungrateful that it was like you were never there."

She drew in a deep breath and then asked us, "Isn't that how we are with Allah?"

I know now that my despair of 2001 was completely my own doing, born from my wronging my soul. But that year, I hadn't yet accepted responsibility fully, although I had taken the first step in this direction by recognizing that I couldn't blame the sorority anymore. I had grown so bitter in my resentment of my sorority sisters that it was eating me up inside. I refused to forgive them because it was the only revenge I felt I had. I kept saying I'll never forgive them for what they took from me and I couldn't wait to see them on the Day of Judgment so I could take from their good deeds and I could pile my sins on them. It hadn't yet occurred to me that I had wronged myself. Like Satan who whispers the suggestion and withdraws, you can blame only yourself if you comply. They hadn't twisted my arm and dragged me, and they certainly hadn't cut open my chest and made me believe that my association with them meant I was saved. I had both gone and believed willingly—on my own accord.

This painful reality hit me suddenly one day after prayer.

Even my concept of forgiveness had been confused. Forgiveness wasn't something you bestowed for someone else's benefit, it was bestowed for yours. Hadn't the Companions and righteous people been known to say, "I forgive so-and-so because I want Allah to forgive me"? And didn't Allah's Messenger teach that whoever shows mercy to others, Allah will show mercy to him? He didn't say, whoever shows mercy to others, Allah promises mercy to the ones whom he shows mercy.

SubhaanAllaah.

Had I not been so resentful of those with whom I had felt "safe," I would have heard my Lord's call to true safety in the Qur'an. *"And We have not created the heavens and the earth and that between them except in truth. And indeed the Hour is coming, so forgive with gracious forgiveness."*

Even as I came to realize that my losses sustained by joining the sorority had been my own doing, there was a vicious turmoil erupting inside as the insobriety wore off, giving way to an excruciating pain that I found difficult to bear. A veil had been ripped from my eyes and I was seeing for the first time the raw ugliness of self.

I tried to turn away from the mirror and say the pain was inflicted by something, *anything*, else. The sorority. Dropping out of school. My husband not saving me. Ghazwa. Wadiah. My parents not embracing me as a Muslim. Marrying William. Marrying so soon. Having two children. Having no money. William going to school. All the violence in the world. The propaganda against the Muslims. Not having enough books on Islam. Sumayyah no longer befriending me. Hadiyah not calling me.

Anything, anything at all, except facing the real culprit.

Myself.

Years later, when I became active in *da'wah*, I saw the same scapegoat and denial in those who would not accept Islam even as they knew it was the truth. They gave a thousand reasons why they couldn't be Muslim, and not one had anything to do with pure Islam itself, or the truth of themselves.

It's amazing to me how powerful illogical fear and denial are as motivators of human behavior, especially in imprudence. A woman will remain with an abusive husband, a man with an abusive wife. A person will support an oppressor, or even become an oppressor himself. A person will kill an unborn child, or abuse the ones who are already born. A person will deny the veracity of something unfolding right before her eyes. Or they will give up their soul to the world even as they know they will meet their Creator and never again return to the earth.

It scares me that it is really that easy to go astray. It is this realization that ultimately softened my heart to my sorority sisters and inspired me to forgive them, and love them even, and blame myself.

Everyone wants to feel secure, safe, in this confusing world. It's terrifying to know that even after you embrace the true religion, the journey doesn't end there. I don't think there is a Muslim alive who doesn't wish that he, like some of the Companions, had been given the glad tidings of Paradise. In the absence of a concrete promise, we hold onto the only thing we can—that we have the chance to be amongst those of every generation whom Allah has saved from misguidance, and who thus will be granted Paradise without ever entering Hell. We certainly don't want to die on disbelief, but even as a Muslim, I don't want to die on misguidance either.

The true religion isn't one in which a person can testify to the truth, go to the *masjid* once a week, and relax in the knowledge that he or she is safe. The true religion doesn't allow one who claims affiliation to simply say "I am saved" or "I believe."

I once heard a lecture in which the speaker said, "Once you make the testimony of faith to enter Islam, then know that you will be tested to see just how true is that claim."

A doctor isn't a doctor because she claimed to be. A surgeon isn't a surgeon because she said she's good with her hands. A teacher isn't a teacher because she said I can teach.

They first have to take a series of exams.

And everyone doesn't pass.

"Do men think they'll be left alone on saying, 'We believe' and that they will not be tested?" This question that Allah asks in the Qur'an is one I reflect on often today. And I still don't feel secure. And I most certainly don't feel "safe."

I was reading a book so aptly titled *Stories of Repentance*, and a righteous worshipper who was heard weeping over his sins was asked, "How is safety achieved?" He responded, "By performing all prescribed acts of worship, by not wronging others, and by repenting to Allah." Upon hearing this, the person wanted to learn more, so he exhorted the righteous man, "Can you please deliver a sermon to me?" And the worshipper replied, "The best sermon you can receive is by looking into your own self."

But these were lessons I learned later. Then, in 2001, I was despairing over what I had done to myself. I had taken baby steps to repenting truly, but I hadn't yet quieted the turmoil that incited so much pain that I felt the need to blame someone else. Fortunately, I was aware that this wasn't correct, but that knowledge alone could not remove my resentment altogether. There were moments, may Allah forgive me, that I even questioned Allah's allowing me to ever enter the sorority in the first place. This was irrational, I know, especially since He had given me so many signs that I chose to ignore, most distinctly during my interrogation meeting itself. This is the test of life, I learned. Allah shows you the Straight Path, and it is up to you to take it or turn away.

I had turned away.

He is not going to block you from the Path, but He also isn't going to remove your responsibility to think and choose it for yourself. Otherwise, there is no purpose at all to life. And if there is no point to living, we wouldn't be here on earth.

But we are here. So we have but two choices: submit when the clear signs reach you, or turn away and deny they were ever there.

And these choices represent both possible states of human life, that of belief or disbelief when being shown the truth of Islam, and that of true Islam or of misguidance when being shown guidance and propriety in understanding and practicing the religion itself.

Although I was taking my baby steps in spiritual self improvement and thus should have expected that I wasn't the only human prone to error and in need of patience in our home, I was completely unprepared for William's influence by the fraternity that would prove a tremendous test for my marriage and faith.

When the fraternity was unsuccessful in convincing my husband to divorce me and marry one of the "saved" (I'm at a loss as to how Annette passed any of their stringent tests, except that she was willing to play part in ruining someone's life), they settled for convincing him that he should at least take a "saved" second wife.

William was still in school, and we were surviving financially mostly because my tutoring was going well. I was even earning enough to pay Arifah for helping me, whereas before she was just doing it for the sake of Allah. The only setback was that the wealthier clients were unwilling to come to me, so I had to take a bus, train, and taxi (rich neighborhoods didn't have bus stops throughout) to get there. The families willingly reimbursed me in addition to my normal pay, but this was taking a toll on me and I was exhausted. We were saving enough to get a car possibly in the next year, but that seemed far off and, besides, I had to worry about today. Arifah, may Allah bless her, allowed me to borrow hers, since she wouldn't need it while she was babysitting Luqman and Rahma for me. So that left only the one day that William watched them that I had to take public transportation.

In the end, William never took their advice, mostly because he simply couldn't. I'd like to say we couldn't afford it and that given his schedule he didn't have the time, but that would be naïveté speaking because impracticality rarely stops a man from doing what he wants. And with the sorority "saved" sisters, they were ever so willing (when it was someone else's husband) to forfeit their Islamic rights to maintenance, equal time, or even the provision of a home. So these financial and logical impracticalities would have been rendered moot points with the candidates being sent our way, or at least sent my husband's way. In the sorority, this had nothing at all to do with me.

I don't know why I didn't turn in my membership badge sooner, or, better yet, I don't know why I had accepted it at all.

William's sole reason he couldn't accept their offer was that he had already agreed before Allah, an imam, and two witnesses that he understood that his doing so would mean my divorcing him. In technical terms, there is no such thing as a "no polygamy" clause that removes the man's option to marry up to four wives. The clause simply secures that if he ever decided to do it, I just won't be one of those wives.

In circles of sisters, this is often brought up, with all the "You know that's right!" and "I ain't the one!" followed by emphatic nods and guffaws of thunderous laughter, and exaggerated convictions like "It can't be me!" If I hadn't gone through what I did, I could probably join in these dramatic displays. But today I am not so at ease amidst such conversation, not because the experience changed my feelings on what I'm willing to be part of, but because it taught me a profound lesson that reiterated for me just how complicated life is. *You can tie his hands, but you can't tie his heart.*

For me, this is poignant because his heart was all I wanted to secure when I wrote the clause in the first place.

I once met a sister who had divorced her husband after he took another wife. When I asked her about it, she said in reflection, "I don't regret my decision. But it taught me a lot." She explained, "It still hurts, *ukhtee*, whether you stay or leave. That's what I wasn't prepared for. I still felt betrayed. I still felt angry. I still felt jealous. But the hardest part was whenever I had a good laugh or wanted to share something I'd learned or read, he wasn't there. I missed him so much that I wished I could just pick up the phone and talk to him, spend a day with him even, just to have him back." She sighed. "That's when I started to wonder if I should've divorced him at all." She was silent for some time before she shook her head, her eyes growing distant in thought. "The reality is," she said, "the moment your husband marries someone else, your life is never the same. Whether you stay or leave."

What made this period of my life a huge test for my marriage and soul was that my husband's heart began to change. I was never clear on whether there was actually a woman behind this change or if he was merely enamored with the idea that he could actually be in a *halaal* relationship with someone else while being married to me, or both. Either way, his barrier to this dream was not in doubt. That barrier was me.

The arguments during this year were so visceral that I felt as if he was ripping my heart from my chest each time he spoke of removing the no-polygamy clause from our contract. His words hurt so much that I felt like I was literally groping for a counterattack that would inflict the same amount of, if not more, pain.

I remember moments in which I felt as if my life itself was falling apart, and I was at a loss for what to do if he insisted and I was actually divorced. I couldn't fathom what I'd do with myself, how I'd live, how I could even go on.

It was then that I realized how much I loved William. I had always thought of myself as not really liking him "like that" and that my agreement to marry him was more indicative of my generosity and pity for him than any authentic feeling in my heart. I felt superior to him, I realized, and viewed his suggestion to alter our agreement as the most vicious form of ungratefulness he could show for all I'd done for him.

Today I know that even if I hadn't felt superior, I would have still felt betrayed and saw his actions as being ungrateful to me. But at the time, this is where my rage was mostly coming from—a feeling of superiority over him, and of course from that natural dislike for it that Allah placed in the heart of every woman.

"It's not even permissible to make the *halaal haraam*." This implication by William that the contract itself was forbidding what Allah permitted was said in hopes of convincing me to go before the fraternity imam and frat witnesses to officially remove the clause from our agreement.

Naturally, I was infuriated.

"What! That's not making the *halaal haraam*. It's fulfilling a contract."

"But it's not permissible to put something *haraam* in there."

"So now monogamy's *haraam* to you?" I couldn't believe he was suggesting that choosing to live in monogamy was *haraam*—unlawful.

"This has nothing to do with monogamy. I'm saying you can't make polygamy *haraam*."

"Am I trying to rewrite the Qur'an? I just don't want it for me."

"How can you hate something Allah allowed?"

"How can *you*?"

Silence and gathered eyebrows. "What's that supposed to mean?"

"Didn't Allah give women choice in the terms of marriage?"

"Yes."

"So why do you hate *that*? Take it up with Allah."

"But this isn't your choice, it's mine."

"When *I'm* in the equation, it's not *your* choice. You can't make *me* do something *you* choose."

He huffed, clearly spent by my words. "What problem do you have with the Sunnah of polygamy?"

I glared at him. "What problem do *you* have with the Sunnah of monogamy?"

If there was one advantage I had over William during this time, it was that he simply could not win an argument with me. I almost always had the last word, and this wasn't because I insisted on it but because we would get to a point where he couldn't think of anything logical to say in response to my words. So the argument would end.

Although I was most often victorious in our war of words, I cannot say I was victorious in the battle most significant to me—that to win William's heart. Rationally, someone might point out that I already had. But that's not what I wanted. I wanted his heart inclined *only* to me.

Another battle I wasn't sure I was winning was the one being waged in my heart and mind. I had begun to wonder, *What if William's right? What if I should remove the clause?*

Today I wouldn't entertain thoughts like these. I know a woman has full rights to lay down some ground rules before entering a marriage. And once she does, she's under no obligation to revisit them, and most certainly not for the man who signed them off and whom she wouldn't have married without them.

But I was still young, still learning, and was thus easy prey in falling victim to the one thing the fraternity had perfected to a science—casting doubt.

Even after leaving the sorority and moving beyond this period of my life, I met sisters who had been taught something similar to what William and I were being taught back then—that a woman's not wanting to live in polygamy was indicative of weakness of faith and an unwillingness to embrace her religion in full.

Today I see it as the other way around. Those men, and women, who have difficulty believing that a woman doesn't have to live in polygamy and nor is she compelled to like the idea for herself—even if it's her reality—are in actuality the ones suffering from weakness of faith, because they haven't yet embraced fully a proper belief in Islam.

Belief in Islam means having full faith in the Wisdom of Allah—in His obligating and forbidding, in His encouraging and discouraging, and in His giving humans no choice in certain matters while giving humans full choice in others. Clearly, one of the matters in which human choice is most extensive in our religion is that of marriage—from the very choice of a spouse, to the conditions under which one will live with that spouse.

Yet even after choosing a mate and laying down conditions, I know there are matters that we cannot choose—like the inevitable tests that will enter our marriages.

Even so, of the unexpected—and expected—marital trials, Allah does not once ask a believer to "love" or "prefer" these trials.

Polygamy is a trial.

If I'm a "weak Muslim" because I don't wish a trial on myself, I say this weakness is closer to Islamic faith than the claim of loving to be tried. It is nearer to righteousness to be ever aware of human weakness in yourself than to suffer from the façade of strength and be unable to live up to your claim.

I choose to be wise.

I do not want polygamy in my life, not because I don't believe in what Allah revealed, but because I do. He promises that He'll test the believers and purge from them those who are not true to their claim.

And I don't know if I'll pass.

I have lived a little, so I know there are women for whom the trial has brought much good, and who wouldn't change their lives for the world. But even these women—with only rare exceptions—are like the believer relieved from excruciating pain who wouldn't take back those years of suffering because of all the good it has brought to her life, and continues to bring.

Certainly, with trial comes recognition of one's purpose on earth, the realization of the crucial affair of the soul, and the increased certainty that we will one day meet our Creator and stand before Him in final Judgment.

Yet no person who believes in Allah and the Last Day will say, "I want Allah to put me to trial." This is what I'd be saying if I claim a love or preference for something in which Allah has placed a different reality in my heart.

If Fatimah bint Muhammad and Ayesha bint Abu Bakr were not excited about this prospect in their lives, how amazing would it be for me, Renee Morris who does not even know her position before the One who lauded their station in Islam, to claim I have something in my heart that even they never claimed.

My heart goes out to those men whose ignorance and weakness of faith inspire the remarkable imagination that their wives, and believing women, will be closer to Islam by claiming to be better than the torchbearers of Allah's religion, expressing a love and preference that not a single Sunnah can be brought, except in opposition to what they claim.

One of the most heated discussions we had that year was when William, under the haze of the fraternity, claimed that my unwillingness to alter the contract was not only indicative of my weakness of faith in Islam but also due to my being "influenced by the West."

This was a claim I had great difficulty refuting in my heart, let alone in words. Who can rightfully claim they are not?

The fraternity had gone over all the ills of women and how their *deen* "ain't right" and how they "just ain't ready for this Sunnah," all the while denying their true desire: the revival of a Western pre-Islamic male "sunnah" that they were compelled to abandon when they realized that the Day of Reckoning is true. One look at their statistical résumé in displaying *their* readiness for this Sunnah is a clear indicator where their true hearts lay all along. But like one who tears typed words from newspapers and magazines and glues them to a paper to convey a message entirely unknown to the typist himself, the fraternity twisted and contorted the words of Allah and His Messenger until they were rearranged in a manner that allowed the fraternity to deliver a message about women in Islam that can be understood only by looking into the lowest desires of their souls.

Like cheerleaders shouting words on the sidelines of the real game and their wearing short skirts and twisting their bodies in gyrations while merely feigning interest in the meaning of their cheers, the sorority sisters closed ranks and nodded their heads in agreement to all the misogynistic absurdity the fraternity, the real "players on the field," claimed of their gender while stripping from these very women their rights in the name of Islam.

"You need to be careful, Renee. Just make sure your ideas aren't coming from the West."

"How do you know *your* ideas aren't coming from the West?"

"This is the Sunnah. This is something the West hates."

"Monogamy is the Sunnah too. Does the West have to hate this Sunnah before it's valid to you?"

"I'm serious, Renee. Think about it. Why do you have a problem with it?"

"I don't. There's nothing to think about."

I crossed my arms. "Why don't you consider why *you're* so obsessed?"

"I'm not obsessed. Otherwise, I'd be married right now to whoever I want."

"I thought you already were."

He sighed in frustration. "You know what I mean."

"No, William, I don't. All I know is that you're giving me hell about something you agreed on years ago. And now you want to go back on what you signed. That's not Islam."

"If I wanted to go back on it, I wouldn't be talking to you. Anyway, some scholars say I don't have to honor that clause. It's *haraam*."

"Then why are you arguing with me? Let me take the sin. Do what you want. I'm not removing the clause."

"But it may not even be valid."

"Are you ready to meet Allah with that on the Day of Judgment?" I regarded him.

"Go on," I said. "Go ahead and convince yourself it's the Sunnah to break your marriage agreement. That's your sin, not mine."

"I'm not saying I'd do it. I'm just saying what some scholars say."

"And if it's only *some*, then that means *other* scholars say our contract is just fine how it is."

I sighed. "But, frankly, William, I really don't care who's right or wrong. I made a decision. And I'll stick by it. If it's wrong, I accept Allah as my Judge. You do the same."

"But why are you so intent on following the West?"

"And why are you so intent on following the *saved*?" I said the last word sarcastically.

"If you're so convinced they're right," I continued, "then why are we having these discussions? Go remove the clause yourself. You know my position, and it's not going to change."

I shook my head. "If I would've known I couldn't trust you, I wouldn't have married you at all."

"I'm not following them. But they do have a point."

"You didn't want anything to do with them until they started dangling women in front of you. I guess now you see the light, huh?" I mocked his eyes widening and tongue hanging out as he stared at dangling women, suddenly inspired to recite their mantra like a robot, a hungry grin on his face, "I am saved! I am saved! O, yes, I testify to the world, *I am* saved!"

I laughed, and because it was funny, William couldn't keep from laughing too.

"But seriously, Renee, look at how the West makes us think of polygamy."

"It's not polygamy they don't like, William. It's accountability. You know as well as I do that there isn't a single man in the West who has a problem with the idea of more than one woman. He just doesn't want the responsibility."

"Or the stigma."

"That too."

"It's looked down upon," he said. "That's what I'm trying to say."

"But I don't look down on it, William. I just don't wa—"

"But how do you know that, Renee? Maybe deep inside you do and don't realize it."

"And maybe deep inside you want to commit adultery and don't realize it."

"That's not fair."

I creased my forehead. "Why not? Because only a woman can have *Western* thoughts on polygamy? What about you? You're from the West too, more than I am."

He frowned at my last words but decided to ignore them. "I'm not the one sticking to a contract that says I don't want to accept my religion."

"But you're intent on breaking one that was made according to that religion."

"See, this is what I'm saying, even the arguing back and forth. This is from the West."

I laughed. "William, humans disagree. Even the Prophet's wives discussed things with him. Please don't pull the women-need-to-be-stuffed-under-floorboards argument with me. You married a person with a mind. Maybe all the fraternity wives got brain transplants in favor of floating molecules, but I didn't."

He started to grin at my words but resisted. "But what about pleasing your husband? Don't you want me to be happy?"

"Of course."

He looked at me affectionately, a smile creasing a corner of his mouth. "Well, it'd make me very happy if you remove it."

This one statement made me consider actually going before the fraternity, and sorority, and removing the clause. Today I understand the reason for my sudden change in heart. Kindness. Letting someone know how much something means to you is so much more powerful and convincing than arguing for what you want. I hadn't yet read books like *Men are from Mars, Women are from Venus* or *The Surrendered Wife*, so this realization was drawn purely from intuition and experience—though I could have used those two books during my years of confusion and despair.

Still, I didn't give in. But I did lower my voice and do the wisest thing a woman could do in softening a man's heart. I stopped arguing and embraced him warmly, giving him a kiss on the cheek. Then, in his arms, I said as sweetly as I could, "And it would make me very happy if we keep it in there."

Despite my apparent fortitude in not wavering in my stance, inside I was falling apart. I was already despairing the horrible mistake of joining the sorority, and I was even blaming my former membership for this trial in my marriage. In my mind, if I hadn't been intent on joining the club in the first place, William wouldn't have these crazy ideas in his head.

Crazy ideas I was beginning to believe myself.

I imagined that I was perhaps influenced by the West.

Today, I think maybe I was. And maybe he was too. There are lots of maybes in life, and this is just one. But I also say, even if I was, as long as that influence didn't involve *haraam*, I have absolutely no problem with that possibility.

Now, when I reflect on the ideas that the club had put into my and my husband's minds regarding women's approach to plural marriage, the imbalance of it all is stunning. In the fraternity, women got the brunt of criticism for being influenced by the West, but in reality much of what was thought of as "Western" was merely evidence of women's nature. What's more is that the group completely ignored the fact that the Western influence was, in many cases, more prevalent in the men than the women.

The great majority of non-Muslim men are not celibate before marriage, and many of them are not even faithful within marriage itself. Promiscuity itself has become a sign of "manhood" amongst many Western men. When these men convert to Islam, they face a drastic life change, not only in their spirituality but in their lifestyle itself. Because the man is no longer part of a religion or mindset that gives him free reign to do what he likes, he is forced to lower his gaze and protect himself from sin, thus submitting to a lifestyle that is tremendously difficult for a person who did not spend his youth guarding his chastity.

Now, in his new religion, Judgment Day—and Hell Fire— is very, *very* real. His only option now as a Muslim is to decide if he wants to submit to his desires, like before, and risk sullying his soul, or make one of the biggest decisions a person can make in life—commitment in marriage. Only this time, it can disrupt, or completely destroy, the foundation of the one he already has. This creates a huge dilemma, especially since in Islam marriage is public. Does he take that step, openly legitimizing desires that he had concealed and lied about in his previous lifestyle, and thus risk sacrificing or disrupting the relationship he already has? Or does he leave the opportunity alone altogether and resist the raging temptations in his heart?

Like my own turmoil that I experienced after withdrawing from the sorority, this pain is not easy to bear, at least not without a culprit to blame. For the men in the fraternity, it became their wives.

Islam alone was difficult for these men. Because in the Sunnah the wife is fully aware of what he is doing and can demand her rights (if she opts to remain in the situation at all), lying is not an option to him like it had been before. For many of the converts in the fraternity, this was difficult to bear, as never before had the woman even been part of the equation.

Because these Western-influenced men were unable to admit that the combined concepts of accountability and his wife actually having a choice troubled them most, their scapegoats became things like "women have weak faith" and "women are influenced by the West," all to avoid admitting that just this once his wife may have the upper hand, even if in nothing other than her holding a place in his heart that would mean his utter crumbling if she leaves.

In my case, the fraternity solved this by not only saying women have weak faith and are influenced by the West, but by adding the interesting spice of, *It's not permissible to divorce him when he marries someone else.* Their favorite hadith was the one that cautioned women against divorcing for no reason. In their distorted view, it was as if a woman in polygamy woke up and decided on divorce with no reason at all for leaving except to say with a bright smile, *Whew! I think I'm ready for a change.*

It was pointless to point out to them that in Islam her "reason" didn't have to concern him at all. She could leave because she simply feared for her soul or was completely unhappy in something that was completely *halaal*, polygamy only one possibility of many. I think it burned up the former "players" to know that she actually had a choice and that this was no longer a game. So the fraternity had to create a new reality for themselves, sitting around quoting Fulan's website in these instances because the Sunnah wouldn't quite give them the censure they wanted to spout at women during the next lecture.

In bizarre desperation, some of the fraternity even pronounced disbelief on a woman who divorced because she didn't want to live in polygamy. Also, in hopes of reviving the Western "sunnah" of keeping the "other woman" secret, they made the amazing claim that the Prophet's wives didn't know whenever he married someone else, even as a famous hadith clearly tells of how Ayesha inconspicuously went to the ceremony of one just to see how the new wife looked, not to mention how the wives talked and met in the house of one another each day.

One of the most heartbreaking memories I have of my years in the club is that of a new Muslim I met one day while attending a sisters' gathering at the group's *masjid*. I remember that the first thing I noticed about her was her demeanor, which was so unlike that of my sorors: Her eyes and face glowed with the excited uncertainty of a person who had recently embraced Islam and was among Muslims for the first time. A cordial smile lingered on her face as she entered the sisters' area, her eyes scanning the faces until she found a place to sit on the carpeted floor. Although I was a bona fide member at that time, my heart ached for her as I realized that she would not be welcomed here. Her *khimaar* was a subtle turquoise that she wore loosely draped about her head, and a hint of her hair and neck were visible beneath the soft fabric. She wore a wide floral skirt that matched her head cover and hung just above her bare ankles. Her shirt, though long-sleeved, was slightly fitting although I knew in my heart that it was likely the most modest piece of clothing that she owned.

I suppose it was my *fitrah*, that natural disposition towards kindness and love for others that Allah placed in each person, that inspired me to, without forethought or hesitation, to get up from where I was sitting and go to her, extending my hand to hers and shaking it before seating myself next to my new sister in Islam.

As I had expected, she was not welcomed at the fraternity house, and Ghazwa and Lisan were the first to let her know. Upon seeing her, they got up as if on instinct and came over to us. Immediately, without greeting or hesitation, they began to bombard our casual conversation. They drilled the young woman as to her identity and affiliation with the "saved." The other sisters offered a more tacit disapproval. Their conversations quieted and they held a distant look of scorn as they stared at the young woman. Some of them wore upturned lips, and others whispered behind their hands, expressing, I knew, defamatory words, even as I could not hear what they were saying.

"Where you from?" Ghazwa demanded with arms folded authoritatively across her chest.

The young woman told her that she was from Bethesda.

"And who you sit with there?"

The woman's forehead creased in confusion.

My heart fell, and I started to say something.

"I'm sorry?" the new sister said.

"Like who you take from?" Ghazwa spoke more slowly this time, her eyes widening with each word, as if mocking the woman's ignorance.

"Ghazwa," I interrupted, "she's new."

"New or not, she need to be on the *haqq*."

I cringed. There was a sudden feeling of déjà-vu as I recalled my initiation dinner at Wadiah's home. I was at a loss for what to do or say, feeling as hopeless and weak as I had at that time. Because I was now getting looks of scorn myself (for daring to make any excuse for a person's ignorance of being "saved"), I shut my mouth. But I offered casual, discreet smiles of sympathy as both Ghazwa and Lisan drilled the young woman on how it was disrespectful to enter the *masjid* and sit down without first offering two units of supererogatory prayer and how it was inappropriate to wear bright colors and tight clothes.

If it hadn't been for the *adhaan* announcing the time for 'Ishaa prayer, I don't think the woman would have had a moment's peace that night. But by Allah's mercy, Ghazwa and Lisan abruptly stopped speaking upon hearing the call to prayer echoing through the small speaker set up on the sisters' side of the *masjid*.

Naturally, the sister's face had now changed to one of confusion and discomfort, but I tried to make up for the awkward encounter by making light of the situation. She laughed at my lighthearted humor, but only out of obligation. I could see her eyes following Ghazwa and Lisan, as if afraid that her interrogators might return any second. I recalled how I had felt with my former roommates and my heart ached for her.

After the prayer, I saw her on a cell phone, a look of sadness and desperation in her eyes as she stood in a far corner whispering into the phone. When I approached her, I saw that her eyes were brimmed with tears that she was using all her strength to hold back. I remember immediately pulling her into an embrace and apologizing for the behavior of my sorors, only vaguely aware of the others glaring at me. Fortunately, I was able to exchange numbers with her before she made her way out of the *masjid* and to her car.

Of course, I never again saw her at the *masjid*. That fact alone is enough to fill me with regret. But what followed in my keeping in contact with her was what would become most heartbreaking in my memory.

It was only by the Grace of Allah that Diane kept in touch after the incident and opened up to me. In our conversations, we never mentioned the encounter with Ghazwa and Lisan, but we both knew that it was one of the major factors in her growing discomfort with being around the sorors, a discomfort that was affecting her commitment to Islam itself.

If I had known then what I know now, I would have put her in touch with Hadiyah or Sumayyah or Arifah. But because I myself was so ignorant as to imagine that that in itself would be a sin (because they were not part of the sorority), I kept trying to soften Diane's heart to the club, convincing her that, despite their lacking character, the likes of Ghazwa and Lisan were the only real Muslims in the world and that she should come back to the *masjid* despite them. As I spoke, I wanted so ardently to give her Hadiyah's number, but I resisted, telling myself not to "follow my desires" and "go astray."

In the end, Diane never returned to the company of Muslims, and I eventually left the issue alone. It wasn't that I had given up convincing her to return to the *masjid*. We merely had a more pressing issue to confront: her disintegrating marriage.

Like the fraternity would later do with me and William, they convinced her husband that he should take another wife—from amongst the "saved." I hadn't yet experienced my own marital turmoil concerning this issue, so I was only distantly sympathetic. I didn't agree with what the group was doing, but my ignorance about Islam prevented me from believing they were doing anything fundamentally wrong, even as her husband spent hours on the Internet searching for potential mates and on the phone talking to ones he was "considering" marrying. I tried to soften Diane's heart to the idea of polygamy, but to no avail.

As I think back to that time, I realize now that it wasn't polygamy that was bothering her. In fact, she had said on more than one occasion that, although this allowance had initially held her back from accepting Islam, she had come to understand the option as a mercy to women once she researched the Sunnah of this marriage in Islamic history. Her understanding of the allowance increased after reading how Islam actually restricted the practice, which had had no limit on the number of wives a man could take before the revelation of Qur'an. She also admired how the marriages of the Prophet and his Companions united races and tribes and cared for widows who'd lost their husbands in battles, making the practice one of the most instrumental in obliterating nationalism and racism and in providing a structured, selfless system to care for all women, young and old.

However, in the fraternity, this selfless, merciful system was effectively abandoned and was replaced by a selfish, merciless system based on the fraternity's ideology regarding matrimony: displeasure with the Islamic Sunnah of marriage itself.

The clearest example of how the fraternity shirked Islamic marital guidance was in their cavalier approach to polygamy: men's addiction to Internet sites and chat rooms that allowed unrestricted interaction between men and women. Under the guise of seeking a subsequent wife, the men would visit matrimony sites with pictures of mostly uncovered women purporting to look for mates. They would chat with these women online and on the phone, and would sometimes meet the women personally, all of this without the knowledge or permission of a woman's family or guardian.

Although the Western approach to matrimony does not include the women's family or guardian until the two have made the decision, the Islamic approach is the exact opposite—a man isn't permitted to even discuss the possibility of marriage with a woman until he seeks permission from the woman's guardian, after which the two decide whether or not they are compatible. Many women on the Internet sites were unaware of Islamic guidelines for marriage, but the fraternity brothers certainly were not.

When Diane objected to her husband spending hours and hours online, she was told, "This is the Sunnah." Diane's husband, like other fraternity members, claimed to have the intention to "help" the women in their faith, despite the fact that the Prophet instructed both men and women to marry for religion—in other words, marry those who could help *you* in *your* faith. Despite scholarly rulings cautioning men against this un-Islamic behavior, the fraternity continued their "marriage pursuits," just as they continued their numerous activities and methodologies that were foreign to Islam.

Today, I find the saddest results of the fraternity's disregard for the Sunnah to be not only the increase in divorce and Hollywood-style marriages (those that last only months, weeks, or days), but, most significantly, the detrimental effects their disregard has on the faith of women influenced by fraternity ideology.

For those people well read in Islam (even if they are not Muslim), the incorrectness of the fraternity's approach to Islam—and marriage—would be obvious, and glaringly so. But for new, unknowledgeable Muslims like Diane, the truth became blurred.

When the activities of her husband didn't sit well with her, Diane was initially aggravated with her husband, but, like most club recruits, she eventually blamed herself—as I would some time later when suffering from my own agony.

"I don't think I'm strong enough to be Muslim," Diane told me one day. Her tone was despondent, an exhaustion detectable even through the receiver of my cordless phone.

"Don't say that," I told her.

"I know it's not right. But I just can't handle it. It's just too much."

"But what about your soul?"

She sighed into the phone. "Renee, that's all I've been thinking about. I just don't know what to do. When I became Muslim, I thought..." Her voice trailed, and seconds later I heard sniffling. "I didn't expect this," she said in a broken voice. "I feel like I'm noth—" At that, she lost her voice, and she cried, unrestrained, into the phone.

I tried to soothe and encourage her. But I was at a loss. Although consoling words were coming from my mouth, in my heart I felt powerless to help her. What could I possibly say to make it better for her? In my ignorance, I felt that her husband's behavior was justified, even if unpalatable, since she didn't have a no-polygamy clause in her contract.

Eventually, she apologized for her crying and got off the phone as she tried to pull herself together.

I called her days later, but her husband answered telling me she wasn't home. I tried again each day for about two weeks before her husband finally told me she had traveled to visit family.

I never heard from her again.

But I did discover, through the sorority grapevine (as they thanked God that her husband *finally* found a "saved" wife), that Diane eventually divorced her husband and left Islam. Although the likes of Ghazwa and Lisan looked at her leaving the religion as a "good riddance," I was heartbroken after hearing the news. Part of me blamed myself. I was the only one she had opened up to, and I had done nothing to quell her doubts about her marriage, or Islam.

Today the feeling of self-blame is even more potent as I realize that I may have been more instrumental than even the sorority in pushing her away from the Truth. In my ignorance, I exacerbated her struggles by justifying the behaviors of the fraternity and her husband instead of countering them with Islamic truths.

At the time, the sorority itself was, to me, Islamic truth.

When I later experienced my own marital struggles, I began to understand the frustration and confusion of Diane. Because I was experiencing them myself.

But I refused to bow out gracefully. After all, I had a marriage contract to point to.

Despite my personal frustrations with the un-Islamic aspects of the fraternity, I do recall moments when I, unlike Diane had been able to, found it almost amusing to witness the antics these men would go through to ensure they could have multiple wives while the first wife wasn't allowed (according to a fatwa posted on Fulan's website) to even *dislike* that her husband married someone else, even if she chose to remain in the marriage and be patient. I imagine that the unsatisfactory results from this particular posting inspired their final act of desperation: the denouncing of the woman's Islam itself.

Just to think they did all of this to avoid the unbearable reality that they often told her of him: *She doesn't belong to you.* If they only knew their greatest chance in keeping their beloved was in respecting her right to a choice and saying, "I love you so much. Please don't go. I don't think I can survive without you" and dedicating every moment with her to putting actions behind those words.

It was almost touching to witness how much they would go through not to lose us, even going as far as to pull rules out of thin air.

Aw, how sweet, I thought at times. *I'm flattered.*

"But I'm also Muslim," I told William. "So the contract stays the same."

I know it may appear that William and I were constantly arguing and that I was feisty and arrogant to my husband during this time. But this couldn't be further from the truth. We had our moments, no doubt, but for the most part our marriage was mellow and intimate. It was only these brief moments that shifted everything for us, but especially for me.

Before he brought up the idea of changing the contract, our evenings and weekends had been spent laughing and joking, cuddling and reflecting, at least whenever he happened to be home. We simply didn't have time to be at odds with each other all the time. We were rarely together as it was. Even after the contract disagreement, we spent our time as we had before, but there was always the painful undercurrent, even if we chose to ignore it for the sake of the moment.

Before joining the sorority, I had read tons of books on marriage in Islam, and I was determined to be the best wife I could be. There were moments when it was difficult to play the role of the righteous wife, but I did the best I could. If we argued, it was mostly friendly discussions that involved societal issues, like interracial marriage in Islam as opposed to the matrimony among non-Muslims. We also discussed our time at MSGT during high school, recalling old classmates and friends.

If there was one thing we argued about concerning our marriage before the no-polygamy clause distraction, it was how little time we had together and how little of William's time was spent with the children. But even these disagreements were not as heated as the polygamy discussions. The children and I were just missing him, and I told him as much.

Twenty-six

"And if you fear dissension between the two,
appoint arbiters, one from his family
and the other from hers. If they both desire reconciliation,
Allah will cause it between them.
For Allah has full knowledge
and is acquainted with all things."
—Qur'an, 4:35

Here is a journal entry dated May 15, 2001, testimony to a profound lesson I learned about what it meant to really love someone for the sake of Allah: *Serve your husband with your heart for the sake of your soul, not with your soul for the sake of your heart.* I had loved William with my very soul in the hopes of our hearts becoming one, and I didn't know how to turn that around.

A month later I asked for a divorce.

There were no arbiters for us during this period because we were the only Muslims in our families, and we feared that our Christian parents wouldn't understand the disagreement enough to come to a conclusion agreeable to us both. William felt we should talk to an imam or someone reputable. I had my mind made up but was open to having a knowledgeable elder intervene.

I had grown tired of the back and forth arguments about the clause and the fraternity's pseudo-Islamic marriage terms disrupting my house. It had taken such a toll on me that I feared I couldn't be Muslim and married to William at the same time. Reading one thing in the Qur'an and hadith and hearing another thing entirely parroted by my husband from the fraternity was causing so much confusion that I didn't know what to believe. I just knew if William was right, I didn't have the ability to fulfill the role of being his wife. At this point, the clause disagreement had become inconsequential compared to the enormities that the fraternity was claiming concerning my Islam and my worth as a woman.

The hurt was immense. I never imagined I'd be in this situation. My parents never divorced, and I admired them like I never had before. To have remained married for more than thirty years seemed phenomenal, even incomprehensible, to me. I wondered how they did it, when I couldn't even make it to my fifth anniversary. And didn't want to.

I had already called my mother to tell her I was thinking of coming home for a while. I didn't mention divorce, she didn't ask, so we left it at that. She sounded genuinely excited, especially since I'd visited only three times in the last four years, and even then it was an in-and-out visit bestowed more out of obligation than desire. William and I would then stay with his parents down the street, enjoying their company for the two or three days we were in the city. His parents were so much more relaxed, open-minded, and respectful of my religion. I often wished my parents were more like his, but he'd tell me not to say that, that I had no idea what I was wishing for.

I know too that my mother missed Luqman and Rahma. She'd only seen them for the couple of hours I'd remained at the house, and that wasn't enough for her. I'd already seen how she'd been with Emanuel but I hadn't imagined that she'd love my children too. Today this sounds ludicrous to my ears, but I really thought my family hated everything about me once I'd accepted Islam. I know now their upset was due mostly to Islam being foreign to them and to a sincere concern for my well-being. I can appreciate that now, but to my young mind they were just being cruel.

After I told her that I was considering an extended visit, my mother called more often to ask how I was doing and to just chat. She never asked any details, and I never gave any. I pretended that I just missed her and Dad and was thinking of returning to school. I hadn't really given school much thought, simply because I didn't even know what was going to happen with my marriage, but it gave me something to talk about. But this excited my mom, a PhD-holder who despised the idea of a woman giving up the opportunity to finish her education. At that point, I really couldn't disagree with her because having a degree right then would have made my circumstance a lot less complicated, at least in the practical sense, especially if my husband and I actually did divorce.

I know now that she knew full well that my marriage was going sour. Now, it's almost comical to think that I actually imagined she had no idea. Any time a married woman wants an open-ended visit in her parents' home without her husband, unless he travels as a career, the reasons usually amount to one.

But I'm grateful she didn't say anything. I understand this too is adult wisdom. She knew just what I needed— normalcy and affection. And, may Allah guide her to Islam, that's exactly what she gave.

One of the stupidest things I did that year was agree to go with William to the fraternity house to discuss my marriage. It was a sort of compromise, that or nothing. I wanted to go to Arifah's parents but William disagreed saying he didn't know them and was unsure if they were knowledgeable enough, especially since they were once in the Nation of Islam. When I pointed out to William that all the frat boys had once worshipped the cross, he just shook his head and said it wasn't the same. The fraternity had "connections" to brothers who knew brothers who were friends with students who sat in classes down the street from Fulan overseas. I thought this was a really stupid frat-thing to say. I wanted to retort, "Arifah's father actually *sat* overseas and shook *hands* with some real-life Japanese. Just imagine the knowledge in his hands alone." But because I had been saying more than I wanted to lately, I kept my mouth shut and decided I could stomach the meeting, at least since this was to salvage my marriage and not to sabotage it.

Or so I thought.

I left the meeting infuriated. I spent the rest of the day mumbling to myself all the things I should have said but didn't.

I was granted my divorce, that was the only up side of it all, and because it was initiated by me, I would be, according to the Islamic opinion I followed at that time, free in only a month. I kept my mind on August, which would normally be my anniversary, but which now represented my ticket to freedom out of the frat madness.

Thank God!

I couldn't wait. I calculated that I should be able to go home the first or second week of the month, so I called my mom to arrange getting a flight for the third week. She agreed and told me she'd talked to some professor and administrator friends of hers at a university in the city and that they would admit me, no problem, and could I have my transcripts from Maryland sent? She'd take care of everything else. I agreed, smiling as I hung up the phone.

It was my first feeling of genuine relief. I felt as if a load was lifted from my shoulders. I laughed out loud so many times in one hour that I know now that I needed a psychiatrist. This was called *depression.*

My being ecstatic was the natural counter-balance to my feeling of utter despair. I wasn't really happy. I was just in dire need of being so. Because I associated all of the causes for my despondence with events related to my marriage, being granted the divorce triggered the opposite emotions, as I saw not being married as the way out of unhappiness.

Of course it wasn't that easy. But I was on this high for two full weeks before reality hit.

One day in late July, I took the stroller and walked to the townhouse community of Bashirah and Jadwa. When I arrived, Bashirah was home but said Jadwa was out running errands with the children and couldn't come over. That was fine with me because I could relax in the quiet atmosphere of her living room with only her and Ihsan and my children. It was really peaceful. In any case, it was Bashirah I was most drawn to because we had so much in common, despite our age difference.

Ihsan was bringing us a tray of cookies and what looked like a fruit smoothie when I suddenly burst out laughing. I heard the jingling of the dishes on the tray as I startled Ihsan, but she didn't drop anything. She set it before me with her forehead creased and a confused grin on her face. Looking at her made me laugh more. Bashirah sat on the couch a comfortable distance from me with her eyebrows raised and an expression that said, *Well, are you going to share the joke or keep it to yourself?*

When I recovered from laughter, my eyes were watery and I was still nursing chuckles.

"What?" Bashirah stared at me, starting to smile but apparently unsure if she should.

"I'm sorry." I chuckled. "I was just thinking of something this imam said."

Her face relaxed and her eyes grew curious as a smile formed at her lips. "Oh. What?"

"That I'm not Muslim anymore if I don't change my contract."

Her smile faded and her eyes grew concerned. "How is that funny?"

"Because it's ridiculous."

"Yes," she said slowly. "But it isn't funny."

"I know." I shook my head. "It's just stupid, that's all."

She nodded with uncertainty, studying me for some time. Then she reached for a drink and handed it to me.

I took a sip as she folded her arms, still regarding me. "What contract is he talking about?"

I set the glass on the tray and glanced at her. "My marriage contract."

She gathered her eyebrows. "How does that have anything to do with him?"

"William and I were going for..." I shrugged "...counseling I guess you can say."

There was a question on her face, but I sensed she didn't want to pry. She glanced at her daughter then to my son entertaining himself on the floor. Rahma was holding a toy as she lay on a blanket next to him. "Ihsan, take Luqman to your room and show him a video."

The room was quiet suddenly, and I realized I had said too much. Clearly, this was Bashirah's way of saying the conversation was too mature for Ihsan, and Luqman. Ihsan nodded and left the room, leading Luqman out with her.

Bashirah looked at me, re-crossing her arms. "Renee, speak English. What are you talking about?"

"We're divorced."

I reached for the glass and took small sips, not meeting her gaze. But I could see her blinking repeatedly.

"What?"

I nodded, smiling as our eyes met. "We're divorced."

She shook her head and narrowed her eyes. "When did this happen?"

I creased my forehead as I tried to recall. "About a week ago."

"Then you're not divorced. You're *getting* a divorce."

I shrugged. "I suppose."

"I know this is not any of my business. But can you please give me a general reason why? I mean, you're so young, you're....what?"

"Twenty-four next month."

"Only twenty-four. Are you sure this is serious enough to divorce over?"

I nodded. "I'm sure. I've never been happier in my life."

She drew in a deep breath and exhaled, grinning to herself. I knew from her expression that a tease would come next. "Renee, you sound like a drug addict pop star in an interview after eloping with her dread-locked drummer."

I chuckled, a bit embarrassed once I realized how my clichéd response must have sounded.

"That line alone can get you admitted to the psych ward."

Shaking her head, she asked, "What's *really* going on?"

"William thinks I should take out the no-polygamy clause in my contract."

"And?"

"I disagree."

She stared at me as if unsure she was understanding. "So you're getting a *divorce*?"

I was quiet. Coming from her, it did sound over-simplistic, and stupid.

"Did you even pray on this?"

I creased my forehead as I looked at her, realizing it hadn't even occurred to me. "No."

She slowly closed her eyes as she shook her head again. "Renee, you don't divorce your husband over something like that. You work it out between yourselves."

I dropped my head slightly, my gaze on the glass that I held with both hands, the pain coming back suddenly. "We tried." I spoke quietly, as if hesitant to speak.

"And that's all you can come up with? That you disagree about a clause? Are you really thinking this through?"

I didn't say anything, my eyes still on the fruit shake. I felt my face grow warm and my chest knot. My eyes began to burn. I didn't want this marriage. I was already registered for school. I wanted a new life. I didn't want Bashirah to convince me otherwise.

She sighed, as if realizing she was overreacting. "Why do you think it's necessary to divorce?" Her voice was calmer, more diplomatic.

"I don't want to live like that."

"Like what, *habeebati*?"

"In polygamy. He knew that before we got married. I told him that. He said okay. I even dropped out of school for him. I don't understand it. We have two children. I gave up everything, I mean *every*thing. And now this? I thought women had rights. That's what I thought. And now what? Now what?"

The tears welled in my eyes, and I set the glass down, my hand shaking as I did. Embarrassed, I quickly folded my hands on my lap, blinking to fight the tears. I hadn't expected to have an outburst.

"Now what, *habeebati*? What's happening now?" Her voice was gentle, evoking the tears. I wiped them away before they could spill forth.

"Everything. I mean." I drew in a breath and exhaled, shaking my head, having difficulty forming the words. "Everything. They bring this girl to him and now all he can think about is someone else. I thought I was special. I thought he loved me." My voice cracked at these last words.

"And why do you think he doesn't love you now?"

"How can he love me if he wants someone else?"

"Is he married to her?"

"To who?" I looked at her in fear, my eyes tear-brimmed.

"No one, I'm talking about what you said. You said there's a girl."

Oh. "No, he didn't marry her. But he wants to marry someone."

"But you don't know who it is."

I shook my head. "There's no one now."

She creased her forehead in confusion. "But you just said there is."

"No. He *wants* to marry someone."

"Anyone." She concluded this, sounding a bit disappointed in me.

"Yes, anyone. But no one yet."

"And this is why you're divorcing?"

"No.... I mean, not only that. It's breaking the contract."

"Did he actually do it?"

"No."

"Then it's not breaking the contract, *habeebati*."

"But he says the contract's *haraam* anyway."

"And you disagree?"

"Of course. That's why I put it in there."

"So this is why the imam says you're not Muslim, because it's in your contract?"

"Yes."

"Who is this imam anyway?"

I told her.

She pursed her lips. It was clear she had heard of him and disapproved of our selection. "Why did you go *there?*"

"William wanted to."

Her eyebrows shot up. "*William?*"

I knew why she was surprised, but I didn't address that. "I didn't want to go, but it's the only people he trusted."

She grew quiet. I could tell things were becoming a bit clearer. As I learned later, it was general knowledge to the Muslim communities in the area that this was bad news. Having a husband involved in the fraternity made trivial problems detrimental. Whereas other communities were bringing in believers, the fraternity was turning them away, often pushing people from Islam altogether, especially women.

For several minutes, we didn't speak. She really didn't know what to say. The added complication of the fraternity made it difficult to give advice. I later learned that this was because the fraternity didn't operate on rational or Islamic terms; they operated on psychological and emotional ones masked with Islamic slogans and the parroting of correct Islamic beliefs. Even if there was someone, like Arifah's parents, who could offer practical or Islamic guidance, the mere psychological brainwashing made distrust an undercurrent of a member's dealings. Thus, a person who didn't agree with everything in the fraternity but wanted to be "safe," like William, would ultimately trust only one of the members, making any sort of good advice and direction an impossibility until the haze wore off. The good news was that the haze almost always wore off—extremism by its nature is self-destructive and short-lived, but the bad news was: *When and at what cost?* Sometimes a person "woke" without a grain of faith in their hearts, or after a mental breakdown.

This—the complete loss of faith—is something that I, unfortunately, can relate to. There was a brief period in my life, following the turmoil in my marriage, that I quite literally gave up. I gave up on myself, I gave up on my soul, and, may Allah forgive me, I gave up on my Lord. But for more reasons than you can imagine, I choose not to recount my experience. But that was the time when the recollection of my *shahaadah* was most painful to me, when I wanted to forget that I had recited it at all. My spiritual degeneration was a culmination of regret, animosity against the sorority, and, most truthfully, the atrophied strength in facing the sins I had committed against my soul.

But it's not at all like you imagine. There's no point where you wake up and feel as if you've fallen from a cliff, or when you say, "I disbelieve." It's a slow, almost imperceptible, shaving of faith that occurs within. There's the listlessness, the carelessness, and finally the giving up. The terrifying verses and hadith about the punishment for this rarely crossed my mind, mainly because, more than anything, disbelief is the forgetting of yourself. Thus, you have no comprehension or desire for what you need most. So you wander in darkness and think it light, and see light as darkness from your contorted vantage point. In a way, it was like being in the sorority all over again, except this time the entire *ummah* was not part of the club I'd forged for myself.

Today people often ask me how I could have gotten involved with the sorority in the first place, especially after seeing how clearly misguided they were. In all honesty, it is very difficult to explain. But I liken it to hearing a vicious rumor that an apparently righteous person is secretly involved in sick lewdness of some kind. The sheer shock value of it leads you to disbelief, but over time you begin to wonder if it's true. Every movement and word of the person suggests that there may be some truth to the claim, even if these possibilities are expressed only in your heart. Imagine then that the person is finally exonerated and you're left realizing that the rumor was a heinous lie. Then shortly thereafter the person opens up a daycare in their home. I've but one question for you: Would you send your young child there? Or would you rather be "safe"?

Years after leaving the sorority, I could detect a new recruit by merely looking her in the eye. Her entire demeanor was abnormal. New recruits were typically fidgety, uncertain, unable to relax in public if speaking to a non-member, constantly looking over their shoulders, startled by certain words or people approaching. Veteran members were simply cruel, often denying the Islamic greeting of peace to a believer or carrying themselves with an air of arrogance and scorn that would become their signature for years to come.

Even now, it's scary to think I had been there once.

"I don't think William will last too long with them," Bashirah said finally, her eyes lost in thought.

I nodded, too ashamed to admit that he wasn't the only one guilty of foolishness. "*InshaAllaah.*"

"Be patient. I know people who've gone through that. It's like the Nation of Islam in a way."

I creased my forehead. "What do you mean?"

"It doesn't last. It has attractive slogans, some pretty good messages, but overall, it's a short-term thing for most people. It doesn't allow you to live a normal life."

I nodded.

"A friend of mine's daughter got involved in that. The girl abandoned every *masjid* and Islamic organization because they weren't part of the saved. She moved overseas only to realize that there's no such thing as she imagined. Every country is filled with the weak and the strong, the knowledgeable and the ignorant, and the righteous and the sinful." She sighed.

"Sooner or later," she said, "you realize this is called life. If someone's ignorant, you teach them. But first you have to learn yourself." She shook her head before she continued.

"I just wish there was some way to tell these young people that there's no easy formula to doing what's right. The only safety is in focusing on your soul and your family."

I didn't know what to say.

"*InshaAllaah*, he'll come around. He's like you. People who want to make something of themselves never last there. It's for people who've lost hope and need to feel better by putting others down."

"He doesn't really agree with everything." I felt obligated to at least give a more balanced picture. "It's just the polygamy thing that's got him."

"There's always a hook. If they got him on anything, they got him."

She sighed. "It's a good thing you're not involved in that."

I bit my lower lip, my gaze on Rahma, tempted to confess but too ashamed.

"I just want my life back."

She laughed then quieted until she was looking at my daughter. "We all do, *habeebati*. We all do."

I was surprised to hear that. "You're not happy with your life?"

She creased her forehead and met my gaze, a smile still on her face. "I'm grateful for my life. Allah has truly blessed me. But everyone has things they regret or wish they would've done differently. I'm no different."

"But you seem so content."

"No one's content, *habeebati*. You just reach a point where you realize there's nothing to do but say, *alhamdulillaah*, and focus on your life."

"I can't wait to get there."

"You will, *inshaAllaah*, as long as you hold onto your faith."

I grew quiet, remembering how despondent I had been lately. "That's what I'm afraid of."

"What?"

"Not being able to hold on. That's why I asked for the divorce."

She watched Rahma for some time. I could tell she was thinking of something.

"Just make sure it's William you can't live with, Renee, and not yourself."

Bashirah's words stayed with me, and I wondered if I had made the right decision. I thought of how William was being influenced negatively, but I also remembered how I had once been too. Was I being unfair by leaving? Was I being impatient?

I thought of how he was listening to the fraternity saying that I wasn't even Muslim if I kept the clause in my contract, and the familiar anger returned. I simply couldn't live with someone like that. William himself had not gone as far as to question my Islam, but he did agree that our marriage terms were un-Islamic. That in itself was troubling and made me uneasy about remaining. What else would he deem un-Islamic? If I gave on this, what else would I be expected to compromise? Would my life gradually be dictated by fraternity terms instead of Islam?

I then thought about Luqman and Rahma. Was it fair to them if we divorced? The prospect of disrupting their lives tormented me. I didn't even know what it meant to be a single mother. I had no example. The stories I heard were not promising, and I wondered if Allah would be displeased with me if I gave my children a broken home.

This alone made me think I should take back my decision. But I was still indecisive.

I took Bashirah's advice and prayed the *Istikhaarah* prayer.

A week later I found out I was pregnant. I cried when I saw the two pink lines on the wand. I took another test and the results were the same.

I wouldn't be leaving in August after all. I called my mother to let her know I couldn't keep my flight but would let her know when I could. She said she would talk to the people at the university to secure me a place for January. I said okay, although I knew it would be at least another seven months before I could even consider coming home.

I talked to William, and we came to this decision. Since the *'iddah* period now ended at the end of pregnancy, I would use these months to determine what I wanted to do. But we didn't take back my initiation for the divorce. It remained in motion. But I knew in my heart that I would take it back. There was just too much to consider now. School itself was out of the question.

But because deep in my heart I really did want out, I decided to stick to my decision. If I had a firm change of heart in my last trimester, I would tell him then. Besides, realizing that I was serious was inspiring changes in William. He'd constantly ask if I was sure about my decision, and I'd say I was. There were moments that I really felt bad for him. I could tell he was deeply wounded. But then I'd think about how much I was hurting, and I'd feel a surge of determination to remain firm. It didn't escape me that not once did he offer to take back his request to alter our agreement. That hurt most.

I visited Bashirah more often and kept her updated as to my plans. She didn't say much except to remind me to pray on it.

One day she surprised me by stopping by the apartment with some freshly baked brownies. I was so happy to see her that I squealed and embraced her. She had never been to my apartment before but she knew where I lived.

"I thought you could use the company."

I beamed. "Come in."

She came inside and we sat on the couch in the living room as Luqman zoomed in and out, entertaining himself in some sort of fighting game with imaginary adversaries. Rahma was sitting on the couch distracted by her toys.

"How are you?"

I shrugged. "Okay."

"How are you feeling these days?"

I wasn't sure if she meant the pregnancy or the impending divorce. "Actually pretty good. I don't even have nausea. At least not so far."

She nodded, her eyes on Luqman. "So you're still going through with it?"

"I'm not sure. For now, I am. The way I see it, if he wants to break our contract, he doesn't want to be married to me."

She was quiet. "Are you sure you'll be happier alone?"

I studied my son for some time. "No."

Luqman fell out on the floor, playing dead. Then he jumped back to his feet and made "pow, pow" noises to get revenge.

"That's good," she said. "At least you know."

"You gave me a lot to think about."

"Well, I just want you to know it isn't going to be a walk in the park."

I looked at her. "You were divorced before?"

She shook her head. "No, but I know how it feels to hurt."

"I'm kind of scared," I said honestly. "But I'm also really relieved. Of course, I have seven months to wait. But that's fine."

"Then you'll have a new baby, and you'll need him even more."

I shrugged. "Maybe."

We were quiet for some time.

"Are you sure this is only about your contract, or is there something else?" Bashirah was speaking in a low voice, not wanting Luqman to hear.

If I were honest, there were other things that were bothering me, but the contract was the only one that affected me as personally as it did. Every marriage has problems, so I chalked up the other problems to that. The truth was that I felt as though I was already a single mother. William was barely there. I know this was partly because of 'iddah and that I was sleeping in the children's room. But he was hardly there before that. Even if he wasn't at work or school, he would be out, and it bothered me tremendously. Part of me was worried about him, but another part wondered if he had already broken the contract. But this was mere speculation, and I couldn't go on that. Still, it was excruciating to even imagine that he was already married to someone else. That's how I knew there was no way I could remove the clause. I couldn't even survive my imagination, how about reality?

"Mostly the clause." I didn't want to talk about my other pain. It hurt too much. I also didn't want it discredited. I didn't know if Bashirah would trivialize it, but there are just some things you keep to yourself. After all, William was still my husband. I owed him his privacy. I was his garment, so I would cover his faults. But my mind drifted after I spoke.

I thought of how even when he was home, he was distant from the children, as if afraid to play a role. I had tried to ask him about his own childhood, thinking perhaps his behavior was related to that, but he refused to talk about it. So I left him alone. But it was a tug-of-war. I wanted him to open up, and he closed up even more. I asked him to be more attentive to the children. He said I was doing fine and was happy with all I'd done. I told him he was still their father, and he would grow defensive, saying he knew that. Still he wouldn't play with them. I had begun to wonder if he didn't have only methyphobia but phobia of parenthood too.

"It's not easy, but neither is being alone."

It took me a moment to register Bashirah's words.

"What's not easy?"

"Your husband marrying someone else."

I stared at her. Feeling my gaze, she met my eyes with her forehead creased.

"You didn't know?"

"Know what?"

"That Jadwa and I are co-wives."

The words were so foreign to me that it took a full minute for me to comprehend their meaning. I started to speak but couldn't find my voice. I just kept looking at her as if seeing her for the first time. *Bashirah?* No way.

"But... how?"

She laughed. "All this time, I thought you knew."

I squinted my eyes and shook my head. "I... had no idea."

"Well," she sighed, smiling, "now you do."

Of course, I asked her a million questions, and I learned this: Bashirah was the first wife and Jadwa, her best friend, had been recently divorced from her first husband and living in a shelter. Apparently, Jadwa's marriage had been abusive, and Bashirah had been trying to tell her to leave him and to accept Islam. Jadwa finally became Muslim and Bashirah asked her own husband to marry her. He didn't want to, but she insisted, even crying at times. Finally, he gave in, but reluctantly.

"You *asked* him to marry her?"

She smiled, but she had a look of exhaustion in her eyes. "Yes, I did."

I was floored. This was something I'd never heard of in my life.

"You're not jealous?"

"Of course I am. I'm human. We can't escape that."

"But I mean..." I didn't know how to phrase what I wanted to ask. "...You're happy with that?"

"I don't regret it, if that's what you're asking. I prayed on it for weeks before I said anything to him."

I just stared unblinking for several seconds.

"But how does it feel?"

She drew in a deep breath and exhaled. "Like being in labor."

I furrowed by brows. "Labor?"

"Yes. Except there's no child at the end."

"That doesn't sound good."

"It's not." She said it so matter-of-factly that I feared I was prying. "At least not in the absolute sense."

"Then why do you do it at all?"

"Because I know it's the right thing to do."

I grew silent, my gaze distant. "You really think so?"

"For me, yes. But not for you."

This surprised me. "But why not for me?"

"It's not something you should be forced into. You have your contract. He should respect that."

"But..."

"*Habeebati*, don't base your life on someone else's. You'll never make it through life like that. That's why we have the *Istikhaarah* prayer. It guides us to what's right for us."

My mind went back to her comment. "But if it hurts that much... I mean..."

"Don't look so shell-shocked. I'm not miserable. I said it feels like labor because it does." She paused. "But I also think that's just how life feels in the end. You can't escape it. You just have to find your rhythm of breathing that gets you to the end."

"But you said there is no end."

"I said there's no baby in the end. There certainly is an end to the labor."

"But how?"

She looked at me, a kind expression on her face. "You meet Allah and find that He's pleased with you."

That night when my imagination tormented me again, I thought of Bashirah's words. *Like being in labor.*

I could relate to that feeling.

I felt like I was in labor too. That's how my marriage felt right then.

Like labor, the pain was so immense, so unimaginable, that no book or person could have described it to me. Nothing could have prepared me for it, not even myself. There was no mental exercise, no Lamaze class that would have given me a true, fitting heads-up for what I was to endure. And no matter what breathing exercise or chant someone may have told me to say, most likely, it wouldn't have worked for me. I had to merely grit my teeth to sustain the pain or to fight a piercing scream, but still, the pain wouldn't go away. And all I could think then was, *Am I going to survive? O God, will I survive!*

But unlike labor, there was no final moment that made it "worth it in the end." Because, as long as I was enduring the pain, there was no end. Yet still, like enduring the pain of childbirth, I found my rhythm, which had been neither rehearsed nor learned, all the while unable to fathom the calmness of my husband whose most crucial sharing in my pain was holding my hand or stroking my back or gazing at me with a look of concern in his eyes, a look so remarkably distant, even if sincere, that I wondered at such moments of the excruciating pain that was felt all alone, even as he was, in part, the cause.

I pushed these thoughts from my mind.

I was being cynical, and ungrateful. My marriage wasn't like that. It just felt like that right then. I had gone through my own hazing, so why couldn't I be patient through his? He had said he was glad to have me back. Where had I gone? Had William felt like he was in labor waiting for me?

Should I do the same for him?

Twenty-seven

*"No calamity befalls the earth or yourselves except that
it is inscribed in the Book of Decrees
before We bring it into existence.
Verily, that is easy for Allah."*
—Qur'an, 57:22

On Tuesday, September 11, 2001, I woke at dawn and started my day as I normally did—with prayer. I had a heavy heart that morning, having reflected on Bashirah's words, and life, a lot. I felt that I should perhaps give my marriage another chance. It saddened me that I would be the one giving in, but as I wrote in my journal a couple of days before: *This is the life of a woman, what choice do I have but to live it?*

I prayed *Fajr* in the quiet of the apartment after William left for the *masjid* to pray there, and I felt a peaceful connection to my Lord. I thought of how He had guided me to Islam and how in many ways William had been part of that. I thought of Luqman and Rahma and couldn't imagine their lives without seeing their father each day. Like so many women before me, I decided that sacrifice would be my station in life. I had to think of others before I thought of myself. If I wasn't happy, it didn't matter. At least my children would be. What was the clause anyway except some words on a piece of paper? They had done nothing for me so far except give me false hope and endless problems in my marriage.

Maybe the fraternity was right. Perhaps there was really something wrong with my faith. I wasn't perfect, and I was only beginning to learn the complications of that fact. It was possible that deep down inside I didn't like the idea of polygamy at all.

I pondered that by thinking of Bashirah's and Jadwa's marriage to the same man.

It didn't bother me. I actually admired them more than before.

No, I didn't have a problem with the idea, I realized. This was about me, like Bashirah had said. I shouldn't be forced into it, especially when I specifically stipulated that I didn't want it before I even entered the marriage.

But Bashirah was right to caution me to make sure it wasn't myself I couldn't live with. I was beginning to wonder if, even after the divorce, I could bear to live with myself.

Because the children were still sleeping, I returned to their room and lay on the feather mattress I had placed on the floor, drifting to sleep wondering if I really had it in me to tell William I changed my mind.

I woke to Rahma stirring, but when I sat up to look in her crib, she had already put herself back to sleep. William was gone to work, I could sense it in the emptiness the apartment felt right then. I lay back down and shut my eyes but felt a pain in my side. For some reason, this jolted me alert, and I blinked repeatedly, my heart pounding. Something was wrong. I felt the pain again, this time in my abdomen, and I sat up.

The pounding in my chest grew more incessant until I scrambled to my feet and went to the bathroom to see if my fears were correct.

There was nothing.

I exhaled in relief and left the bathroom, but I couldn't bring myself to rest right then. I wandered into our bedroom and looked around it, a lump developing in my throat as my eyes grazed the bed I no longer used. I wondered if all of this arguing and disagreeing was even worth the trouble.

I sat on the end of the bed and picked up the remote. I rarely watched television, so I'm not sure what made me press the power button and wait for the screen to come to life. I felt the pain again but ignored it. It was most likely stress.

Mentally, I planned my day. I would go to Bashirah's after the children woke up. I couldn't bear to be in the apartment all day, not today. Anyway, I needed someone to help me through my change of heart. I wasn't sure if I was being too lenient in something in which I should remain firm.

I thought of Arifah but decided that it was Bashirah I should call. Bashirah was older, more experienced, and plus, I'd already cried to Arifah a dozen times. I didn't want to keep droning on about the woes of my life to her. I wanted to enjoy her company as a friend.

I was only half aware of what was being shown on television. Tragic images were so common these days that it was difficult not to become stoic. So I watched with a sense of detachment until the burning building collapsed.

Right then, I felt as if my heart fell to my stomach, evoking a pain so intense that I clutched my abdomen and bent over. It was at that moment that I knew this wasn't a thousand miles across the ocean. This was happening just hours away.

When the pain subsided slightly, my eyes were glued to the screen. *O God, O God!*

The whole world seemed to shift beneath my feet, and I felt as if I would pass out. But I steadied myself on the bed, afraid to move. I watched unblinking, unaware of the passing time until Rahma began to cry.

But right then I was struck with more pain and felt a sensation that I was sure was confirmation of my earlier fears.

In the bathroom, I doubled over, knowing what was happening but unable to think what to do. I was terrified to leave my house to go to the hospital. The world was falling apart. I didn't want to be out there when it finally caved in.

I lay on the cold tile floor moaning, wondering if this was how it felt to be in a country at war. I imagined women miscarrying and dying from it because there was no medical care. I imagined women getting caesarians without the aid of anesthetics, and I rolled my eyes to the ceiling in pain.

Rahma cried louder, but I couldn't move to get her. I needed help. Instinctively, I thought of calling William, triggering a realization that aggravated the pain.

The pregnancy was over. So was our marriage.

It felt surreal. It couldn't be over so soon.

But it was. This was what I chose. I said I would be free at the end of pregnancy.

Now I was.

My chest tightened in panic. What was I supposed to do?

Eventually, the aching subsided enough for me to tend to Rahma. By then Luqman was awake screaming too. It was as if we all were panicking and hurting at the same time. Even my children knew our safety was threatened that morning.

The phone rang as I was making breakfast for Luqman. I was too weak and terrified to fill my stomach with anything right then.

"Is everyone all right?"

It was William sounding panicked.

"Yes." My voice was amazingly calm, considering that my response wasn't entirely true. But then again, I knew he wasn't asking about my health, but our lives.

He exhaled in relief.

"I'm coming home."

Before I could tell him what happened, he hung up.

By then I accepted the bleeding as part of the tragedy of that day. As I sat at the table next to the kitchen, I watched with a sense of detachment as Luqman ate oatmeal and Rahma nursed. I had no idea what William planned to do when he arrived. Certainly, he couldn't undo the collapsing of the building—or the collapsing of our shared life. But I also knew I couldn't pretend that nothing had occurred.

When Luqman finished breakfast, he zoomed from his seat and began running around the living room as if nothing tragic had altered our reality. Rahma began looking at him, a childish grin on her face as she kicked her legs in glee. I decided to put her down and get dressed.

I wasn't getting dressed to go out. I had no intentions of leaving the apartment. For all I knew another plane would fall from the sky on my way to the bus stop.

I was getting dressed because I knew this home no longer belonged to husband and wife. It belonged to William Garret. I needed to leave.

William's arrival was in no way inconspicuous. The door banged open and he stood in the doorway as if coming to rescue us from a burning building.

"You're sure everyone's okay?"

I nodded, my eyes growing distant from where I sat on the couch, the stabbing sensation returning.

He looked relieved as he stepped inside and closed the door. He immediately came to embrace me, but I leaned out of his reach.

"What?" He sounded aggravated.

"I'm losing the baby." My eyes welled as I said this, and slowly they met his.

First his face was concerned. He opened his mouth to ask if I was okay, then realized there was more to this than my physical state. His eyes widened until his face bore an expression I couldn't recall seeing until then. Trepidation and panic.

He, like I, never imagined this moment as real. It had been so distant in my mind. Never once did I think the pregnancy would end before nine months. This was odd because with Luqman and Rahma I was worried sick about the slightest thing going wrong. I monitored my meals and vitamin intake so compulsively that I would set an alarm to remind me to eat a certain meal. I imagined deformity, prematurity, even fetal death. Why it had not occurred to me that these were possibilities during my 'iddah too, I'll never know. At that moment, I remembered only that I had prayed to Allah. In my upset, I thought grimly, *And this is what He decreed.*

It was the worst possible time for anyone to be alone, and I had to sleep somewhere else even as I was too terrified to open the front door. I couldn't imagine how I'd bear sleeping without William in the next room.

"We have to go to the hospital," he said, still looking at me.

At his words, and his use of "we," the moisture was evoked from my eyes. In that moment, I saw his arm twitch. He wanted to reach out to me but knew he couldn't.

For several seconds we just stared at each other, a flood of thoughts and emotions shared in absence of words.

I'm sorry, my heart cried. *I'm sorry. O God, I'm so sorry.*

His eyes welled too, but he turned away, looking at his son who was still running around oblivious. "Luqman!" I knew all the hurt he was feeling was put into his son's name, and I covered my face with my hands, as if my heart was being tugged at the sound of his voice. "Get your shoes on. We have to go." Luqman stopped running, stunned as he looked wide-eyed at his father, who never spoke to him like that. *"Now."*

William drove me to the hospital in a car he had borrowed from a friend. During the ride, neither of us spoke. I felt as if someone was suffocating me twice—first with losing my husband, and second with the threat of the car being swallowed up by the earth like the Twin Towers had been destroyed by the plane. I was uneasy and wanted the normalcy of my life back. Even if all we would do was argue about the contract, I wanted to relax in the safety of my husband's arms again.

I went through the routine of the emergency sign-in and admission only remotely aware of my surroundings. The diagnosis I already knew, so I merely nodded vaguely as they told me I'd miscarried. As was routine in cases like these, the doctors performed a D and C, a minor surgical procedure to make sure that all remains of the fetus following the spontaneous abortion were removed.

I didn't stay long at the hospital and met William at the door to my room when I was discharged. Part of me had accepted my personal predicament at that moment, and my mind went immediately to the tragedy occurring outside the hospital walls. I didn't know if it was even safe to drive home. Because of the pains, I hadn't been sure what was going on. I thought I heard something about an attack on D.C. and that part of the Pentagon had already been destroyed.

The nurse who was discharging us was a pleasant-looking Black woman with a short perm who reminded me of Natasha. A gold crucifix glistened from her necklace just above the top button of her white coat. She smiled at me as she handed me the paperwork to take home.

"You take care of yourself," she said.

I met her eyes, wondering if her advice were at all possible, given that our country was at war.

"Is everything all right now?" I asked, my voice hopeful and fearful at once.

She looked at me oddly, as if she didn't understand why I'd ask about what she had just said. "Yes, just stay off your feet for about a week, and you should be fine."

I shook my head. "No, I mean after the attack."

As the meaning of my inquiry registered, the professional cordiality faded into an expression of scorn that

I interpreted as my words reminding her of what she'd hoped to forget. I felt bad as she contorted her face, and I wondered if I'd overstepped my bounds. Perhaps she had lost a loved one today.

Her narrowed eyes confused me, but I watched for some hope of information as her nose flared and lips moved in reply. "I don't know," she said so cruelly that I winced. "You tell me."

I creased my forehead in confusion and was only vaguely aware of William trying to get my attention to tell me it was time to go. But I couldn't break my gaze from hers. She was still looking at me, now wearing an expression of tenacious disgust, refusing to even blink as she continued to look me in the eye, challenge and fury in her gaze.

Finally, I felt William tug at my arm, which shocked me into alertness because he had been keeping his distance respectfully until then. He held me by the elbow, touching the cloth of my *jilbaab* instead of the skin of my hand.

In the car, he huffed after I sat in the passenger seat and he had secured our children in their car seats.

"What were you thinking?"

I stared at him in confusion. "Thinking about what?"

He glared at me. "Asking her that?"

I blinked as I gathered my brows, not comprehending his words.

"About the attack in New York."

"What's wrong with finding out? I wanted to know."

His expression softened as he continued to stare at me, a look of pity in his eyes. "You don't have any idea what's going on, do you?" It was a rhetorical question. I wasn't supposed to respond. But in keeping with my sincere ignorance, I did.

"No. Do you?"

He breathed, as if wanting to laugh but couldn't. Instead, he shook his head. "Ray," he said, triggering a warmth in my heart at the sound of my nickname, "they think Muslims did that."

It took me almost thirty seconds to understand his meaning. "*What?*"

He nodded. "Yes. That's why I wanted to make sure you're okay. There have been a lot of hate crimes in the area."

"*What?*" I still couldn't believe what he was saying was true.

"Yes, Ray. Everything's different now."

I sat back in my seat, exhaling in the motion. I stared out into the darkness beyond the dashboard. This was too much to fathom.

"Some nutcases killed all those people, so now Muslims have to pay."

I shook my head in disbelief, still gazing into the night. "But no Muslim would do that."

"I know."

I thought back to the woman's face and was suddenly overcome with shame. Now it made sense. *You tell me.* Little did I know, verbal harassment—and terrorism—would become common against Muslim Americans and Muslim nations for some time.

Years later a friend of mine would tell me a coworker came to her amid the country's varying terror color alerts, and the coworker said in all sincerity, "This is really confusing. Can you guys just give us some idea when the next attack is going to happen?"

"Ray," I heard William say next to me, "you need to watch yourself. They've turned this into a war against Islam."

Twenty-eight

*"...And you will surely hear from those who were given
the Scripture before you and from those who associate
partners with Allah much abuse.
But if you are patient and fear Allah,
Indeed, that is of the matters (worthy) of determination."*
—Qur'an, 3:186

I find it perversely amusing—in a way that incenses heat
in my chest, and I find myself fighting tears of helplessness
instead of humor—that I can no longer walk the streets in
safety because my presence makes others feel unsafe. I
could remove my *hijaab*, the simple piece of cloth that
ridiculously defines my threat to them, and make them feel
safe.

They don't even deserve a trial, I read in a paper the
other day before tossing it aside in disgust. And my mind
reeled, *Then how would you ever know they were guilty in
the first place?*

And then a sickness came over me as I realized that this
country, post-911, had become guilty of exactly what the
perpetrators were—terrorism. And because grief and fear
was a more dangerous combination than war itself, that
meant that everyone, even the elderly neighbor who needed
a metal walker to take a single step, would fit into either one
of two categories at the sight of me—those who wanted to
harm me, and those who felt a sense of justice at seeing me
harmed.

On October 13, 2001, I wrote this journal entry: *The
most difficult war to fight, let alone win, is the war to combat
ignorance.* This entry was inspired by a phone call I had
received earlier that day. I had always kept in touch with
my sisters, at least in the minimal sense. At least once a
year, Patricia and Courtney would each receive a call from
me, that obligatory call inspired more by guilt than my heart
being moved toward cultivating familial connection.
Usually, it would be in Ramadan, when I knew the months
had passed faster than I'd realized and that Allah would call
me to account for keeping the ties of the womb. In the last
two years, Patricia received more frequent calls simply
because she was much more personable and mature than
her younger sister.

But that morning, Courtney called me. At that time, I
was living in the same apartment I had been at the time of
the miscarriage. William, may Allah bless him, said he
would move out and pay the rent until the end of the year—
after which I imagined I'd have the stomach, and guts, to get

on a plane to fly home to my parents. We were technically, in Islamic terms, divorced, but no paperwork had been filed to make it official in the courts. Needless to say, neither William nor I was inspired to enter any government building and ask for anything during the current political climate, if it wasn't our lives or the lives of our children at stake.

I was so surprised to hear her voice, and pleasantly so, that I didn't detect until later that her initial greeting sounded rehearsed and obligatory, as if a precursor to the real purpose of the call.

"Oh, wow, I'm so glad you called," I'd said.

"Really?" It was a flat tone, as if she found my comment amusing but couldn't muster the energy to laugh. I interpreted it as the subdued affection we felt obligated to put up as a shield from the innate love we had for each other as siblings.

"Yes. This is such a surprise."

"Hm."

The line grew quiet for a few seconds.

"Mom says you're coming home to go to school," she said.

"Yeah, actually I am." In my mind, I said *InshaAllaah,* as I normally did when talking to someone who wasn't Muslim.

"Why?"

I sighed. "I miss everyone." Courtney was the last person I would tell the truth to.

"Hm."

Quiet again.

"Are you going to wear all that stuff?"

This was the first indication that the call wasn't inspired by her desire to keep in touch. My smile faded. "Yes... of course."

"Hm."

Huh? "Why?"

"Just wondering so I can arrange my schedule."

My pleasantry returned and I smiled into the receiver. "You're coming to visit?"

I heard her breathe, the beginning of scornful laughter. "Not if you're there."

It was as if my smile fell from my face. I sat down on the couch, unsure if I heard her correctly. "What?" I was stunned.

"I *was* coming for Christmas and New Year's."

I contorted my face. "Then don't let me stop you. I can find somewhere to stay while you're there."

"Hm."

She was beginning to aggravate me. But I reminded myself that I was Muslim and therefore had to be the "bigger person." I took a deep breath. This wasn't going to be easy.

"You know," she said as if she was suddenly inspired to share a reflection, "I was watching the news and saw someone who looked like you."

My jaw clenched. *Don't get upset. Don't get upset.* "Oh? That's nice."

"No, it isn't actually."

I couldn't stand it anymore. "Is that why you called? To insult me?"

"No." She sounded pleased that she'd gotten under my skin. "I called to ask you not to insult us."

"*What?*"

"I just hope you're not selfish enough to come home and say you're a Morris. To us, you're not anymore."

I had to take a deep breath and exhale slowly. "Who's *us?*"

"I guess you wouldn't know, huh? You've all but disappeared since you married that stupid drunk."

"Courtney, you really need to get a life." It was the dumbest thing to say, but I couldn't get my thoughts straight right then.

"I could if people like you wouldn't keep taking people's."

Rage built inside my chest. "You have no idea what you're talking about."

"Yeah? Turn on the news, and you'll see what I'm talking about. Then again, you don't need to watch the news since you already *know* what's going on."

I was suddenly reminded of the nurse saying to me, *You tell me.* I tried to stay calm. "Honestly, Courtney, I imagined that you actually called out of the goodness of your heart. I see now that I was wrong."

"No, you were right. I care about my family's safety. That's why I called. I just hope your sudden interest in coming home isn't related to what happened in New York."

What! "You've lost your mind."

"No. *You* have."

"Have you ever considered turning off the TV and just listening to your stupidity?"

"You *would* think I'm stupid."

I had no idea what she meant, but by then I knew it wasn't a compliment.

I sighed audibly. "Is there anything else you'd like to say? I'm kind of busy right now."

"Just one thing." She sounded as if she were talking through gritted teeth.

I rolled my eyes.

"I hope they take all of you and put you in concentration camps like they did in that movie."

Shocked, I opened my mouth to say something, but no sound came out.

My parted lips were greeted by the sound of a dial tone in my ear.

Angry thoughts flooded my mind right then. I couldn't imagine that I'd ever thought she'd be open to Islam, or human dignity itself.

This was a scenario I'd imagined in my head more than once. My father, my mother, Courtney, and perhaps even Patricia, staring at me, a visceral pain in their eyes, as the truth of Islam gripped their soul. *Why didn't you tell me?* And my silence, my averted eyes, my shoulders shrugging, my stilled tongue saying something entirely different from the truth: *Because you never let me speak.*

These days I'm silenced before I even part my lips. It would be easier if I disagreed with their motives. But I actually understand. I am even less inclined than they to hear the sound of my voice in all its peculiarity and weakness, even as my words unveil a veracity they have no ability to refute.

What's strange is that my conviction isn't any less. It is, in fact, more heart-felt than ever before. But so is my human empathy. I know they have no desire to hear what I have to say, or at least what I'd say if I had courage to speak, and I'm too ashamed to burden them with my human flaws that I have difficulty having patience with myself.

If I could just say a few sentences, it would be easy. *This is the truth. If you submit, there is Paradise as a reward. If not, I fear for you the arrival of a Tremendous Day.* But this isn't the hard part. The difficulty is in not merely speaking, but in living, in being an example, allowing this to carry more weight than words. This is the burden I have difficulty bearing, knowing that my responsibility to teach, to warn, is upon me not because I am an exemplar in any sense, but because I have submitted, and am thus responsible, in spite of myself.

I know too that no one is worthy of emulation in the complete sense. The time of men receiving divine words and guidance direct from the heavens has long since passed. Yet I know also that this, earning my status as instructor and guide, is what is expected of me, and rightfully so.

I don't like confrontation, disagreement, or even being the cause of someone's unrest, as ironic as that sounds. So I live the saying, *Live and let live*, even as I know salvation's treatise has no such theme, at least not in my meek application of the adage.

But I see the fraying of the lines I've drawn for myself, feeling the anger and resentment rising at the sight of someone from my past, one who carries herself as if she knows it all, saying words like *I don't care what they think,* or *They can go you know where, this is the haqq.* I often have to resist the urge to walk up to her and call her bluff. Because I know of all stances, hers in the easiest—and weakest.

If I had the audacity to deny the humanity of everyone, even myself, I'd have no hesitation in my words, no shame in my speech, and no wisdom to resort to when I speak. I simply wouldn't care. I would have divided the world quite decidedly into two camps: me and them. And my camp would be the only one deserving of patience and respect.

In truth, such stiffness is a barrier, not so much between one and the world, but between one and herself. It allows one to overtly fulfill obligation, while perverting all the empathy and wisdom that are quintessential to obligation itself. It allows one to live in denial of basic truths, like it *does* matter what they think, or it is you who might end up where you're saying they can go.

You can use superficial strength to protect your cowardice but for so long, but then, what will you do in the end to protect yourself from your self?

Despite our prior consistent planning for my return home, I didn't call my mother for a month. I was so hurt and offended by Courtney's call that I began to consider my options in D.C. William was constantly asking me to take him back, and although he had told me that he was about to marry someone else, from the sorority no doubt, I began to consider accepting. It would be easier than sustaining the constant attacks upon my religion at home.

At moments I was filled with rage at the mere thought of my family. Why had my mother invited me home if she really didn't want me there, or if she couldn't accept me for who I was? I was terrified to walk around in *hijaab.* I feared for my life. But that didn't mean I wanted to be pressured to take it off and hide under the guise of The Church. Who did they think they were anyway? They had no right to harass me like they did. Didn't they know I already had enough pain in my life?

They didn't of course. They had no idea. Or, at least, they had no official confirmation if they suspected the truth.

I thought of Horace and Audrey and wished they were my parents, if only for that moment. Oh, how much I'd love to sit with a mother and father who asked sincere questions about my faith instead of parents who feigned a desire to see me with plans to strip that faith from me when I arrived.

The unrest that built inside me was tormenting, because I didn't have much of a choice. Had I still been married, I could have withstood this humiliation with a bit more fortitude, and dignity. But right then, I had no one, *no one* but myself. I needed my family right then. I was a mother.

A *single* mother. Yet I couldn't even comprehend how to do this alone.

I stressed over my predicament until my head hurt, wondering if I was willing to not only remarry William and forfeit the very clause that inspired our parting, but reenter the marriage as a second wife.

It's funny how a change in predicament can inspire an entirely different point of view. Young, single, and childless I would have scoffed at such an option. But now I just wanted the guarantee of a roof over my head and food on my table each night. I swear, if a financially stable brother—married or single—came and proposed right then, I'd marry him without a contract at all.

I cried so much that Luqman more than once asked me if I was "cwying to Allah" because we needed money again. It tore me apart that this wasn't too far from the truth.

One day shortly before Ramadan was scheduled to begin in mid-November, my mother called.

"Is everything all right?"

She was asking because she hadn't heard from me in so long.

"Yes, ma'am, it is." But even I could detect that I wasn't convinced.

"Did you confirm your flight?"

"No..."

"Why, honey? School starts in two months." She sounded worried and disappointed.

I was quiet. The familiar anger built as I thought of her real intentions in bringing me there. But I remained calm. "I don't know if it's a good idea if I come."

She grew quiet, I sensed, mostly because she needed some time to comprehend my words.

"Why not?"

"Mom, Courtney called." I said this as if I was uncovering a plot they were keeping from me.

"*Courtney?*" She said this as if I was speaking Chinese.

"Yes, a few weeks ago."

"What did she say?"

I told her, my voice flat and devoid of emotion, a sharp contrast to what was erupting inside.

"Oh, *Renee*," she sang with so much pity that my throat closed. "I hope you're not paying attention to her."

I had expected my mother to come to Courtney's defense. For some time I didn't speak. "But she said this was what you and Dad wanted too."

"Renee, please tell me that's not why you haven't called."

I grew quiet, embarrassed suddenly. I wondered then if Courtney was more similar to the sorors than I'd realized. She had actually made me believe that someone had said and done something they had absolutely no knowledge of, let alone guilt in.

"Listen," my mother said when I didn't respond. "If I want to say anything to you, I'll tell you myself. Right now, we're worried about you and want you home. I've already talked to the school and they said you can start in January. And, honey, you know I'd be more than happy to watch the children for you."

Immediately, my thoughts went to my Islamic garb. Normally, I wouldn't care. But with the new political climate, I wasn't so sure I wanted to be in Indiana wearing what would look like what Afghani women were forced to wear. I also didn't like the idea of being Muslim on a college campus right then. My mother was sincere in her intentions, but this was something she couldn't hope to comprehend. To her, I was just Renee, her daughter, returning to school. To them I'd represent something else entirely. And I wasn't sure I was ready for that.

"Okay..." I said.

"Renee?"

"Yes?"

"Please don't let someone make you ashamed of who you are."

I knew she wasn't speaking only of Courtney. After all, the whole world, it seemed, was against me right then. And I couldn't say I was doing a good job of not feeling ashamed, even as I knew their assumptions were incorrect.

"I already told the school you're Muslim, if that's what you're worried about. And they said they're looking forward to meeting you."

Right then, all my fears and anger and resentment filled my throat and eyes. I could hardly breath from the relief I felt right then. "Thank you," I whispered because I was having difficulty finding my voice.

There was a long pause, which was good, because I was overcome with emotion right then.

"Do you still wear that veil on your head?"

My heart sank as I registered her sudden question, my cheeks now wet with tears. I wiped them away with the back of my hand, my heart pounding in realization that this was the moment I had dreaded. A second of hope, and then this. I should have expected it.

When I spoke, my voice was between a moan and a whisper, as if afraid what the response would evoke on my mother's end. "Yes..."

"Good. Forget what the people are saying. I know who you are. And I'm proud of you for sticking to what you believe."

I broke down in tears, and despite my best efforts to hide this pitiful outburst from my mother, I heard myself sniffling and breathing audibly like a child. "Thank you, Mom," I croaked in the only voice I could find in my throat.

"No, honey, thank *you*. I'm sorry for what we put you through. We love you, Renee. Don't forget that."

Submission

"And whoever fears Allah,
He will make for him a way out
And will provide for him
from (sources) he could never imagine.
And whoever relies on Allah, then He is sufficient for him.
Indeed Allah will accomplish His purpose.
Verily, for all things has Allah appointed a due proportion.
---Qur'an, 65:2-3

~

Twenty-nine

"Something that has continually surprised and touched me is the unshakable conviction of every one of the sisters I spoke to—that the pain, tears and heartache have all been worth it. Not one of them would take back their shahaadah if ever they had their time again. They are prepared to go through the trials and tribulations to achieve their goal: to hold on to their religion, to hold it close to their hearts, for its beauty to permeate their lives, their bodies and their souls and so gain the pleasure of their Lord and His Love and to one day see the beauty of His Face."
—Na'ima B. Robert, *From My Sisters' Lips*

I returned to my home in Indianapolis in the last week of November 2001 during the month of Ramadan. I cannot lie and say that the year thereon was smooth for me, but I also cannot say that it was as painful as earlier that year, or even the years before. I was reunited with my family—my mother, father, and two younger brothers Michael and Elijah, who were now eleven and fourteen and were absolutely enamored with the idea of a "little brother" in the house. Whenever I coached Luqman to say *Uncle* before their names, Michael would grin ear-to-ear and eye his brother, as if saying, *Is this for real?* and Elijah would maintain a straight face despite the pride glowing his eyes, shrugging in that manner typical of teenage boys thinking they're men, as if saying, *Yeah, of course.* Emanuel didn't call them *Uncle*, so this was really new. Rahma was too young to inspire much excitement, but she got her share of attention too.

My father was still obviously deeply troubled by my acceptance of Islam, but for the most part he kept his thoughts to himself. Occasionally, he would be gruff and ask me what was the point of all this "starving," kissing the floor, and walking around "like a mummy." I'm human, so I was offended, but I wasn't perturbed, mostly because my mother was there to say, "Oh, sweetheart, leave my baby alone."

My mother's reversion to terms of affection when referring to me reinforced the feeling I had when I had hung up the phone—that she really did miss me and want me back, even if I wasn't, at twenty-four, the Renee Morris she had envisioned me to be. But that didn't stop her from being determined to make up for lost time. She was more excited about the prospect of school than I was.

I learned also that my mother's change of heart wasn't inspired only by her desire to have her daughter back.

While I was gone, she had some religious lessons of her own. Both my aunt Marcella and my uncle Marvin had accepted Islam. This was a complete surprise to me, as I hadn't seen them since Darnell's funeral. There had been moments that I thought of them, but I never brought myself to ask about them, mostly because I didn't want to know. I imagined them to be wallowing in depression and taking medication to merely function enough to pour themselves cereal and milk.

When my mother told me the news, it was right before they were coming over for dinner during the last days of Ramadan. She was grinning as she prepared the food, her eyes lit up with pleasure as she knew this would be exciting news to me.

"What?" I said after she told me. I almost cut myself from where I was dicing meat (*halaal* meat, no doubt) on the counter at an angle to where she stood stirring a pot of sauce at the stove. I grinned so wide that my cheeks hurt. "How?"

"That," she said, pointing the wooden stirring spoon at me, a sly smile on her face, "I'll let be a surprise."

I creased my forehead, unable to contain my happiness. "A surprise?" I couldn't imagine how their story could be more surprising, or pleasing, than the fact itself.

When they arrived, my aunt was wearing *hijaab* and I squealed like a little girl, running to hug her. I held on for a full minute, crying like a baby because I was not only happy to see her but because I was happy to see her doing so well. Her face glowed with a spiritual illumination that I would recognize as a signature of many believers for years to come. My mother's brother had a glow too, and I was still crying when I hugged him. I was at an absolute loss for words.

My father was in the living room, unable to partake in the excitement, but he did give a terse nod of acknowledgement when his eyes met theirs. Apparently, they visited often and he couldn't pretend to be as pleased to see them as I was, especially since they had influenced his wife to actually be happy for their conversion to Islam. Later I realized that my father, in his own way, was happy for them too. We all had been worried about them after Darnell's death, especially since Marcella couldn't have more children. It was a relief to my parents that they had found something to keep them positive and afloat. Apparently, my fears about their crumbling hadn't been too far from the truth. Before they found Islam, they were about as despondent as two people could possibly be.

"So, tell me," I said eagerly at the dinner table, too excited to realize I was speaking with food in my mouth. "What made you consider Islam?"

They grinned at each other, and Marvin nodded that it was fine with him for his wife to tell. "Well...," she said. "Actually, you."

My jaw dropped (which wasn't so great because I hadn't even swallowed my food). I pulled myself together, swallowed, and gathered my eyebrows. "Me?"

"Not you directly, of course." She was smiling. She went on to explain that my mother visited them often, along with my brothers, and one day she was crying and Elijah asked my mother if he could speak to his aunt alone. This struck my mother as odd, but because she felt it would be good for Marcella, she agreed.

My heart sank, anticipating the conclusion, my eyes darting to my father, who glanced at me sideways, lips pursed in disapproval. But I could tell he wasn't as upset as he had been initially. I looked at Elijah, who dropped his gaze to his food, fighting a grin on his face but unwilling to meet my eye because it would mean acknowledging that he had broken his promise. But I wasn't upset. I was just surprised. And, okay, a bit embarrassed because I knew this meant my parents knew.

"And he said, 'Can you keep a secret, auntie?'" Marcella laughed a bit. "And I told him I could. So he said, and I quote, 'You're sad because you don't know why you're here.'

"Of course," she said, "I didn't know what on earth he was talking about, but I was so down, I was willing to hear anything, even if from a child.

"So he said, 'I'm going to tell you a story you can't tell anyone until you go to college. That way you won't be here anymore. Do you promise?'"

I smiled, gazing fondly at Elijah, remembering how I said he couldn't say anything until he was about to go to college, because then he wouldn't be living with our parents anymore.

"I found him amusing even though I was depressed, so I agreed, thinking this ten-year-old was really something for his age. It was just comforting seeing how serious he was about helping me. I thought I was just enjoying his company. But then he said, 'Before God put Adam's children on the earth, He did something very important.' He looked at me and said, 'Auntie, do you know what it was?' I told him I didn't, so he said, 'He asked us all to say He is the only Lord. And you said it too, auntie. You and Uncle Marvin too. My Dad and Mom said it but they don't know yet. I'll tell them when I go to college like you.'"

She laughed, and my mother and I did too. My father huffed and rolled his eyes, looking at me in disapproval again.

"Then he said, 'God made us say this so we can't say anybody made us pray to pictures like the one you have right there.' And he pointed to the Black Jesus on my wall. 'You don't remember this, auntie, because God put it in your heart. But when you hear me talking, you know I'm saying the truth.'"

I sighed and stared at my brother, but he wouldn't meet my gaze. He was looking at our aunt and stuffing food into his mouth, his cheeks bulging as he chewed.

"And the funny thing is," Marcella said, "he was right. But what got me was when he said, 'That's why you're sad. You're not praying to God like you're supposed to.'"

Tears welled in my aunt's eyes as she stared lovingly at her nephew. "And I tell you," she said, shaking her head. "Those words saved my life."

She wiped her eyes, and I wiped mine too. I laughed. "I told him it was a secret."

"Yes, he told me that," she said. "That's why we talked alone. But I'm the one who broke the promise." She grinned. "I told my husband about it before I went to college."

She and I laughed, and my mother smiled proudly as she looked at her son.

"And of course, some secrets are just too good to keep."

I shook my head in amazement. This was indeed a surprise.

"But how did you learn everything?" I asked.

"I still don't know *every*thing," she said with a smile. "But I asked around, met Muslims. I guess Islam never really attracted me until then. I always associated it with the Nation of Islam."

At the mention of the Nation, we grew quiet momentarily, immediately reminded of Darnell.

"But I found out I was wrong."

I nodded.

"Later on Elijah told me William was Muslim too, and that surprised me, I must admit."

My smile faded at the mention of his name, but I tried to hide it, the sides of my lips still creased. "I wanted to ask him about his conversion, but he wasn't here so I asked his parents instead." She shrugged. "They didn't know much, but what they told me was intriguing."

For a moment, I didn't know what to say. "But when did you convert finally?"

She creased her forehead, "It was, what...?" She looked at her husband. "1997 or 98?"

He squinted his eyes and nodded. "Yeah around then, a couple of years after Reggie."

I was bringing food to my mouth and halted it in mid-air, inches from my lips. My heart pounded in my chest. "After Reggie what?"

She looked at me oddly. "William never told you his friend became Muslim?"

I nearly dropped my fork. I set it down, feeling a pulsing in my head. I have no idea why I reacted so dramatically. But I did.

"No." My voice sounded more offended than I intended. But it was too late.

She shrugged. "I thought you knew. Reggie said William was the one who taught him."

I felt my face go hot. "When did Reggie become Muslim?"

"It was...I forget which year, but it was the same year you got married."

Instinctively, my mind raced back to the last time I'd seen Reggie, and it actually had been the summer I married. "*Before* I got married?"

My aunt didn't know what to say, my mother, father, and uncle looking at my aunt and each other, as if trying to decide what was okay to say. Then they averted their gazes and continued eating, leaving it up to Marcella to decide for herself. Apparently, they had been under the impression that I already knew the story.

"Yes," my aunt said finally, not looking at me.

I sensed there was something else they weren't saying. "*What?*" I demanded, knowing I had crossed the bounds in talking to my aunt like that.

"Sweetheart, it doesn't matter now." It was my mother's voice.

"What doesn't matter now?"

She sighed, looking at my father, who shook his head in disappointment. He then stood abruptly. "I have some work to do."

My mother locked her gaze with Elijah and Michael, giving them "the look," inspiring them to stand, then leave. Elijah, knowing if it wasn't for his ears, it wasn't for Luqman's either, tugged Luqman's arm and said, "Come on, man, let's play some Gameboy."

"Gameboy!" Luqman squealed as he hopped from his seat.

Rahma was asleep in her playpen in the living room. My mother had bought it before we arrived. It was obvious she was excited about her role as both grandmother and babysitter come spring term at the university.

A knot tightened in my chest. My first thought was that Reggie was dead. I felt my stomach churn. "Mom, please." I couldn't take this anymore. I had faced Darnell's death, so I could face my former best friend's.

"Sweetheart. It's nothing except that Reggie had called before summer vacation and told us he was Muslim."

She looked at my aunt, who said nothing but shook her head, clearly disturbed by something.

"And?" I was growing impatient.

"And he asked your father again, if he minded if he married you."

I felt sick, suddenly remembering how Reggie was always trying to call and talk to me that summer, but I resisted, preferring William's company instead. I had no idea Reggie was Muslim, and William hadn't told me. I grew infuriated for some reason, but this didn't make any sense. I didn't even like Reggie then.

Or did I?

"So what did Dad say?"

She shrugged. "He was very angry about Reggie leaving The Church, and, honestly, I was too. That's why we gave you such a hard time."

I grew quiet, leaning back in my chair with my arms folded. "But what did Dad say?"

"He had already told Reggie yes, of course. You know your father always loved him like a son. But he did let Reggie know that he didn't like the idea of you two being Muslim."

I bit my lower lip until it hurt, my gaze growing distant. I wondered if William knew all of this. I had a feeling that he did.

"We would have told you, but we thought you and Reggie had already discussed this. We had no idea you didn't know." She sighed.

I dropped my head and shielded my eyes with one hand as my elbow rested on the table.

"But even when you married William, we had no idea what was going on. We didn't even know you talked to William like that. We were really confused, so we told Reggie what had happened and asked him what was going on and..."

I drew in a deep breath. I could take this. I was strong. "And what?"

"He just sat in a daze for a long time, and that's when we knew something was wrong. But still," she breathed audibly, "before now, we had just assumed you chose William instead."

There are three sides to every story when a man or woman feels the other is wrong. His side, her side...and the truth. This is something a friend of mine told me years later when I was recounting the woes that led me to my present reality. I laughed as I realized she was right. But it wasn't "his" or "her" side I had wanted the night my mother told me of the summer I eloped with William. I wanted the truth.

My instinct was to call William immediately and demand an explanation, but I know now that this was irrational and unjust. But at the time, I had every intention of picking up that phone and giving him a piece of my mind, until Marcella said, "Renee, it's the last ten days of Ramadan. Don't waste them thinking of this."

Her words reminded me that Allah is my Lord, and that it is His pleasure I want most. So instead of going upstairs and calling my ex-husband, I went upstairs, performed ablution and prayed to my Creator, asking Him to give me better than I lost.

Eventually, I told my family that William and I were divorced according to Islam, and that it was just a matter of paperwork through the courts to make it official.

I hate divorce. I really do. It's not something I wish on anyone. But I also realize that it is often necessary and can ultimately bring a lot of good.

Naturally, I was now curious about Reggie and what had become of him, but I would be lying if I said I still didn't love William and want to remarry him. Living with someone does that to your heart, even as it undergoes so much pain.

Because William had a right to his children's life, we were not strangers while I stayed at my parents' house, and he called periodically to check on the children, and me. But I never brought myself to satisfy my curiosity on the story of Reggie. Besides, in time it faded in significance, and the truth of what really happened between my ex-husband and former friend didn't even matter to me anymore.

One day a couple of months into my first term at the university, I received a postcard from William in the mail. There was no return address and no signature on it, but I knew from the note and handwriting that it was William and that he knew I'd know. It said simply, "Men have PMS too (pre-manhood syndrome). I'm sorry. Will you forgive me? I still love you."

I knew he was already remarried to someone and had been for several months, but I couldn't bring myself to ask who. I knew, as I know now, that I had every right to know, especially since she would be a stepmother to my children. But the pain of this knowledge alone was too much to risk aggravating by knowing details. Still, my mind was going crazy in curiosity, and my heart was going crazy in jealousy. I discovered then what Bashirah had meant by the feeling of being in labor, because in my mind and heart, I felt like William's wife, and now I was left to find my rhythm of breathing knowing that each night he was with someone else.

I didn't visit Marcella and Marvin as much as I would have liked because I was too busy with school. But they visited the house often, and we talked a lot about Islam. According to my parents, Elijah was "too young" to make the decision of changing religions, so they told him he would have to wait until he was eighteen to decide if he really wanted to convert. This disturbed me greatly, but I didn't say anything, at least not to my parents. Privately, I told him he wasn't a child to Allah. He said he knew that, and that he considered himself Muslim already but he would let them know when he was eighteen. When I asked him if he prayed, he said he did and was even teaching Michael about Allah and Islam. Naturally, Elijah's knowledge was very basic, and he wasn't as consistent with his prayers as he should have been, but I was proud of him for his efforts and asked Allah to keep him firm.

Gradually, I learned what Reggie was doing with himself. He was an elementary school teacher in D.C., where he lived and had gone to college, and that he came home every summer to work at an academic youth program, which paid well. I learned too that his parents were very disappointed in his conversion and were constantly nagging him about returning to "the life of Christ."

I thought of Reggie often but couldn't muster anything in my heart for him except curiosity and pity. It still inspires tears in my eyes to think of how he had worked so hard to do everything right, even talking to my father for permission, only to lose me without ever being given the chance to say how he felt.

I finally got up the nerve to submit the paperwork for the divorce, especially after I discovered whom William had married—Annette—and was planning to marry another sorority sister as his second wife. But Annette was against the marriage (imagine that) and was being "unreasonable" in how far she was going to prevent it. All this I learned from William in late April (during my studying for final exams) when he called my parents' house one day to check on the children. As I'm sure many former couples do, we got to talking like old times, and he started to complain to me.

"With you I can understand. It was in the contract. But what's her problem? She needs to check her intentions."

"We all do," I said, hoping he caught the hint.

He didn't. "This is ridiculous."

"I suppose you've already made up your mind?"

In my mind, I saw him smiling. "Yeah, you know me."

"Yeah," I sighed, shaking my head. "I do."

A pause. "You get any mail recently?"

"I got a postcard a long time ago." I wasn't in the mood for beating around the bush.

"Oh... What do you think?"

"That whoever sent it had the wrong address."

I heard him chuckle. "Yeah?"

"Yep."

"Why's that?"

"Because I'm nobody's fool."

"Come on, Renee. You can't hold a grudge forever. I thought you'd be over it by now."

"William, it hasn't even been a year. And this isn't a grudge. This is my life."

"*Our* life."

"Not anymore."

"So you really aren't going to take me back?"

"Didn't you read your own postcard?"

A confused silence. "Yeah..."

"You're not the only one with PMS. I have it too. But mine is post-*marriage* syndrome."

He laughed. "You always were a bit headstrong. I like that."

I frowned, realizing his comments were crossing the line. "William, I have to go."

"No, wait..."

"What?"

"Renee?"

I was getting irritated. "Yes, William."

"I meant what I said."

"I know."

"No, I mean the last line on the card."

I still love you. My heart softened, and I knew too that I felt the same. But I wasn't about to go back and be a third wife. I just didn't want that for myself, especially since it seemed like he planned the whole thing. Now, if I remarried him, the clause would be a moot point—I would be entering polygamy. I don't think he imagined that I would never come back. It pleased me that I would surprise him by doing just that.

"Like I said, I have to go."

"You never answered my question."

"I didn't realize you asked one."

"Do you forgive me?" His voice sounded so regretful and sincere that on my emotions alone, I would have taken him back right then.

"Yes."

"Really?" His voice rose in anticipation.

"Yes, really." I wasn't joking. I did forgive him. It wasn't doing me any good holding onto the pain.

"So you're coming back?"

"I didn't say I was coming back, William. I said I forgive you. I went through the haze myself. I know *inshaAllaah* you'll be out soon too."

He grew quiet. "It's not a haze, Renee. You shouldn't say that."

I creased my forehead. "It *is* a haze."

"A lot of the people you're thinking of left."

"That's funny, because I wasn't thinking of any people at all. I was talking about all the craziness."

"It's not craziness though. They're calling to the truth."

"Islam is calling to the truth, William. From that perspective, I agree with you. Their other ideas, I'm not so sure of."

"But some people are not following the Sunnah. We have to be safe."

"William, why are you talking to me like I'm in kindergarten? I know that. I just don't feel safe with that group."

"Who do you sit with now?"

I gritted my teeth. This was really ridiculous. "I sit with my mother and father," I said. "Usually around dinnertime."

"This isn't a joke."

"I'm not joking. I really do."

I heard him breathe in frustration. "Ray, you can't jus—"

"Don't call me that." I don't know why it offended me right then, but it did. He had no right to call me by my nickname anymore.

"Okay, Renee, then. I'm just saying you can't dismiss the truth just because some people are doing wrong."

I groaned. "Did you hear me say I doubt the truth?"

"But you said the group is wrong."

"I said I don't feel safe with them."

"But it's the only group on the right path."

"When I'm speaking of a group, William, I'm not talking about the one mentioned in hadith. I'm talking about that *group* of people I met in Maryland. That's an entirely different issue."

"It's not though. They are that group in the hadith. They're the only ones who—"

"William, I'll make this easy for you. Call your fraternity friends and let them know I *sit with* my parents, who don't even believe in Allah. If they want my social security number, they can have it so they can make sure they have the right Renee Morris when they add the thousandth page to their off list."

"I really wish you could see that—"

"I see William. I see that your *group* of friends have really made you believe they represent all the people on the right path on the face of the earth. To be honest, I really expected more of you. I really thought you'd be the last one to fall for something like that."

He was silent for some time. "You shouldn't stereotype."

I knew what he meant, and at that moment, I was embarrassed because he was right. I shouldn't stereotype.

Had I not stereotyped years ago, perhaps I would have realized that everyone has problems, regardless of their race, and perhaps, then I would have taken a bit more time to decide if I wanted to marry him. I was beginning to realize that part of my disappointment in him was because I expected more. I guess in a way I didn't expect him to be so *human* and flawed. Years later, I would do a study on people who grew up worshipping a White man as God, and the results were stunning. They held similar stereotypes and expectations as I had, from beauty to intelligence to just being a "good citizen." The results were strikingly different for those who had worshipped God as Black or had grown up in the Nation of Islam or who worshipped no image at all.

"I'm sorry. You're right."

He sighed. "Just think about what I said, okay?"

I contorted my face in offense. "I'm finished with that group."

"I'm not talking about the group. I'm talking about me."

I sighed, feeling sorry for him then. "No, I'm sorry William. After what I went through with those sisters, I pray to Allah I'm never misguided like that again."

"But Renee, a lot of them are gone. Now, we have some brothers there who sat with some students of scholars who sat with Fulan overseas."

His words incited a headache. "Okay, William. Thank you. I'll think about it."

When I hung up I groaned and rolled my eyes, swearing I never wanted to hear Fulan's name again in my life.

A week later, I asked my mother to find me a lawyer to make the divorce official.

Thirty

"And reverence the wombs (that bore you).
For Allah ever watches over you."
—Qur'an, 4:1

One day during the first week of August 2002, shortly before I turned twenty-five, I was sitting on the back porch of my parents' house reading a book that I had borrowed from Marcella about the history of the *Ka'bah* in Mecca, the first house of Allah, built solely for His worship. Luqman was running around in the grass playing with Emanuel, who had arrived with his mother for a visit a few days ago. Courtney was also home for a few days, but I had stayed out of her way because her scorn was so potent that I feared harm from just being within feet of her. She was home because she knew Patricia would be, and because she wanted my parents to meet her boyfriend aptly named Christopher, who was oh-so-interested in The Church. He had seen my father's sermons on television and was inspired, blah blah blah. I couldn't understand how he was so inspired by the calling of Christ while his girlfriend was more moved by that of the devil. I just assumed that the old saying was right. Opposites attract.

I was being cruel. But that's how unnerving it was to be in Courtney's presence. There was no dearth of cruelty in her behavior or vocabulary. She was so pathetic that even my *father* once told her to shut up when she was talking to me. I have no idea till today what that poor guy Chris saw in her, but they ended up marrying.

On the first day she arrived she brought up some silly thing she saw on television, asking me what I thought. "Do Muslim women get beatings for not pleasing their husbands?"

I feigned sincere consideration. "You know, I really don't know. I'm still learning a lot myself. But there *is* a book called *The Complete Idiot's Guide to Understanding Islam.* Your answer may be there, especially since it was written just for you."

So it's understandable why I was outside reading instead of relaxing inside enjoying the wonderful company of my entire family reunited in one place.

"Renee?"

At the sound of my name, I looked up from where I sat on the cement steps. For a second, I just looked, too shocked to react at all. It took me a second to recognize his features beneath the beard from where he stood at the fenced entrance of the yard. He wore a cream colored *thobe*, and he looked a bit taller than I remembered.

Although I registered all of this, all I could think was, *MaashaAllaah*. And I don't know a Muslim woman alive who doesn't understand all that is conveyed in that simple expression. Till today, I've never seen any man, on television or on a sports field, as handsome as a believer with the light of Islam on his face. The beard accents this beauty, and humility illuminates it. Reginald Mathews had that humility and light. At that moment, may Allah forgive me, I completely forgot that I was supposed to lower my gaze.

I remember a gathering where a sister had said that she had a weakness for dark-skinned men, and she asked us what we thought most attractive in a man. Another sister smiled and said what I've held as true ever since. "The best looking man to me is the one in *sajdah*."

"*As-salaamu'alaikum*," he said, lowering his gaze from where he stood about ten feet from me, an awkward smile on his face.

I returned the greeting and realized that I too should be averting my eyes. I looked at Emanuel and Luqman playing in the yard. They stopped only momentarily to see who was there, then continued their activities.

"So..." He didn't move closer, and I understood that was his way of maintaining a proper distance. There was no *comfortable* distance that day. We both were too distracted to be comfortable at all.

I glanced at him but realized that wasn't a good idea, so I returned my attentions back to the children.

"How does it feel being married to Billy Bob?"

I laughed, immediately reminded of Darnell's nickname for William, especially when he felt William had done something stupid. I wondered if Reggie resorted to the nickname for the same reason Darnell had once.

"Well, I'm not anymore, if that's what you're wondering."

"No, I'm not wondering. Your parents said you weren't."

I nodded, unsure what to say. I looked at him right then and saw that he was looking at me too. We both turned away. But in that moment, I saw the hurt in his eyes, and my heart ached for him. It was as if he had aged ten years in the last year alone. I wished I hadn't been so hasty in marrying William. If only I had known...

"What about you?" I said. "Did you find your soul mate yet?"

"Yes, I did."

My heart fell, but I kept a straight face. "When?"

"When I knocked on her door almost twenty years ago and asked if she could come out and play."

SubhaanAllaah. Some men know just the right things to say. I couldn't keep from grinning.

"Do you think she'll mind reconsidering?" he asked.

"Reconsidering what?"

"Marrying me."

I sighed. "Maybe. But she isn't allowed to date anymore."

"I know. But I want a date anyway."

I was a bit taken aback by this. I didn't say anything, but I was unable to temper the flattery nestling in my heart.

He spoke again.

"Because I need to rearrange my schedule around it so I'll know how long we have together before I leave."

On August 10th, 2002, Reginald and I signed the Islamic contract for marriage and scheduled a formal ceremony for the following July, giving our families, particularly our mothers, time to arrange a ceremony that they would like. It would be the first wedding in both my and Reginald's family —Patricia and I had eloped, Courtney was not yet married, and Reggie had never before taken that step. It also gave time for the court's paperwork to go through (William and I agreed on an annulment), to allow Reggie and I to marry legally too.

Aunt Marcella offered to overlook everything to ensure that everything would be according to Islam at the formal wedding, and that the men and women would be separated during the festive part.

Reggie had asked me if I wanted to put the no-polygamy clause in the contract, and I said I didn't. This surprised him and he assured me that he didn't mind.

"No," I said, sighing on the phone. "I really don't want it in there." Thinking of Bashirah and Jadwa had softened my heart. But, most significantly, I didn't want any reminders of what I'd gone through with William. Besides, I knew it was only Allah who controlled hearts and I was under no delusion that I could control Reginald's. "But I do want it to say that you can only pursue it with my knowledge and approval."

He agreed.

"What do you want as your *mahr*?"

I thought back to the book I had been reading when he had walked into the yard. I knew then what I wanted as my dowry. I smiled into the phone. "I want you to take me to Hajj."

He agreed again.

We spent the two weeks we had until he had to return to work and I to school holding hands and taking walks around the neighborhood. He also spent a lot of his time playing with Luqman and Rahma. It was awkward to see how at ease he was with my children, and they with him. I'd always imagined that divorce would traumatize them and prevent them from opening up to a stepparent.

I was wrong.

Seeing Luqman laugh and wrestle with Reginald reminded me of what I had always wanted from William. With Reggie, I didn't have to ask. It was second nature. We decided that they should call Reggie *Amu*, which meant *uncle* in Arabic, and that's what Luqman would shout whenever he wanted to be chased. "Amu, catch me!"

Undoubtedly, it was an adjustment for Reggie to go from being single to having a ready-made family, but his love for children and his determination to make a place for himself in their lives pushed him through. There were moments he would grow pensive, wishing he had done things differently so that it was he, not William, who married me back then. I also sensed a tinge of jealousy whenever the children spoke to their father on the phone. But whenever I asked about his feelings, he'd say, "I'm just grateful I didn't lose you completely."

I thought of how Reggie had been there for William and Darnell when we were young, and I wondered at his big heart. I didn't realize how much he was dedicated to making a change in people's lives until I heard him talk about his teaching and some of the students he'd inspired. Some had even become Muslim although they were in only the fifth grade.

I kept wondering what it was that I had doubted in him in the first place.

During the summer that we married, Reggie and I talked about everything, even the fraternity.

"That's sad," he said during a walk one night after the children had gone to sleep, his hand gently gripping mine. "I don't see how anyone thinks it's the Sunnah to slander and backbite believers."

"I know."

He sighed. "But just make *du'aa* for them. They think they're right."

I rolled my eyes playfully. "Don't I know?"

"You know, Ray, we should be grateful to Allah for guiding us. There's so much confusion out there."

I nodded, remembering my initiation dinner.

"It's not only them, Ray. There are lots of people who are confused."

"I believe you."

"I even met some really nice brothers, but I find out they're into some really strange stuff. Chanting themselves into trances. Thinking that their sheikhs have some secret knowledge that even the Prophet, *sallaallahu'alayhi wa sallam,* never taught or knew about. Calling on the Prophet in *du'aa.*"

I wrinkled my nose. "Really?"

"Yes, you wouldn't believe it if you saw it. It's like they get this high off it." He shook his head. "Men and women are alone doing this stuff sometimes. And I'm not talking about husband and wife."

I was silent momentarily. "I thought the fraternity was bad."

"Well, they are. But it's a lot of bad out there." He was quiet for some time.

"The funny thing is," he said, "they spend their time doing the same stuff the fraternity does, except they do it nicely."

I laughed. "I've certainly heard that before."

"Really. They have all these pamphlets against the people of the Sunnah, calling them all kinds of names. But they smile at you while they do it. You'd think they don't have a mean bone in their body." He laughed. "Until you ask if what they're doing is the Sunnah." He shook his head. "You'd think they'd say yes and explain how, but they actually got upset with me and never invited me back again."

"Good for you."

"Yes," he said sincerely. "It was good for me. *Alhamdulillaah.*"

His eyes grew distant. "I almost married one of the sisters though."

My jealous instinct shot through me. "Really?"

"Yeah, she was nice. But when I saw how she was more into the sheikh than me, I knew something was wrong."

"Maybe she thought he had a lot of knowledge."

He shook his head. "No, it was more than that. She was always talking about how she felt so close to him, and how he was her and she was him, strange stuff like that."

My eyes widened. "Woe, that's kind of out there."

"You tell me."

He went on, "One day I asked if I could meet the sheikh and she got all quiet and said there was nothing wrong with him and that he was trustworthy." He creased his forehead. "It was weird, like she was trying to hide something. I even called her one night, late, and she wasn't home." He looked at me. "You know where she was?"

"No..." I stared at him in disbelief.

He nodded. "With the sheikh. At a so-called 'private session'."

"Hmm. Are you sure they're Muslims?"

"That's what they say, but of course some of them aren't. When you start praying to the Prophet and saying the rules of Islam are only for the ignorant masses, then you're talking another religion entirely."

"Wow." I didn't know what else to say.

He drew in a deep breath and exhaled. "So be thankful. You could have been caught up in that."

"True."

We were silent until my mind drifted to how little time we had.

"I'm going to miss you," I said.

"And I'll miss you more." He smiled. "But I waited this long to marry you, I can be patient for now."

I leaned my head on his shoulder and we walked in silence, enjoying the comfort of each other's presence. The crickets chirped and lightning bugs winked in the night, as if reminding us just how much they understood that Reggie and I belonged together.

Gratefulness and regret are parts of one whole, I wrote in my journal the day my father officially approved Reggie's proposal to marry me. *One rarely exists without the other.*

These words were inspired by my realization that I had been guilty of ungratefulness more than foolishness in my years of youthful zeal. The ungratefulness had inspired within me a self-righteousness that veiled my eyes from the path that had lain before me all along—that to which I had been directed in my father's church. Today I'm amazed that I didn't see it before then, that I couldn't appreciate it when I needed it most. Had I been more cognizant, more tempered—more wise, I would have followed my father's spiritual directives calling to purity, to spiritual truism, to God himself. Because I was distracted by happening upon what my father had been guiding me to all along—the Truth, I missed the message of what this discovery was supposed to bring about—a betterment of self.

You can ask the world to respect you for who you are on the inside, my father had told me once, *or you can show on the outside what's inside, so that they have no choice.* In my youthful naiveté, I missed this message entirely. After embracing Islam, the religion to which my father had unwittingly guided me in his love of Christ, I strayed from the path of this blessed Prophet more grossly than I had before I happened upon the Truth. I had accepted in my heart Allah's religion, but my limbs had not yet followed suit in bearing witness to the very definition of Islam itself—submission. In my ignorance, I blamed my parents for rejecting Islam, not realizing that it wasn't the Truth they were recoiling from. It was me.

It was as if I had again sought love within while stripping my body from its garments without, meanwhile expecting others to not judge me for the only thing they could—what I was showing them. This time, my love within was my belief in Allah, and my garment was the exemplification of the true religion, in word and deed. And, once again, I had sought self-worth in stripping the garments from my body instead of clothing myself in dignity to reflect my internal spiritual growth.

All the while demanding with my tongue what I did not with my actions—respect.

For, truly, as I learned from my father, there are only two types of respect in this world—the kind that is given from the goodness of a person's heart and the kind that is earned by the virtuousness of a person's actions. *And the wise person puts himself in the second category before he expects others to put themselves in the first.*

I had not been wise.

But my parents had been.

I was embraced back into my childhood home even as I had not put myself in the category of virtue or wisdom. Yet, amazingly, I felt superior to the ones who had taught me every lesson that allowed me to be guided to the Truth. I hadn't yet realized that my religion was, to them, merely a label reflecting little truism in the ostensible sense. In this way, I and the sorority were one. Even today, I believe that Allah allowed me to exist under the haze so that I could witness conspicuously what I could not of my heart.

My parents had not wronged me. My sisters had not wronged me, not even Courtney herself. Courtney had become to me what I had been under the haze, and it was up to me to choose whether or not I wanted to be patient with myself.

On August 9th, 2002, my father had been sitting in the living room reading from the Bible in preparation for a sermon when I approached him hesitantly. It was late at night, and Luqman and Rahma were sleeping, as were my mother and siblings. The house bore a quietness that transformed a mere breath into disruption. So I held mine as I beheld the copper brown of my father's face as it was illuminated beneath the lamp next to the couch.

For a moment, I just studied him. In that pause, memories were evoked of days gone by, of moments irrevocable, and love immeasurable. I thought of his daily guidance that demanded us to be the best of ourselves, to be beacons in a world of darkness, and to be sincere when all sincerity was lost. I thought of how it was his call to righteousness, his call to purity, his call to true religion itself that allowed me to accept, with a heart swelling in belief, the religion of Islam.

My eyes welled as I recalled the rage I felt when he told me that his was a religion of love and mercy whereas mine was a religion of hate and vengeance. And I realized, now, that he had only spoken of what he saw—not in my religion, but in me. Negativity had been my way of life then, a testimony to my truism of self, and a dishonoring of both my childhood faith and the faith of Islam that I had embraced.

"Daddy?"

At the sound of my voice, he lifted his gaze, noticing my presence right then. Till today, I recall that his eyes were luminescent, creases forming at their corners as his lips spread in display of genuine pleasure in finding me opposite him in the room.

He placed his pen in the crease of the Bible, closed it, and set it aside.

"You're still awake?" he asked, grinning.

Shyly, I grinned too then lifted a shoulder in a shrug. "Yes, I guess I am."

"Sit down."

I entered the room and sat next to him on the couch. I felt his arm around me a second later, the sweet scent of his cologne tickling my nostrils and reminding me of my days as a child of The Church.

For several minutes we sat in silence, and I relaxed under the weight of his arm, each of us lost in thought.

"I'm sorry," I said in a broken whisper.

My father pulled me closer until my head rested on his shoulder.

"I understand now what I did wrong." The tears slipped imperceptibly from my eyes, and I bit my lower lip.

He remained silent but stroked my shoulder, assuring me that he understood.

Several minutes passed before he spoke.

"I'm proud of you, Renee."

His words evoked more moisture from my eyes.

"I always have been."

I sniffled and lifted a hand to wipe over my face.

"I was young once, so I can't fault you for being who I was myself. I'm just grateful that you're beginning to see what some never do." He drew in a deep breath.

"Enlightenment," he said, "isn't learning something your parents don't know. It's appreciating that you were enlightened only because your parents already were."

Thirty-one

"Labbayk Allaahumma Labbayk,
Labbayka laa shareeka laka Labbayk
Innal hamda wanni'mata laka walmulk.
Laa shareeka lak."

"O my Lord, Here I am at Your service! Here I am.
There is no partner with You. Here I am.
Truly, the praise and the provisions are Yours, and so is
the dominion and sovereignty.
There is no partner with You."
—*Talbiyah* recited during Hajj

People often ask me to recount my Hajj, but like so many others who have completed the journey, I have difficulty finding the words. I am still learning from the experiences of those blessed days of January 2003 when Reggie and I answered our invitation to Allah's House, even as the trip was a sacrifice financially and practically for us both. Reggie was a teacher, and I a student, and we would miss three full weeks. Fortunately, his school and mine were flexible, but we had a lot of catching up to do when we returned. But our mind wasn't on that as we recited the *Talbiyah* of Hajj.

Our tongues were wet with the *Talbiyah* when we arrived in Mecca to perform *'Umrah*. We made seven rounds about the *Ka'bah* followed by walking back and forth between the mountains of Safa and Marwa, just as Prophet Abraham's wife Hagar had done centuries ago while she was searching for water for her son Isma'eel. We drank from the blessed water of Zam Zam, the spring that had gushed forth at the heel of Isma'eel as he cried out in thirst.

As our Hajj group entered a gate of the Haram, the holy *masjid* enclosing the *Ka'bah,* I recited the prayer, "O my Lord! Open to me the doors of Your mercy." When our group leader pointed to an area on which dozens of people stood supplicating to Allah, he said, "That is Safa." The mountain was visible beneath where people sat, even as it was sheltered in the immaculate marble-floor building of the Haram. We then reached an area that led to some descending steps stationed between tall pillars.

"And that is the *Ka'bah.*"

I lifted my gaze under the sunlight and beheld the black structure draped in cloth, exposing red bricks at the marble floor. I sucked in my breath and felt something inside me give, and the moisture welled behind my lids. I could hardly believe I was here.

Scores of believers circumambulated the House, and I could hear the sounds of *du'aa* and *Talbiyah* coming from the throats of hundreds of Muslims. I saw people with skin as rich as dark chocolate and others with complexion as white as milk. I saw others with eyes like ebony and others with eyes the color of the sky. I saw short and tall, young and old, healthy and incapacitated, those walking on two legs, and those using their arms to move forward because they had no other limbs. I saw children on the shoulders and backs of parents, and still others walking on their own. I saw tears in pilgrims' eyes and heard the whimpers of others, all of them reciting praises and prayers to the One about Whom I bore witness when I said, "*Laa ilaaha illAllaah.*"

The tears flowed freely then, and I faltered in my step just slightly as I made my way toward the crowd rounding the *Ka'bah*. I felt my husband supporting me with his arm, and I glanced at him and saw that his cheeks too were wet. His eyes rested on Allah's House, and I saw his jaw quiver as more tears escaped his eyes.

We rounded the *Ka'bah* together, he and I, each of us reciting our own prayers, begging of our Lord. At the Black Stone, we raised our right hand in its direction, because we were too far to touch or kiss it. At the Yemeni Corner, we prayed, "Our Lord give us the best in this world, and the best in the Hereafter and save us from the punishment of the Fire!"

We spent many nights in the large tents of Mina, where the women had a tent and the men another. I met sisters from America, Pakistan, Malaysia, Saudi Arabia, and China, each holding her own story of the sacrifice, determination, and hope that had brought her to the blessed city to answer Allah's call.

I spent a day on Mount Arafat, praying to Allah and asking Him to guide me on the right path. It was there too, on this mountain, that I reflected on being in the sorority and how I had been unjust to my sisters in Islam. I remembered that a person could not enter Paradise carrying in her heart even a grain of pride, that disease that caused the children of Adam to look down on others and reject truth.

I saw too that I was carrying more than a grain.

I had said with my tongue that the mistake of the sorority was in forgetting that all people were prone to err, including oneself, and that the sorority's sin was in dismissing the benefit of someone in whom Allah had placed much good.

Yet, in my criticism of my sorors I had committed the same crime.

As my heart yearned for Allah's forgiveness, my heart softened to Ghazwa, Lisan, and Wadiah, and Annette too. I wanted Allah to forgive me, and my faith wasn't complete unless I wanted the same for my sisters in Islam. They were my mirrors, reflecting an image of myself, even if the glass did not enclose what I wanted to see.

Today, I see the glass for what it was—a reflection of me.

And I can look myself in the eye and say, *Yes, I was a soror,* because I know repentance begins with being honest with oneself. And I don't want to live in dishonesty anymore.

Yet, I know that in those words there will be many who find fault and inspiration for endless discussion of how they could, or would, *never* be like me. Others will laugh and cast a defamatory label that separates them from the sorority's sins.

All the while forgetting that each believer, righteous or sinful, is merely a reflection of what you could possibly be.

Within so many of us is pride, injustice, lack of humility, criticism of others, and the writing of our own terms of right and wrong. In this way, we become part of a fraternity or sorority that we have formed—or pledged—in our own lives.

Sometimes the only member is oneself.

Who does not look down upon a single soul in this world? Whose heart is graced with a humility so great that they, without fail, admit wrong each time a truth becomes clear? Who among us has not moved her tongue to speak ill of one who believes in Allah? And who has not, even for a single moment, judged her sister by standards she set for herself? And who can claim that she, upon seeing the blessings of another, has never felt even the slightest flicker of envy in her heart?

In truth, Ghazwa and Lisan merely represent two matters inexorably connected to each of us: the soul's unrelenting internal battle, and the movement—or stilling—of the tongue each day.

Prior to Hajj and spending a day on Arafat, I failed to realize this and had thus formed a single-member sorority in destroying the only life over which I had any control—my own.

It is easy to sit back and laugh or scorn the sorority, because this reaction incenses the sin of pride rusting our hearts. Our mockery and arrogant regard for the "misguided" offers a pseudo-comfort in the nest of our own lacking lives. We are like the one who swears that Allah will not forgive so-and-so because the sin is too reprehensible to forgive, and meanwhile it is possible that Allah announces above the Heavens, *Verily, I have forgiven so-and-so but I have not forgiven you!*

Or perhaps, we are like those mentioned in the Qur'an, who upon entering Hell Fire will say, *What is the matter with us that we see not those whom we used to count among the bad ones? Did we take them as an object of mockery, or have our eyes failed to perceive them?*

Today I am moved to still my tongue and heart that flutters about restlessly in criticism of others, lest I commit a sin greater than the one of those I scorn.

How soon we forget it is the sin of pride that transformed Iblis into Satan himself.

And how soon we forget that the sin we see in others may merely be Allah putting before us a mirror to show us what our own hearts cover within.

I know now that a pure heart that carries not even a grain of pride heeds effortlessly this simple advice offered by a righteous scholar centuries ago: *Do not leave your house and happen upon anyone except that you assume that he, or she, is better than you.*

I know too that a pure heart does not find humor in the mistakes of others. I know also that a pure heart never feels safe from even the most heinous sin. And I know that even as I am horrified at the utter audacity of another person's disobedience, there is possibly an even more horrific transgression lurking in my own heart.

O Allah! Hearer of Prayers, Forgiver of Sins,
Turner of Hearts!
I ask You to forgive me and my husband,
and to preserve us upon Your Religion.
And I ask You to forgive Ghazwa, forgive Lisan,
pardon Wadiah and Annette.
They came to You reciting Your Oneness after the
darkness of disbelief.
And they came to You seeking the Light of Islam.
They heard of a man calling to Your worship,
And they responded to the call.
They sacrificed the comfort of their families
and dedicated their lives to You.
O Allah! You know the hearts of humans better
than we know them ourselves.
You know that we ever fall short in purifying them
and in dedicating them to You.
So I beg you not to call me and my husband, or Ghazwa,
Lisan, Wadiah or Annette, to account for what we did in
ignorance, and I testify before You that
I forgive them for any harm. And I ask You, O Allah, to
remove from my heart and theirs any animosity, hurt, or
sense of resentment against anyone who believes.
O Allah! You are the One Who
shows Mercy without measure,

The journey to Hajj taught me so much about my religion, myself, and my soul that I am at a loss for how to explain all I learned, and am still learning today. I can talk of the rites, but I cannot speak of what my heart felt as my limbs moved in fulfilling them. The completion of the fifth pillar of my faith truly exemplified that learning the rites is rudimentary, yet performing them with sincerity and patience is monumental.

Hajj for me was about focusing on my personal duty to Allah while establishing a camaraderie with my brothers and sisters at the same time. It was about overlooking the faults of others, focusing on the self, and reaching deep down to draw on faith and faith alone. It was about finding my place amidst thousands of people who had come for the same goal.

This was excruciatingly difficult because pilgrims often grew aggravated with me, shoved past me, and nearly trampled the very life from my flesh. Yet, all the while, I had to bear in mind that my Hajj would not be accepted if I showed the slightest bit of anger or argued with a single soul. There were moments, I cannot lie, that I felt the fury rising inside my chest and my lips nearly parted to unleash what was raging within. But then, I was reminded of the Prophet's words about the qualities of a blessed Hajj, and I immediately calmed.

Is this not a lesson to take with us to our homes, to our "sororities"—and to our souls?

I think each hajji has a personal story, an anecdote from Hajj, from which they draw a lesson that they'll never forget. For me, this lesson was one that occurred, incidentally, after I had completed my rites of Hajj. I often wonder why Allah decreed this experience for me, even after I was no longer a pilgrim, and today I believe that it is because without this final lesson, I could not truly return home anew.

As is customary for most groups, ours remained in Saudi Arabia for a week following the completion of Hajj. During this time, we stayed in a hotel at the Haram and enjoyed purchasing souvenirs and praying our prayers at Allah's House.

One day, Reggie said that there was a local scholar inviting our group to his home (it was a home he owned in Mecca; he actually resided in another city). There would be dinner and a short lecture for whoever wanted to come. Sisters could come too because his wife would be there to receive them.

Naturally, many of us were exhausted from Hajj itself and thus chose to stay at the Haram. But Reggie felt that it was too good of an opportunity to pass up. So we went, although I was too shy to say I was tired myself.

When I arrived, I met the scholar's wife and some of her friends and family. Not all of them spoke English fluently, but the scholar's wife could although she had an accent that made her words difficult to decipher. She told us about her children, her grandchildren, and her husband, who she shared spoke better English than she. We ate and chatted and the scholar's wife asked some of the Americans to share their stories of accepting Islam.

Amidst all of this, someone shushed us and said, "Shhh. Sheikh Fulan is about to speak."

My heart fell, and I felt my stomach go sour. I couldn't believe I was actually sitting in the house of the very sheikh whose name I never wanted to hear again in life. But because I was a guest and was compelled to be polite, I listened as the intercoms were adjusted on our side. When they were, Sheikh Fulan began his talk. Incidentally, it was about the Sunnah and remaining firm upon the right path.

Although I no longer felt any animosity toward the fraternity or sorority, my heart filled with dread, and I braced myself for the moment he would ask us to testify that we were saved.

But instead, I heard what would become the most memorable part of the Hajj trip for me:

Know, brothers and sisters, that Islam is easy and the religion is clear. It is based upon worshipping Allah alone and establishing the prayers. If a person fulfills these matters sincerely, know they are your brother or sister in faith. This is Islam. The right path is found through these matters, but they bring no benefit if you do not guard your tongue and overlook faults in the people of Tawheed.

A lot of the youth today imagine that safety is achieved through affixing a label upon themselves. Beware that this is a trick from the Avowed Enemy, as Allah's religion is not a religion of slogans and labels, but a religion of sincerity, action, and good character. A lot of the youth also spend their time seeking the faults of their brothers and sisters, but know that if you spend your time seeking faults, it should be those of your own soul.

It is not permissible to question a believer to test his commitment to the Islamic creed. This is not the methodology of the Sunnah or that of our righteous predecessors. When you distract yourself from the focus on your own soul, you will find the wrong path before you, and if you do not return your focus to yourself, your destiny is but ruin. Know too that no one is free from error, so do not waste your time labeling others according to their mistakes. Their affair rests with Allah. As does yours.

So fear the coming of a Day after which there will be no more. And fear the coming of the day in which your soul will depart from your body, and there is nothing left for you except the good or evil you leave behind.

That day, I learned too that Fulan had been told about the fraternity and had known nothing of them. But he did recall youth coming to his classes seeking rulings against others who had made apparent mistakes. He had cautioned them against this but was unaware that there was widespread error involved, let alone in his name. My husband shared that a student of the sheikh said that Fulan had been overcome with tears when he first learned that it was his name that was used in spreading confusion amongst the youth.

I learned also that the "ruling" that the fraternity interpreted as a call to kindness as they continued in their misguidance was not a ruling at all. It was a response by several scholars of the Sunnah, Fulan among them, to the confusion caused by the fraternity, reminding the believers that kindness and good character, in addition to correct *'aqeedah*, were integral parts of Islam. This kindness was not merely in how words were spoken, they said, but in what those words were. The scholars' response also reminded believers that patience, offering advice, and thinking well of Muslims was the Sunnah, not abandoning people based on disagreements and mistakes. Above all, their advice was a call to the Sunnah itself, that of seeking beneficial knowledge, acting upon that knowledge, and fearing Allah.

It turns out too that Sheikh Fulan has no website at all.

That day made me reflect a lot on hearsay and the injustice of believing it at all.

Today, I feel renewed as if I returned to America with a new heart, body, and mind. I pray this is a sign of my Lord accepting my Hajj, so that I can have the reward of Paradise when I die.

In showing our commitment to a new life, and our hope that we were indeed forgiven our sins and were starting life anew, Reggie and I changed our names upon our return. I chose Rayan, the name of a gate of Paradise, and he chose Abdullah, one of the most beloved names to Allah that meant "servant of Allah."

A year after Abdullah and I returned from Hajj, William left the fraternity for good. I'm not sure exactly what happened, but I know that when he left, he was no longer married to Annette, who has a daughter from the marriage, and that his second wife bore no children from the union but remained his wife for only a few months after he and Annette divorced.

Today, William and his parents live in Saudi Arabia, where Horace and Audrey accepted Islam and went to Hajj with their son. William is remarried to the daughter of an American mother who converted to Islam and a Saudi father who met William shortly after he relocated in the Kingdom.

Abdullah and I have two daughters, Fatima and Habiba, and I am pregnant with our third child. We plan to relocate in the next few months to Saudi Arabia ourselves, where we already have a villa waiting for us so that Luqman and Rahma can see their father each day and Reggie and William will be neighbors again.

I was packing for this move when I received a phone call from Wadiah, whose voice broke mid-sentence because of her crying into the phone. She then asked me to forgive her for all she had done, evoking memories of my call to Sumayyah. I then grinned, my heart warming as I recalled my Hajj and *du'aa*, and I told her, "*Ukhtee*, I already have."

Epilogue

*"Indeed there is within the body a piece of flesh which if it
is sound, the whole body is sound,
and if it is corrupt, the whole body is corrupt.
Verily, that is the heart."*
—Prophet Muhammad, peace be upon him (Bukhari and Muslim)

Today when I mention the sorority or hear other
believers discussing similar trials, people often say, "Thank
God I found Islam before I found the Muslims." For me this
is an awkward declaration because I don't think of Islam as
belonging to the Muslims at all, and I don't think of their
actions as adding or taking away from its veracity for me. In
response, I think, *Thank God, I was graced with Islam,
despite the faults of the Muslims—and the more potent faults
within myself.*

My lesson isn't one in which I now look at my Muslim
sisters and brothers and thank Allah I didn't meet them
until a certain time in my life. Mine is a lesson that inspires
me to look within and it is there I levy blame. I know now
that when you're tested in your faith, you exhibit what's
deep within your heart, even if you're unaware of what's
there. So my lesson of being Muslim this long is quite
different and is noted in my journal entry that I wrote upon
returning from Hajj:

*In times of severe trial, there is only you, and
that most vital, and often forgotten, piece of flesh.
In hardship, it is the heart, of all pieces of flesh in
the body, that will betray you first, and most
ostensibly. So it is the pinnacle of wisdom to forge a
pure alliance with it before then. Care for it,
nurture it, and purify it with sincere love, devotion,
and humility before your Creator, and yourself—so
that at such times it will be your spiritual fortitude,
and not your spiritual, and emotional, cause for
ruin.*

My ruin during my years in the sorority, I know now,
was a result of the actions of my own hands, not those of
anyone else. But I could, like I had during my resentment
toward the sorority, blame others for my spiritual
crumbling. Or I could, like those who turn away from Islam
altogether, blame the actions of professed Muslims for my
forsaking of the Creator. I could point to the television, to

the newspaper, or to the "bad" Muslim I saw, or heard of, to excuse—and ignore—my responsibility of self.

Yet, your experience is not representative of reality at all, except that within yourself.

It was during Hajj that I discovered this simple truth. Whenever I found myself growing impatient, I noticed others pushing and bickering, their behavior aggravating my impatience. Whenever I found myself reflecting on a sin I'd committed, I merely felt a push or heard an argument, the behavior of others inspiring nothing except a prayer for their forgiveness, and mine. When I tired of walking, I found myself counting how many more rounds or rituals I had to go. When I found myself engrossed in a heartfelt prayer, I felt as if I could go on walking forever, and I didn't want it to end.

Upon returning from Hajj, my life changed dramatically, and the personalities like those I'd met in the sorority disappeared completely from my life. I grew so accustomed to my new circle of friends that I nearly forgot the sorority existed at all. My new sisters in Islam represented in life and deed what the sorority had in words alone—that of the true "saved sect" of believers following the footsteps of the early Muslims.

My sisters in Islam apologized for the slightest mistake, covered the faults of others, rushed to help a believer in need, reminded each other to avoid sins of the tongue, and, most significantly, they inspired an increase in my faith because they reminded me of Allah and the Hereafter each time we met.

I remember one day reflecting on the virtues of my new companions and I wondered why I couldn't have met them while I was in the sorority—when I needed them most.

A moment later Allah gave me my answer in the words I'd heard from Hadiyah before I accepted Islam.

Consult your heart. It is there you will find your answer.

~

About the Author

Umm Zakiyyah was born in 1975 in Long Island, New York, to parents who converted from Christianity to Islam after they married. She graduated in 1997 with a Bachelor of Arts degree in Elementary Education from Emory University, and she currently teaches English grammar and writing to high school students. Umm Zakiyyah is the recipient of the 2008 Muslim Girls Unity Conference Distinguished Authors Award.

~

CPSIA information can be obtained at www.ICGtesting.com
Printed in the USA
LVOW13s0517110414

381277LV00001BB/118/P